Catherine Feeny

Catherine Feeny was born in 1957. After doing an undergraduate degree in English in the UK, she spent three years at Vanderbilt University in Nashville, Tennessee, teaching, and studying for her M.A. On her return to England she became interested in alternative politics and, with her partner, Raymound ffoulkes, restored and set up a radical theatre in Canterbury during the 1980s. After spending several years in a small village in rural Burgundy, they now live in Brighton. Catherine Feeny is currently working on her second novel.

SCEPTRE

The Dancing Stones

CATHERINE FEENY

SCEPTRE

Copyright © 1995 by Catherine Feeny

First published in 1995 by Hodder and Stoughton
First published in paperback in 1996 by Hodder and Stoughton
A division of Hodder Headline PLC
A Sceptre Paperback

10 9 8 7 6 5 4 3 2 1

British Library Cataloguing in Publication Data

Feeny, Catherine
  Dancing Stones
  I. Title
  823 [F]

ISBN 0 340 65751 0

Typeset by Palimpsest Book Production Limited,
Polmont, Stirlingshire
Printed and bound in Great Britain by
Cox and Wyman Ltd, Reading, Berkshire

Hodder and Stoughton
A division of Hodder Headline PLC
338 Euston Road
London NW1 3BH

This book is dedicated to the memory of my darling mother, Patricia Mary Brewer, whose incomparably witty and original use of language was my first, and will always be my greatest, inspiration.

ACKNOWLEDGMENTS ∫

I would like to thank my partner, Raymond ffoulkes, not just for his help with the manuscript, but also for the encouragement and the constant discussions; Sara Menguc, my agent, for her faith in my work and her wonderfully good advice, Georgia Glover, and my editor, Carolyn Mays.

I would also like to acknowledge the help, support and advice of the following people: my sister, Sarah Feeny Welch, and my brother-in-law, Norman Welch; my father, Patrick Feeny; Felicity-Ann Hall; Amanda Shepherd; Graeme Duncan; John Butt; Sarah Taylor-Moore. Thanks too to the good people of Diges, for providing a sane and gentle place in which to work.

It has not always been possible to trace copyright for some of the passages quoted in this book. The publishers apologise for any inadvertent infringement and will be happy to include an acknowledgment in any future edition.

ACKNOWLEDGEMENTS

Ring the bells that still can ring.
Forget your perfect offering.
There is a crack in everything.
That's how the light gets in.

Leonard Cohen

a time to weep and a time to laugh,
a time to mourn and a time to dance

Ecclesiastes Chapter 3
Verse 4

Scandinavian bards, story-tellers and learned men
have spoken less of the goddesses than of the gods . . .
The wives of the gods remain practically always in the
background. The number of goddesses seems to have been great
enough, but of many of them we know scarcely more than
the name . . . Only one seems to have been revered by all
the tribes: she who in old German was called Frija, in
Anglo-Saxon Frig, and in old Norse Frigg.
Indeed the very name Frija is only a former adjective,
raised little by little to the dignity of a proper name.
It meant the 'well-beloved', or 'spouse'.

New Larousse Encyclopedia of Mythology

Prologue ∫

Magpie Cottage 13 The High Street Wyley

June 11th 1985

> *Dear John,*
> *I took lunch today with Lady Polly King, in the course of which I suggested to her that, this year, it might be appropriate to commence the opening of the Manor grounds with a general blessing, given by yourself, followed by a procession to the stone circle, at the head of which would be a large, wooden crucifix, which I volunteer to make. Upon the crucifix will be a model of Jesus, to remind people of the passion of Our Lord and His consummation of the Forces of Darkness. I have already bought the red paint at the D.I.Y. shop in Rocester.*
>
> *All this after Homer's speech, of course.*
>
> *Lady Polly graciously agreed to my idea, especially in the light of recent events, which have confirmed that the Devil is nigh and we must be ever vigilant. I imagine that she is troubled, as all Christians must be – excepting perhaps yourself and Sara, who are so much more modern than the rest of us – by an ever-present image of The Dark One in the midst, as it were, of our little community. On a day that the stones are allowed to dominate she and I feel that Christianity should put in rather more of a showing than it usually does.*
>
> *This year's roses, by the way, look to be the best ever.*
>
> *With regards in Christ,*
>
> *Marjorie Sand*
> *P.S. Perhaps you could lend me Martha for an hour or two to help me make the cross?*

1

Melanie Flowerdew

Melanie Flowerdew kicked open the door to Martha's bedroom with a bare foot. Jesus! What a stink! She thumped across the clothes-strewn floor to the window and flung it open. A blast of morning air rushed in. She breathed deeply. Roses. Honeysuckle. And all the other flowers that had survived Grandma's vicious pruning and Martha's stupid theories.

Melanie turned back to the room and felt the sunlight start to warm her spine. Havoc, as usual. A depressing crud made up mainly of soiled t-shirts, almost every single one of them bearing the smiling representative of some endangered species. And other things, too, that weren't exactly designed to cheer you on your way: about seven different varieties of homeopathic and herbal tranquillisers to help Martha withstand the stresses and pressures of working at Wyley Rectory; *Women Who Love Too Much* fallen open at what was probably a favourite page; *Every Time I Say No I Feel Guilty* – though when had Martha ever said no in her whole fucking life? Last week's copy of *The Rocester Gazette*, choc-a-bloc with pictures of dead treasurers.

Why did she do it, she asked herself for the fifty billionth time? Why had she picked up this habit of always feeling compelled to check up on her mother by going into her room when she was out?

Melanie sighed noisily. There was no use kidding herself.

Part of it was just plain nosiness. Inherited from Grandma, no doubt. Grandma was the sort of person who'd go through your knicker-drawer to see if you were taking the pill, though there was never any danger of Martha doing anything that sensible. Grandma was probably enjoying her last earthly resting place wafting among the household nooks and crannies, lodging in keyholes.

But it wasn't just nosiness; there was some other reason and Melanie often wondered what it was. Maybe it was to make sure that Martha really had gone out and wasn't, in fact, lying on her pillow, o.d.'d on chlorophyll. Maybe it was because she hoped that Martha had fucked off, put all her belongings in her battered old rucksack and simply gone. Maybe it was because she was frightened that she had.

Anyway, there was never anything interesting to see. Not even anything really horrifically nasty. Martha's speciality was the unspectacularly nasty. Her make-up, for instance. The glittery scarves she got from Oxfam. Her taste in men. Though here, you had to hand it to her; she did, at times, veer towards the spectacular. Right now she was excelling herself. Who on the planet could imagine anything more revolting than Sergeant Brian Tulliver?

Melanie walked over to Martha's unmade bed and sat down on it. The smell was stronger here but the fresh air was doing what it could to eradicate it. She looked in the mirror, surprised, as always, to see her own reflection there, and not someone else's.

That was because she *had* seen other people: that was what Martha's friend Joodi said. Martha had met Joodi at Demeter Foods. Joodi was wispy and had a pierced nose. The hole went septic every summer, when she had hay fever. Melanie, Joodi claimed, was an old soul which had returned to Wyley because of Wyley's stone circle. Had she ever glimpsed the outline of other, different faces beneath her own? Well it didn't matter really because her subconscious had.

Why, Melanie had asked, would she spend four thousand years coming back time and again to this dump when it was bad enough being here for one whole Sunday afternoon?

'Because of the stones,' said Joodi. 'I'd guess you were around when they were building the circle. I can sort of tell about these things. It's from the stones you've gained your age-old wisdom.'

Well that made some kind of sense at least. It certainly wasn't from Martha, and it certainly wasn't from Grandma, and it certainly wasn't from the people of Wyley, who were light on any sort of wisdom, even the spanking new.

I am me, Melanie thought, and immediately experienced a loss of solidity, felt herself become only a fuzzy formlessness of swarming particles which the reflection in the mirror – so utterly and unmistakably there, so rooted and assured – stared at with its green eyes. She could make this feeling happen in the stone circle too, lying bang slap in the middle, under a sky with just a tiny silver aeroplane, or black and crammed with constellations. But there it was even better because there was no reflection. You really were nowhere at all and anything was possible.

And then Grandma's voice jumped in, ruining it, making the atoms scramble back into line, sternly asserting the dull reality of just Melanie looking at herself in the mirror. 'So self-dramatising, adolescents. Don't believe you're unique. They all think like that. All the time.' Well, maybe adolescents and old souls had that in common.

It was strange that she bore no resemblance whatever to Martha, Melanie thought, watching her pale hand smooth down her black hair. It was something she was eternally glad about. Martha was bony with knobbly knuckles. She had small, sharp nipples and thin, gingery-blonde hair that tailed off into two points just below her shoulders, a sort of physical manifestation of the way she spoke, not quite finishing her sentences, presumably because she didn't have the energy to go on. Melanie's father's genes must have overpowered Martha's. Whoever he was. Melanie didn't suppose she'd ever find out now.

She bent down and picked the copy of *The Rocester Gazette* up off the floor. Friday, June 7th 1985. If you wanted evidence that nothing ever happened in the area, here it was. The annual opening of Wyley Manor, its garden and grounds, wasn't till the end of the month but, even last week, they were already harping on about it. Except for the two stones in the church meadow, this was the one day of the year when people were allowed access to The Wise Lady of Wyley, 'Wyley's very own ancient stone circle,' as the article put it, and the journalist was acting like they were being done some enormous favour:

> *'Happy Birthday Lady Poll'* Wyley *villagers will be singing on Sunday, June 30th to Lady Polly King when Wyley Manor grounds are thrown open to the public once again to celebrate Lady Poll's birthday on July 2nd. Lady Poll, widow of Sir Horace King and mother of 'Commentator' writer Sir Homer King, confided to* The Gazette *that this year's roses look to be the best ever.*
>
> *'We're all quite excited,' she said. 'This year's roses look to be the best ever.'*
>
> *Lady Poll's horticultural interests are well known to Wyley-dwellers (she is Patron of the Wyley Horticultural Society) but two years ago reached a wider public when her garden was photographed by* Country Manner *magazine along with some of Lady Poll's gardening tips.*
>
> *'If the weather holds we expect a bumper turn-out,' she told your reporter. And if this sudden influx is a headache for village bobby Brian (Tully) Tulliver, he certainly isn't telling!*
>
> *'Lady Poll's birthday is a community event' was the word from the Wyley police station last night. 'Everyone wants to help celebrate the eighty-ninth of a very special lady.' And anything special planned for next year's big nine-oh? 'We'll have to see,' he smiled.*

There was a picture of the old soak, which must have been taken a hundred and fifty years ago, or from a distance of half a mile, though she still looked as if someone had taken a blow-lamp to her. To illustrate her excitement Lady Poll was holding a basketful of roses and a pair of secateurs, and not quite succeeding in not looking as if she was wondering what the hell they were for. The best roses ever. They had said that last year. They would say it again next year. Everyone in the whole of Wyley said it every fucking year. How good could a stupid rose get? The truth was that the roses stayed exactly the same.

And this year there wouldn't even be the excitement of Lady Poll falling off the edge of the rostrum like she did last year. Sir Homer would have seen to it. They'd've set up some protective fence or electric barrier or something, so no matter where Lady Poll lurched to she'd be bounced back to the middle of the stage.

Melanie pulled a hypnotist's face and spread her hands into two, wavering spider's webs.

'I command you, oh Lady Poll, by the Sacred Wisdom of The Circle, to do something exciting at the opening of the Manor grounds to the public again this year.'

The brilliant thing was that everyone had known it was going happen. They had watched, with horrified fascination, those still shapely legs, topped by that incongruously pudgy body, tottering forward, much too near, tottering back, tottering forward, nearer and nearer. No one had said a thing. No one in Wyley ever said a thing. You could've exploded them one by one and they wouldn't have objected, out of awe for the event. Lady Poll about to go splat in a cloud of emerald chiffon was as nothing compared with the social censure that would have fallen upon anybody who had shouted 'Watch out'. And down she went. And everyone shouted 'Oh! Oh!' In high voices, as if they were surprised. Except for Melanie, who doubled up with laughter then hot-footed it to the Manor to call an ambulance. Everyone was ultra S-H-O-C-K-E-D and the story went that Melanie had run away out of shame, like her mother before her. No one ever asked themselves how it was that an ambulance turned up.

It was all one great big fucking charade, really. The Emperor's New Clothes. Except in Wyley the Emperor fared a whole helluvalot better than the little boy. Christ, you only had to look at the village school that they all wanked off over like it was some kind of great triumph.

A couple of years before Melanie and Martha came back to Wyley, when Grandma was still alive and kicking, Rocester Council had pulled out its funding and said all the kids could get on the bus and go to primarys in Rocester. Not our precious darlings! Not among rough little boys with names like Wayne. So the parents wrote petitions and pestered the council and got them to advertise it, rather than raze it to the ground and sell off the land to build Barratt Homes, like they'd planned. It was bought by a couple of money-grubbing prep-school teachers called Speed, who wanted to run it privately. Local M.P., Thomas

Bright, had come down and made a speech at its new opening about community spirit and family values and all pulling
together. The whole lot of them, including, of course, Grandma,
were beside themselves with joy and self-congratulation. And
every day you could see a row of forlorn little sods, whose mums
and dads couldn't afford Wyley Primary, queuing up for the bus
to Rocester, which was always late.

That was Wyley for you. A talent for the selfish and ineffectual.
God, you could tell Martha had been born here. At the moment
her favourite t-shirt, now festering on the carpet at Melanie's
feet, was one with a picture of a toxic toad on it. You would have
known it was poisonous, even if the writing underneath hadn't
informed you, because of its livid colouring and its malevolent
expression, which might have been some hippy artist's idea of
how a toad would look if it could smile. A brush with this toad
and you were a goner. To Melanie's way of thinking it was
one animal that the world could just about rub along without.
There were many more endearing, more deserving creatures
that Martha could have emblazoned across her tits, if she had
to be a walking billboard. Ones that might elicit sympathy and
commitment. But no.

The vegetarianism was worse, though. Melanie had pointed
out a trillion times that feeding poor Hame organic baby food,
the colour of pus, and then weaning him onto solids – if you
could call them that – in the form of mashed mung beans and
lentils, was not going to mean that any cow was going to live
that would otherwise have died. Cows were bred for meat. If
she and Hame didn't get to eat them it didn't mean no one else
did. Ineffectual.

And, similarly, back in the sixties, nobody profited from
the fact that Martha Blandish screwed whoever she felt like.
Especially not in 1968 when she had conceived a child with
some poxy stranger in a sleeping-bag at a rock festival and
named it Melanie Flowerdew.

Why, she had asked her mother a million times, couldn't she
just have called her Blandish? And Martha had replied, a million
times, with a silly smile on her face, that she had wanted Melanie
to have a special name of her very own. This was the line Martha
always took and Melanie had believed it when she was a kid but

as she got older it dawned on her that it wasn't for that reason at all; it was so that her mother didn't have to feel that she had that much to do with her being there; so that she didn't have to feel responsible. By the time Hamish was, equally thoughtlessly, conceived – with Paul Stevens, wimp, who was really a poet (unpublished) but who worked in a bank in his spare time – Martha had given up on the idea that Melanie's own separate name was any great shakes and so she went and called Hamish, Hamish Blandish. Poor little sod.

It would have been better really if they'd both ended up in the circle, like the other one. Well, her at least, the cuckoo in the nest. Not Hamish.

Hamish was the best thing that had happened since they'd come back to Wyley two years ago. Melanie was fifteen then. Grandma was dead and in a canister. The house was Martha's and Martha was three months gone. They undid the lock and staggered into the kitchen with their suitcases. Martha dropped the canister onto the kitchen floor. It split apart and a draught from the open front door blew the ashes across the floor and up, up into the air, over the curtains, the draining board, the big wooden table. Over every damn thing in fact. Grandma had always been wary of draughts. Martha burst into tears.

'I couldn't keep hold of it. There's too much gravity. I was going to put her in the garden and now she's gone.'

But Grandma was actually very far from gone. She was clinging to everything, as Martha would have known if she'd been the one to clear her up.

Grandma who, Melanie now noticed, was at this very moment eyeing her from the top of a shoe box, her helmet of grey curls jammed down firmly onto her head. Melanie pushed the box towards her with her foot. She hadn't noticed this shoe box before. It must be one of the lower strata, shot to the surface by a frantic looking for something. She picked it up and put it on the bed.

Under Grandma there were other photos. Hamish. Hamish. Another Grandma. Then some maps. Wyley Parish. Rocester Parish. Wyley Parish, 1960. A pair of gloves. A scarf. One earring. And then something strange and unexpected: a picture cut out of a newspaper. Melanie turned it over. The other side was only part of an advert, so it must have been the photo that Martha had kept it for. The date of the newspaper was at the bottom of the advert page. May 1970.

What was surprising was that Martha had cut it out at all. Martha was a hoarder of clothes, beads, pills, make-up, perfumes – she had at least four sticky old bottles of patchouli on her dressing-table – but she actively disliked pictures and photographs. The t-shirts were as far as it went, and they were because of The Cause. There were only two paintings in the whole of the house, and they both belonged to Melanie. There was the clown she'd got for Hamish. It hung on the wall opposite his mobile – Martha didn't mind mobiles. And there was the watercolour of the stones in her bedroom. Dangerous, unlucky, Grandma would have said, whose own pictures were mostly of bowls of fruit and dead pheasants. The first thing Martha did after she'd recovered from the trauma of seeing Grandma dispersed across the kitchen was to take down all Grandma's pictures. Which would have made the place look pretty bare if it weren't for the beams.

So why had Martha carried this cutting with her, carefully enough not to lose it, through one and a half decades of petty tragedy and minor disaster? She didn't possess a single photo of Melanie. Melanie had taken the two of Hamish, and the ones of Grandma. Martha had probably felt too guilty to throw them out. But here, folded neatly in half, and deliberately stored away, in very good nick, considering how ancient it was, was a photograph from a newspaper.

It was a street scene. London, probably. A girl was looking in a shop window. She was wearing a short skirt, boots, and had long, straight hair. She'd got ugly, thick black lines all round her eyes and her eyelashes were clumped together and spiky. Men walking past turned to stare at her. As well they might. They wore flared jeans, denim jackets, and strange sort of waistcoats that looked as if they'd just hacked them off a passing sheep.

Melanie supposed it must have been fashionable at that time to go round looking like you'd been beaten up or had recently slaughtered something, but why the hell had Martha kept the picture? Melanie stared and stared at it. If it had been a sealed box she would have rattled it.

'Wee wee.'

Melanie quickly put the photo back where she'd found it.

'Wee wee,' Hamish repeated emphatically.

'Oh shit. Can you hang on a sec?'

Hamish looked dubious.

'Oh shit.' Then Melanie spotted, in the corner by the bed, Sergeant Tulliver's helmet. Well that explained the smell. She should have guessed. It was the rank, stale, oniony pong that always hung around the policeman, combined with the sad, broken aroma of recent sex.

Melanie ran over and grabbed the helmet.

'Here Hame, you can use this.'

She popped him down on it and carefully lifted his grubby nightshirt, on which was written 'Tots For Toads'.

'Finished.' Hamish stood up.

'Good boy. Do you think I'll have to empty it, or do you think it'll just soak in?'

They both stared at the helmet gravely for a couple of minutes.

'Well, that's saved me a job. I'll just put it in the garden to dry. Then we'd better get you dressed, hadn't we?'

And she picked Hamish up and tossed him in the air because, suddenly, she couldn't bear to think about Tully, and she couldn't bear to think about Martha, and she couldn't bear to think of them having the kind of sex she knew they had together. Martha was stupid enough to be in love with Tully, stupid enough to marry him. Imagine what that would do to Hamish. Imagine what that would do to all of them. Love and sex. Untried, they were already spoiled. Martha had spoiled them. The room reeked of their failure. By the Sacred Wisdom of The Circle Melanie would never never never fall in love, she promised herself. She would never never never have sex with anyone.

Melanie lowered her face to Hamish's gingery curls, inhaled the sweet newness of his body, kissed him noisily.

'Melly,' cried Hamish, in a fit of amusement. 'Melly! Melly!'

'No,' shouted Melanie, throwing him into the air again. 'Smelly. Smelly. Smelly Tully. Smelly smelly smelly.'

2

Wyley

There was a note from Martha on the kitchen table. She suggested that Melanie and Hamish should meet her at the Rectory at the end of the morning. They'd go to Demeter Foods during her lunch hour, buy a whole pile of things they didn't need and couldn't afford, and have lunch.

Melanie hated eating at Demeter. It had a few sanded tables at the back of the shop with bowls of brown sugar on them. They did fruit juices, herbal teas, sandwiches, and a selection of really horrible yoghurts made of goat and ewe's milk, cows being just too normal to be ecologically acceptable. One time Melanie had found a caterpillar in her carrot and walnut sandwich. She showed it to Martha, who said it was just proof of how very organic the food was at Demeter. Melanie said either something was organic or it wasn't, and didn't caterpillars deserve the chance not to be eaten along with everything else? Then Hamish threw up and a cadaverous female, with a caved-in nose and bony fingers – they were all like that there, probably due to the filth they ate – came and wiped it up with a recycled J-cloth.

Well, at least today they weren't going to be treated to the sight of Martha's breakfast, so there was some hope of them keeping their lunch down. The mess she put in her bowl every morning reminded Melanie of the bottom of Hunca Munca's cage when it needed cleaning.

Melanie felt in her jeans pocket.

'Let's have a picnic breakfast today, Hame. We'll buy something from Gimble's and eat it by the stones.'

They went out the front door and stopped in the front garden to admire the yellow roses, which were Hamish's favourites. While he talked to them and prodded them gently, Melanie gazed idly down the street towards the village school, silent for the summer.

Here Martha had begun her not-very-lengthy education. Melanie had been there too, for a few terms, and Grandma's entire schooldays had been spent at Wyley School. They wouldn't be able to afford it for Hamish, and the Rocester schools were a jungle, so God knew what would happen to him.

Now, in term-time, the milk-white Wyley mothers clustered by the school gates, while their children ran around on the grey tablet of playground, surrounded by Victorian railings with sharp spearpoints at their tips. The mothers were all what Grandma would have called 'newcomers'; their husbands were commuters. They gossiped and assessed in their cottons and sandals, each with a child, too young for school, dragging one of their arms into a hypotenuse.

When you thought about it, there weren't many people who had been born in Wyley living here now. The old village families – the Webbs, the Trannocks and the Atters – who intermarried, interbred (not usually in that order) and lay side by side in Wyley churchyard, now mostly lived on the Rocester council estate. Past the village school you could just about see the war memorial with the names of Webbs, Trannocks and Atters jostling together beneath the Latin inscription, *Pro Patria*.

Melanie opened the garden gate, hoisted Hamish onto her hip, and turned down the path that crossed the village green. The village's small, oval pond was perfectly still and flat, and reflected the cloudless sky. The path brought you out in the High Street, between the post office and the Rose and Crown.

The Rose and Crown was another thing that had changed. Thanks to the efforts of Wyley's more prominent busybodies, it had got boring.

It was a large pub – or coaching inn, as it now described itself – with crimson and white climbers scrambling up its Tudor brickwork. Inside there were two bars that had once been the public and the saloon, but now there was no difference between them. In the larger one there was a long fireplace, with a snug. Thick black beams were plastered with shining horse-brasses. It specialised in real ale and flower wines. People drove down from London to eat ploughman's lunches and show off in its garden, which was at the back and had a view of the green and the cricket pitch.

Four years ago the Rose and Crown had been run-down and gloomy. Boys from the Rocester council estate gathered outside on their motorbikes at chucking-out time, revving their engines. Grandma complained about it constantly – though, living where she did, she could hardly have been greatly affected – and most Saturday nights Marjorie Sand phoned the police. On Sundays they had a really loud live band, which Martha sometimes went to hear when they were staying with Grandma. That was put a stop to when Miss Evans from the post office got the Environmental Health round to measure the decibels.

One thing no one could stand in Wyley was to see anybody else enjoying themselves. They preferred events where everyone pretended to.

Not long after the decibel test the pub was sold to Simon and Veronica Tarrant, who had made a killing in the city and had always *longed* to own a real country pub.

Veronica, cool, pretty and very yuppie, with short brown hair and a large, off-white Habitat apron, had old-fashioned flowers planted in the Rose and Crown's garden. Her mutton pasties got a write-up in the *Telegraph's* food column, which was written by a girl she'd been at school with.

Simon had a tortured accent and an innocent, public-school face. He wore very new jeans and a striped t-shirt with wide sleeves, presumably in order to create a relaxed ambience, though he was really the kind of man who looked a pillock in anything other than a suit. He set up a game called bat and trap and was always wanting to tell you how to play it. Martha tried to get Melanie to have a go at it one time when she took her and Hamish for lunch there. She was all in favour of the introduction of old traditions.

But Melanie had preferred it when the Rose and Crown had

the games room, in the building to the side of the garden, which had probably once been a barn. The floor, originally covered in lino, had had long, gaping areas where the flagstones showed through. In wet weather it flooded. The billiard table was bleached, and tilted when you leaned on it. It was lit by a single light-bulb. The old landlord let you hang out there as long as you wanted and didn't mind if you smoked. Eventually though, fed up to the back teeth with Marjorie Sand's complaints and Sergeant Tulliver's visits, he got rid of the billiard table and turned it into what he called 'The Family Room'. He put a lampshade on the bulb and bought a few junk shop chairs, but it was never a success. Only the most hardened of drinkers went there with their children, on the days it was too cold to leave them in the car.

Simon and Veronica had changed all that. Within six months of their arrival the barn had been completely re-wired and spot lamps had been placed on the walls to bounce a diffuse light off the beams. The lino was removed and a floor of seasoned oak was placed over the flagstones. They put in a wood-stove.

The room was now used mainly for wedding receptions. It wasn't unusual to see a row of rented cars waiting outside, or an old-fashioned carriage, pulled by a blinkered dapple-grey, their stupidly-costumed drivers smoking cigarettes and looking at their watches.

A fortnight ago Martha took Melanie and Hamish to the Rose and Crown after work and asked to see Veronica's catering prices and made Melanie look at them too.

That was when Melanie realised that Martha was thinking of marrying Tully. This was Martha's way of introducing her to the idea, letting her get used to it.

She'd done the same sort of thing when Tabitha had to go to the vet to be put down. The cat box had sat in the kitchen, waiting, for the best part of a week, so that Tabitha wouldn't be frightened when the time came. When the time came she was scared shitless. Poor Tabitha. Martha fed her on Eco-puss from Demeter. Poor Tabitha. Melanie's eyes prickled.

She imagined Martha in white and Tully in uniform, processing out of St George's beneath an archway of crossed truncheons, the church-bells ringing hysterically. They'd go away somewhere to screw ferociously for a fortnight. Then he would take possession of the household. Underwear would begin to find its way into the laundry basket. Doors would need to be locked. The last grains of Grandma would be reached for with a brush under the dresser. You would come upon him, unexpectedly, in the kitchen, standing by the fridge in sky-blue nylon underpants with ridges, drinking milk from the bottle. There would be curls of ginger pubic hair stuck on the bar of soap on the edge of the bath. There would always be a vague need to be careful – to be frightened.

'Well, Melanie, what do you think of it?'

Melanie couldn't speak, so she shrugged. Veronica gave her a brief, acidic glance.

It was the sort of pretentious crap you'd expect. All very self-consciously British. Veal and ham pies, Whitstable oysters, homemade pickles. No bridge rolls or vol-au-vents. Meat without cruelty, organic, macrobiotic, vegan and veggie could be arranged to order, Veronica told them. Veronica said that she got some of her girlfriends down for the day whenever they did a reception. They weren't waitresses, of course, but they liked to help out for a bit of fun. Melanie could just imagine the snots.

Did they know that they'd had a string quartet evening as well, with a glass of wine and amuse-gueules? Everyone had had such a fabulous time they were doing it again next year. Along with the May Ball. Fifty pounds a double ticket, which included a buffet and a glass of champagne at midnight. Lots of Simon's old Oxford chums had come down for the last one. Some of them had even dressed up in Petit Trianon costumes – shepherdesses, milkmaids. It had been such a laugh they'd decided to have a fancy-dress evening later this month – they might have seen the posters for it? – a free Buck's Fizz for anyone in fancy dress. The theme was 'A Midsummer Night's Dream'. They also intended to have monthly, tickets-only dinners, cooked by guest chefs and with a seasonal menu. Mrs Blandish should come along with Sergeant Tulliver.

Mrs Blandish. Veronica would have to be blind, deaf and dumb not to know the truth.

Melanie put Hamish down and looked up at St George's clock. It said ten-thirty. It always said ten-thirty. Soon after

John Feather had become rector of Wyley he'd tried to get it going. He'd got Martha, who'd just started working for him, to phone a special clock-repairer who advertised in *Country Manner*. There was a copy of it lying around because everyone had bought it to read the article about Lady Poll. The clock-repairer was very young and had gained his interest in crafts at Bedales. Wyley couldn't have been more impressed if he had actually managed to repair the thing. Wyley valued craftsmanship highly. Lots of the mothers had part-time jobs in antique shops in the surrounding villages, or in boutiques that did natural yarns and hand-knitteds, where they dyed wool with beetroot out the back.

'Do you want to go in the church, Hame?'

Sometimes Hamish liked to look at the stained glass window behind the altar. Melanie liked to look at it too, because Wyley got so hot under the collar about it. The window was about a billion years old. Tourists came and admired it, which meant that it sold cream teas and postcards. And of course Wyley felt it had to wank off over anything to do with its precious Heritage. But it also, unmistakably, depicted the stone circle. Heaps of people in Wyley believed that an image of the circle was sacrilegious or, at best, unlucky to have in the house, so it was doubly awful having it perched right above their holy altar. Marjorie Sand was all for taking it out and smashing it to pieces.

Hamish shook his head.

'Cwisps.'

'Okay, we'll get you some.' Melanie bent to tie a shoelace that had come undone. Hamish watched her. As she stood up she became conscious of a small twitching in Magpie Cottage, the movement of a duster among the china street-sellers in the bay window.

'Do you know who lives in Magpie Cottage, Hamish? Don't look. Don't look. She'll see you. A witch!' The blue eyes rounded and Melanie realised her mistake. 'Not really, Hame. Only joking. Just silly old Marjorie Sand. Just Marjorie Sand. She's too silly to be a witch.' Angel of Death, more like, the way she kept coming and praying all over Grandma when she was dying, and laying on hands. Hamish looked unconvinced. 'And Martha's working in there,' Melanie added, to divert attention, pointing at the Rectory, almost opposite where they were standing.

As she spoke the Rectory cleaner, Joyce Atter, who got the bus in from Rocester twice a week, emerged from the Church Hall. It was the morning after Brownies, so she stopped to sweep up the fag-ends that the waiting fathers had smoked by the door, dumping them in a black bin-bag that she dragged behind her.

'They's that scared of the stones,' she shouted to Melanie, noticing her and Hamish over the other side of the road.

'Who are?' Melanie shouted back.

'Brownies. Guides. And others. Some of 'em won't come have their babies weighed in winter. "Make it earlier," they say. "Too dark." Rapists. Murderers. Muggers and suchlike. But it's the stones they's scared of. Brownies won't walk home without their dads. Guides won't neither. There's people, as should know better, put it about that the stones move around the village. Worried they'll find one follering them home. Said the same when I was a kid. So I get to sweep up fag ends.'

'Stupid,' shouted Melanie.

Joyce Atter shrugged. 'Who's to say they don't? Just doesn't need putting about, that's all. Summat's up though. Never seen them so jumpy. Never seen so many cigarette butts. Something's on its way, and they don't like it. Still, it's an ill wind.'

Melanie glanced down at Hamish. He didn't appear to have heard. Or if he'd heard he hadn't understood. Poor kid, he hadn't had much of a day of it, what with witches and walking stones.

'Hey, Hame, want a piggy-back?'

But now there was some sort of commotion going on at Callan's Butchers. A small crowd was forming outside and there was shouting coming from within. All along the pavement people had started to come out of their houses and were standing, with folded arms, asking each other what was happening. Marjorie Sand emerged, in pale pink rubber gloves, and fell into a tête-à-tête with Miss Evans in front of the post office.

With Hamish on her back, Melanie squeezed through the crowd and finally made it to the front of the group inside the shop. Stretched out on the floor among the blood-spattered sawdust, a girl, only a bit older than herself, was opening her eyes. Melanie recognised her. She was one of the au pairs. Almost all the mothers had them. You saw them sitting on the benches round the village green, talking brokenly to each other, surrounded by prams and toddlers, while their employers did yoga in Rocester, or took the train to London to be waxed.

'Stone,' she said.

'Keeled right over,' said Tom Callan, a meat cleaver in his whopping fist, looking down at the girl as if he would like to chop her up into pieces. 'Tried to grab some sausages to stop her fall. They won't stand up to that. Weren't made for it for one thing.' He pointed angrily at a string of pale sausages trailed across the floor.

'She says she's stoned,' said Miss Sayle, who was fat and had no mouth and ran The Wise Lady Tea Rooms. 'It's legal in Denmark.'

'Well, it ain't legal here,' said Tom Callan, twisting his cleaver round and round.

'Are yer hungry love?' shouted Joyce Atter, who had come up behind Melanie. 'Maybe you should get her to the tea rooms and Miss Sayle can give her a cuppa?' she suggested to Tom Callan.

'Not if she's stoned,' said Miss Sayle firmly. 'And anyway, we've just started doing luncheons. There's a cover charge.'

'What in God's name is going on?' One of the mothers had burst through the crowd. She stared accusingly at the girl, who was struggling into a sitting position. 'Where is baby? What have you done with her? Where is baby?'

'Stone,' the girl repeated.

'What? What?'

'Perhaps she means she's left the baby by the stones,' said Melanie.

'Left the baby?' The mother's livid face turned on Melanie as if it were her fault.

'You can see the stones from here when there aren't all those people. I used to do the same with Hamish. Grandma and Martha did the same with me.'

'Martha? Martha Blandish?' The woman's sharp, crimson lips pulled tight. She turned her back on Melanie. 'Is this true? *Écoute* Chantal, *as-tu laissé bébé près de les pierres?*'

The girl said nothing.

'She's right, Mrs Blade, the pram's out there, in the church meadow,' said someone who was standing by the door.

'Well, it's not good enough. I shall be informing the agency. *Tu comprends? Ce n'est pas assez bon.* Children disappear, you know.' She flounced out of the shop.

'So do parents,' shouted Melanie, before she could get out of earshot. 'Mean cow,' she added, evoking disapproving glances from Tom Callan and Miss Sayle.

'Can you stand up now, love?' asked Joyce Atter, offering a hand. 'I'll walk her down to Doctor Oliver's. It's probably only her menstruals.'

'See what I mean?' she remarked to Melanie out of the side of her mouth, nodding in the direction of the nearest stone, beneath which a group of mothers had lifted the baby from its pram and were inspecting it for damage. 'Something's up. Something's about to happen. The first to be told is the innocent.'

'What a feast, Hamish.'

They were lying in the sun with their backs against the wall of the churchyard, eating smoky bacon crisps and drinking the fizzy orange that Martha said would make Hamish hyperactive.

'When I was young Gimble's wasn't a supermarket, it was a greengrocer's. There were ladies who'd fill a paper bag with apples for you and flick it over and twist the ends. And when Grandma was young.' Melanie started chanting and Hamish beat time with a chubby hand; this was a ritual they'd established. 'There was a cobbler and a baker and a fishmonger. There was a barber, who was also a bookie. There was a hairdresser and a draper's. *Two* sweetshops. And a dairy that made its own ice-cream.'

Probably wasn't quite such a dump back then.

The sun disappeared momentarily. There was no one in the church meadow except for Melanie and Hamish. The pair of stones subsided into a dull slate-grey. The sun reappeared and they became silver. Hamish dropped the half-eaten bag of crisps and rolled up into a tight little ball.

Melanie rolled over and flung herself, floppily, onto her back, arms splayed outwards. She groped for her can of orange and took a slurp from it. It dribbled down her chin and under her t-shirt. Hamish had fallen asleep.

The church meadow. The only bit of the circle you could be in without trespassing. Though you did, as John Feather's article for *A Guide To Wyley* pointed out, get 'glimpses' of some of the stones from the folly footpath, which was just outside the village, at the end of the byway. Glimpses! John Feather was such a goody-goody, but then all rectors were probably.

Melanie closed her eyes. At least John Feather liked the circle. He'd got interested in it when he was writing that article, and he had even gone to the bother of doing quite a bit of research on it.

According to John, The Wise Lady of Wyley was one of around seven hundred stone circles in the British Isles. It was thought that there were, originally, more than twelve stones in its outer ring – which was pretty massive anyway – but some had been used by the Romans to make a temple of Venus, on top of which the Normans later went and built St George's.

John had gone to Rocester library, and ordered stuff from the Rocester bookshop, and managed to unearth some local legends, a few of which Melanie had heard already.

People used to think the stones danced on Midsummer's Eve and, if you entered the circle at dawn of Midsummer's Day, you were supposed to vanish. They said you'd hear the sound of the cuckoo at that time as well, and it meant the arrival of Frija, a Teutonic goddess. She was associated with fertility. Apparently a whole pile of Wyley villagers got pissed off about the circle's pagan connotations in the eighteenth century and managed to pull one of the stones over, which showed that they hadn't changed a whole hell of a lot, but Wyley people were still performing rites, which might have been to do with Frija, up to the end of the last century.

What John couldn't say, in spite of his research, was what the circle was for, and why it was called 'The Wise Lady'. Not that that stopped him speculating. He thought the name might be because the largest stone, at the southernmost reach of the circle – 'The Wise Lady Stone', it was known as – did look a bit like a woman bending her head. He thought that the entire thing might be a whopping astrological clock, or a temple, or a place for ritual sacrifice, or even a kind of storehouse of psychic energy, which was what Joodi and Martha went for.

And then, like a good rector, he finished with a paragraph of theological contortions, saying that the stones were somehow to do with Jesus really, and telling you that, anyway, the circle was mostly on private property and you weren't allowed to trespass.

Melanie smiled; people did trespass though, in spite of warnings. Not regularly, not methodically, but they did. The circle was a magnet that drew things towards it. That was why, though Wyley had dwelt among the stones for over a thousand years, a quarter of the circle's lifetime, they were still a topic of conversation. The village had never quite got used to what they could come up with.

Of course there was always gossip about lost virginities. How many hymens had been broken in the stone circle? Must have been hundreds. Could have been thousands.

The way it worked was that the girl, or perhaps both of them, got frightened. They clung closer and closer together. They freaked themselves out on eternity until, in contrast, their bodies were hot as cauldrons. Try it out now, while there's still time, ordinary, day-to-day time. Stupid really. A lot of marriages had been necessitated in the circle, the couple marching up the aisle of St George's and flying away, to finish off in Benidorm what they had begun under the auspices of The Wise Lady.

Round Wyley they didn't say, 'Fancy a fuck?' They said, 'Want to go and look at the circle?'

Well, that was one thing that definitely wasn't going to happen to Melanie.

A few weeks ago Sergeant Tulliver got called out to pick up a loony who'd got out of the bin at Rocester. Lady Poll had spotted him through a pair of binoculars in one of the fields belonging to the Manor Farm. He was found in the circle, hanging onto a stone, screaming something about the coming millennium. Marjorie Sand said he was drawn there by the devil. What the devil was trying to achieve with the madman she was hazier about. When Melanie asked, she retorted that the whole event had left Lady Poll quite poorly. She'd had to go to bed for the afternoon with a hot water bottle and a toddy.

This didn't seem any great shakes for one who was supposedly capable of causing eternal damnation. Especially since Lady Poll would have enjoyed the toddy.

Melanie laughed to herself. Just another bit of debris drawn into the circle's gravitational pull. And then there was the story someone had told her a very long time ago, so far away on the edges of memory that she could put no face, no voice to the narrative. They were walking through the dew, very early on a warm summer's morning. They were gathering mushrooms. It was sunny, but with quite a thick mist, or they wouldn't have been out there in case they were spotted. They had just bent down to pick a particularly lovely mushroom, had felt the soft, fleshy coming away of its stalk from the earth, when they became conscious of a presence. At first they thought it must be the Manor gardener, Mr Mulch, but, as they straightened, they saw that it was a woman. She was at the heart of the stone circle and her robe was made of mist, threadbare with grass and flowers. The sun was shining on her and she was smiling. If you believed it, John Feather's goddess.

Who had told the story? Who could say? There were more people who liked those stories when Melanie was very young. She had almost believed that there was a doorway to somewhere else, just across the fields.

Grandma didn't like the stories, though. Grandma was vehemently literal, except when it came to the all-pervasiveness of malevolence. She had that in common with the newcomers: afraid of the circle and irritated by it. Irritated because the stones had nothing to do with Wyley really. The village was there because of them; they were not there because of the village. Wyley, when you got down to it, was just passing through.

Grandma was the enemy of ambivalence and inconsistency. She, like the mothers, like their commuting husbands, whose shiny cars whipped the hedgerows as they raced home to gin and tonics, wanted to know exactly where she was. She wanted to be sure about the level of decibels surrounding her, to be certain whether a thing was good or bad, to know just where she stood in terms of history. But the stones resisted all that. The stones had moods and could become strange. They glistened in a fragile, too-bright sunshine. On wet days they were jagged teeth. Against snow they were black crows. They never gave or demanded anything, never made judgments – or suspended them, either – showed little effect of lashing centuries of weather. They couldn't be surprised or shocked because they had already witnessed everything. Wyley's God was younger than they were.

Metamorphosis. Change. Uncertainty. If Melanie really was an old soul, this was why she kept coming back to them. They confirmed a fact that it was easy to forget: not everywhere had the same values as Wyley. Not every time had believed the things that most people believed now.

And maybe – did she really feel, or only hope it? – the circle would draw into its orbit something that brought the possibility of things being different.

'Wake up sleepy head.'

Melanie shook Hamish gently until his eyes opened.

'Look at you. You're all covered in grass. Stand up and I'll brush you down, then we'll go and see Martha.'

She helped Hamish to his feet and flicked her hand quickly over him. She'd thought she could manage it, but there was no way she could avoid thinking about the rumour, the circle's most horrible story.

It wasn't that she really believed it. It wasn't that anyone could really believe it. It was just another of the sort of bad things that Martha had a way of picking up. You didn't have to believe it because it begged all sorts of questions: why hadn't she been arrested, for instance? And was it likely that she would have been allowed to have other children? It was patently and utterly ridiculous, as Martha would have explained, if Melanie had ever asked her about it. And she must ask. It was very important that she should. If it wasn't true she didn't want to believe it any longer.

The hairs on her arms pulled into little goose-pimples. But what if it was true? What would she do then?

The story went like this. On a very snowy day, towards the end of a very cold winter, one of the Manor farmworkers went to the field where the circle was, to see if any of the sheep had started lambing. As he neared the circle he thought one of them had because there was a lot of blood on the snow, near to The

Wise Lady. When he got up to it, however, he realised that there was no lamb there. Instead, cold and pale and quite dead, there was a human foetus. Self-aborted. Some said the mother was Martha Blandish.

3

The Rectory

Sara Feather and Martha Blandish had spent the morning sorting jumble in the study at the back of the Rectory. Great, musty piles of it, incongruously tattered for Wyley, as if, somewhere among the latticed windows and yellow thatching, poorer, less careful people lived and it was they, and not the visible citizens of Wyley, who had put jumble out in black bin-bags, to be collected by Sara in her Morris Minor. Outside, in the formal borders of the Rectory garden, the heads of Renaissance roses hung limp in the translucent heat. The riotous hedgerow was motionless, the tip of one of the stones just discernible, peeping over it. The blue-green hills in the distance were smudgy with the haze.

'Gosh,' said Sara, raising her eyes to the circular, wooden clock that hung next to the bookshelves. 'Nearly time to call it a morning I think.' Then, as her eyes moved to the window and took in the glory of the Rectory garden, where she would sit out and have a lunch of ham and tomatoes with her husband, when he got back from seeing Marjorie Sand, she was assailed by the familiar sensation of how undeservedly lucky she was to live here. A sentiment which, though she was only dimly aware of it, was shared by quite a number of Wyley's parishioners.

The Rectory, a perfect example of Georgian architecture with its yellow, gravelled yard and its pale, seemly brickwork was too grand, they claimed. It would, they felt, have been more suited to his calling if their rector had lived in a purpose-built bungalow, or at least a residence smaller than their own. Of those adhering to this opinion Marjorie Sand was the most vociferous; Magpie Cottage, though exquisite, possessed only two bedrooms. Why, she eternally asked Lady Poll and Sir Homer, did the rector and his wife need four? It wasn't as if they had children.

Lady Poll concurred but Sir Homer maintained that the dignity of the rector's accommodation reflected well upon the village as a whole and also, of course, upon the Manor. Homer King was of the belief that Wyley Manor could be said to have a certain priority should it need, for whatever reason, the cooperation of the Rectory; the pew at the front of St George's church did not, as it once might have done, have the honourable name of the King family engraved upon it but his family did, ineradicably and consistently, occupy that pew when it knelt before God. Besides, the Manor was very much larger than the Rectory.

Sir Homer might have been more inclined to agree with Marjorie Sand had an immodest rector possessed furnishings incongruous to his station – and there had indeed been some unpleasantness in the past – but in John and Sara Feather he could find nothing to take exception to. On his infrequent visits to the Rectory he had observed that the bookcases were filled mainly with paperbacks, not the bound volumes of the Manor library; the pictures on the wall were black and white prints, most of them of inoffensive landscapes. The desk was full but not frantically cluttered, which would have been too low church for Homer King's taste, and the photograph on it of John and Sara, surrounded by a bunch of smiling people in duffle coats was, in its uniqueness, a permissible piece of frivolity. Sir Homer was not to know that it was taken at an event organised by Christian CND.

'John will be home soon. I wonder how it's gone,' Sara added, hastily stapling a price to a last pair of gloves and putting them with the heap of clothes on the carpet. She blinked excitedly; John was another unwarranted blessing. If there were some ways in which she was less fortunate, she thought to herself, she was jolly lucky in others. But then an expression of sadness crossed her doughy, peg-doll face because it was this bad fortune that had brought John and Sara to Wyley, that and something

John didn't know about, something more mysterious, about which, though she didn't know why, she felt a little guilty.

It had all happened because, from the outset, Sara and John had planned on having children. It was one of the subjects they had discussed during their engagement, when John was just coming up to his finals at Exeter and Sara got the train down to visit him, staying with married friends in their small spare bedroom. For it had been a proper engagement. A bicycling by rivers sort of engagement. Shared favourite tea-rooms. Letters in blue ink, not felt-tip. An old-fashioned engagement, jammed full of projects and expectations.

After their wedding, finding themselves in a quiet hotel bedroom, overlooking a choppy Cornish sea, had been surprising, as if it were something neither of them had quite believed would happen.

Sara's twenties had gone by, and it was when she reached her early thirties that it had become obvious to both of them that something was wrong. They went to doctors, who did tests and said there was nothing the matter. It was just a question of relaxing and a baby would come along. The doctors spoke to both of them, but it seemed to Sara that it was mainly her they looked at.

She had felt then, as she felt now, looking glumly at the jumble, that it was her inefficiency that had let the side down. Not active failure, just not being quite good enough. Lying on the doctor's table, white legs splayed, resembling, she imagined, the frogs' legs she had once seen in a French supermarket, she had decided it must be her fault – though 'fault' was a word that neither of them spoke; they only thought it. Women were more complex. There was more to go wrong if you were dealing with complexity. She was simply not offering what the sheer fact of her femininity had promised. Worse still, the professional side of the deal was being threatened by an overwhelming need to collapse into a watery state. To be pitiful.

Not that she ever did collapse. In fact, the afternoon after that humiliating examination, the cool, itchy gel still between her legs, she had manned a stall at a Bring-and-Buy because someone had dropped out at the last minute. When, later on, John, ever the gentleman, asked her about her visit to the doctor her reply had been non-committal. 'Not very pleasant, but it didn't last long. You know how these things are.' But he didn't, and she would not have been so impolite as to tell him.

She should have felt a kind of grim pride at not making a fuss – it would have been some consolation – but she knew of old that those who can and cannot successfully make a fuss in this world is laid down in canon law, and that she was of the latter group.

They worked in a poor parish in London, in the inner city. People arrived at the house at all hours of the day and night. Their front door was always open, the kettle on the gas stove was always steaming. They wiped the noses of bawling toddlers, drove people to hospital, keeping the back seat of the car covered with an old sheet to protect it from bloodstains. They filled in forms, telephoned the Social Security several times a day. Their nostrils filled with the sour-milk smell of poverty.

They were useful, happy and childless. Then Sara spotted the living in Wyley.

She remembered that day now, as she sat in the sunny room, listening for John's footsteps. It was her guilty secret.

It had been raining. Of course it had been raining. She'd put the telephone down at the end of a long and hopeless conversation with the woman at the DHSS who she always hoped she wouldn't get, and looked up at the streaming window. A sad line of Jamaicans were queuing at the bus-stop. She looked down at the desk again, to see what she had to do next, and that was when she saw it. It leapt out at her from the open page of what John called 'the trade mag'.

Wyley.

The telephone burst into life yet again but, for once, she ignored it. Her whole body had started tingling. For a moment, blushing at the idea, she thought she was, quite unexpectedly and for no reason, about to have her first ever orgasm. But the tingling did not peak and diminish. It continued, unabated, as if her entire skin surface had, unwittingly, tuned into some distant radio station. Facts about Wyley, that she had never known she knew, delivered themselves into her consciousness.

There was a window in the church there, older than anyone could reliably guess at, she told John later, when she drew the living to his attention, and there was a stone circle; its name was The Wise Lady. Wyley lay in a fertile valley, among a landscape of undulating hills and curving footpaths.

'You've visited Wyley then?' he asked.

'No,' she replied. 'I've just heard about it.'

The feeling had lasted about five minutes and then the front door had opened and someone had called and it had subsided. At the weekend, when they drove to Wyley in the Morris Minor, Sara wondered if it had ever really happened.

'Goodness, are you sure you really want to? It will be a bit muddy and we haven't any wellingtons we can lend you,' said the departing rector when Sara asked to see the stones in the church meadow. He was the ascetic, bookish variety, who believed incredulity to look intellectual.

'Mine are in the Morry,' said John, 'if you don't mind my not coming with you.'

'Not at all. I'll just pop out for a moment.'

So she'd slopped to the meadow in outsize wellies and had found the stones, bigger than she'd imagined them, blackened by rain, though now the sun was shining dazzlingly, with blown blossoms scattered at their feet.

'I know it's silly,' she said at lunchtime, describing the sight as they ate shepherd's pie with the rector and his wife, 'but it made me think of all sorts of other pagan things. Pan, Aphrodite, Attic revelry and all that. Not at all English, really.'

'Paganism has never been particularly English,' said the departing rector, disapprovingly.

That afternoon, on the way back to the city, they had told themselves that the problem had probably been London and things would be different in Wyley. John applied and got the living. They had been here two years now and Sara was thirty-eight. Whatever had beckoned her to Wyley had failed to keep its promise – if something had indeed beckoned, if something had indeed promised. Or not kept it yet.

'I'll just do in the nursery, then I'll leave you in peace,' Mrs Atter had said, earlier that morning, carrying the Hoover into the room adjoining John and Sara's.

'The nursery?'

'I mean the small spare room, love.'

'Was it ever a nursery?'

'Not that I know of.'

For a moment it had been tempting to read it as a message, though Mrs Atter was an unlikely Gabriel and Sara did not merit angelic visitation. But this was superstitious, and Mrs Atter was probably just thinking of another house she did.

By and large John and Sara fitted in to Wyley – but then Sara would have fitted in anywhere that John was. Transplant her to the mouth of the Nile and she would, within a week, be organising parish breakfasts and flower rotas.

Wyley had welcomed them, not with open arms exactly, but with the civility due to those whose credentials are proven. Now, once or twice a week, depending on the season, Sara arranged flowers beneath the window that she had thought about that day in London.

She had grown to love that window.

There was a funny little shelf beneath it, one of those odd stone bits of churches that you always felt were there for some now forgotten reason. Certainly it wasn't terribly useful for its allocated purpose. It was much too narrow. Vases were prone to falling off it and smashing on the flagstones.

When she arrived in Wyley Sara decided it would be better not to bother with flowers under the window. They weren't really necessary. But Marjorie Sand, who had homed in upon them and, at that time, was eternally present, insisted. The purpose of the flowers was not decoration. It was to hide the depiction of the stone circle, luckily placed at the bottom of the window. That it was there at all was a disgrace but it could be partially masked with hollyhocks and gladioli in summer; in spring great sprays of blossom; at Christmas large quantities of evergreens (excluding mistletoe). Wyley expected it and would otherwise be disappointed.

The need for sturdy, fleshy sorts of flowers made the vases more precarious. Sara bought some stainless steel ones and kept a dustpan and brush tucked away in a corner. St George, who hovered above the stones, his two feet, in their jewelled slippers, pointing in the same direction, looked as if he was walking upon flowers. It was a nice effect, but it always seemed to Sara a shame to block out the circle.

'There's more gravity in Wyley than in most places,' said Martha, finding Sara kneeling on the flagstones, surrounded by battered lilacs, one time when she'd come to call her to the telephone.

'Yes,' said Sara, misunderstanding. 'People are rather serious.'

'No, real gravity,' said Martha. 'Things fall over, get dropped easily. Like I dropped my mother's ashes.'

Sara cast her mind back to school science. Wasn't gravity the same everywhere except at the poles? Perhaps it did vary, she couldn't remember. Something in her felt compelled to make a sensible comment. The rest of her just nodded.

'Oh,' said Martha now, interrupting her thoughts. She was sitting on the carpet, lifting to the light a framed picture of The Wise Lady stone, holding it away from her. Sara moved closer to admire it.

'Now that is nice.'

It was done in soft charcoal. The artist must have drawn sitting directly under the stone. The peak of The Wise Lady dissolved into a swirling mist and appeared distant, while the wall of rock in the foreground was close, dark and intimidating.

'It doesn't seem to be signed.' Sara turned the picture over and then back again. 'No, wait a minute, there's a letter in the corner here, a "B" I think, and there is a date, '67. Well, that doesn't tell us much.'

'No one will buy it,' said Martha.

'Somebody must have bought it in order to be throwing it away,' reasoned Sara.

Martha put the picture down and wiped her fingers on her skirt.

'I don't have much to do with the stones any more,' she said. 'Not since I got pregnant – with Melanie I mean. Before that I'd been going to go to art college. But I got pregnant, so I never went.'

'You should do it now,' said Sara, picking up a pair of pink socks that she had just spotted under a chair. 'You're lucky to have a talent.'

Martha sighed. 'It's not possible to do these things with children. For a while I thought maybe, when Melanie was grown up, then I might, but then . . . I didn't have the heart for it any more somehow . . . It would mean London, anyway.'

'You could move. You could sell your mother's house.'

'Yes, I'm lucky I have a house of my own. But, well, it would be the same problem. No qualifications and three of us to support. Jobs are hard to get. I'm lucky to have one.'

'We're lucky to have you,' said Sara hastily, embarrassed and envious. 'But I do see what you mean.'

'And then of course there's Tully.'

The two women looked back at the picture.

'If nobody buys it I might keep it,' said Sara.

'Stones attract travellers,' said Martha, reaching for a cardboard box and putting the picture in it and covering it with a cardigan. 'The police think they're moving towards us.'

'What, New Age travellers, coming here to Wyley?' Sara was startled. 'I thought they went to Stonehenge and . . . What's that other place called?'

'Glastonbury. They do,' said Martha. 'But there's always the possibility. Tully says they might read Sir Homer's article in *The Commentator*.'

'Do New Age travellers read *The Commentator*?' asked Sara, doubtfully.

'Some, probably.'

'Well if they do it'll be pretty clear to them that the stones are private and they'd be far from welcome.'

'Tully says the stones are a threat to law and order, but I think it might be fun if they came,' said Martha.

'Well,' said Sara, starting to gather together her unused labels, 'I don't know that a stone can really threaten anything in particular. But it is all rather unfamiliar. Goddesses and whatnot. Frija in all her Teutonicness.'

'Wife of Odin,' said John Feather entering the room. He was wearing jeans and a sweatshirt. Sara beamed at him encouragingly. If she were a dog she would have wagged her tail. She could tell from the expression on his handsome face that he was irritated.

John pushed his dark hair back from his forehead.

'I looked her up when I wrote that thing for *A Guide To Wyley*. There really isn't much else to say about her. I wish to God I hadn't written that article now, though. Especially the last paragraph. I thought it might put paid to Marjorie's complaints about the stones, appropriating the whole caboodle for Christianity. Instead I appear to have merely fuelled her enthusiasm in her crusade against paganism and the forces of darkness. God knows what she'll come up with next. I shudder to think. If Marjorie had lived in Wyley all her life I'd be tempted to believe that it was one of her ancestors who organised the pulling down of that stone in the eighteenth century.'

Sara twisted her pale lips sympathetically.

'No go then?'

'No go I'm afraid. She still wants to pursue the ridiculous idea. I tried to get her to change her mind but whenever I came up with anything convincing she said she wouldn't want to disappoint Lady Poll on her special day. The whole thing is so ridiculous. Imagine parading around with a crucifix. Especially in Wyley.'

For John Feather knew the boundaries of his parishioners' belief and was well aware that the limits of his jurisdiction were Sunday and the interior of St George's church. Should he trespass elsewhere, other than for the occasional Mother's Union Meeting or jumble sale, he would receive a hostile welcome. Apart from Marjorie Sand, who believed in Christianity with an unappealing ardour, there was no one in the rector's flock who imbued their weekly visit to the parish church with any more significance than they gave to other English notions, such as the sacrosanct nature of private property or the desirability of a class-system.

Nor was there any requirement, or, to be more accurate, any wish for John and Sara's help in practical matters. When the phone rang, when people called, it was to fix dates for weddings and baptisms, to discuss the organisation of charitable activities, times of bell-ringing practice. Split lips after unlucky tumbles – of which, if the rumours were true, there seemed to be rather a lot lately – were dealt with by private doctors. Marital discord was the province of solicitors.

If a rector had not been on hand to christen them, marry them and bury them it is true that the citizens of Wyley would have felt the lack but they never felt a lack of, or need for, moral guidance or judgement upon ethical dilemmas. There were no ethical dilemmas in Wyley.

John rolled his sleeves up and wiped the sweat from his forehead. He'd gone for a walk after the interview with Marjorie, and he always walked briskly. It hadn't been a pleasant walk, unfortunately; everyone appeared to be rather jumpy, and something strange had happened: he'd met Mrs Blade coming out of Dr Oliver's and she'd asked him to bless her baby.

'Jason is baptised, Mrs Blade,' he'd said, puzzled. This wasn't something that had ever happened before in Wyley.

Mrs Blade had scissored her lips into a nervous smile.

'I don't think one can have too many blessings, rector.'

So he'd done it, quickly and furtively, feeling rather stupid, surprised at the relief it seemed to give her. But then he was always forgetting the literalism of his parishioners.

Unbeknown to most people, including Sara, John had, during his first year at Exeter, come up with a faith that was based upon the idea of giving God the benefit of the doubt. Having done this, and with the desire to do some good within his society, it had followed that the most apposite medium for the fulfilment of this desire was the Church of England. He liked and appreciated its rituals. Even in Wyley's assured brides, with wedding lists at Harrods and jobs in PR, there appeared to be a desire for the kind of mystical endorsement of human activity that only ritual could give. In whose name these endorsements were made was, to John Feather's way of thinking, important culturally but had nothing to do with any kind of objective historical truth. The truth was the ritual. If he had lived in Wyley four thousand years ago he would probably have been the High Priest of the stone circle, though this was not a thought that he confided to Mrs Blade, as she got into her Volvo.

He was not ashamed of the nature of his faith but he saw little to be gained and much to be lost by informing his parishioners of it. The most apathetic members of his congregation would scream blue murder at the idea of a rector who did not agree wholeheartedly that Christ was a man who had been alive two thousand years earlier, as real as Homer King or Prince Charles. And since for John Feather the medium was the message, there was no reason to alert his flock to historical niceties that they would resent and misinterpret and ultimately reject.

Which was why Marjorie Sand was such a thorn in John Feather's flesh. Her insistence that the church should encroach on areas that most of Wyley did not consider its concern placed him in an awkward situation. As rector he should go along with Marjorie's more excessive ideas; not to do so would be to show a lack of enthusiasm that would be suspect even amongst those who did not agree with Marjorie themselves – it was, in a sense, his job to support her hyperbolic faith, if only to reassure the parishioners that, although most of the time he didn't manifest it, he did actually feel that way himself. On the other hand he really did not believe what Marjorie Sand believed and it was galling and, indeed, dishonest to pretend that he did. Furthermore he knew that if he paraded around a crucifix at an event as hallowed as the opening of the Manor grounds to the public he would be bitterly resented even as his faith was admired.

Sometimes he wished he hadn't come to Wyley. Life had been much easier in the inner city where your task was clear and where people were much more interested in whether you could help them fill in their social security forms than in why you did so. It wasn't as if coming to Wyley had made any difference.

John glanced briefly at his wife, who was putting things away in drawers, thinking sadly how plain and colourless she looked in her skirt and blouse and the beige sandals that showed her wide, pale feet that resembled two saucers of stale milk.

She suffered, of course, from comparison with Martha, whose face had always struck John Feather as being like that of the most sternly beautiful of Renaissance Madonnas, the ones who suckled their baby in the full knowledge of future sorrow. And Martha radiated sexual energy, which Sara did not.

With his handsome, intellectual face, his thick, dark hair and, oh best of all, the chill aura of clericism, John Feather had had to become accustomed to fielding the attentions of lonely Wyley mothers, whose husbands worked late in London and whose au pairs were out tasting the delights of Rocester. But these offered no temptation, no promise of excitement or danger, nothing huge or ugly or uncontrollable. They were gas flames who burnt blue and cold. Whereas Martha . . . He was glad she never smiled at him specifically.

Sara wore things that seemed to her to match. Martha appeared to put together her clothing the way that some birds made their nests, including a little bit of whatever might happen to be lying around: today, an Indian scarf woven with silver, a short, full skirt with a black, sleeveless t-shirt above it, with a picture of a whale on, under which was a strange old garment in faded, cream lace. It would be nice if Sara . . . John searched through his brain for the words and only came up with ones that he instinctively disliked when he heard them in the mouths of his female parishioners: 'did more with herself'; 'made something of her better features'; 'dressed up a bit'.

He rejected these thoughts as unworthy of him. The fact that Sara did not do these things was the very reason that he had married her; it was what had told him that she would make a suitable rector's wife. And he had been correct for she had never failed to keep her side of a bargain that she did not know she had made. In all sincerity John Feather appreciated this. Because of it he endeavoured at all times to treat her with courtesy and kindness. He was, perhaps, kinder to her than he might have been if he had loved her.

To make up for his uncharitable thoughts he went over to where she was standing.

'Gosh, look at this. Wherever did it come from?' He held up a vast grey brassiere that had once been white.

'Gosh!' echoed a voice behind him, nastily. John turned. It was Melanie, lolling by the bookcase, resting Hamish against her small hip, which was projected for the purpose. She was smoking a roll-up.

'The door was open so I came in. I'm surprised you aren't scared of burglars with all this jumble in the house.'

'Hallo, Melanie,' said John.

'Oh that.' Sara looked at the bra quickly. 'Miss Evans at the post office. It belonged to her mother who died in a home just outside London at the end of last year.'

'Do you think anyone will want it?'

'Probably not, but one is always surprised.'

'Oh, Melanie, I do wish you wouldn't smoke,' said Martha.

Melanie took a drag and looked around her boredly. John Feather was wearing, as usual, a blue sweatshirt with the sleeves rolled up. Perhaps he thought the only way a rector of Wyley could justify that kind of clothing was to constantly give the impression that he was just about to start doing some kind of manual labour. Martha scrabbling about among a pile of old knickers; that must make her feel at home. And Sara.

Why, she wondered, for the millionth time, running her eyes down Sara's shapeless form, reaching the bottom of her pleated cotton floral skirt and arriving at her blueish legs, beaded with dots of congealed blood and a brown running-stitch of scars, did Sara persist in shaving her legs? Even quite thick hair would be preferable to this scene of hopeless self-mutilation. For a moment it occurred to her that perhaps Sara's bodily hair was of a phenomenal thickness such as to make its eradication highly desirable but, looking again at Sara's neutral features, this explanation seemed too interesting to be likely.

'I thought the poor got the dole,' she said, kicking at a poxy sweater, with beige half-moons under the armpits where perspiration had bled it of colour.

Sara's face became slightly pink. 'They do,' she replied, in a self-consciously sensible voice. 'But it isn't enough, especially if they have children.'

'They shouldn't have children then, if they're so hard up.' With a glance at her mother.

'Well they do, and that's that. We can't take their children away from them, can we now?'

Melanie shrugged.

'I bet they spend the money on tellys and videos.'

Sara pursed her lips. 'I suppose some of them do,' she said, putting on her sensible voice again. 'But not all of them.'

'Why not just give them the clothes instead?'

Sara did not reply but shot a glance at Martha who, sensing that she was expected to intervene wailed, 'Oh, Melanie, can't you think of other people?' with one of her I'm-going-to-have-another-nervous-breakdown looks.

That was good, coming from Martha, who had campaigned to save everything and anything except for people.

Melanie ignored her. 'So how's things with Marjorie Sandbox?' she asked John Feather.

John pulled a wry face. 'She's not budging. Says Lady Poll would be disappointed.'

Melanie took another puff on her cigarette and blew the smoke out of the corner of her mouth.

'Lady Poll my ass.'

Martha looked at her desperately, but said nothing.

'You're right about that,' said John, unmoved. 'It's not anything to do with her really. It's Marjorie who's cooked the whole thing up and I can't think of anyone other than Marjorie who can make it go away.'

'Go and see Sir Fat-arse. He's not going to want his yearly pontification upstaged by you and Jeeezus and Marjorie Sand.'

Melanie paused. John contemplated her. Leaning against the wall, she was staring at him with her large, green eyes, her lips slightly open, as if he were the most stupid mortal on the planet.

'Golly, that's a thought.'

'Golly, it is,' she mimicked. She puffed her cheeks full of air and blew upwards, disarraying her straight, black fringe for a moment, as if to suggest that the things that she didn't think of just didn't get thought in Wyley.

4

The Manor

'The mad people are getting nearer; I can sense it,' said Lady Polly. 'I should know: I was born in an asylum. It's given me an eye for them.'

She paused, and Crispin Turner, the farm manager, paused also.

'In an asylum?' he said, turning his full-lipped, almost pretty face to look at her.

Lady Polly admired his peachy skin for a moment.

'Oh yes. Though I once turned heads on the Cote d'Azur, I was born in the grounds of a lunatic asylum. In Yorkshire it was. My father was the gardener there.'

'You still turn heads, Lady Polly,' said Crispin.

'He grew daffodils. Dispirited blooms I always thought them. Didn't like being in the grounds. Too chill. Too shady. There was a black wall, so high it met the clouds, which were also black. He grew rhubarb, too. For the inmates' bowels. Most efficacious. I sometimes witnessed the results of it. That's one of the things about the mad people: they are so relaxed about their bodies.'

She started to walk on, and Crispin Turner walked on also. Across the faultless lawn went Lady Poll, her lips moist and violet with age, rouge on her cheeks, loose white powder beneath it that she had applied that morning with a vast, downy powder puff. There was no natural blush to exaggerate, only broken veins beneath the snowy coating. Her eyebrows were too dark a brown. Her hair was the colour of a baby duck. She resembled an unsteady clown, who had tremblingly applied ill-chosen make-up. The Wyley children, the small Octavias, Violas and Tarquins, were afraid of her. Her strange and costly gown was turquoise, green and purple.

'Did I tell you, Crispin,' she asked, 'that I apprehended a mad person a few weeks ago?'

'No,' said Crispin. Though she had, and he knew about it anyway.

'No cause for admiration,' said Lady Poll, with assumed modesty. 'I was watching for them with my binoculars. I watch twice a day, night and morning. That's when they will come: night or morning.'

'Not afternoon?' asked Crispin.

'Oh no,' said Lady Polly. 'In the afternoon they have their naps. It's the stones, the horrid stones, that draw them. They reveal my location. Low profile is impossible if you own a stone circle. All the way from Yorkshire he'd come. Tell me, if you can, how he found me. Marjorie's wrong, it's nothing to do with the devil. And you may be sure, Crispin,' she jabbed an orange fingernail at him, 'that one was merely the tip of the iceberg. The others will be coming, too.'

There was a pause, during which Lady Polly spotted a solitary daisy and pierced it with the sharp heel of one of her radiant stilettoes.

'Though it is possibly the case,' she continued, 'that if it weren't for the mad people I might not have been so fortunate. As a gal I was – how can I put it? – passionate by nature. In the asylum my curiosity was satisfied. After which I was always – or almost always – reluctant for physical contact. They like that, the upper classes. Keeps 'em interested.'

'Um,' said Crispin Turner, who was himself an aristocrat.

Lady Poll fell silent. Two sparrows squabbled in the yew hedge at the end of the garden. She remembered how, all those years ago, armed with this patina of frigidity, and blessed with peerless beauty, she had set her sights higher than the job selling ladies' hats, which would otherwise have been her social destination, and had aimed for, and won, a country manor.

Her success had been due to a well-thought-out strategy; after some consideration it had come to her that the most likely place for a gardener's daughter to encounter a member of the landed aristocracy was The National Gallery in London – especially when it was raining. She sold her umbrella and, sure enough, a particularly heavy April shower blew her Horace King.

There had been shock in his family when it was revealed that a northern girl of the lower middle-classes was to combine her humble genes with the Kings' so venerable ones. But this had diminished in the light of her ladylike manner and her willingness to forget everything that had happened to her before that day among the paintings, that had ended in tea at the Savoy – or to appear to.

'How hard it is to forget things, Crispin,' Lady Poll remarked, apropos, it seemed to him, of nothing, in the Manor garden, nearly seventy years later.

The hat shop and its accompanying vista of genteel semi-poverty. How possible it had been then; how narrowly avoided. At night, in her dreams, during those early days of marriage, Lady Polly King, whose frocks were described in *The Tatler*, presented creation after creation to scornful ladies with cigarette holders and laughing lips – desperately, as if by selling enough hats she might reach the magic number that would free her. In the morning she would phone a girlfriend and they would go out and buy gowns together – and hats – and drink martinis. Alcohol was new, and somewhat risqué.

But the hats never left her. Nor did the mad people. As she spoke to Crispin, Lady Poll scanned the horizon for signs of their arrival.

She had tried to drown their clamour with gin and It, looking out over the Mediterranean and the sunshades, only to find that the gossip of the bright young things was less sharp, less piercing than the murmur of the mad people's distress, or their pleasure. The haunting belief that they would return to reclaim the life that, behind dripping walls, had been denied them, was stronger than the cocktails they served in that bar in Nice that Horace and Polly went to most evenings during their honeymoon. Even now their naked faces entered through chinks of sobriety, demanding ever heavier doses to shut them out.

Because of the mad people, Lady Poll's beauty promised more than it was disposed to give, but Horace never upbraided her for it. And when, rather late in the day, her son Homer made his appearance, he was not to know that not all mothers were physically revolted by the touch of their offspring.

'You must have many happy memories of Sir Homer's boyhood,' said Crispin Turner, softly.

'Sir Homer,' said Lady Poll, 'went to Eton.'

'I know,' said Crispin, his lips pulling outwards into a slight smile. 'So did I.'

'Then you must have known him.'

'Only by reputation. I'm much younger than he is. Tell me about him at Eton.'

But Lady Poll had spotted Mulch, the gardener, doing something he shouldn't and had begun to totter, speedily, in his direction. Crispin followed.

'It's very hot out here,' said Lady Poll. 'Makes one thirsty.'

'You were telling me, Lady Polly, about Sir Homer at Eton.'

'Mulch, Mulch, Mulch!' screeched Lady Poll, as they neared him. 'How often have I said? How often?'

'Sir Homer, Lady Poll,' breathed Crispin Turner, so close to her ear that she felt his scented breath entering its crevices.

'Funny child,' she said, stopping. 'Didn't notice him much.' She turned and faced Crispin, giving him a full view of her crumbling features. 'You see, I was more interested in dresses.'

Inside the Manor, in his book-lined study, behind his heavy desk, sat Sir Homer King, the topic of this lopsided conversation. The study smelled of wax polish and dry sherry and, even on this richly warm June day, retained that slight chill that proclaimed the walls to be of a thickness only now attainable by the extremely rich. Homer King who, as he exasperatedly replaced the telephone receiver, resembled nothing so much as a very full jug of cream.

He had just received a request from John Feather to come and discuss with him some ridiculous idea that Marjorie Sand and his mother had had in relation to the opening of the Manor grounds. He was due in about twenty minutes and the outcome of their conversation would doubtless result in unpleasantness between himself and his mother, which was something Sir Homer usually avoided, due to its tiresomeness.

Feather's call had been followed, in quick succession, by one from Sergeant Tulliver, who had insisted on reading him, in its entirety, an illiterate missive he had received from police headquarters in Rocester, the subject of which was itinerant hippies. The constabulary was apparently of the opinion that, having been denied access to Stonehenge, the hippies might turn their attention to other stone circles. If this happened, the Rocester police force at least would be quick to take preventative measures.

'You will have to translate for me, Sergeant, the meaning of action taken "accordant with the phenomenon before it has a chance to multiply".'

There was silence on the other end of the phone and then a slight huffing and puffing.

'I believe, Sir Homer, it means that you may be confident of the force's best efforts.'

'Well that is reassuring, Sergeant Tulliver, and how elegantly the concept has been expressed.'

'Thank you, sir,' said Tulliver doubtfully.

But, in spite of his sarcasm, Sir Homer was alarmed. He lifted a copy of *The Times* from his desk and gave a second, brief perusal to an article on this very topic that seemed to bear out the police force's conviction of a need for concern.

How many such people were there? Sir Homer wondered. On this the article was not very informative. Tens? Hundreds? Thousands? This seemed preposterously unlikely. And why couldn't the wretched individuals just give up? Sir Homer, if the majority of the nation had wished it, would have been willing to forego his Christmas celebrations in St George's.

Sir Homer thought, with a shudder, of the television reports from Stonehenge the previous summer. It was the memory of them that had inspired a recent piece he had written for *The Commentator*, in which he had roundly denounced hippies, rock festivals and trespass upon stone circles in general, and his own in particular. At the time of writing, however, he had believed that last year's events, so manifestly unpleasant for all parties – police and hippies alike – must have marked the end of the entire 'phenomenon'. It had never occurred to him that it might, on the contrary, 'multiply'.

Sir Homer closed the newspaper and looked, with relieved satisfaction, at the picture on the front of it. 'Conservative M.P. for Rocester, Thomas Bright, arriving at Downing Street today for a meeting with the prime-minister.' Sir Homer sighed with pleasure. How well Thomas had progressed since his days at Eton. How truly gratifying to know that Sir Homer and Thomas Bright had a peculiar bond of friendship. This intimate tie alone, combined with the returning calm of Sir Homer's study, seemed proof against any anarchic desire to destroy the given order of things. He hoped that Thomas would soon make another visit to Wyley Manor; he spent most of his time in London or at his grange in Dorset.

The last wind that had blown Thomas to Wyley had been the re-opening of Wyley Primary. What a pleasant event it had been. How roundly Thomas had been applauded when he had made his feelings known about hanging, and when he had said how tired he was of hearing people knock the nuclear family. Afterwards Thomas and Homer had managed to get away and had dashed to a little restaurant in Springham and had a delightful meal of foie gras followed by veal, washed down with an aged claret.

The reminiscence had brought back Sir Homer's equanimity.

In search of inspiration for other pleasant cogitations, he looked out of the window to the Manor garden, finding there, however, sights that evoked a mixture of emotions.

The dull, wizened, stumpy form of Mulch, the unlikely creator of all the garden's vivacious beauty, returning to his work in preparation for the opening, was a satisfying evocation of rural industry. This was marred though by the vision of his mother, whose liver-spotted hand Crispin Turner was now raising, gallantly, to his rosy lips.

Ever more Lady Polly reminded Sir Homer of a picture he had once seen of a hundred-year-old parrot. Turning to commence a progress along a regiment of roses she stumbled and Crispin intercepted her in mid-air, before she fluttered to the ground. Sir Homer gave a tut of annoyance and made a mental note to speak to Cook and Miss Trannock to see if it could be ascertained exactly where Lady Poll was getting her alcohol.

'Your mother, Sir Homer, should be dried out and then given a course of counselling,' the young locum had said who, in the absence of Dr Oliver, had attended Lady Poll when she came out of hospital after her fall from the rostrum.

'Dried out? Is my mother a dishcloth, Doctor? And are you suggesting to me that she would profit from discussing her existence with a social worker, a quarter her age, who has gained his "qualification" at some dingy polytechnic?'

No, this was not what the locum was suggesting. He left hastily. A letter of apology was sent by Doctor Oliver on his return from holiday. There were certain malaises in Wyley that the private sector was better equipped to diagnose.

Sir Homer had never considered why his mother drank; he was not greatly interested in why people did things. He knew she did and that she always had done; though, since the wretched business of the madman in the circle, her consumption appeared to have risen dramatically.

At night, when he walked through the fields, Sir Homer frequently spotted his mother at the window with her binoculars. Once he had heard her shout 'They're coming! They're coming!' across the silent meadows. It would clearly not do.

This morning, over elevenses in the drawing-room, which today had consisted of bitter black coffee and homemade macaroons (he took elevenses in his study on the days they had cream eclairs because his nerves were just not strong enough to watch his mother eating one) Lady Polly had made an alarming statement.

'I have a feeling that something exciting could happen this year at the opening of the Manor grounds, Homer.'

Sir Homer profoundly hoped that she was referring to the nonsense she was organising with Marjorie.

At any event, she was not going to be permitted to move about on the rostrum. Her gait was just too unsteady – which was understandable in one's eighties, everyone in Wyley recognised that.

And as for peeping and prying among his mother's motivations, Sir Homer was loath to tamper with a stable situation.

He had discovered long ago that secrecy could be desirable, that repression had a purpose.

Sir Homer remembered, as a child, the horrible excitement, when she was out, of evading Nanny and creeping into his mother's closet. Closet: even now the word was thrilling. To be among the drop-waisted muslins and cloche hats; the metallic sheaths that scintillated in Paris and London; soft, skin gloves and long dust-coats; silk slippers, dyed tangerine, mauve and palest lavender. A rush of colour. The occasional brush of an ostrich boa. The creamy presence of perfumed silk. Tissue-thin olive gold shifts twisted into ropes and knotted. But, best of all, the nasty, lovely secrets of crumpled piles of peach-coloured crêpe de Chine: deeply female; deeply clandestine. Hidden, he knew, from the eyes of his father.

Sir Homer imagined that alcohol had effaced what few memories his mother had ever had of his childhood. He watched her now, with Crispin beside her, his open face and vigorous body a startling contrast to her decrepit one. Even penniless the second son of a viscount evoked respect, and envy.

All his life Sir Homer had felt a certain nervousness about his own station in society. Not that he feared it should ever be wrested from him; it was rather that his mother's lowly and, worse, eccentric background meant that Sir Homer could never quite feel that his feet were as firmly planted on solid earth as he would have liked. It must be a factor in certain decisions that, were it not for his mother's upbringing, he might have made differently.

He adhered, for example, to a gentlemanly conservatism, rather than the kind that was currently in vogue and was perhaps more advisable for those with aspirations. But to aspire was to suggest that you felt that your position within the class-system was movable, and who would want to move other than those who had started low, or at least lowish? So he made it his business, in his weekly column, to stand for, or appear to stand for, those Tory viewpoints which could be termed enduring, even while his natural sympathies lay elsewhere, with men like Thomas. So, too, in his occasional pieces, which he merely signed 'The Epicure', he tended to review not new, fashionable restaurants but older establishments, whose impeccable pedigrees were well-known and undisputed. It was for this reason that he avoided the refurbished Rose and Crown, and thereby any assocation with the City brashness of the Tarrants.

These were not problems that Crispin Turner experienced. Though he could not expect, as Sir Homer could, upon the death of his remaining parent, to inherit a country manor, a considerable number of investments, and a large estate. Nor did he already possess, in his own right, as Sir Homer did, a spacious flat near the Palace of Westminster, where he was accustomed to laying on interesting entertainments.

There was no doubt that Crispin had used his talents sensibly. The management of the Manor Farm brought with it a little tied-cottage. Within reason Sir Homer permitted him a small amount of experimentation – he was morbidly interested in organic vegetable production. In the fullness of time he would undoubtedly win the hand of a relatively affluent local lady, which was the most he could expect now that the trust, which had paid for Eton and Wye College, had dwindled to nothing. His prospects in this respect could only be enhanced by his association with Wyley Manor.

Sir Homer's eyes rested on the cool woodland that prevented the inhabitants of the Manor from having to look at the stones when they were downstairs.

The respect that the Manor inspired was another cause for Sir Homer to detest and resent the presence of the stone circle. Even without the hippies it had always struck him as brash. It attracted the wrong sort of attention; attention which could only undermine the King family's expensively-acquired status. Madmen running here, there and everywhere; his mother prophesying some kind of visitation. Why had the ancient people taken it upon themselves to uphold what they saw as eternal verities when there were so many other things they could have found to occupy themselves with – killing dinosaurs, gathering berries, making fires or whatever?

The desire to worship was absent in Sir Homer and not even kindled when he piously buried his head in his hands on Sundays in his own special pew. The desire to be worshipped was a more lively blaze. However he explained it to himself, the real problem he had with the stones – when he considered them in daylight – was that there was nothing about them that included him in any way. They would be there when there was no longer a Homer King to resent them. He owned them but, irritatingly, they proclaimed by their very presence that, even in England, ownership is not always enough.

In the corner of the study Chummy, Lady Poll's miniature whippet, stood and trembled. It had been put there at Lady Poll's command, for a reason that Sir Homer had been unable to fathom – perhaps fear that it would catch sunstroke. He turned and looked at it with irritation.

Its thin, rat-like tail was tucked tightly between its legs; every bone of its fragile body was visible. It resembled one of those unappealing, small, transparent fish that people insisted on keeping in aquaria; the ones whose liver and kidney and lungs, or whatever a fish possessed, were completely and tastelessly revealed. If they had to have a dog – and who of any eminence possessing a country residence did not? – why, he wondered, had his mother chosen this mutant breed? As if it could read Sir Homer's mind the dog's trembling doubled in speed so that the whole solid room seemed to be shaking with him. On good days Sir Homer could see in Chummy a relationship to those stone dogs who, on medieval tombs, made convenient foot-stools for their dead, stone masters but today it occurred to him that anyone perceiving this link might feel that it indicated, not Sir Homer King's innate aristocracy, but a certain queasiness about his situation.

Averting his eyes from the distasteful creature, Sir Homer looked out once more, beyond the garden, across the fields. A figure appeared at the Wyley end of the folly footpath. Sir Homer was startled. Could this be a hippy? But no, as the man strode purposefully along the path he realised that it was only John Feather.

Sir Homer rose and went to the window. One of Lady Poll's silk scarves lay forgotten across the back of a burgundy leather sofa. Sir Homer picked it up and pressed it to his face. It smelled of Joy by Patou. He watched John Feather getting nearer, running it slowly back and forth between his legs, then dropped it quickly when he realised that Crispin Turner was gazing directly at the study window. He couldn't have seen, because of the reflection.

5

Midnight

Midnight, and Wyley Manor was iced with moonlight. Homer King opened the French windows softly and stepped onto the blue lawn, his mind thick with the residue of thoughts that the day had inspired: the circle, his mother's dresses, his social position, but most of all Thomas Bright, his smallboy, his love of Etor. Before him lay the Manor garden and, beyond the neat crenellated yew hedge, Wyley parish, a maze of hedges and ditches, a series of divisions and barriers. Double locks and burglar alarms. Neighbourhood watchers.

The woodland was only a tangle of darkness now but he could see, in his mind's eye, the stones beyond it and how the milky light would be gathering on their peaks and trickling down their veiny undulations. In his groin there was a pulse stirring. Sir Homer glanced back at his mother's darkened bedroom to check that she was not watching. Further down the slight valley the pale blue iris of a television moved distantly in Crispin Turner's cottage.

He walked across the grass, leaving bottle-green footsteps on the dew, and tunnelled under the yew hedge, through a tight-fitting hole that was otherwise used only by rabbits. It would have been easier to have gone up the drive to the Springham road and met the footpath. Easier but more visible. Besides, these urges, when they came, didn't take much notice of hedges, fences or ditches; they usually meant he had to send his suit to the dry-cleaners. He also had an intense dislike of that thin, dry, unwelcome footpath, which bisected the field in which he now emerged, gave the villagers a right to cross his land, and ventured too close to the folly. The villagers called it 'the folly footpath'.

'What I find puzzling, Sir Homer,' said the fat and energetic archaeologist, who had arrived, uninvited, at the Manor one Sunday morning, two years earlier, 'is the folly footpath at the end of the byway just outside the village. The byway must once have been a road – presumably, in the eyes of Rocester Town Council, it still is, because it appears to have been tarmacked, though not very well, fairly recently – but it ends at the stile, just fizzles out into the footpath.'

'There is nothing puzzling about it,' said Sir Homer, with glistening bonhomie, handing her a gin and tonic. 'The byway simply stops at that point.'

'Possibly, Sir Homer, though it is unusual for roads to lead to nowhere,' said the archaeologist, vigorously, taking a quick sip from her heavy glass.

Sir Homer raised his eyebrows but the archaeologist went on speaking.

'I prefer to believe that the byway must once have continued right into the circle itself. There is a gate into the field at exactly the right point to support this theory. Doubtless one of the earlier owners of the Manor objected to the road – or track as it would then have been – for some reason and constructed the folly footpath as a compensation for terminating what must have been a very ancient access. Findings of artefacts in the field that contains the stone circle would appear to bear this out.'

'Artefacts?' asked Sir Homer lightly.

'Arrow heads, shards of cooking implements, that sort of thing. Whereas the folly footpath has offered nothing of interest. You can barely even glimpse the stones from it.'

'But Professor Morrow, I dropped a cuff-link myself this very morning. You are not claiming that this means anything?'

'It bears witness to your presence, Sir Homer. Do not underestimate the pull the circle will have had for Wyley's early, and indeed later, inhabitants. There are those who claim, for instance, that the figure depicted in the window of Wyley church is not, in fact . . .'

'Professor Morrow, can I offer you another gin and tonic? And can I invite you to dine with us?'

'Thank you, Sir Homer, but I have made some tongue sandwiches, which I intend to eat under The Wise Lady, if you will permit it. Pathways are enticing. They have a way of reasserting themselves. I like to believe that the evidence of so many people doing something purposeful in one place refuses to vanish.'

Permission had been granted, with beaming reluctance, and Sir Homer had considered what Professor Morrow had said, and pondered it in his heart. He knew, for he was no fool, that she had been right about his cufflink and the intimate bond between his location and its resting place beneath the floorboards. He did not suppose for a moment that the lives of other men did not have similar motivations and causal sequences to his own, though largely unfathomable and achieved less gracefully.

As he stumbled his way, damply, towards the folly, Sir Homer thought about the hippies. He could no more have communicated with these individuals than he could have embraced his mother, achieved the same rank in society as Crispin Turner, walked hand in hand with Thomas Bright through the corridors of Westminster in his best silk cocktail frock.

Why should others not suffer gracefully their exclusions, as he suffered his own? Why should hippies believe themselves to be above the rights of ownership? Why should professors – even those from Cambridge – expect to stomp about his meadows with their trowels? Because a road had once existed, did it mean that it had to exist forever?

It was tussocky underfoot. A few sheep bounded away into the darkness and vanished. Sir Homer thought again of closets. Interesting, desirable, secret places within the figurative versions of which, if the press were to be believed, all manner of people lurked, doing nothing but wish they were outside in the revealing sunlight. This struck Sir Homer as unimaginative and unlikely. One appreciated the light because of what the light could offer. One appreciated the darkness similarly. The darkness had offered him Thomas Bright. Daytime was not so lenient.

Sir Homer paused as he remembered that other, long ago, midnight, with its sudden, white throwing open of sheets, the soft, thin outline of golden hairs, that clear invitation, which he had accepted. He remembered how they had been the talk of the school the following morning.

How unresilient gossip is, Sir Homer reflected, as he continued towards the folly. All now utterly forgotten.

From that day onwards those sheets had been thrown open repeatedly. The arms that had thrown them grew muscles and the voice that had invited deepened but the moment remained intact, in spite of the weight of calendars; secret, beautiful and exclusive, in spite of Thomas Bright M.P., grown up, married and sometimes dubious.

Sir Homer learned to avoid indulging or exploring the duality of his nature; that is to say both dualities at once. Public school taught him how to separate the two lobes of brain more utterly than nature originally intended, to erect a frontier that was seldom open. Discreet neighbours, the two components of his personality hardly ever met. By means of a skill that is peculiarly English, Sir Homer was able to deal with a nature that might otherwise have been problematic.

He even had two names – or two that he felt to be real. His full appellation was Homer Randolph Horace Plantagenet King. Sir Homer's grandfather, Randolph, would have quite liked one of his names to be Wyley, in order to hammer the family more securely into position, but even he had to admit the negative aspect of its connotation. Norman was clearly unacceptable, Tudor had something of the 'Neo' about it, so Plantagenet was chosen to round things off. A nod to the monarchy; an attempt at ancestry with Randolph and Horace; a toe in the landed-since-time-immemorial with Homer, for his godfather, who was laird of an ancient and dismal castle, with walls four feet thick to protect it against anyone deranged enough to wish to attack it, overlooking a loch so chill that those who fell into it while fishing salmon died within minutes.

Two real names only, though. Homer, for the suited, respected, daytime individual who had, this morning, conversed with Sergeant Tulliver and John Feather, lunched with his mother at one, and talked on the phone with his editor at *The Commentator* during the afternoon. Flora for the other, in the night, in the closet.

Sir Homer now stood at the door of the folly, where he paused and admired its stony curlicues that the moon had turned to metal. It must be late eighteenth century or early nineteenth. Certainly there was something Gothic about it. Supported by four weathered stone pillars, the roof was a puffy canopy scattered with rather camp representations of stars and planets, topped with a perfect sphere, which was presumably meant to be the sun. One day he would have to get it properly dated. As far as he knew, his grandfather had never asked about it when he purchased the Manor at the turn of the century, and the previous owners were now long dead – Randolph King was not the kind to interest himself in follies of any variety.

Sir Homer removed a silver key from his pocket, unlocked the door of the folly and entered. In the corner was the big trunk, with 'King' written on it, that had travelled in the guard's van when he went to school, placed there, with much straining, by Mulch, supervised by Nanny. Mulch who, now he thought about it, had looked identical then to how he did now. Which must mean that, if Mulch had been seventy in 1940, he was now – Sir Homer did some slow calculations – a hundred and fifteen. This did not seem terribly likely but it did not seem terribly unlikely either.

He abandoned the thought and stood, instead, at the one window, drew back its thick curtain and looked out across the silvered field, feeling Flora completing her occupation of his body.

Flora, his – horrible word – transvestite personality. Not irresponsible exactly but not really responsible, because that was another horrible word, redolent of mean little bills on spikes; of tiny Mr Taylor, the Chief Executive of Rocester Council; of Thomas Bright's wife, who made Oxo cube gravy; of Homer King's various deadlines; of the management and supervision of Lady Polly: everything that Flora closed the door upon.

You stepped into moonlight, you clicked off the lamp and nothing afterwards really counted. Or it counted as dreams count, as the theatre counts behind its proscenium arch. Afterwards Sir Homer always remembered this foreign country of his existence as he would a holiday, had he taken holidays, or as the intimate, dark, colourful interior of a cinema when standing again in the harsh, desiccated daylight.

For weeks, months even, Flora could subside, almost be forgotten, then something would summon her forth: a visit from Thomas, or merely the thought of him; the touch of a beautiful fabric; a glimpse of something mysterious or sensual.

Flora could love while Sir Homer could merely, at best, esteem – except in the case of his mother who he need not esteem but must say (only very occasionally and, mercifully, only to other people) that he loved. Flora had leapt, fully-grown, into existence when those sheets had revealed Thomas Bright, naked and erect, and Homer King, compelled to silence on the topic of the beautiful – except in the forms in which it was deemed to exist at Eton, such as military uniform and the smile of the Queen Mother – had realised that, whatever Thomas Bright was, he wanted to be the receptive opposite.

Flora ran over to the trunk and flung it open. Two rubber bosoms bounced up at her. She gave one of them a playful pinch, scrambled, feverishly, out of jacket, waistcoat, shirt, tie and collar, and put them on.

Smooth stockings – silk, not nylon – the soft shimmer of muslin as it fell over her head and slipped down her body, rubbing her thighs, floating outwards into the fullness of the skirt. Why did women, how could they ever, have given up these fabrics, these magic tissues? Even the names were beautiful: organdie, organza, tulle, chiffon. Incantations, love potions. Compare: denim, nylon, polyester. Sterile, emotionless, masculine. No sense of romance. No whiff of joy.

Twenty minutes later Sir Homer left the folly, crossed to the edge of the field and disappeared into the woods, from which he emerged, his pink pumps soaked with dew and the hem of his skirt somewhat bedraggled, into the outer ring of the stone circle. In the faint mist the stones were great dark masses that seemed to be steaming, the grass beneath them a vast, polished auditorium upon which they cast grey shadows.

The cold-shouldering irritations of daylight, of the responsible hours, were now transformed into a ring of gleaming erections. This was the greatest reason why Sir Homer feared them. The presence of the circle upon his land, upon his noble acres, was similar to a murderer having, not the corpse itself, but a photograph of the corpse, in his immediate vicinity. This was why he protested so much, afraid that others would penetrate its secret. Sometimes it seemed likely to him that the circle had been created by an early band of transvestite homosexuals, in far off times when discretion was less of a priority.

Both penis and anus, how could he resist it though? How could he not feel, not know, that here was a celebration of himself in its purest form?

Sir Homer entered the circle on tiptoe, dipped into the lowest curtsey his portly form would permit, and began to dance. Swooping and diving and breathing heavily, interspersing his movements with little leaps, his skirt grazing the meadow, he cavorted. Beneath his pumps, under the earth, inside the circle, he felt a sort of buzzing.

A quarter to one, and many of the citizens of Wyley were sleeping the sleep of the just, while others were finishing the day's occupations or preparing for the one yet to come, hoping, uncertainly, that it would be identical to all the others that had gone before it. Uncertainly, because there was a strangeness in the air that was unfamiliar to them.

The sky was so odd, to start with. It was crammed with a preternatural number of stars, right down to the horizon, so that the whole of Wyley, its church, its fields, its houses, its circle, seemed surrounded by a kind of visible, sizzling static electricity. You could even hear a low humming. The lights were flickering and there was also a funny sort of vibration.

Melanie, who was sitting on the churchyard wall, smoking a roll-up and watching a strange woman dancing in the stone circle, felt it under her fingers. She'd never experienced anything like it before, but presumably it was what got nutters like this one going. Still, if they wanted to dance in Sir Fat-arse's circle, let them. She flicked her cigarette away. Its little orange end twirled in the air four times then died in the grasses.

Melanie sighed. She'd had to get out of the house, it had been making her feel so shitty. Tully was there, in Martha's bedroom, and the screaming was awful. There'd never been noise like that with the others. She'd gone to check it wasn't scaring Hamish, but he was all right, fast asleep, though God knew how he managed it with all that racket. Tomorrow Martha's arms would be covered in bruises.

It couldn't be normal to do it like that. Or maybe it was. Melanie wasn't in much of a position to have got a handle on normal, what with Martha and Grandma and the succession of wimps and losers who'd tramped through her existence. Christ, and now Martha was thinking of marrying one of them. Melanie pulled her lips tightly together and threw her shoulders back because she could feel a sob in the pit of her stomach. The thing you had to do was to think of something else very quickly. Her brain chucked up at her the photograph of the woman in the shoe box that she had looked at that morning and almost forgotten, those silly, spiky eyelashes, the pretty face. She rubbed a fist across her watery eyes. If the woman in the picture had done that she'd have ended up with a black line along her face and a dirty smudge on her hand. Probably, though, she'd never had cause to snivel and ruin that perfect make-up. Probably she was continuing, somewhere, a compact, orderly, self-contained existence. Melanie sniffed hard. The thought was comforting.

Coming out onto the balcony of her darkened bedroom, Lady Polly also felt the vibration, as she tried to steady her elbows on the wooden railing in order to stop her binoculars bouncing so. But to her it was a less unfamiliar sensation – a gin bottle lay on the bedroom carpet, quite empty. Something was coming and going within the twin moons of the lenses. A glimpse. Why, it was surely Homer. But no, it was a woman. A madwoman. Lady Polly dropped the binoculars with a muffled cry, staggered back into the bedroom and, after much fumbling, managed to illuminate a ruched lampshade. Her pink telephone was on the bedside table. She picked it up and spent some moments speaking to the dialling tone, then she laboriously started to dial Crispin Turner's number, using her fingernail. Before she had quite finished she dropped the receiver, sank onto the zebra-skin bedside rug and fell asleep. She did not hear the lamp keel over.

In his little tied cottage Crispin Turner's television screen turned into a confetti of coloured dots.

Simon and Veronica Tarrant were drinking dandelion wine with Simon's old chum, Jolly, in the closed bar of The Rose and Crown. Jolly had thrown his rounded chin backwards and his cravat was quivering.

'Listen to this, Si. Just too bloody funny. Your Midsummer Night's Whatsit's Do, Sebastian Rundle's coming as Titania. Haw haw haw.'

A fluted glass slipped from Veronica's fingers.

'Oh shit. Silly me. Oh well, Joyce can deal with it in the morning.' Veronica looked at the thin shards at her feet. 'Are the lights dipping, or is it my imagination?'

'Vero's wet herself,' said Jolly. 'Haw haw haw.'

'Probably a storm somewhere,' said Simon.

In St George's church, unseen and unheard, a metal vase, staggering under the weight of cabbagey, crimson roses, tipped and fell off the shelf under the window and dented.

From her flat above the post office, Miss Evans tried to phone the electricity board to complain about the flickering, but the phone went dead, so she returned to her knitting.

'Knit one. Purl one.' Among her stitches her wandering brain twined endless, sticky, decapitated heads of the smiling monarch. She composed a letter. 'To Whom It May Concern. I wish to draw to your attention the untimely diminution of the electricity supply in the centre of Wyley yesterday.' There was a sound outside the window. She laid down her knitting and the tight little ball of powder-pink wool rolled off the humpty and under the dresser. The street was deserted except for deaf old Bill Webb, escaped from the Council again probably, drinking out of a beer bottle, which he threw into Marjorie Sand's ornamental wheelbarrow.

In Callan's Butchers Tom Callan's knife shook as he sliced through a leg of lamb, slipped and nicked one of his monstrous fingers. Swearing, he raised it to his lips and sucked at it. Next door, in the kitchen of the tea-rooms, a gobbet of all-fruit jam fell from Miss Sayle's spoon onto the linoleum. She scooped it up and put it into a metal bowl for the coach party due in the morning.

Marjorie Sand had just voraciously gobbled down her last fairy-bun and was now at prayer behind Laura Ashley curtains studded with rosebuds.

'The wicked may sprout as thick as weeds and every evil-doer flourish, but only to be everlastingly destroyed, whereas you are supreme for ever. See how your enemies perish, how all evil men are routed.' A bubble of saliva rose and burst from a little hole at the edge of her lips.

'You raise my horn as if I were a wild ox, you pour fresh oil on my head; I was able to see those who were spying on me, to overhear what the wicked were whispering.'

She quivered and the saliva trickled down her cheek and onto her nightgown. She wiped it off with a Handy-Andy and continued.

'God preserve my son, Seymour, and let the right questions come up in his examinations at Oxford. Hold, in your everlasting arms, my dead husband, Dennis, who now bathes in thy glory. Smash into pieces the window in St George's, which is an abomination to thy name, and reveal unto us the whereabouts of the porcelain thimble that Lady Polly King was going to give to me if she found it. Let the pagan perish in his sin that he may burn forever in eternal torment. Amen.'

The cold floorboards beneath her knees shivered. Vibrations ran up her bony legs.

Fresh compost, leaf-mould, horse manure. Mulch made notes carefully, laboriously. Page after page of springs and summers recorded on paper, memories of colour in stubby pencil. He raised his wrinkled nose and sniffed the air. The table trembled beneath his twisted hands. Good growing weather.

'Golly.' Sara Feather swirled the water round in her mouth and spat into the sink. 'John, are we having a minor earthquake or something?' But, even as she said it, she felt a slight tingling throughout her body.

'Probably just blasting,' called John from the bedroom.

Melanie took a sharp intake of breath. The humming had suddenly become very much louder and the churchyard wall was shaking. She looked behind her at the village. It was plunged in darkness. She turned back to the fields. The whole earth was juddering. She leant forward and peered into the night, trying to work out what the fuck was happening.

The dumpy figure had disappeared from the circle but, on the horizon, two sets of lights had appeared. As they got nearer she saw that they belonged to two rickety, not very large buses. Melanie kept her eyes on the direction from which they had come, wondering if there'd be others, but none followed. There must be only the two of them. She swivelled round as they came chugging up the high street, sounding like they were going to conk out any minute, and caught a glimpse of spray paintings of water and fishes up and down their rusty sides. They continued past the war memorial and down the Rocester road, then they vanished. Melanie let out her breath, but they appeared again a moment later, bobbing along the uneven tarmac of the byway that led to the folly footpath, where they stopped. The lights stayed on a minute or two, then they were extinguished.

Melanie stroked her hands along the churchyard wall. It wasn't vibrating any more. A dim glow behind her told her that the electricity was on again in Wyley. The humming had ceased. It was very silent. Whatever had been expected appeared to have arrived.

6

The Travellers

The first thing was the colours. They were not the colours of England. They were the colours of India, Indonesia, Central America. They were the colours of dreams, of acid trips, the visuals of the high-pitched screaming of heavy-metal guitars. They spilled down the sides of the Aquarius Bus and the Pisces Bus. Uncompromising primaries. The water sloshing from bursting waterfalls and rivers, from big-bellied clouds all over the Aquarius was so fucking blue. It was the blue of: what colour's the sky? Blue, of course. So I dip my paintbrush in the Blue Paint. Except this wasn't painted. This was spray-canned by thonking great men in yards full of crashed cars. It said, 'fuck you, with your shades and nuances, from those who don't take no for an answer'. The Pisces Bus', in massive, sunshine letters, with an oceanful of orange fish, starfish, catfish with long red whiskers, flying fish with wings, had at the bottom, curving where the metal curved to the shape of a muddy front wheel, 'The Bus Crazy Barratt Family', in Celtic script. With an addition, an arrow pointing straight ahead and 'Gone to Afghanistan. Back for the Millennium'.

But the colours didn't stop there. They'd rioted into the woodland side of the byway, where a purple washing-line had been hung between two trees and clothes had been pinned to it with green and blue clothes-pegs, everything slightly stiffened,

as if it had got wet and dried out many times. A t-shirt with a
spiky marijuana leaf and 'Drugs Not Jobs' printed on the front
of it. A square, batik scarf in shocking pink and rose. Faded indigo
jeans. A blue whale, hanging from its tail fin. Not a lot different
to Martha's clothes line, really, including the whale, which must
have got thrown up on.

There were logs to sit on around a smouldering fire, and
woven rugs with holes in them where the powdery earth
showed through. There were painted flower-pots with blazing
geraniums in them; across one of the rugs dried flowers made
and half-made into garlands; a jam-jar full of clover and cow's
parsley. Between another pair of trees, a yellow hammock, with
an embroidered design in purple wool on it.

Then there were the smells. Diesel predominated. Out of the
top of both the buses poked metal chimneys from which came
thin wisps of yellowy smoke that smelled of cider-apples. The
pale blue smoke of the fire was more intense, sweet and earthy.
Incense, joss-sticks and patchouli combined with the musty scent
of Indian fabric.

And the silence. The camp was sleeping, a deep, exhausted
sleep. The birds had not yet started to sing in the woods, which
still held onto the night's mist. A cuckoo called in the distance.
A tatty old dog quivered on a paisley-patterned cushion with the
ghost of running, growled at a dream, wagged his tail, rolled on
his back but did not wake.

Melanie stood in the centre of the camp, frightened and
entranced. Throughout the long, hot night, she had convinced
herself that the buses would be gone in the morning – if,
indeed, they had ever been, if it was not just the intensity of
her longing that had grabbed Wyley and shaken it. But what
she saw had nothing to do with her. Other, stronger forces were
at work.

She bent and picked up one of the garlands. A woven circle
with mauve and orange flowers and dried seed-heads and grasses
inserted into it. The crown of a bride or a goddess. She dropped
it quickly, in an attempt to avoid the thought that was pushing
itself upon her: these people had something in common with
Martha. The colours, the flowers, the smells; for the first time
ever Melanie could see what Martha was getting at with her

collections of shells and feathers, roses wilting round the place, misguided t-shirts.

Four years ago Grandma had paid for Martha and Melanie to spend a fortnight in Crete because Martha was in one of her great depressions. There, for one whole afternoon, while everyone else was on the beach, Martha had trailed her round the Minoan museum in Heraklion. For form's sake Melanie had pretended not to like it, gone on a bit about the sunshine outside and how they could go to museums at home, where it rained all the time. But she had liked it. She had followed the culture, from case to case, until it reached its zenith when everything it produced was weird and exuberant and beautiful. But after that it all changed quite suddenly. Something had happened. The things in the last cases were still trying to look the way they had looked during the best time, but they were only clumsy echoes. The people seemed to have half-remembered what they were trying to do but they'd forgotten its substance.

That was what being Martha must be like, though Melanie had never known that before, because she had never seen the proper version. Her life a clutter of relics and artefacts, approximated at ideas, all left over from a better earlier existence. No-one appeared to have suggested that the real Minoans had gone off and continued to do their thing somewhere else, but perhaps they had. What had changed for them? And why had Martha stayed behind when she could have gone, too?

Wyley felt very far away, bleached out of existence. The circus had come to town. The gypsies were passing through. The fair was setting up. The carnival was filling the streets. By some sleight of hand, by taking itself seriously, the frivolous had become serious and the serious had become frivolous. Stick figures. Dolls in a puppet show. Punch and Judy. Marjorie Sand the crocodile and Sir Homer King the magistrate. Hamish the baby.

Reversal is the first magic. The second is identification.

And now, although she did not know it, Melanie was walking towards the third, most difficult, magic.

She had thought that the hammock was empty and that everyone was sleeping in the buses. Whatever was weighing it down was clothes, or bedding; the corner of a blue coverlet with a procession of small, green elephants tumbled from its side. She bent over it curiously and then jumped backwards with both hands to her lips. A fizz of adrenalin bubbled up through her body and she felt slightly dizzy. There was someone in it, and he was dead.

She looked again. A pair of hazel eyes stared up at her from a face quite similar to her own so that she felt, for a moment, as if she were lying in the middle of the stone circle where, instead of seeing only the expressionless sky above her head, she was meeting her own reflection in masculine form. The image pulled the ground away from her, her feet sliding towards their imagined position. Thin sheets of glass were slipping from her hands and breaking repeatedly on the ground. The pieces of glass were pieces of herself, and there was no point in trying to gather them up because the tight little ball of selfhood that had been her way of managing to cope, had been shattered. Without this unknown person, she would never be intact again, and he was dead.

And then his naked chest lifted with a deep breath and Melanie realised that he was not dead but asleep, and that people could sleep with their eyes open, which she should have thought of sooner because Wyley proved it daily.

She reached into her back pocket for her tobacco and Rizlas, quickly made a roll-up, and lit it, blowing the smoke away from the boy so the smell wouldn't wake him.

He was about eighteen. His chest was hairless and quite strong-looking. There was an elaborate tattoo on one of his outstretched arms, a curly sun rising over grasses filled with pointy mushrooms and butterflies and marijuana leaves. There was a thin white scar just below his rib-cage. His hair was black and curled slightly, like her own, and came to just below the nape of his neck.

The expression on his face was angry and defiant and a little confused; probably, Melanie thought, the confusion was something he kept hidden when he was awake. It was the kind of expression that Tully was going to hate, if he ever saw it, and he'd probably make sure he did. She'd seen the way Tully's fists twitched when she looked at him like that. Melanie flipped the cigarette onto the ground, stamped on it, blew out hard to get rid of any residue smoke and then lowered her lips towards those broad, vulnerable lips that were also kind. She was two inches away when the boy spoke.

'What're you playing at, Curdie?'

Melanie ran through the camp, getting tangled in a crimson rug, tripping on one of the logs, knocking over a jam-jar of dandelions, hearing her footsteps break the silence, wake the woodland and start up the dawn chorus. She didn't know whether she was laughing or crying.

Josh woke because Curdie was holding a mirror over his face and bringing it nearer and nearer. It was early. The birds were just cranking up, which was a drag because he'd hoped to get some decent kip after yesterday. It had taken forever to get here because Karen had lost the ley-line three fucking times, at which point Paul had said why not follow the map and pick the ley-line up at Wyley? Paul didn't believe in ley-lines and Karen knew it. Maps, she said, were an imperialist construction. They were following the pathway of the stones, not some fucking B-road put there by a fascist government. So they stood around arguing and then Ralph said that the tank on the Aquarius was leaking. At least it hadn't rained. Rain was the worst thing. Rain was the real pisser.

Josh heard voices. Paul and Miranda were coming out of the Pisces. Curdie must have woken them, too. Which was fair enough, since they were his parents. Paul started to put wood on the fire while Miranda stretched out on the rug, her eyes closed, her face lifted towards the sunlight. Josh moved in the hammock and she raised a flat hand in his direction. He waved back, though she wouldn't see him. There was something magnificent about Miranda. Large-boned and Nordic, you wouldn't have thought she was forty.

'Curious people, I imagine. Or childrun. Nothing is missing,' she said in her Danish accent, so sharp and precise it always made Josh think of flint. She had learnt English once and once only, back in the sixties, when she had left her farming community with a DJ from Sheppey, who had somehow got washed up there, and gone to live with him in Croydon where she'd got work in a pub. Since then her English had discarded nothing. Her vocabulary had neither changed nor extended to ambiguity. Whether this was because Miranda herself was incapable of anything other than complete honesty, or because she considered her acquisition of the language a job completed, it was hard to say.

The DJ auditioned for Radio One and didn't get it. 'After that he tried to wallop me.' Which proved unwise. Miranda was just under six foot. She gave the DJ a black eye and cracked one of his ribs. He took her to court on a charge of grievous bodily harm.

'It would be true to say, would it not,' asked her defending solicitor, 'that you feel remorse for what you have done?' His eyes were begging. 'No,' Miranda replied. 'He was a right fucking bastard after he failed that audition.'

She spent nearly two years in prison, emerged politicised, went back to the pub in Croydon, where she sweated her guts out for eighteen months to get together enough money to travel to Goa. No one had ever given her anything. She had never expected them to.

'In Goa,' she said, 'I learned to make magic potions. I extended my stay by posing in the nude for an underwater photographer.' In 1976 she came back to England and met Paul at a party in London.

As Josh watched them, Paul turned away from the now crackling fire and gave Miranda's sand-coloured hair a gentle tug. They were an unlikely pair, really, but they generally got on. The first night they slept together they conceived Curdie. That was what Paul said gave him the impetus to drop out of Oxford and start earning a living. Not that Miranda ever asked him to do anything for her. When she discovered she was pregnant she assumed that this, like everything else, was something she'd do alone.

She didn't do it alone, though. From what Miranda said it sounded like Paul, as usual, had tried to take over. The one thing he couldn't do was actually give birth but he read most of the alternative literature on the topic. When Miranda was in the last stages of labour, in a rural squat just outside Brighton, he tried to help her to deal with the pain by explaining to her that the sexual aspect of childbirth was something that was wilfully overlooked. He explained that what she was now experiencing was very similar to the movement the vagina makes during intercourse. 'Think of it,' he finished, 'as the ultimate orgasm.'

In spite of her weakened state Miranda managed to land him a powerful kick, right in the nuts. Hearing his cry the radical midwife, who'd been downstairs in the kitchen having a joint, came upstairs to see if she was needed.

'Shared labour,' she said, looking at Paul doubled up in the corner as Curdie's head began to pop through between Miranda's strong thighs. '"Rite of couvade" it's called in some cultures. The man takes on the woman's suffering in a ritual enactment. Never seen it so convincingly done, though.'

They moved to another squat, this one in the centre of Brighton. That was where Josh met them. He'd just come off the Convoy. Miranda was working at 'Infinity'. She'd recently spent a few weeks in prison again, after being arrested at Greenham. 'All crime is political,' she said. They were in CND, Miranda was involved in the Brighton Women's Centre, Paul was in an anarchist group. They were members of Non-Violent Direct Action.

Josh remembered them now, poring over maps to figure out how to disrupt Cruise. Both of them tall, both of them strong-minded, or pig-headed, depending on how you looked at it. After two years on the road their activities struck him as static, everything around them felt nailed down. Miranda told him to 'keep your fucking notions to yourself'. Paul explained that organisation was the key to anarchy. Josh said that was a contradiction in terms. 'Only apparently,' said Paul. Josh asked what the fuck that meant and Miranda made a gruesome Danish porridge to help him to convalesce. 'The liquid in your lungs was a build-up of aggression.' It was pneumonia that had stopped him moving.

In June 1984 Miranda went to Glastonbury and bought a ticket in a raffle run by 'The Bus Crazy Barratt Family', who had got together a newer bus for their journey to Afghanistan, and were raffling off their old one. Miranda had known she would win, so she wasn't surprised when she did. She named it the Pisces for the cycle that was just about to give way to Aquarius, and drove it back to Sussex without tax, insurance or a driving licence, and parked it in a friend's garden, where it died.

The friend put up with it being there for a couple of months, after which he got a bit fed up with it, so he phoned Miranda, told her he wanted it out and that his mate, Ralph, would get it going for them, for not a lot of cash, and keep it parked up near his place until they needed it.

That was how they met Karen and Ralph, which was how the Pisces and Aquarius convoy got started. By September it was ready to roll but only Josh had any real intention of going on the road. It just happened that, in October, Paul had the traumatic experience that made him feel he had to get out of Brighton. The phantom shitter had set fire to Karen and Ralph's caravan and they'd had to move to the squat, though there really wasn't room for them. Everything pointed in the same direction. Miranda said that it was a time of leaving.

'You are not much of a guard dog, Nelson,' said Miranda to old Nel. She was scraping some of last night's leftover lentils into his bowl for him. Nelson didn't much like lentils but he'd eat them if there wasn't any dog food. 'What would you do if there were robbers? Wag your tail at them? Do you think that would make them split?'

Josh started. 'Split.' The word shot through him. How did Miranda do it? Did she know somehow? Could she tap into what you were thinking? 'Split.' The word that had been running through his mind ever since they'd decided to come to Wyley. An old, dated, ridiculous word she'd learned in a pub in Croydon; a word everyone else had left behind. Except for Josh. He didn't use it but he thought about it a lot. It was the only thing he could be sure of about his other visit to Wyley. If it was Wyley. He couldn't even be sure of that.

It had happened such a long time ago. The early seventies. Josh was younger then than Curdie was now. He remembered that his mother was still pretty and happy in those days. She still looked like the picture of herself she'd put up on the kitchen wall. The picture hadn't been bubbled or damp-stained then, or pulled away from the sides of the frame so that the backing showed through. Her clothes and make-up hadn't been funny. They'd fitted the time the way the picture fitted the frame.

She'd been particularly happy that day because of the man who was with them. Here it was all hazy. The man was dark, that was all Josh could remember, but Josh hadn't been interested in him. There were two things in his mind. One was his mother's beauty, the yellowness of her hair in the sunshine. The other was the fair that they had been going to go to until the man showed up. It was the last day of the fair and they were going to miss it.

They had driven through the countryside in an open-topped car. The man and his mother shouted to each other above his head; the wind caught their voices and blew them backwards so Josh imagined them leaving a trail of words behind them. Where were they going? Josh thought it was Wyley but he couldn't be positive. There were so many similar names and so many similar places. England was crammed with them. He could have asked his mother, if it weren't for what happened that day, but then if it hadn't happened he wouldn't have wanted to ask her. It was the day that hacked his life in two and nothing was the same after.

They'd stopped for lunch in a big but grotty pub. They'd had to sit in the garden because of him, though it wasn't much of a garden. The grass was long and scrubby and the table they sat at was rickety and covered in bird shit. You could see the cricket pitch but no one was playing. The landlord was nice and told Josh there was a games room. He made it sound quite exciting but it turned out to be gloomy and damp, with only a billiard table that he couldn't reach over.

Josh was bored, sulking and wishing something would happen and then something did happen and he wished it hadn't. There was a woman standing by their table and the man had leapt up and his chair had fallen over onto the grass. There was a lot of shouting, and everything was horrible and the word 'split' was knifing through the air until he could almost see it, cold, metallic and glinting in the sun. Josh hadn't imagined it could get more horrible, but then the shouting stopped and there was a very large silence, and his mother and the woman had their arms round each other and they were both crying.

Josh rubbed his face angrily and, lowering his hand to the ground, felt it meet the velvety bed of earth and pine-needles. He pushed hard and the hammock started swaying. As it swayed it creaked: Wy-ley, Wy-ley. But it could have been somewhere else. It could have been anywhere in England.

They must have got back, though he remembered nothing of the return journey. The man disappeared and never came again, and his mother disappeared too, but slowly. She was still there literally, of course, but, bit by bit, her personality vanished. Exactly what had happened remained a mystery. For some while Josh believed that a lot of thinking about that day would help him figure out the bits that he had enough information to figure out, but it was time that told him all he was likely to know in the end. One day, when he was thirteen, he suddenly realised that the man must have been his father and that his mother's personality had faded away because she didn't feel it was worth living without him.

So this was love. Two, four, seven years later and still Josh wasn't enough, life wasn't enough. She went to her job at Sainsbury's, with the horrid badge with her name on, and then came home and made him a meal, after which she ate popcorn and watched television in the dark. Popcorn was almost all she ate. She drank only soda-water. She got thinner and thinner. So this was love.

There were things Josh couldn't figure out, of course: who the woman was; why they were both crying, why his father never came back again and why, after that day, his mother always tried to stop him going to the fair.

He did go, though, every June. The fair measured his height, his strength, his toughness for him. Perhaps he'd got travelling in his blood. Best of all he loved to walk around the backs of the caravans, into the dark suburb behind the lights, away from the ringing bells, the shouting, the smell of fried onions and candy-floss. Here was the network of cables and gasping generators that gave life to the wonderful machines, lit the metal touch-papers of dodgems, breathed life into the million small swings that spun outwards as they moved. He liked to wonder, among the quiet, slightly rancid alleys of squashed grass, what the people in the caravans – the wives, the children, the men who did the loading and unloading – could be doing. In almost all of them he could make out the blue aquarium light of a television. Were they watching the same dull programmes that his mother watched at home? Surely not. The broadcasts they received came from somewhere else, some distant planet whose people sent messages only to them.

It was the fair that gave him sex, the only sex he was capable of. He'd tried it with a girl once, in a phone box, after one of his mates had got hold of a bottle of vodka. She was someone's cousin, and she'd drunk quite a bit of it herself. The inside of the phone box smelled of fag-ends. She pushed his hands up under her jumper and he tried not to recoil. Two horrible words came into his mind, 'Female Biology'. He felt his zip being pulled down and then a strange, cold sucking. Female biology: his mother, fading away because of love, the way nobody believed people actually did any more. Love. Heterosexual love, that was making his mother a skeleton. Nothing happened and Josh knew it never would. That night he smashed up the kitchen and kicked a hole in the telly. He hated her. She'd ruined it for him.

But then, a few months later, at the fair, he'd fallen over a cable, splat onto the grass, and the door of one of the caravans had swung open.

'Christ, you look a mess. Come in and I'll mop you up.'

Josh stepped into the caravan and the door closed behind him. It was darker inside than he'd expected, lit only by one small paraffin lamp. Looking at the man, Josh guessed he was about thirty-five. He bent and set a match to a small stove.

'Never gets that warm in England,' he remarked. 'Take your shirt off and I'll dry it by the stove, then you can brush the mud off it. Don't be shy.'

Josh wouldn't have been, but now he was. As he unbuttoned his army-surplus shirt the man watched him. Josh became aware of the smoothness of his own skin, of his body as a thrusting, arching thing, and then his face was in the pillow of an unmade bed and everything was happening quite quickly behind him. He could have stopped it, but he didn't want to because at last someone else was taking the lead; there were no quizzical eyes looking up at him, wanting him to perform, there was no empty flat that he had to fill with presence. His body was being penetrated, it was a snake swallowing something, working it down with its thin, pliable bones, trusting that it would nourish, would make up for the fact that he did not, could not, love a woman. He came on the sheets, said he was sorry, laughed and then cried.

There were several such encounters after that. They still happened sometimes. They were not what Josh really wanted, but they gave him a kind of happiness. He always remembered that first one best, though. Afterwards the man had made them something to eat and told Josh a bit about himself. He said he wasn't really a fair person, he was an artist and photographer, whose special subject was travellers. It may or may not have been true. He said that governments had never liked travellers because they were hard to keep track of and because they brought news of other places where things might be different and better. Look at any oppressive regime and you'd find they put a restriction on movement.

Josh had never thought about this before. Nor had he really thought *like* this before. Travellers. Oppression. These were distant words that the man had brought near to him. As the man spoke, Josh imagined the whole world as a milling mass of people with different destinations. Muslims going to Mecca, Jews to Israel, gypsies to Stes-Maries-de-la-Mer and Appleby. People being stopped at borders, shot on frontiers, swimming across lakes and rivers, climbing mountain paths, clinging to boats at sea. These were the first political thoughts of his life.

The next day he stood by the M2 and stuck his thumb out without expecting much. It was June 18th, 1981. He was picked up by a van of people on their way to Glastonbury. It was the first year of the Pyramid Stage. It was the year of Aswad and Hawkwind. He never went home again.

The problem Josh had with women, said Paul, derived from equating sex with love.

'The problem you have with women,' said Miranda, 'is because it wasn't a woman. It was a littul girl, who knew nuthing about intercourse. I will sleep with you, Josh, and you will see that you will have no problems with your erection.'

Female biology. Josh didn't believe her and he couldn't bear to fail again. Next time it would kill him.

Ralph emerged from the Aquarius in his blue boiler-suit, which was covered in diesel, followed by Karen, panda-eyed with yesterday's kohl, her hennaed hair in a million rasta-ish tufts, a spider stud in her nose. Carmine was sucking at her breast, a baby born to the sound of whales' song in a caravan in the Sussex woodland. Not what you'd expect for a vicar's grand-daughter, but Carmine had never seen her grandparents. Karen's dad had chucked her out once he knew she was pregnant.

Josh swung out of the hammock and went and had a pee behind a tree. They'd have to dig a shit-pit later. It was one of the first things they did when they were planning on spending more than a day somewhere. That was why Josh felt so angry whenever he thought about Karen and Ralph's phantom-shitter.

The bit of woodland where Carmine was born belonged to a friend of Ralph's. The council wouldn't have liked it if they'd known anyone was living there but there was no reason for them to find out; no one from the nearby houses got hassled about them, except for one person, and he wasn't likely to do anything because he'd built an illegal extension to his bungalow. Well, that was what they thought.

It was a lovely piece of woodland. Josh used to go down there a lot when Ralph was working on the Pisces. The diesel engine was what Ralph did. Sometimes he slept under one of the buses and you had to be careful to check he'd woken up before you pulled off in the morning. When he went on a cross-channel ferry he liked to have a kip up near the funnel, with his ear against the deck, so he could hear the heartbeat of the engine, he told Josh. He had a quiet, muttery, hesitant voice, that was too easy-going for stress or emphasis.

'That neighbour of ours, we reckon it's him, "the phantom shitter", Karen calls him, well he comes and has a shit on the middle of the footpath every morning. Must get up early. I mean not that I get up early, but Karen, she's usually up, well, quite early. He can't complain to the council about us, but there's people from the cottages in the opposite direction to him who use the footpath. Karen clears it up because what he wants is for people to think it's us.'

Eventually Karen got it into her head that they should get up extra early and catch the phantom shitter. The first morning she set her alarm Ralph took too long to wake up and they missed him, though not by much. There was a steaming pile of shit at the usual place on the footpath in the woods, where some of the trees were just barely starting to turn to their autumn colours. The next day they caught him. They hid behind a bush and came out once he'd got his trousers down and was well under way.

'You. Listen,' said Karen. 'We know what you're doing and we want that fucking mess cleared up.'

When they went back after breakfast, miraculously, it was. Ralph managed to get the Pisces started and they wrapped Carmine in her little shawl and went shopping at 'Infinity'. The Pisces broke down on the way back, so it was early evening by the time it rattled into the clearing where the caravan was. Or had been. Everything they owned was in that caravan: Karen's guitar, Ralph's manuals, all their clothes, the wooden cradle they'd made for Carmine out of a drawer they'd bought at a jumble sale. The only thing he hadn't burnt was the Aquarius, and he'd slashed one of its tyres.

You don't call the rozzers when you've been living somewhere illegally and you've got two untaxed vehicles, one of which has a dodgy MOT. They could have got their own back by telling the council about the man's extension, but that would only have involved him in hassle, not real loss. After the morning's humiliation he'd probably decided that was a risk he was willing to take. Anyway, why add to the destruction?

Josh walked over to the fire and crouched on a log. Paul had boiled a kettle and was making a pot of red zinga for the others and a mug of coffee for himself. Karen was lighting a flattened roll-up in the other direction to where Ralph was sitting. You had to be careful with matches around Ralph.

'Where's Curdie?' asked Josh.

'Asleep,' said Paul. He picked up a copy of *The Commentator* that lay at his feet and took a quick sip of his coffee. 'Listen to this. Will you just listen to this?' He put on his hanging-judge voice, though his accent was posh enough anyway. '"Wyley Manor, which I will in due course inherit, also possesses a stone circle. It is not open to the public for the same, judicious reason that English Heritage and the Wiltshire police now see fit to limit public access to Stonehenge."'

Nobody listened much. He'd been reading it to them constantly ever since it came out. Paul always bought *The Commentator* because he liked to know what the other side was thinking.

Before that they hadn't been quite sure where they would go for the solstice. They'd thought of trying to get to Stonehenge – even if they didn't make it they'd be bound to meet up with some of their mates on the road – but that had never felt quite right, somehow. It wasn't just Stonehenge that was the issue. It was all stone circles. They were a source of immense positive psychic power, left as a gift by the ancient men and women who had built them; they belonged to everyone. Ideally the solstice should be celebrated in every single stone circle, so that this power for goodness could be thoroughly tapped into.

Josh had written an article on this subject, and sent it off to *Planetary Pathway*. He'd made a list of lots of stone circles that nobody usually thought about and urged people to try to get to them. Wyley was one. Whether the article had been published or not he didn't know. *Planetary Pathway* was actually one bloke, called Kristof Smit. He was German but he'd lived in England since the early seventies. He spent the summer travelling round the festivals in a horse-drawn caravan. He had a long beard and looked like a troll. Most of *Planetary Pathway* he wrote himself, not because he was a show-off or because of a lack of contributions, but because he was so hard to find. Josh had given his article to someone from the Legalise Marijuana Campaign who was going to a Spring Tree Festival in Wales and thought that Kristof might be there. He didn't know whether it had reached him.

Then Paul had bought *The Commentator* and read the article by this shit, Homer King, who thought he owned the circle at Wyley, and it became clear to them all the direction that they were being pushed in. Karen started to sense the tingley gravitational beckoning of a ley-line and, when Paul and Miranda looked at their map, it turned out that it was coming from the direction of Wyley.

'Of course we'll be the only ones there, which will mean a sharp down-turn in my annual revenue,' said Paul. 'But I'll live with it.' He had studied Politics, Philosophy and Economics at Oxford. Paul's destiny was supposed to be the Civil Service. At the end of his second year, just before he met Miranda,

Paul's father had called him into his study to discuss his future.

Paul always described his father as 'kind though unenlightened. He is the sort of man who can use the word "patriarch" without guilt, irony or humour.' Paul's father delineated, at some length, the options in life that Paul could reasonably expect.

When he had finished Paul asked, 'Have you read the Bible, Father?'

His father replied that he had, or rather, must have done, though not very recently.

'Then you will remember the part in which Satan takes Christ to the mountain-top and offers him the kingdoms of the earth?'

Up till then Paul's father had been unaware of Paul's speedy political evolution. From the beginning of his time at Oxford his tutors had encouraged him to read round the subject, but he had read rather further round than anyone had envisaged. In the space of two years he had left Conservatism, briefly considered the Liberal Democrats and the Labour party, rejected them, moved through various forms of Marxism until he arrived at his present political stance, which was Anarchy. He had also become a Buddhist, in theory though not in practice.

Sometimes Josh couldn't help feeling for Paul's dad.

'I see you are set on squandering your talents,' the old man remarked.

'Not squandering them,' said Paul, 'channelling them in different directions.'

He became a drug-dealer, which was a sound move because his posh accent might otherwise have made him unpopular. A drug-dealer in Brighton was never going to be lonely. He dealt grass, acid and coke and he was right, he was good at it. He did it because he needed the dosh and he didn't think drugs were harmful. He didn't do it because he wanted to look cool; those were the ones who ended up inside, which was something Paul definitely didn't want to happen.

The traumatic event which made him want to get out of Brighton was related to his dealing. It took place on October 12th, 1984.

Paul had just done a fairly large transaction with some blokes who lived in a small flat near the front and he'd stuck around to have a smoke with them. They were sitting there, shooting the breeze, when one of them heard something.

'Christ, what's that?'

They closed the curtains and switched off the lights, then looked out. There was a helicopter circling. 'Oh shit, look down there.' The street was full of flashing blue lights. From the other side of the building came the sound of police sirens.

'We could chuck it down the bog,' Paul suggested. He was supplying; they were only buying.

'Two ounces down the bog. You're joking.'

'Anyway, it's three floors below us, they'll be on the stairs,' said the other.

They stood in silence. 'I didn't know they got out helicopters for drug-dealers.'

'We could throw it out the window,' said Paul. He was supplying; they were only buying. 'Then look for it later.'

'Oh yeah, into the hands of a waiting rozzer. Jesus, there must be fifteen police cars down there.'

Paul wasn't easily rattled, but he was rattled now. Barely breathing, he waited for the sound of heavy footsteps on the stairs.

'We could hide it.'

'No point, they'll just trash the place.'

Paul was getting pissed off. 'Do you want to get caught or something?'

'Buy it back and you can put it wherever you want.'

'I didn't know they got out helicopters for drug-dealers,' said the other one.

Suddenly, Paul realised that they didn't, or not for small-time drug-dealers. Nor did they fill the road with police cars. It was the dope. It did that sometimes. It could make you paranoid, so that you believed that all the aggressive forces of the universe were pointed in your direction. Once his mind had calmed down a bit, he also remembered that the Tory Conference was going on only streets away. Something must have happened.

Something had happened. A bomb had gone off at the hotel hosting the Conference, killing and injuring some, but sparing the Prime Minister, which is a tendency of bombs the world over.

The trauma had been great, though. After that Paul kept waking from nightmares in a cold sweat. Round Brighton it was easy to forget quite what you were up against, the sheer might of the forces of law and order, how, if they came looking, there was nothing you could do about it. They could crush you underfoot, and they would. Bearing that in mind, it wasn't logical to go on the road, but Paul needed to get the hell out. They all did, for their different reasons.

It was late October when the Pisces and the Aquarius finally left Karen and Ralph's woodland, bouncing along the pot-holed track, clanking and revving. They filled the narrow country lane, and then they came to the main road and they were really rolling. In the Pisces they'd got Bob Marley on full blast and Miranda was passing round a tin of hash brownies. It was already starting to get cold. The stove was burning. Miranda was wearing a vast jumper, the colour of bluebells, knitted by an old aunt in Denmark. They were heading for Wales to winter with the Tepee People at the Rainbow Village.

'Stop the bus, Paul,' Miranda shouted after they'd gone about ten miles. 'There's a girl hitching in that lay-by who's going in our direction.'

Josh looked out the window. She was thin, with bare feet and wore a wrap-around patchwork skirt, very old, and a t-shirt covered by a drooping cardigan. Her thumb was stuck out and she had a tattered piece of cardboard in her other hand, on which was written 'Anywhere'. She had no bag or rucksack. She said her name was Emily.

Emily came down the steps of the Pisces, where she usually slept, and lowered her body heavily onto one of the rugs. Miranda chucked her a large cushion and she leant against it, locking her hands together beneath her vastly distended stomach. She didn't know she was pregnant when they picked her up and didn't even realise when she started being sick in the mornings. It was Miranda who told her. Emily was a ha'penny short or, as Paul put it, had two houses deep in the woods. She was a drongo as well, never did a thing except, occasionally, a bit of stealing, though rarely anything that was useful to anyone.

She lived her own, strange existence adjacent to the rest of them. They'd probably have been better off without her but she wasn't much of a hassle, really, except when the rozzers got on to her, or when she pinched Carmine awake to see her eyes open. Now she started rolling a joint. Miranda poured her a glass of milk.

Josh took a slurp of his red zinga, feeling contented. The Wise Lady wanted them here, that much was certain. She had sent out her message through his own brain, when he was writing that piece for *Planetary Pathway*, to Karen, by means of her ley-line, and even using the medium of that Homer King shit and his article in *The Commentator*. They'd been brought here for a purpose. Perhaps he'd even find out what had happened that day long ago in Wyley, if it was in Wyley: that was the first thing he needed to be sure of.

'What were you playing at with that mirror, Curdie?' he asked, as Curdie bounded out of the Pisces, his long plait half-undone from being slept on.

'What mirror? I've only just got up.' He turned his brown, dirt-stained face to Miranda for verification. 'Haven't I, Miranda?'

'If Josh believes you, you have no need of my confirmation. If he doesn't, why should my evidence convince him?'

Curdie looked confused; it was a heavy number for an eight-year-old.

'No sweat, Curdie, I believe you. Course I believe you.'

But what was it, then? His own spirit, wandering in the woodlands while he was sleeping, drawn out of his body by its proximity to the whopping power of the circle, a little late getting back?

'There was someone in the camp early this morning,' said Paul. 'They don't seem to have done any damage.'

'Unless it was them who knocked over my dandelions,' said Curdie.

Josh was startled. Someone in the camp, watching while he was sleeping in the hammock. Who were they, and why were they looking at him?

7

First Acquaintance

As the grandfather clock in the hall pompously struck eleven, Sir Homer entered the drawing-room of Wyley Manor.

The French windows were open and the scent of roses and honeysuckle was wafting into the room; a small breeze stirred the blue velvet curtains. It was a light, spacious room with flowers in vases and a marble fireplace. Sir Homer lowered himself into a fawn-coloured armchair with a contented sigh. Precisely on cue Cook brought in the tray, which she carried fiercely, as if fearing that, at any minute, it would be wrested from her. She set it down on the low, walnut table and exited silently.

'I think,' said Lady Poll, who entered now, on the arm of Crispin Turner, 'that I shall have a sherry.' She'd changed for elevenses and was wearing a shapeless gown of thin silk, speckled with yellow and turquoise. She said this every morning and Sir Homer did not reply. She said it with a conspiratorial, slightly surprised air, as if this were a one-off event, a bit naughty and not to be repeated. Though, of course, it was repeated throughout the day.

'I have invited Crispin to join us, Homer, because of the lemon biscuits.' She gestured in his direction and Crispin made a slight motion of his head, designed to indicate his awareness of the privilege. 'A large sherry, I think,' said Lady Poll, tipping a cut-glass decanter. 'I need something to wake me up.'

She seated herself on the matching sofa. Chummy leapt up beside her and farted softly.

'Really, Mother.' Sir Homer paused in his task of pouring coffee into a china cup. 'That dog is a most distasteful creature.'

'Don't be nasty, Homer.' Lady Poll took a sugar lump from the bowl and placed it in Chummy's smelly mouth.

'It has quite put me off my biscuit.'

'He, Homer, he. Chummy is a he.'

As if to bear this out, Chummy presented a thin, wet, pink erection.

'Goodness, Homer, whatever have you done to your hands?' Lady Polly exclaimed, before Sir Homer could speak again, causing Crispin also to turn his head and stare at the red scratch marks on Sir Homer's hands, with interest rather than concern.

Sir Homer, discomfited, opened his mouth to deliver some hasty explanation but, at that moment, to his relief, there was a commotion in the hall, announcing the arrival of Marjorie Sand. Marjorie Sand was the kind of person who could not arrive anywhere without a commotion.

'No really, Cook, no coffee for me. Really no. I don't want to disturb them if they're . . .' On certain vowel sounds her voice had a curious, hollow quality, presumably due to the air captured in her cheek. 'Certainly not fresh. Just warm it a little. I'll just pop in and see if they aren't too . . .'

Sir Homer leapt to his feet and straightened his waistcoat and watch-chain. Crispin Turner's glassy eyes followed the movements of his stubby fingers.

'Marjorie. Sit down. Is Cook bringing fresh coffee and more biscuits?' He did not like the woman but affability came effortlessly to him, when he wanted it to, and he was eager to change the focus of attention.

'She said she was, but I really didn't want to . . . How are you Lady Polly?'

With an assumed modesty, she sat on the edge of the armchair into which she had lowered herself gawkily. She always judged it flattering, and maybe politic, not to appear too sure of the security of her position at the Manor; though elsewhere – in St George's, for example – she let there be no doubt concerning her certainty as to whether or not she belonged.

Homer King contemplated her as she gratefully accepted a cup of coffee from the fresh pot that Cook had emphatically presented, and helped herself to some thin, yellow cream from the china jug. She was not a handsome woman. She had the dowdy bearing of a spinster teacher from an Angela Brazil; though thin, she seemed to fill a lot of space; her stooped aspect gave the impression that one side of her body was longer than the other. She mainly wore beige.

'I came to see if you'd heard the awful news.' She reached for a biscuit from the plate that Cook had replenished.

'What awful news is that?' asked Sir Homer cordially, also taking a biscuit. Marjorie usually had some awful news to relate, to which they were not yet privy, and it customarily took the form of minor fires, broken windows, miscarriages and abortions and, before the Rose and Crown changed its clientele, boys on motorbikes.

'You mean you haven't heard?'

'Haven't heard what, Marjorie?' asked Lady Poll, a little sour after her first sherry, getting up to help herself to another.

'"The heathen are come into thine inheritance: Thy holy temple have they defiled and made Jerusalem an heap of stones."'

'What on earth are you talking about, Marjorie?'

'The camp in the lane, at the end of the Folly Footpath. A group of pagans have arrived. Of course it was only to be expected, sooner or later.'

'And what is it they want?' Lady Poll seated herself again.

'One can only guess, of course, but Martha Blandish says they probably want to celebrate the midsummer solstice at the stones. We are a Christian country, a Christian country, and yet the Dark One has been permitted to nestle in our bosoms and penetrate our community. I've just come from the Rectory. The Feathers are being dangerously ecumenical about it, of course, but the Wyley mothers are being most sensible. Mrs Blade's baby had a nasty experience with the stones yesterday and Mrs Blade – who is a very nice woman – had the baby blessed by the rector. The presence of the Dark One was made manifest in the centre of Wyley last night – I don't know if it affected the Manor – and today all the mothers are making provisions. John offered a group blessing – though he was unwilling enough to do that – but the mothers want their children to be blessed separately. The Rectory is full of them. Most wise in the circumstances. Oh, if only Seymour were here rather than at Oxford reading Greats.' She glanced, pointedly, at Crispin Turner, who might not be aware of the impressiveness of her son's whereabouts.

'And how would that help?' said Sir Homer, with a surprising amount of anger in his voice. He had gone rather pale. Seymour Sand was a singularly unattractive individual, with a large, pasty head, small, gold-rimmed glasses and a demeanour of extreme piety. His voice had broken when he was ten. He did not, however, usually evoke such emotion in Sir Homer.

Everyone except for Crispin jumped, and Lady Poll slopped some sherry onto Chummy's quivering back.

'Seymour is a constant source of spiritual strength,' Marjorie replied, rather offended.

Sir Homer looked down at his scratched hands, which seemed to have the whole story written upon them: how Flora had been summoned by memory and by the beauty of the night to dance in the stone circle. It was rare for her to impinge upon his daytime consciousness, the very fact was alarming.

Now it seemed to him that other, stronger forces, of which he had been unaware, might have been at work in the moonlight; forces which he felt, with a terrified certainly, would not sprinkle their demands for indulgence lightly between the solid weeks and months; and that these were somehow bound up with the presence of the travellers.

If Sir Homer were not very careful, someone would divine his secret.

'I am going to speak to Tulliver and see what can be done. This is insupportable. Quite insupportable.'

'Oh, it is,' said Marjorie Sand, solicitously, in case she had gone too far.

'Yes, indeed,' said Lady Poll, who did not really understand.

'You could talk to them first, I suppose?' Marjorie Sand did not really consider reasoned discussion an option but enjoyed the thought of the drama of such an event: the rude and defiant hippies face to face with the magisterial Sir Homer. As with her religion, she liked her social prejudices confirmed by illustration.

'There is nothing to talk about. Nothing to discuss. The stones are on private property. The camp in the lane is almost certainly illegal. Laws exist to protect people against such invasions and they must be used in this instance. I have nothing to say to these people – whoever they are and whatever they call themselves.'

But here Sir Homer was wrong. Within seconds he discovered that he had very much to say. For at that moment Lady Poll's sherry glass fell from her freckled hand and she let out a faint scream.

'They're back. The mad people are back. They've come for me.'

The others followed her frightened gaze to the end of the garden, where a strange sight met their eyes. A head was appearing through a hole in the yew hedge, followed by a long arm, carrying a plastic container. The container was placed on the grass and then, with a bit of a struggle, the other arm and the rest of the body appeared. A tall man pulled himself to his feet and looked around him interestedly. He was followed by another man, or boy really, with long, curly hair. He was wearing filthy black jeans. His feet were bare. The top half of his body was covered only by a torn leather jerkin. He too was carrying a plastic container. Last to emerge was a girl with strange woolly hair. The three of them stood and talked for a moment and then the two men made their way towards the French windows and the girl disappeared around the side of the building.

'I was young,' cried Lady Polly. 'What else could I do? It's a mad person. There was one out last night. I remember it now. I tried to phone you, Crispin.'

'Be quiet, Mother,' said Sir Homer sharply.

Lady Poll burst into tears.

'Lady Polly,' said Crispin softly, 'these people have not come for you. They are merely a form of gypsy. What they appear to want is water.' He placed an arm lightly upon her shoulders. The sobbing began to subside. 'Perhaps another sherry?' he suggested.

'Hallo,' said Paul, who was now standing at the French

windows. 'I hope you didn't mind us using the hole in the hedge. It looked like an established pathway, though it isn't very big. We imagined you must use it as a quick route to the fields.' He stamped each foot on the ground quickly, to get the dust off his sandals, and stepped into the drawing-room. Josh put down his container and lolled against the open window, a sulky expression on his face.

'"A quick route to the fields"?' Sir Homer exploded. 'Do we look like the kind of people who are in the habit of using holes, for that or anything else?' He felt his brown dampen. Already his fears were being realised.

'I can't say, really. I don't know what people who are in the habit of using holes are supposed to look like. We came up here because we've got a couple of requests to make. One is for some water. The other is to be allowed to have a solstice celebration in the stone circle.'

Sir Homer opened his mouth to speak but he was interrupted by a subterranean sort of sound. It was Mulch, who had appeared behind Josh, followed by Karen, who was carrying two pink roses.

'She's cut my roses.'

'The fucking secateurs were just lying around,' said Karen, burying her nose in a Constance Spry. 'Anyway, if you think this lot here believe they're your roses you're kidding yourself. This bloke,' with a nod at Sir Homer, 'reckons it all belongs to him. You ask him.'

'Flowers belong to everyone,' said Paul, placatingly. 'They are all our roses.'

'No they are not,' said Sir Homer, relieved that the discussion was moving onto firmer territory. 'This is my garden, in which you are trespassing, and those are my roses, which you have stolen. It is my stone circle, to which you will not be given access.'

'How much does he pay you, then?' Karen asked Mulch.

'You and your like are tools of the Workings of Darkness,' yelped Marjorie Sand, grabbing at the crucifix which dangled limply at her throat.

'She's picked my roses.'

'No, *my* roses, Mulch,' said Lady Poll, unexpectedly. She had now recovered her composure, thanks to the sherry and Crispin's reassurance. Lady Polly had never been able to train Mulch out of this sense of ownership and it had long been a bone of contention between them. On the day the young female journalist, just out of Oxford, had come down to interview Lady Polly for *Country Manner*, Mulch would have quite hogged the limelight had not the journalist been of a character to understand the eccentricities of old gardeners.

'And, while we are on the subject, it is my Manor, my garden, and my stone circle, Homer,' she added. 'I am not dead yet.'

Sir Homer felt a chill run through the whole of his body. This was a completely new development in the relationship between himself and his mother, and a totally unwelcome one. What could possibly have inspired it?

'It's not your fucking circle because property is theft,' said Karen. 'The whole lot of this place is stolen from the people.' She glared at Josh for support, but he said nothing.

'Wyley Manor was not stolen,' said Lady Poll, loftily, 'it was bought by my father-in-law earlier this century, and so was our title.'

'Mother!' Sir Homer was aghast.

'Is that really the case, Lady Polly?' asked Crispin Turner.

'It is indeed,' said Lady Poll.

What evil magic was at work in Sir Homer's orderly household? First the exacerbation of his mother's ghastly obsession with her unfortunate childhood, then her sudden assertion of ownership of her possessions, and now the family history dredged up, in all its undesirable newness. Sir Homer turned to the three travellers.

'Get out, or I shall phone the police.'

'Can we have some water first?' asked Paul.

'No you cannot. If you choose this way of life you must be willing to abide by its consequences. And I should warn you that I, on behalf of Wyley, am today going to take immediate action to have you and your companions moved on.'

It was the voice of authority, Sir Homer reminded himself. The accent that ruled the world and lead the armies. It was him and Thomas Bright, M.P. for Rocester, in the vanguard of the struggle against anarchy and socialism. It was just unfortunate that the tall traveller had that accent too.

'Water belongs to everyone. It falls out of the sky. Nobody owns the sky,' said Paul.

'The Manor water does not come out of the sky. It comes along pipes and is charged to my water bill.'

'Well I could give you tenpence towards it.' Calm, quiet, reasonable, with a slight, disingenuous smile. Appropriating the qualities that were bought at Eton, honed at Oxbridge, designed to be used for the service of queen and state. Hitherto Sir Homer had tended to view the idea of class solidarity as the preserve of the more menial members of society – it was something so natural to the higher born that it scarcely needed thinking about – but now he felt a tremendous sense of betrayal.

There was a quiet knock on the drawing-room door.

'Miss Flowerdew, Lady Polly,' said Cook. 'Shall I show her in?'

'And who is Miss Flowerdew?' Lady Poll asked.

'The one who got the ambulance when you fell off the rostrum,' said Melanie, who hadn't waited in the hall.

'I don't know you,' said Lady Poll. 'Who are your father and mother?'

'My mother is Martha Blandish. She's a single parent.'

'And what is a single parent?'

'An unmarried mother, Lady Polly,' said Marjorie Sand.

'How unusual.' Lady Poll looked genuinely interested. 'Does she work in a hat shop?'

'She works at the Rectory, Lady Polly,' said Marjorie Sand.

'There is always a danger,' said Lady Polly. 'And what have you come about, Miss Flowerdew?'

'The flowers for decorating the church for the opening of the Manor grounds. Sara Feather was going to come and choose some for Mr Mulch to cut the day before, but she's busy, and so is Martha, so I got sent. Somebody's got the Wyley mothers all wired up about the devil or something and the Rectory's full of them. I wouldn't have come if I'd known you were entertaining, though.'

In the French window Josh grinned. He couldn't see the speaker, because she was hidden by the open door, but he liked the way her sharp voice contrasted with the twittered, spluttered bickering. It had been bloody stupid to come, of course, he'd known that from the offset. It was Paul's idea. They couldn't just assume that Homer King hated hippies and travellers and didn't want anyone in his stone circle, even though he'd written an article saying exactly that. Instead they had to give him the benefit of the doubt and approach him in a reasonable manner. It had worked about as well as Josh had thought it would.

'Goodness,' remarked Lady Poll. 'Everyone wants my flowers today.'

'These are not our guests, Miss Flowerdew,' said Sir Homer. 'And I would be grateful if you would make that clear to the people of Wyley.'

'I don't think I need to. The stone circle has never been exactly available.'

Josh slipped silently into the drawing-room. Melanie took a step forward. A sudden strange breeze grabbed one of the French windows and slammed it against the brickwork. A pane shattered and broke where Josh had been standing. Everyone turned. Melanie and Josh's eyes met. Melanie blushed. Josh watched the colour form at the centre of her cheeks and spread outwards until it covered her whole face. He smiled at her, but did not take his eyes away. She had watched him. Now it was his turn.

Marjorie Sand gave a little scream. 'It's the powers of darkness.'

'Cook, go and fetch Miss Trannock to clear this up,' said Sir Homer. 'And you,' addressing the travellers, 'have two minutes in which to leave.'

'Do I get to see these poxy flowers or what?' asked Melanie crossly. She had dropped her gaze but couldn't resist glancing up again to see if Josh was still looking. He was, but this time she couldn't read his expression.

Sara Feather was very rarely irritated by her husband. She was not of an irritable disposition to begin with and, given the circumstances of their marriage, it would have been inappropriate; so it was a new sensation to find herself irritated by him today.

Perhaps it was because of all the commotion at the Rectory. But the commotion had been calm compared with what she had experienced in London. How could she be ruffled by a few worried Wyley mothers when she had watched the victim of a racial stabbing die on her sitting-room floor? Maybe it was Marjorie Sand stirring things up, going on and on about the devil, until he was so real to the pop-eyed children that they burst into tears every time somebody new knocked on the door. Or maybe John was actually being irritating.

It was the way he stuck to that ridiculous blasting story that Sara found so maddening. Blasting what, for heaven's sake? For the first time ever, in the middle of the night? It was scarcely likely. In fact, it was wrong, as John must be aware. However, having found a semi-plausible untruth, that almost everyone showed signs of being willing to accept, he persisted in it.

'Just blasting, Mrs Sprunt,' he said, as he held a reassuring hand over the hairless head of Paris Sprunt and gave his blessing. At first he had been reluctant. Now he looked as if he was rather enjoying it. Christ among the children, thought Sara, and then was taken aback by her own venom.

She was taken aback too by her sudden fierce sense of loyalty to the stone circle. It was the circle that had caused the events of the night before, that much was obvious. It was the circle that had sent her its message at their dismal parish in London. She had not imagined it because, last night, it had been repeated.

Sara thought of her first sight of the stones in the church meadow, their damp, vulnerable beauty, the sunlight and the blossom. They were so *undemanding*.

'It was the stones that shook the ground last night, John,' she wanted to say. 'Oh, and by the way, it was the stones that brought us to Wyley.' What she did say was, 'It's quieter now, John. Martha can deal with things, I think. Melanie's up at the Manor looking at the flowers for me, so I'm going to go to the church and plan this year's display.'

'All right,' said John, without looking at her. 'See you later.'

Sara calmed down a bit as soon as she stepped out of the Rectory. When she unlocked the door of St George's she was met with a surprise. Not a vase was standing. The vibrations of the night before must have knocked them over. Usually it was just the ones beneath the window that fell.

Sara made her way to the front of the church.

'Oh, how pretty.'

The vases on the altar had fallen backwards. On the flagstones below St George there was a mosaic of blooms and shed petals, pieces of broken pottery. The whole effect was very pleasing. Sara contemplated it and, for a moment, felt tempted not to replace the vases on the uneven sill. The poor circle, hidden away as if of negligible importance, seemed to have been so lovingly placed there by whoever had made the window.

'Hallo.'

Sara swung round. The voice had come from just behind her.

'Goodness! You made me jump.'

It was a girl, with a filthy face and hands, straggly hair and bare feet. She was massively pregnant.

'What are you doing?' she asked.

'Well, I'm about to clear up this mess and then I'm going to think about how to decorate the church for the opening of the Manor grounds this year: Wyley's big event.' Sara looked curiously into the girl's face. There was something not quite right about it.

'Does the church belong to the Manor?'

'Of course not,' Sara replied. There was a lack of mobility in the girl's features, a dreamy, otherworldliness about them.

'So why do you decorate it?'

'Oh, I don't know. Tradition, I suppose.' Sara realised suddenly that the girl was simple. 'You're from the camp, aren't you?' She looked at the girl's stomach. It was hard to keep her eyes off it. It was so tight and bulging, so blatantly fertile; a complete life ready to be delivered up to the doubtful ability of this girl to care for it. 'When are you due?'

'I'm not due. I'm here now.'

'I mean the baby. When is the baby due?'

'I don't know. Miranda says soon.'

'Have you seen a doctor?'

'Miranda gives me herbs.'

Sara looked away quickly. She went and got the dustpan and brush and started to sweep the flagstones. The irritation had spontaneously returned. Her hands were trembling.

'Is Miranda a qualified doctor?' she asked, in a controlled voice.

The broken glass made a sad sort of sound as she collected it in the dustpan.

'I don't know.'

'I could arrange for someone to look at you.' She could barely trust herself to speak.

'I don't want to be looked at.'

'If not for yourself, for the baby.'

'The baby is happy. It kicks.'

'You could lose it if you aren't careful.' Sara thought of the way a newborn's hand opened and closed, as if it could feel the air held within it. She thought of John blessing Paris Sprunt.

'You don't get babies by being careful.'

Sara said nothing. The girl was right. It was the perfect description of her sex life with John, after all, and it hadn't got them a baby. A surging sense of the unfairness of everything welled up inside her. She wished the girl would go away now.

'What happened to your legs?'

'Oh.' Sara ran a hand down her skirt. She felt old and awkward. 'I suppose my hand slipped. It's nothing much. Suffer to be beautiful and all that.'

The girl was silent for a moment and then, 'Who's she?' she asked.

Sara followed the direction of the pointed finger, noting the thick line of dirt beneath the fingernail. Saint George stared down at her in his flowered robes, his long, waving locks twisting about his shoulders.

'That's not a she,' Sara replied, going back to her sweeping. 'That's Saint George. This is Saint George's Church.'

'Are you sure?'

'Of what?'

'That it isn't a woman.'

'Well, I should be. My husband is the rector here. And all the people of Wyley, I promise you, are very much of the opinion that that is Saint George and that this is Saint George's church.'

'They could be wrong,' said the girl.

Sara was conscious of a great tiredness, as if all her life she had been cheering a losing team. She put down the dustpan and brush and leant back against the altar. When she eventually looked around, the girl had gone.

Did she drink milk? Sara wondered. She would, and orange juice. The girl probably smoked. Sara wouldn't, and she would give up her glass of wine with Sunday lunch. The girl probably took drugs.

How much better a life it would have had if it had been John and Sara's child. She imagined its toys strewn across the blank kitchen floor. The playgroup and then the little village school. Secondary education at the good school in Rocester, the one whose catchment area skirted the council estate, flinging its friendly arms out to embrace, instead, the villages with their beamed houses, the restored mills and renovated cottages. It was unfair, of course, but how easy it would be to tolerate unfairness if your children profited from it. Perhaps not Oxford or Cambridge, but Durham or Bristol or Exeter.

Sara blinked and her reverie ceased. For a fleeting second she had the strange sensation that this girl had stolen her and John's baby, like those gypsies in stories and songs who take the beautiful child away from its parents and off to whatever mythical place they are going.

8

The Police

By early evening most of Wyley, with the exception of Sergeant Tulliver, had had some kind of contact with the travellers – though, admittedly, not all of it at first hand. It was, moreover, Homer King who had alerted the sergeant to the travellers' presence, by phoning him at the Wyley police station – a dull, 1950s council house, specially adapted for its purpose – which was also his home.

This was just before midday. The sergeant was sitting at his desk, behind the narrow counter, sleeves rolled up, sweating profusely and squeezing a blackhead when the phone rang. It was Homer King. Something to do with the old bag's birthday, probably.

'Good morning, Sir Homer. Nice day. What can I do for you?'

'Good morning, Tulliver. I daresay you've heard.' The voice was crisp and businesslike. Sir Homer did not squander his charm on public servants.

'Heard what, Sir?'

'The camp in the lane, by the Folly Footpath. New Age Travellers is what the wretched people call themselves I believe.'

'Oh yes, Sir Homer. We have the matter in hand.' Sergeant Tulliver lied with practised ease, as policemen need to do sometimes, in order to reassure the public.

Sir Homer was not reassured.

'What are you doing about it?'

'Well, Sir, we are looking into the legalities of the situation prior to taking action.'

'They have trespassed on my land and one of them has stolen some of my roses. I am willing to take that to court, if you think it would help matters.'

'I will certainly take note of it, Sir, but I'm afraid the courts would be disinclined to view trespass with a view to picking flowers with appropriate seriousness.' Sergeant Tulliver smiled to himself but kept the smile absent from his voice. A true authoritarian, he would have defended to the death the beneficiaries of those privileges of which he did not partake and which he resented to the not-very-profound depths of his being.

'Well, I suggest you do something as soon as possible. The residents of Wyley are not likely to take kindly to something like this. I cannot tolerate it, Sergeant. This interest in my circle is most unwelcome. I cannot tolerate it. If the force does not act quickly I fear I will have to concern myself directly.'

'Be assured of our very best efforts, Sir Homer.'

Sergeant Tulliver put down the telephone and his smile vanished. Sir Homer was right. Something did need to be done or Wyley would be overrun with hippies and he would be held to blame. It was irritating that Homer King and, presumably, others besides had heard about the situation before he had. If it got out, the speedily critical Wyley-dwellers might claim he had not been on top of things at a time when preventative action could have been taken. He swiftly dialled the station at Rocester, only to be informed that they were fully appraised of the situation in Wyley and were presently examining the legalities of the matter. This, at least, he had got right.

The next thing to do was to go to the camp and see if the travellers could be frightened off – not likely. In Tully's experience, even if they could barely read or write or speak English, even if they'd just got off the last banana boat, these sorts of people knew the law like the backs of their hands. Added to which, these situations were the danger area where the force was monitored by people who did not know how hard it was to be a policeman; people who should mind their own bloody business.

Sergeant Tulliver would have set out immediately, but the phone rang again. It was Mrs Gough, on behalf of a group of Wyley mothers, who gathered together once a week, just to get away from things for three or four hours – leaving their toddlers with Mrs Pleasance's Ludmilla, who was a treasure – over a bottle of plonk one of them had usually brought back from somewhere and some brie and grapes. Well, as it happened, today was the day of the girls' get together and they were all extremely concerned.

The policeman listened with increasing impatience. In spite of his outer demeanour of respect and deference he had a chip on his shoulder when it came to Wyley's au pairs and burglar alarms, its Range Rovers and foreign holidays. Would the stupid bitch ever get to the point? Still, she had a nice voice, though. Probably worked as a hooker before she landed Alexander Gough, who was rolling in it.

'. . . and she pinched it!' Mrs Gough finished, her voice rising to a squeak. 'Not hard, but it woke up and started crying. And then she had the nerve to ask for money. Of course, Mrs Lime didn't give her any. And after that the girl called her a fascist.'

'And?' Tully was at a loss. It hadn't occurred to him that not everyone viewed being called a fascist as just another part of everyday life.

'Well, isn't it illegal?'

'What, Madam?'

'I mean isn't it abuse or something?'

Sometimes Tully marvelled at the way the public viewed the law as something small and pliable, specially there to deal with their own little grievances. While he sympathised with the desire to rid Wyley of all undesirables, he found it hard to believe that Homer King or the Wyley mothers could seriously consider that minor nuisances to themselves would have sufficient force under the law. The major nuisance of the camp being there at all was a different matter, but in order to eliminate it you had to find something they were doing that was properly illegal – not just something other people would rather they didn't. That was the bind, the irritating restraint with which a policeman had to learn to live. Tully would quite happily have hanged everybody who had ever called him a fascist, but British society at least did not usually work that way.

'Was it said in a threatening manner?'

'Well, I think it was pretty threatening to say it at all.'

'I'm afraid, Madam, there's not a lot I can do unless there is evidence of a definite threat. A lawyer could always argue that the term "fascist" is a political appelation no different from "Conservative", for example.'

'You are not seriously telling me, Sergeant . . .' This continued for nearly a quarter of an hour. In the background Sergeant Tulliver could hear the gentle hum of women's voices, the soft clink of their glasses. Simultaneously he started to feel peckish and a bump began to form under his blue trousers. '. . . could perhaps put a barbed-wire fence around the stones, or something electric, so that nobody could possibly imagine that there was any chance of celebrating anything whatever in them.' The Sergeant's mouth watered at the thought of the unopened tin of spam on his kitchen table.

As soon as he'd put the phone down, however, it rang again. It was Marjorie Sand, wanting to know how long it would be before the travellers were moved on. The next caller was Miss Sayle, from the Wise Lady Tea Rooms, where the travellers had eaten some toasted cheese and tomato sandwiches and then had had the cheek to question the bill. Marjorie Sand phoned back after that, to say that she was starting a petition and trying to organise a prayer-vigil. After he'd got rid of her the phone rang again. This time it was Sara Feather.

'I'm calling because I'm worried, Sergeant Tulliver.'

'You mean about the camp, Mrs Feather.'

'Not entirely. I mean, yes, the camp, but mainly the children – if there are any. Well, I know there's one pregnant woman. I don't know the legalities of the situation, but I'm frightened that things could get out of control.'

Tully was not completely sure he had understood.

'We hope to move them on as soon as possible, Mrs Feather. Obviously it all has to be done correctly, but the Rocester office is doing its best to ascertain the situation of the travellers *vis-à-vis* the law.'

'That's not what I mean, Sergeant Tulliver. What I'm trying

to say is, we don't want anyone getting hurt or anything. People can be so silly. We don't want any harm to come to the baby.'

'Pardon?'

A slight confusion entered Sara Feather's voice, as if she were finding it hard to say what she was feeling. 'What I mean, Sergeant Tulliver, is that certain people seem to be getting very worked up. They are talking as if any means at anybody's disposal would be justified in getting the travellers to move on.'

'Well, it isn't,' said Tully, reluctantly, trying to imagine what kind of damage Mrs Feather imagined Miss Sayle from the tea rooms or Marjorie Sand could wreak upon the travellers.

'I know that. I just want to be sure that they do, too. It may be that they don't entirely understand.'

A bleeding woman telling him his job.

'I'll do what I can, Mrs Feather, but people think what they want to think.'

'I must say I am at a bit of a loss to understand the force of the reaction. It's almost as if . . . as if . . . Do you know how many travellers there are, Sergeant Tulliver?'

Tully improvised. 'We are not yet aware of the scale of the problem, Mrs Feather.'

'Ten? Twenty?'

'I'm afraid I would not be at liberty to divulge even were I to have a precise figure.'

'Well, if you need a hand . . .'

That was the trouble with things like this, thought Tully, as he got some margarine out of the fridge. He had decided to have his lunch before he went to view things. It would probably be the only chance he'd get, if the rest of the day was like the morning. With burglars, child abuse, rape, murder, you knew what the public wanted. All you had to do was give it to them; which could have its difficulties but, as long as a result was delivered fairly swiftly, everyone was happy. But this was what they sometimes called a grey area of policing. The law wasn't automatically clear and opinion could be divided. Christ knew what Martha would think, silly bitch. You did one thing and half the people screamed that you should have done the other. Still, Tully thought as he put an oblong of spam on his slice of Mother's Pride, you couldn't please everyone: that was the nature of justice.

He was just finishing his sandwich and swallowing down the last of his pineapple juice when the phone rang yet again. It was Simon Tarrant from the Rose and Crown.

'I was wondering, Sergeant, if you wouldn't mind coming rind for a few minutes. We've had a bit of trouble here. I'd like to talk to you about it.'

At that point Sergeant Tulliver decided to abandon his visit to the camp until later in the day. It was bloody obvious the hippies weren't going anywhere, and it might be a good idea to establish a police presence on the street. Community policing, they called it. He would ask people for their help, tell them to keep an eye out, make them feel important, like he had done with the Neighbourhood Watch. They'd liked that. It had given all the Wyley busybodies a lasting reason to spy on their neighbours. Any kind of information, he'd said. Doesn't matter what it is. Could come in handy. Could be important one day. And anyway, how can we serve the community if we don't know the community? If we don't try to cater to its own special needs? It hadn't unearthed much and he hadn't really expected it to, but it had cemented them together. They had believed they were participating and they needed to believe that now. The station in Rocester would soon come up with some ideas about what to do. The big boys could decide the ins and outs, the rights and wrongs, how to proceed, whether to proceed; when you got down to it, it was up to them. But Wyley could think it was playing its part: that when it peeked out from behind its reproduction William Morris curtains it was fulfilling its social duty.

Sergeant Tulliver put on his helmet and set out to play his role of village bobby.

Until the Tarrants arrived the Rose and Crown had smelled of crisps and mild and, usually, vomit. When Tully walked in there would be a furtive hush and the very walls would exude hostility. He had rather liked it like that; had enjoyed glancing round the bar with the knowledge that he could throw anyone out at the drop of a hat. Now it smelled of dandelion wine and the mutton pasties that Veronica, helped by a French au pair, was making in the kitchen. Tully removed his helmet.

'Can I orfa you a larger, Sergeant?'

'That's very kind of you, Sir. Just a half.'

'Would you like to sit outside?'

The pub garden was empty, though several tables still had the remains of lunches on them, lipstick-stained glasses, plates of oyster shells.

'So what's been the problem, Sir?'

'There's a cemp jest outside the village.'

'Yes.' Tully managed to suggest, by his tone of voice, that he had been privy to this information since the beginning of time.

'About five of them came in here. I didn't want to be rude so I said we couldn't serve them because of the dog. Of course we do usually allow dogs but it was jest an excuse. Anyway, they weren't awfully sensitive and they said that the dog wouldn't mind waiting outside if we could let it have some water. So then I had to be more direct. I said I was refusing to serve them a drink. They asked why and I said I didn't have to give them a reason.'

'Absolutely.' Tully gave an approving nod.

'Obviously, Sergeant, we have a reputation to maintain. We see the Rose and Crown as a bit like a French café or brasserie.' Tully had never been to a French café or brasserie, but he nodded again. 'We've worked hard to get it up and running,' Simon continued. 'We spent months just doing nothing but talking to interior designers and architects, garden specialists . . . You can probably imagine what a nightmare that was. And I wouldn't say the job's finished yet. We're in the process of building up a jolly nice sort of clientele by establishing annual events, like this Midsummer Night's Dream Do we've got coming up in a few days. We know the stone circle's here, of course, but we're not really in that game – tourist buses and what have you. It would be too ghastly for words, and not what we came here for. We see the circle as a sort of backdrop to Wyley; aren't much bothered whether it's there or not, to be honest with you. Except that now it's interfering with the whole *feel* of what we're wanting to achieve. Our Midsummer Night's thing gets ruined by hippies turning up and there's a whole lot of dosh quite frankly down the toilet. Atmosphere goes to pot, needless to say: fairies, woodland revels, whatever – haven't read the thing myself but Veronica's batty about it – how do you equate that with a lot of filthy anarchists in buses?'

'Has Simon being making the situation clear to you, Sergeant?' asked Veronica, who now approached the table. As she spoke she fingered a thin gold necklace. 'It was an awful drag trying to get rid of them.'

She did not add that it was she, and not Simon, who had eventually got their message across by saying, with a sweet smile on her face, 'You people really are a lot of revolting fucks.'

'Good afternoon, Mrs Tarrant.' Tully stood up politely. 'Yes, I think I understand what's required. What I'll do is warn these people off making another attempt to come onto your premises, now that you have made your feelings known to them.'

'Yes, do that, Sergeant Tulliver,' said Simon, rising also. 'And make it very clear, eh? There's a good fellow.'

After lunch had been washed up and John and Martha had settled down to some paperwork, Sara Feather decided to brave Wyley High Street. Perhaps by now, she told herself, things would have quietened down a bit.

She soon discovered that they hadn't. In fact, Wyley was more than usually busy. There was an air of excited expectancy. People who were accustomed to huddling in the privacy of their back gardens had brought deckchairs, tables and rugs onto their smaller front lawns and were sitting there, all ready to be horrified and insulted. Those whose lopsided Tudor gems nestled among apple orchards on the furthest reaches of the village seemed loath to go home and were gossiping outside Gimble's, their children's ice-lollies dripping onto the pavement.

The village was festooned with notices, which had erupted throughout the morning, giving it a strangely festive atmosphere. As well as the usual Neighbourhood Watch stickers, with their unlikely racial assortment, and the Rose and Crown's Midsummer Night's Dream Evening posters, there was now a 'No Travellers' sign in each of the local shops and in the Wise Lady Tea Rooms. In the front gardens, behind the basking home-owners, there was an assortment of homemade 'No Trespassing' notices and the odd, more lateral, 'No Dogs'. In the ornamental wheelbarrow belonging to Magpie Cottage was a dainty 'Sign Petition Here' and 'Come And Pray With Us', though to judge from Marjorie's almost hourly phone calls, 'Us' seemed something of an exaggeration.

Queuing up outside Callan's, Sara looked over at the church meadow. Silver-grey in the sunlight, the stones made her think of wild, moorland horses, constrained by the soft domesticity around them. Except that one forgot – it was all so very normal – that Wyley was not gentle. She looked back into the shop where, in front of a row of dripping carcasses, Tom Callan, blood-smeared and wielding a great hatchet-like knife, was waxing lyrical on the subject of those who had sacrificed their lives across the battlefields of Europe. And what kind of people had the world been made safe for? Useless layabouts who lived off the dole and who had never done a day's work in their lives. A pale group of mothers, perspiring delicately from their shaven armpits, was murmuring agreement. Callan lifted his hefty arm and sliced through a great chunk of meat as if it were a human neck.

Safe? Sara was astounded. But the baby wasn't safe; just look at the intolerance expressed in Wyley High Street. If only because of its mother's way of life it was destined to be born into a hostile environment. She began to feel angry. Surely it wasn't right that anyone should be able to subject a child to that kind of existence? There should be laws to protect it. When her turn came she hastily bought some lamb chops and hurried on.

'Some of your shortbread, Miss Sayle.' Sara looked round the Wise Lady Tea Rooms, which was packed to bursting with a mixture of Wyley mothers and tourists, staring wonderingly at the beams and knick-knacks, and elderly ladies cutting buns with small knives. 'Business is good I see.'

'Which is a miracle, considering,' said Miss Sayle grimly.

Were you allowed to have a baby without any kind of pre-natal examination, Sara wondered? If a girl showed herself to be irresponsible – or not able to be responsible – couldn't the social services take away her baby and give it to someone else who was more trusted by the community, someone who would be able to look after it better and provide the things that would otherwise have been denied to it?

Sara took her bag of shortbread, paid and started to walk back to the Rectory. But then, she told herself, the social services probably had no idea of what was happening. They weren't going to do anything unless they knew about it, and they wouldn't know unless they were informed by some concerned individual.

Before crossing the road she looked back towards the stones, half expecting them to give an indication that they endorsed her line of thinking. Could it be that it was because of the traveller's baby that the circle had brought her to Wyley: on a sort of rescue mission? But the sun went behind a cloud and, beneath her gaze, the stones metamorphosed into hard lumps of neutrality.

It was a relief to close the Rectory's elegant door behind her. Sara took her shopping into the kitchen and put it down on the pine table.

'Want a coffee?' she called to Martha and John, who were in the study. There was no reply but, a moment later, Melanie appeared with Hamish.

'Oh, hallo Melanie. I didn't know you were here.'

'Martha wants me to do some shopping for her. In case I should ever have any time to myself. John says he'd love a coffee. Martha says do you have any tisanes left, because she's decided to stop taking caffeine?'

'Oh dear. No, I don't think I do.' Sara waved her arms stupidly, in a helpless and guilty gesture.

'Doesn't matter. If Martha decides to behave differently from the rest of the civilised world that's her problem.'

'Well, perhaps she'd like some lemon squash.'

'Not a chance. She'll say it's full of toxins. I wouldn't bother if I was you. Though I suppose,' she added casually, 'I *could* go and pick some mint from the garden, to make a fresh tisane. If you've got any.'

'Golly, yes, we've got heaps. What a good idea.'

'Come on then, Hame.' Melanie slouched out. Sara put the cups on a tray and a few of the shortbreads on a plate.

'Martha, I'm awfully sorry. We've run out and I don't think they sell them at Gimble's. Next time I go to Rocester. Anyway, all's well that ends well: Melanie's going to make you a mint tea, out of fresh mint, no less. She's gone out to the garden to pick some.'

Martha was wearing a strange garment that was somewhere

between tights and trousers, over which she had put a thin, pink skirt. Her t-shirt was plain white, with a row of buttons down the front, but had a funny, jagged edge and was very short. She looked surprised and was quite plainly touched.

'Melanie's doing that for me?'

'Oh, it's a good idea,' said Sara. 'I should do the same thing, really. They say caffeine's bad for you, don't they?' She glanced at her husband, who was buried in his correspondence. 'Going well?'

'Not badly.'

There was silence for a moment. Sara took a quick sip of her coffee. She felt calmer now.

'The villagers are out for blood, I'm afraid. Marjorie's got a notice up about her petition. I imagine they'll all sign it.'

'What'll she do with it then?' asked Melanie, who entered now, Hamish balanced on her hip and Martha's cup in her hand.

'Thank you, Melanie,' said Martha. Melanie shrugged.

'Send it to Thomas Bright, I suppose,' said Sara.

'Thomas Bright,' said John, putting down his pen and pushing his chair back, 'will almost certainly respond positively to their demands, especially the most extreme – he's shaping up into the most rabid right-winger; some of his comments in the press about AIDS-sufferers have to be seen to be believed – but there's nothing he can do in the short term. In the end it's going to be the legal position that counts and, judging from the lack of developments, that appears to be complex. Marjorie's been on to me as well,' he added. 'She wants to hold some sort of Nuremberg Rally in the church hall. I've managed to prevaricate for the moment, but she'll be pestering again soon and I'll have to come up with a plausible explanation as to why it's not possible.'

'You could just say you don't like the idea,' suggested Sara.

'You hoping to gain some new parishioners?' Melanie's hard little expression was somewhat undermined by the fact that she was holding a piece of shortbread for her stepbrother, who was licking the sugar off it.

'You mean the travellers? Not really. Though of course they're welcome.'

'I wouldn't say "of course",' said his wife quickly. 'Wyley doesn't seem to feel that there are as many mansions as we do.'

'Well, anyway, it's not an issue. I imagine they're Buddhists or something.'

'Oh, I don't think this lot are Buddhists,' said Sara, 'I think they're pagans, or pantheists. That's why the stones are important to them.'

'There seems to be this assumption in the village,' John was entering his stride, 'that, if they weren't here, these people would somehow disappear off the face of the earth; that they could get work and live in houses, like other people. But where would these houses be? And what work? Most of them will have left school when they were sixteen. They won't have any money. As things are they have a camp in the woods. They wake up among fields. If they didn't have their buses, the chances are they'd be living in bed-and-breakfast accommodation. And that's not pretty, I can tell you. And, incidentally, they would be costing the state a darn sight more money than they are at the moment.'

'I'm not sure it's fair on the children, though,' said Sara. Eight months, at least, probably nine. Would the girl even know what to do with it? 'Which reminds me,' though she had thought of little else for several hours now, 'one of them's awfully pregnant. I think it really calls for some kind of involvement.'

'I'd tread carefully,' said John. 'You might not be welcome. This is England, remember. We do still have a National Health Service, which they can use if they want to.'

'I'm not sure they do want to. Perhaps they're nervous of the kind of reception they'll get. But I'm sure we could ask Henry Oliver to have a quick look at her. Just to be certain everything's all right.'

'Well, let them take the lead.'

'You're talking about her as if she's a monkey in a zoo,' said Melanie. 'If I was her I'd tell you to get lost.'

'Melanie,' said Martha, 'I think you should apologise to Sara for saying that.'

'But it's true.'

'There's no need for apologies,' said Sara sensibly. 'I do understand, Melanie. Of course I do. It's just for the child.'

'I don't see what the child's got to do with it.'

'The girl's got nobody to care for her. She's a single parent, remember.'

'Like Martha.' Melanie appeared to be genuinely angry.

'No, not like Martha.' Sara felt a bit flustered. It had all been much clearer when she was thinking about it privately.

'And she's not alone. She's got the other travellers.'

'Once you have children,' said Sara, 'your life isn't your own any more.'

'They do make a difference, Melanie,' said Martha quietly. There was an awkward silence.

Then, 'I know,' said Sara, brightly, feeling as if she wasn't looking very good somehow, 'what we could do is go down to the camp and sort of welcome them to Wyley.'

'Don't you think that might strike them as somewhat ironic?' John asked. 'Considering two people, to my knowledge, have tried to get them arrested and Homer King has even refused to let them have any water from his taps?' For Sir Homer's heroic act was generally known about now, had indeed been common knowledge within an hour of its performance, and had confirmed Wyley in its belief that it was privileged to have such a personage in its midst.

'All the more reason to show them that not everybody here is like that. And we could broach the subject of the doctor at the same time.'

'Bearing gifts,' sneered Melanie. 'What are you going to take them?'

Sara thought a moment.

'Well, there's a few things I wasn't going to put into the jumble sale.'

'Jumble sale rejects. They'll be over the moon.'

'Beggars can't be choosers. And anyway, they're probably very resourceful with old odds and ends.'

'I've got some organic carrots,' said Martha.

'Harvest Festival,' said Melanie. The vegetables from Demeter looked like someone had shat on them and were full of worms. They took about an hour to prepare.

'You'll come, won't you Martha, to help me carry things? And you Melanie?'

'Of course she will,' said Martha, who was looking excited.

'I thought you wanted me to go shopping.' Melanie's heart started to pound a fast, regular, quickening drumbeat. She felt cross with it, as she had felt cross with almost everything and everyone since she had run away from the camp that morning. Ambushed into this terrible, aching tenderness, she even almost felt angry with the boy who had created it. Surprise had been the clincher. It would never have happened if he hadn't surprised her. Now she was vulnerable to the perfume of the mint, and the hum of bees in the garden. Everything could go splat in her face from now on. Her brain was busy making connections and underlining significances. Christ, she'd even bothered to argue with Sara Feather.

'You can do that afterwards.'

'Great. This is supposed to be summer, remember? In summer people have fun.'

'This is fun.'

'For who?'

Sara Feather ran round the house gathering up useless objects to give to the travellers and Melanie was sent to get the shitty carrots. John found an old shirt he didn't want any more. Sara packed it all up in boxes by the front door so it looked like something left out for the dustmen.

'Well,' she said, in her most practical voice. 'It isn't much but it's the thought that counts.'

'Is it?' said Melanie. 'In that case it's surprising Wyley hasn't managed to blow them off the face of the planet.'

'They'll probably be thrilled,' said Sara. 'You can't understand what things like this mean to the poor.'

Thrilled. Where did Sara find these words? Melanie looked at her dull, happy face, her boring dress. She had got something terribly wrong: these people weren't poor.

As Melanie, with a box – John Feather was looking after Hamish, who had fallen asleep – trudged behind Sara and Martha she considered what John Feather had said about bed-and-breakfast accommodation. Sara could do her Lady Bountiful routine but the fact remained that John had been right: there would be a difference if you made these people stop and live normal lives. Then they would be poor.

Martha wasn't well off but the three of them lived in a pretty house with a view of a village green. The mothers, outside the school, complained to each other about how broke they were: 'No Ibiza for us this year, we're just renting a cottage with friends near Truro.' But they weren't poor, not even near it. They could make choices about their lives. And so could the travellers. Maybe they wouldn't be able to if you made them stand still, but now they could. Real poverty was when you couldn't make your own decisions. So Sara Feather's idea of taking them gifts was a ridiculous charade; as ridiculous as if you'd given them to the mothers.

Melanie tried to avoid thinking about the camp's beautiful colours; she tried to avoid thinking about the boy, because she really truly couldn't bear it, but they came back to her again and again. This was opulence; this was richness; the ability to change environments, make Martha a little more understandable, magic Wyley away, not be a let-down and a disappointment. To think that there were people whose top aspiration was to have as much money as Homer King and to own some place like Wyley Manor.

Oh puke. Oh puke puke puke. They'd done it again. They'd taken exhausted old clichés like Grandma might have trotted out: 'Money can't buy you happiness, you know,' and made them new and relevant.

'The thing people don't remember about the sixties,' some half-dead old hippy said on some gormless documentary Martha watched one time, 'is that, as an era, it was intensely practical.'

'Oh yes,' Martha cried delightedly. 'It was.'

'So how come you got yourself knocked up?' said Melanie. And that was the end of that conversation.

'Gosh,' said Sara, as they neared the buses. 'I didn't think it would be like this, did you?'

'Sort of,' Martha replied.

Sara was flabbergasted. She had expected something more squalid. She had thought the atmosphere would be indolent, but there was a sense of activity; rather strange activity, not terribly productive, or some of it productive and the rest of it . . . not unproductive, but . . . They must have found water somewhere because several containers of it had been placed in a shady spot under a tree. They had put up a hammock, which the pregnant girl was lying in, rocking slowly. Someone had filled the branches above her head with spiders' webs made of wool. A species of stew was bubbling on a grid, balanced on bricks and set over an open fire. The grid, on inspection, turned out to be part of an old wrought iron fence.

Sara tried to imagine the kind of mentality that fused together such weirdly disparate elements. 'First I must get some water and then I must put some spiders' webs in the trees.' It struck her as curiously religious. In a way, now she came to consider it, the sort of outlook you could imagine the people who made the stone circle having. Sara blinked to shake off the enchantment. She made herself think of the posters in Wyley, Marjorie Sand's petition, the Nuremberg Rally.

She glanced around. There didn't seem to be many travellers. A naked baby was lying in a cardboard box. Its mother was tickling it with a piece of grass. There was a young man, with curly dark hair, lying on a rug. An arm was visible, sticking out from under one of the buses. A tall blonde woman was playing a guitar. Beside her a child was preparing a salad. It looked a tortuous procedure, all done on the lap, with no table and no chopping board, and with an evident attempt to use as little water as possible for washing the vegetables.

'You know, you can always come and get water at the Rectory,' Sara said spontaneously. 'I can run you back in the Morry Minor. In fact,' she racked her brain for some other ways to help the baby, 'if one of you wants to come and do a bit of work for me in the garden, I can pay them.'

The travellers looked up.

'I'm the rector's wife, Sara Feather. This is Melanie, and her mother, Martha. We've brought some bits and bobs as well that we thought might be useful,' Sara plunged on. 'Carrots and baby clothes. I know you're expecting a happy event.' Even to her, her voice sounded loud and intrusive. 'Actually, I was wondering if you would like me to get you a doctor.'

The blonde woman stood.

'Nobody is ill,' she said. 'But I will come and work in your garden.'

'Oh, I know that,' said Sara. 'I meant a check-up, for your

friend who's pregnant. I've mentioned it to her already, but she wasn't too keen on the idea, so maybe if you . . .'

'If you have already discussed it with Emily, and she has said no, what more is there to say on the matter? When shall I come to the Rectory?'

Clearly there was going to be no co-operation from the travellers on the subject of Emily's baby. It had probably been foolish to expect it. Sara Feather decided that, as usual, she was going to have to rely on her own resources.

'Nine-ish tomorrow,' she replied. 'The Rectory is easy to find. It's just next to the church. If you get lost, ask anyone. Or rather,' she added quickly, imagining the likely result, 'or rather, don't . . .'

'I am good at finding places,' said the woman. 'We know we are not popular in Wyley.'

'People can be silly sometimes.'

'Yes, they can.'

While this was going on Melanie managed to avoid looking at him. Instead she watched Sara making an idiot of herself: now she was starting to unpack the boxes, commenting on the contents, holding up poxy little frocks with ribbons, shaking a well-chewed rattle. Melanie's gaze wandered over the jam-jars full of flowers; the garlands had progressed; the geraniums had been watered, their scarlet petals danced in the heat. She knew that he was watching her. The colours were even brighter now; the wood was noisy with birdsong; the child's blunt knife hacked at a ruby-red tomato. Wouldn't Hamish love to come here?

'You do this now, Josh, I'm sick of it.'

Josh.

'In a minute, Curdie.'

'Why not now?'

'In a minute.'

Melanie allowed herself to look. Not at his face at first, but at the curve of his arm where the spiky sun rose above tangled grasses, then at the smooth structure of his neck, his lips, his cheekbones and then, at last, at those beautiful eyes which were staring admiringly at . . . Martha.

Melanie dropped the box she had been holding. It met the ground with a soft crunch, fell open and its innards spilled out. Josh did not turn. Melanie appeared to be as invisible to him now as she had been to his unseeing, sleeping eyes early that morning. Melanie looked at her mother. She had crumpled onto the ground and was sitting cross-legged, the sunlight had caught her hair and made the pale gingeriness into coppery gold. Seen like that, Melanie realised, you could almost describe her as beautiful.

She studied her curiously, trying to understand Martha's almost infinite sexual appeal, that strange quality of which she had only ever witnessed the effects, for it sounded at a frequency too high, or too low, for the female ear to hear.

Melanie hated her.

Josh spoke.

'Can you tell me some things about the village?'

'Me?' Sara lowered a shirt that she had been holding up so that the sunlight went right through it. It was hardly surprising she asked the question, he was still looking at Martha. 'I can try. To do with the stone circle?'

Josh shook his head. 'About how it's changed since, I don't know, the early seventies, say.'

'Why do you want to know?'

'Just interested.'

'Well, you'd be better asking Martha. I'm a newcomer.'

Martha, thought Melanie, was like a planet that gathered up every bit of crap that came near it: Hamish's father, Paul Stevens; Tully; Melanie's father; numerous forgotten others; Josh.

'My family has been here since the beginning of time,' said Martha.

'It's about the pub.'

'The Rose and Crown?'

'No, not the Rose and Crown, the other one.'

'There isn't another one.'

'Not any more, but there was a while back, right?'

Martha shook her head. 'Not here. You must be thinking of another village. There are lots of villages like Wyley.' She smiled. 'Wyley has changed, of course. When my mother was young you could buy everything you needed here. There was a cobbler and a baker, a fishmonger, a barber, a hairdresser's and a draper's. There were actually two sweetshops and a dairy that made its own ice-cream. But there was only ever one pub.'

So it wasn't Wyley after all. That weird event with his mother and probably his father and the mysterious other woman had happened somewhere else. The Rose and Crown, or what he'd seen of it before they got chucked out, wasn't the pub he remembered. That was a village pub, a bit tatty, dull to a child, but he'd probably like it now. This one was some rich shit's image of what a village pub would be like in an England tailored to suit his discriminating imagination.

Josh yawned. He was tired though it was not late; eight, eight-thirty perhaps, the sun had lowered in the sky but wouldn't set for a while yet. They should have known better than to mess with Babylon – you always got asked to leave, ripped off, refused things – and, since it was in Babylon that his past had happened, why go to the trouble of trying to figure it out? The explanation would be simple enough: it was probably just another one of straight society's typical fuck-ups, which weren't greatly different from its successes. If his father hadn't buggered off, Josh's mother would probably be like Martha, the one who told him about Wyley – they were the same age, about, and not that different in looks – it was only bad luck that things worked out the way they did. Let it be, leave it behind.

Josh looked back at his book, but his curiosity wouldn't vanish, nor would the events of the day. He turned the book over and, instead of reading, drew runes in the earth with his index finger.

He couldn't love a woman. He didn't know how. He wished he did. He wished he hadn't had to hurt Melanie.

After she had gone he had instinctively inspected his body, almost expecting to see purple burn-marks where Melanie's eyes had touched it. If it hadn't been for Martha it would have been impossible not to look back, but once Martha had got hold of his attention he was able to keep it fixed upon her, even while he experienced Melanie's pain and confusion as if they were happening to himself.

Josh lay down, and he must have fallen asleep. When he woke up there was a tension in the camp. Right next to his face was a big, shiny boot, a long, blue, rank-smelling trouser-leg. Dead on time, right when you'd expect him, a messenger from Babylon.

'Who's in charge here?' asked Sergeant Tulliver, looking round the camp. It was like a kid's fancy-dress party. Grown men and women done up like Indian peasants. He felt cool and relaxed and in control. He had put on a clean shirt and he was wearing his helmet in order to give himself extra authority. There was silence.

'I asked a question. You don't want me to have to take you all down the station and ask you there, do you?'

'On what grounds?' It was a girl who had piped up. She was wearing a yellow and purple skirt covered in little diamond-shaped mirrors. Her eyes were circled with black, like Cleo-fucking-patra; there was a spider in her nose and her hair was like a Jamaican's, except red; at one tit she'd got a baby. Tully was shocked. It was obscene, in front of a stranger, to have a boob hanging out. He imagined describing it to the lads down at the station and them saying what they'd do if their girls did anything like that.

'Nobody's in charge,' said a tall man, old enough to know better. 'We don't believe in leaders.'

Sergeant Tulliver was rather stumped.

'You always talk like that?' For the man had a voice like Sir Homer's. It crossed Tully's mind that it was being put on.

The man shrugged.

'Leaders are a creation of the patriarchy,' said the girl.

Tully didn't know what she was on about. 'You got MOT's for those vehicles?'

'Somewhere. They might take a bit of time to find, but I can look for them.' A strange, small, filthy, rat-like person in a boiler-suit covered in diesel.

'You do that, sonny.'

The boy disappeared inside one of the buses. Sergeant Tulliver stood, silent.

The boy came out of the bus with the MOT's. Of course they were in order. Tully handed them back and looked slowly from face to face, turning his head to take in a washing line, a mangy dog, the poxy buses. Nobody averted their eyes.

'Get this straight,' as he spoke, Sergeant Tulliver fingered his truncheon. 'Nobody wants you here and the sooner you fuck off someplace else, the better they'll like it. In the meantime, I've had a complaint from the owners of the Rose and Crown. They say you've been in making a nuisance of yourselves. You go there again and I'll have you down Wyley nick before you can say knife, and you look to me like the kind of people who'd try to resist arrest. That clear?'

At least there weren't many of them, thought the sergeant, as he trudged back to the village. Out of the corner of his eye he could see the stones in the church meadow, first at a distance and then growing with his nearing footsteps. Obstructions to the smooth running of things, they were as undesirable as all such deviations from the norm. Sometimes, at night, he dreamt of them, springing up everywhere, moles, cancers, grey toadstools, in the middle of towns, at busy intersections, diverting the traffic, or blocking the road altogether, so that you had to go down unvisited lanes, ever more narrow, ever more bumpy.

When he reached Martha's it was a relief to see his other helmet lying by the front door. Although it seemed a pretty odd place to leave it, it struck Tully as a good omen, the symbol of his authority and, at the same time, an indication that he had got a firm footing in Martha's cottage.

When Martha opened the door to him, however, his newly buoyant mood departed. She looked at him with a dazed expression and he wondered if she was depressed. Tully didn't have much time for Martha's depressions but, for the moment, he had to put up with them.

She led him into the sitting-room where there was a partly drunk bottle of cider and a tumbler on the floor. Martha had got her old mono record-player up and running – she was quite handy with a screwdriver – and the plaintive wail of some sixties female filled the room. Tully realised in an instant what was up. It was the travellers.

'Do you think it could ever happen again, Brian?' she asked without preliminary.

'What's that, love?'

Martha pointed to the record-player by way of reply, adding, 'We were all so happy then. That festival. Melanie. Going to the camp with Sara Feather reminded me of it. Nothing after that even came close.'

'She doesn't sound very happy, sounds more like a dog howling to me,' said Sergeant Tulliver, pointing his thumb at the record-player. 'You been to the camp then?' Martha nodded. Tully experienced a growing anger. He had thought he'd left everything to do with the travellers behind in the byway and now, here they were, transported to Martha's cottage, might as well have brought the stones along with them. He had the sensation of being right in the middle of a whole lot of things he didn't understand. During the Summer of Love Brian Tulliver had been looking forward to starting his training for the police force. With this thought, however, he rallied. He was in charge, after all. Just let them put a foot wrong, just let them even think of going back to the Rose and Crown. He realised, with sudden inspiration, that that was a good way you could get them: by creating more and more little restrictions, more and more things they must and mustn't do, until they broke the law just by breathing.

'This is now, love,' he said, getting up and pulling the needle off the record, with a satisfying ripping sound. 'This is now, 1985.' He grabbed her hand and pulled her up the stairs to her messy bedroom.

'No, Brian, that hurts too much.'

Melanie heard her mother's voice issuing from behind the closed door. Good, she thought. It was hard to believe that, earlier in the day, she had felt that she was beginning to understand Martha, and had even been to the bother of making her a cup of her shitty tea. Good, she thought, as the screams began – pain, pleasure, who gave a fuck? She would never never forgive her. Nor would she have anything more to do with the travellers. Everything was over.

9

Magic

'This herb garden is very old,' said Miranda. 'It was used for medicine and spells as well as flavourings.'

'How can you tell?' asked Melanie, watching the butterflies rising and alighting on the leaves and flowers.

'The selection mainly, and the arrangement. There's basil, it's wonderful in salads, but it is also a charm against dragons.'

'Handy.'

'Rosemary protects against witches' spells. Sage, savory and thyme are all medicinal as well as culinary. The parsley, over there, is good for the liver. Whoever planted this garden knew what she was doing. A white witch, probably.'

'Could you do magic with these herbs?' asked Melanie, hating the interest in her voice, hating herself for being there at all, sitting on the ground, watching Miranda's strong hands working on the dusty earth.

'Oh, yes.'

'Could you make, I don't know, some sort of cliché stuff like a love potion for instance?'

Miranda gave her a quick, perceptive glance which Melanie pretended not to see.

'I could, but I wouldn't.'

'Why not?'

Miranda straightened and brushed her hands on the side of her shorts.

'Magic,' she said, 'isn't for every occasion. It's there for when nothing else will work.'

'But if, in that case, nothing else had worked?'

Miranda did not reply to the question, instead she smiled narrowly and said, 'The way to achieve things is not to cry out and wallop and pull in the other direction; follow the direction they are already going, instead. Remember the Colorado River made the Grand Canyon.'

'What?'

'I have got a magic herb that I will share with you, though.'

She reached in her back pocket and brought out a small plastic bag, a crushed box of matches and some Rizlas.

The smoke was so hot Melanie could feel it burning her throat.

'Hold it in as long as you can.'

After a few puffs Melanie experienced a slight floating sensation. The colours in the garden became more distinct, more clearly outlined and, at the same time, looser, as if each atom had pulled itself a little further away from each other atom. Distant sounds came into the foreground, then subsided. She played with making them close and then far away.

'Your mother's very young. She must have been about your age when she had you,' said Miranda.

'I suppose so.' Melanie hadn't really considered it and she didn't want to think about Martha now. For a moment she tried to imagine herself having a baby and failed. It was not the kind of thing she expected to happen.

'Why are you here?' she asked instead.

'We're going to celebrate the solstice at the stone circle.'

'Why?'

'Because we were told to.'

'Not by Sir Homer.'

'No. By the people who built it.'

It was mad but it wasn't any madder than Marjorie Sand parading around with a crucifix. As an image it was considerably more appealing.

'How did they tell you? Cosmic rays?'

Miranda ignored this. Instead she looked thoughtful, as if she were trying to formulate what she wanted to say. She took a big drag and started to talk as she was blowing the smoke out.

'If you think of time, not as a number of years, but as a number of generations, then we are about sixty generations from the people who erected the stones.'

'So?'

'If we stand at this end of time and the builders of the circle stand at the other, we can't communicate with them. They're too far away. We don't know what they thought. We can't understand their language. But if they speak to their children and grandchildren, and they speak to the next generation, sixty people isn't very many. They'd fit in a not very big room. That's the way the culture is carried. Not just by books. Probably not even mainly by them. I guess it's women, mostly, who've sent the message through the generations. Your mother says your family has been here a very long time. Maybe they were your ancestors.'

Melanie imagined this row of individuals, all of them with something to say. Miranda was right: the other end of time, in either direction, didn't seem very far off. In her mind's eye she saw the women passing on the message, wrinkled, freckled hands, which the bones showed through, reaching out to young ones, not yet worn down by a lifetime's labour. But then it was all spoilt as she realised that what she got was Martha and Grandma.

'My mother's never given me any messages from the culture,' she said gruffly. 'Nobody's told me anything.'

She turned her green eyes to meet Miranda's.

'She probably has and you don't remember yet,' said Miranda.

'Yet?'

'Important things get forgotten and remembered again. Look how much this silly old world's got to remember. One thing she's given you is an example of fortitude.'

'Fortitude? Martha?'

'How much does she get paid at the Rectory?'

Melanie couldn't work out what that had to do with it, she'd thought they were talking about ancient wisdom.

'I don't know,' she replied, confused, then realised that

Miranda was no longer listening to her and, instead, was staring at the Rectory.

'Shit,' she was saying, 'this stuff must be stronger than I thought. It feels like tripping.'

Melanie followed her gaze.

'The basil and rosemary haven't worked,' she said.

It was Marjorie Sand, entering the garden through the door which gave onto it from the house. She was followed by John Feather. Both of them seated themselves at the garden table. Marjorie Sand was supporting, with her right hand, a massive crucifix, which was attached to a broom handle. The Christ was plastic and looked as if it had been bought from somewhere, but the cross itself was quite evidently homemade and was much too big for the Christ, who was somewhat dwarfed by it. Marjorie had hammered him on with tin-tacks and embellished the scanty blood with more in a darker colour, placing a few realistic drips on the broom handle as well.

Marjorie's voice carried to them across the garden.

'And why has Sir Homer decided it is inappropriate? Why, after I have constructed this beautiful crucifix – I had to send off to some nuns in Basingstoke for the Jesus, you know – why has he forbidden it? What envoy of Satan has been poisoning his ear?'

'Marjorie,' John Feather managed to sound both calm and desperate, 'it's really only a flower show.'

'It would have claimed Wyley for the Forces of Light. It would have made the hippies go away.'

'Christ himself,' said John, adopting the tone of voice that was deemed appropriate to a cleric in such circumstances, 'wandered the earth for three years.'

'Not celebrating pagan festivals and listening to rock music,' replied Marjorie Sand. 'No, John, that will not wash; it was only due to unfortunate historical circumstances. If he arrived now, I think you would find he would behave rather differently. Frankly I am amazed and I must speak my mind. The Rectory has been very far from avid enough in its condemnation.'

'Of what, Marjorie?' John was becoming irritated.

'All this. All these Workings of Darkness.'

John sighed. 'What exactly do you expect me to do?'

Marjorie pounced. 'You can do a full exorcism in the stone circle.'

'Marjorie, this is 1985, not the Middle Ages.'

'Bell, book and candle. I've phoned Father Przdka, at Saint Gontran's Of The Perpetual Misery, in Rocester, and he's willing to pass on some helpful tips – one can make an exception, just this once.'

John Feather appeared to decide to try a placating tone.

'None of this is appropriate now, Marjorie. Maybe it was in the past, when they were ignorant and irrational, but now we know more and so we can understand impulses such as the one to exorcise . . .'

'The impulse to exorcise?' said Melanie.

'. . . so that we no longer feel compelled to act upon our fears and visceral compulsions. There will be no parading with the crucifix and no exorcism of the stones. These are things I cannot permit.'

'You will, at least, allow us to have our public meeting in the church hall?' asked Marjorie.

'The Nuremberg Rally,' said Melanie.

'We've got Homer King lined up to speak, Sergeant Tulliver, I myself and who knows who else? We hope to create a lot of fervour.'

'I am afraid,' said John, reluctantly, 'that I cannot permit that either.'

There was a nasty silence.

'May I ask why not?'

'The roof is still not repaired. It lets in a considerable amount of rain when the wind blows from the east.' John sounded uneasy.

'But it hasn't rained for weeks and weeks and I think we can assume that Jesus will keep the weather fine for the meeting. Besides, Silver Threads had their Coffee and Chat night in the hall only a fortnight ago.'

'To be honest, then, Marjorie,' said John, trapped and embarrassed, 'it's because I don't think the church should be taking sides.'

Marjorie Sand was flabbergasted. 'The church should not take the side of Light?'

'I am afraid that it is not clear to me which side that is.' John rose. 'And now there are things I must get on with.'

Now Marjorie stood up, waving the crucifix agitatedly.

'The Manor will not be happy about this, John, not happy at all,' she hissed. 'Lines are being drawn in the dust, be careful that you find yourself on the inside. If you cannot lead your flock to The Promised Land I shall find myself obliged to take over. Woolly liberalism has had its day.'

'Goodness,' said Sara Feather, standing aside as Marjorie stormed past her, then stepping into the garden, looking cool in a gingham frock.

'I would never have believed things could get into this state,' said John, burying his face in his hands exhaustedly.

'Well, you have gone along with it: the Guide to Wyley and then blessing the children. That will have been taken as encouragement.'

'Don't you start,' said John to his wife, for the first time ever, and went back to his study, slamming the door behind him.

'Oh, shit,' said Miranda.

Melanie picked a sprig of mint, rubbed it between her fingers and sniffed its fragrant perfume.

'That's only Marjorie Sand,' she said. 'She's batty, but harmless.'

Miranda opened her eyes wide. 'You think that woman's harmless? You must be crazy.'

'What do you think she's going to do, come at you with an axe in the middle of the night?'

'She doesn't have to, does she?' Miranda returned to her weeding with increased vigour. 'She gets somebody else thinking it's okay to slash our tyres or shit all over our geraniums, and they do it.'

'Nobody listens to Marjorie Sand,' said Melanie.

'She's having a meeting. You think people won't come to it?'

'John isn't letting her use the church hall.'

'She'll find somewhere, they always do, and there'll be nobody to stand up for us. John Feather is a good enough man, but weak and ineffectual; people will not listen to him. His wife,' Miranda shrugged, 'she lives inside her busy head. Your mother . . .'

'She wouldn't,' said Melanie quickly. 'Why not go and defend yourselves?'

'What we said would make no difference. We are not the problem. The problem is Wyley.'

John Feather sat in his study for the remainder of the morning, his chin resting on his knuckles, looking out of the window. He did not pray because he believed that prayer was merely an intense, introspective communication with one's own feelings, and he was not, at that moment, inclined to explore those in any particular depth. Instead, he thought.

At one, Sara brought him a cheese and tomato sandwich and a cup of coffee. She was friendly, but not apologetic. Why should she be? Of course she was right and, at some stage, he would have to tell her that: he should not have blessed the children, he should have stood by what he believed – but wasn't that exactly what he had done? To bless or not wasn't an issue to John Feather, the action meant only and precisely what the mothers believed it to mean. And yet, and yet, if people took what you offered as symbols quite literally, if they used them to justify, oh God, those words that had been stashed away under the heading 'Hyperbole' and were only occasionally wheeled out to describe what people in safely-distant countries sometimes did – evil, injustice, prejudice, inhumanity – what then?

The tips of the stones, visible above the hedge, glittered in the sunlight. Their presence oppressed John Feather, as if someone were standing before him with raised eyebrows, waiting for him to admit that there was more to be said on the topic. Yes, he confessed eventually, to them and to himself, with the sense that it was being wrung out of him, he had felt power. The Wyley mothers believed that he could control the forces of darkness, so did Marjorie Sand – though here there had been no temptation to comply, it was all too ridiculous and melodramatic – but with the mothers, one gesture from him had helped put an end to fear. It was Christ-like in its simplicity, the kind of dignified ritual you could imagine the High Priest of the stone circle performing. It was his magic, to give or to withhold.

This presented John with an idea which eased his nagging conscience: he would use the power rather than be ashamed of it. Tomorrow was Sunday, and he would preach a sermon that would work a transformation in Wyley. All the meanness, all the stupidity of the small community was floating to the surface, the scum at the bottom of civility and conventional behaviour, but maybe people were unaware that this was happening. If he lovingly pointed out to them the error of their ways, from his position of authority, then they would be bound to listen. They were a captive audience, after all, they would not have any choice.

John got out some paper and his fountain pen and started to work. Half an hour later a loud knock on the door made him jump. Before he could speak, the door opened and Sergeant Tulliver walked in.

'Your lady wife said you was busy, but this is police business, I'm afraid, Rector.'

'Oh, of course, Sergeant,' said John, laying down his pen. 'Sit down. What's happened?'

The policeman sat, but did not answer the question.

'Nice place this,' he said.

'We like it, though it's probably a bit large for us, really.'

Tully did not contradict the remark.

'Well, Rector, so the meeting's not going to be in the church hall. Do you mind telling me why?'

For a moment John Feather did not understand, then he said, amazed, 'Is this the "police business"?'

Tully nodded. 'Could you answer the question please, Sir?'

John shrugged. 'As rector the yea or nay concerning the church hall is my responsibility,' he said coolly. 'Frankly I do not want the church to be seen to be taking sides in what I consider a far from clear-cut situation.'

'So, it's nothing to do with the church roof?'

'No, nothing.' John reddened.

There was an ominous pause, after which Tully leant forward across the corner of the rector's desk. 'Let's get down to brass tacks then,' he said. 'I've had a phone call from the station in Rocester and it looks like things aren't as simple as we hoped they were going to be. Luck of the devil these bloody travellers, if you'll excuse my French. Seems it might not be possible to move them on because there's nowhere else round here for them to go. It all hinges on that, or mostly that. That means they could be in Wyley for quite a time. The way I see it is, the nicer they find it, the longer they'll stay. And nobody wants them to.'

'Nobody appears to.' The ironic tone was lost on Tully.

'The church and the police force have always worked together.' Tully gave a brief smile. 'We're all part of the same thing, really, the efficiency of the social mechanism, I think you'd call it. In order to express a united front the church hall's the most appropriate place.'

John Feather felt a chill run through his body at the realisation that he was being, in some slight way, threatened. It was not his first unpleasant encounter with the police but it was the most unexpected. It seemed incongruous to be sitting in his own, bright study, where nothing was awry, and feeling as if it had suddenly filled with marsh-water.

'I can't do that, Sergeant. I have already given you my reasons and I am quite happy to give them to anyone else who inquires.'

Tully looked down, regretfully, at his chewed fingernails. 'Can't help feeling, Rector, that Sir H. isn't going to be at all happy about this.'

John brushed his hair back from his forehead with a hand, that he noticed, had become sweaty with the nastiness of the interview. 'While I have great respect for Sir Homer King,' he said, 'the business of the church is no concern of the state, and vice versa . . .' No, that wasn't right. 'Or rather . . .' Under the policeman's insolent gaze he became confused. 'Anyway, Sir Homer King is not even a representative of the state. He's just a landowner. What he feels is really not relevant.'

'I'm sure you're right, Rector,' said Tully with a smile. 'All a bit over my head between you and me, and I'm as sure as you are that the Manor wouldn't want to interfere; just occurred to me that maybe Sir H. etc. might feel that this big Rectory was better suited to a family man, someone who'd understand how much you worry about kids, if you've got them. Mrs Sand says Sir Homer was at school with the bishop,' he added casually.

At that moment John Feather looked up and saw his wife and Martha standing at the open door. Sara's face was frozen in its expression.

The sergeant shrugged, as if none of it had really mattered that much after all. There was a pause, then John stood up.

'It seems to me, Sergeant Tulliver,' he said, briskly, eager for the policeman to go away, for Sara not to look like that, to be allowed to return to the safety of his sermon, 'that what you really need to know is how long the travellers are planning on staying. If it's only for a short time you have no problem, really. If for longer then you might want to think again.'

'I have already spoken to them, Rector. They were most uncooperative. People like that are short on respect for the law.' He shook his head.

'They might be frightened,' said Martha.

Tully turned to her.

'What would they be frightened about, love?'

'I don't know. A new place. Different people,' said Martha nervously.

'Law-abiding people don't have nothing to be nervous about,' replied the policeman loftily.

'I know. It's just. I mean . . .' Tully did not look away. 'Why don't I go and talk to them? I could find out a bit about them, ask how long they're staying.'

'That's a good idea,' said John Feather, quickly.

Tully considered the matter. Wyley was becoming restless and it really did look as if his hands were tied, at least legally speaking, when it came to forcing the travellers out. Martha probably wouldn't get much out of them one way or the other, but she might as well have a try. Any information she brought back would be potentially useful. On a personal level there might be results as well; something was up with Martha, which he would possibly sniff out if he let her have her own way on this one. It wasn't just the sodding music, it was deeper than that. It was more as if . . . Tully's brain struggled . . . as if she was still somewhere else, a place he couldn't get her back from, that she found nicer than Wyley.

'All right then, love.'

'I'll go on Monday morning.'

'No talk about the ins-and-outs, though. We don't want to alert these people to their legal rights. Don't want to get their hopes up over nothing.'

The insincerity of this statement was so blatant that John Feather was speechless.

'I won't say anything about their legal rights to them,' said Martha, pleased to be back in Tully's good books. 'I promise.'

Legal rights, thought Miranda, who had paused under the study window with her wheelbarrow and was leaning against the warm brickwork, rolling a joint and listening to the conversation.

10

The Church

Cook appeared, as was her habit, at eight-thirty, in the master bedroom, with Darjeeling tea and the *Sunday Times* and *Telegraph*. Sir Homer, as was his habit, drank the tea and scanned the papers for references to himself. That there was one today, in the *Times*, was no surprise to him: a journalist had phoned the previous morning. As it happened they had had a most pleasant chat, for the journalist had been at Eton at the same time as Sir Homer, though he had only been a new-bug, so of course they had never spoken.

'Talked to Tommy Bright the other day,' said the journalist. 'Quite the P.M.'s pet at the moment. You two are still in touch, I daresay? How could you not be?'

'Yes, indeed,' Sir Homer replied. 'You should phone him for a comment.'

'Might just do that. Anyway, sorry about the hoo-ha you've got down there. I'll do my best to up the pressure.'

The system was functioning and, with every hour that passed, with every new piece of evidence that the status quo was rallying round, Sir Homer became calmer.

He had replaced the receiver with a renewed sense of reassurance, which was increased by the fact that, when the travellers had left his premises the day before, Flora seemed to have departed with them. As was her habit after a foray into consciousness, she had returned to the shadowy domain that she usually occupied, in which she shared the half-reality of the dead, the photographed, those whose names one cannot remember. As a result, Sir Homer now rather regretted his somewhat hysterical phone call to the Wyley police station. Inspired by the sudden, unwelcome appearance of the travellers and by Flora's apparent decision to impinge on daylight, he had been led to forget how thoroughly he had Flora under his control and had momentarily mislaid his trust in the establishment's ability to deal with the undesirable.

Events, it was true, were not progressing with great speed, but public opinion was running high and the police station in Rocester would soon take action. So Sir Homer had been informed by Sergeant Tulliver, early the previous afternoon, when he telephoned to advise Sir Homer of the questionable stance that the rector was taking. Even this, however, need not cause alarm: with the Manor's tacit approval, and the useful information Sir Homer might be able to give, the policeman was hoping to nip all extremism in the bud.

The travellers would soon be on their way and so any nervousness had been completely unfounded. All Wyley wanted was for the travellers to leave, a desire identical to Sir Homer's; the village was completely incurious about what they thought, felt or believed, about the circle or anything else. The public meeting need hold no worries and was, in fact, an excellent idea in Sir Homer's opinion, even if it had been thought of by Marjorie Sand.

Sir Homer sipped his tea and read with satisfaction:

'A group of New Age Travellers are reported to have arrived at The Wise Lady of Wyley, the stone circle belonging to Commentator writer, Homer King. In a recent article, Sir Homer launched a blistering attack on the convoy phenomenon. M.P for Rocester, Thomas Bright, within whose constituency the circle falls, yesterday expressed concern and outrage at the presence of the encampment.'

Sir Homer washed and shaved and presented himself in the dining-room, where breakfast was laid out in chafing dishes on the side table. He lifted lids: kedgeree, kippers, scrambled eggs, devilled kidneys. Sir Homer chose the kidneys and took his place at the head of the table, where he helped himself to toast and poured some coffee.

He was just about to pierce a plump little kidney with his fork when his pleasure was alloyed by Lady Poll staggering in, her complexion resembling papier-maché.

'It has come to my attention, Homer,' she said, falling into her chair, obviously simultaneously still drunk and hungover, 'that you have agreed with John Feather to dispense with what I had viewed as an integral part of my birthday celebration.'

'Namely?' said Sir Homer, knowing perfectly well what she meant, and pushing the tines sharply into the bulging offal so that four little beads of blood appeared.

'The general blessing and procession to the stones with the crucifix. John Feather told Marjorie yesterday morning and she phoned me in the evening, when she was quite sure that nothing could be done. She was most upset. As indeed am I.'

She fumbled for the coffee pot until Sir Homer, seeing she was going to spill it or burn herself or something, reached for it crossly and poured a coffee for her. He picked up his knife and cut into the abandoned kidney. Pink inside. With his fork he placed a piece of it onto a slice of the toast and popped it into his mouth.

'Feather's a sensible fellow about most things,' he said, having regained his composure, 'though his attitude to the wretched camp will have to be dealt with. On the opening of the grounds I must concur with him. It is, after all, a secular event.'

'Marjorie says there are no secular events,' said Lady Poll, slopping coffee into her saucer.

'There's Hickstead,' said Sir Homer, 'surely she couldn't claim that was a religious occasion. Henley, Glyndebourne,' warming to his subject, 'Wimbledon, the opening of the Houses of Parliament, the start of the grouse-shooting season.'

He was rather pleased with himself but Lady Poll dropped her cup, flooding Sir Homer's plate, and started to cry. The kidneys and the toast were completely ruined. At that moment there was a quiet knock on the door and Crispin Turner entered.

'I wanted the crucifix,' wept Lady Poll. 'I thought it would frighten away the mad people. I thought it would stop me remembering everything.' Then, noticing Crispin's tactful presence, 'Crispin, thank goodness you're here to protect me.'

Crispin glided to her side and patted her hand with his smooth fingers.

'There, there,' he murmured. 'There, there, Lady Polly.'

'I do not like you, Homer.' Lady Poll seemed invigorated by Crispin's presence. 'I never have done and I never will do. I am sure I would have much preferred the other one.'

The younger man's eyes met Sir Homer's sympathetically. Presumably Turner was 'the other one', thought Sir Homer crossly. He did not mind his mother disliking him, nor did he blame Turner for the favour he found with Lady Polly, he just wished his mother would be a little more discreet. True aristocracy almost automatically implied mutual antipathy; it also demanded, however, the pretence that this antipathy did not exist.

'Sir Homer,' said Crispin Turner, 'Lady Polly seems not quite herself today. Perhaps you would like me to escort her to her room and check that she is comfortable?'

'Thank you, Turner.'

With that, Sir Homer abandoned breakfast and went to his study, in order not to have to witness the undignified progress up the stairs. At least it was a relief to know that the burden of his mother could be foisted off upon Turner, who, at present, seemed willing enough, but anyway had no choice in the matter.

Sir Homer had seated himself at his desk and was just beginning to make notes for a forthcoming article, when he became aware of a quivering in the far corner of the room. It was Chummy. He laid down his pen and contemplated the creature.

Chummy was a dog with a talent for getting shut in rooms, and then having what Lady Polly termed 'little accidents'. Sir Homer glanced round, hastily, for little accidents, but saw none. In spite of this, however, he was surprised to feel a strong, hot anger welling up inside him; the same sort of anger that he had felt at the mention of Marjorie's son, Seymour Sand. At that moment Chummy seemed, as Seymour had done, to be the symbol of all that was undesirable, irritating, constraining; all that was not the moonlight, all that was not . . .

Sir Homer quickly picked up his pen and started writing. Outside his study the banal sounds of the house were only just audible, but he registered Cook's footsteps mounting the stairs to his mother's room.

'Cook.' Sir Homer opened the study door.

'Sir Homer?'

'On no account is my mother to drink any alcohol today.'

'This is a bowl of chicken broth, Sir Homer.'

Sir Homer returned to the study.

'What's that?' asked Lady Poll, as Cook entered her room. She was lying in bed, wearing a copper-coloured satin nightgown and a matching bed-jacket. Crispin Turner, who had discreetly withdrawn to the corridor while she changed, was now seated on a velvet chair, which he had placed by the bed.

'Broth, Lady Polly.'

'Made with feet and necks and gizzards?'

Cook said nothing, but laid the tray down on the bedside table and left the room.

'At the asylum,' Lady Polly remarked, 'they had broth for supper on Sundays.'

'Perhaps, Lady Polly,' replied Crispin Turner, 'it would be more palatable with a little something in it.' He drew a small silver hip-flask from an inner pocket.

'Oh yes, Crispin,' said Lady Poll, 'I think that would help a lot.'

'There is a similar drink,' said Crispin, as he poured the vodka into the broth, 'which they make in the United States. I believe they call it something like a "gunshot".'

'Indeed?' said Lady Poll, taking the bowl and starting to drink the broth quickly.

'There is something you said, the other day, Lady Polly, that puzzled me,' said Crispin. 'Maybe you could satisfy my curiosity?' Lady Polly did not reply. He glanced at her and, seeing that she was listening, continued. 'You said that your father-in-law – Randolph King, I think?' Lady Poll nodded. 'Randolph King bought Wyley Manor at the turn of the century. That is not what is generally believed in Wyley.'

'No,' said Lady Poll, laying her spoon down in the empty bowl. 'In Wyley it is believed that the King family has been here for very much longer. Since the Manor was built, in 1594, to be precise.'

'But there is a row of portraits, down the staircase, from, if I am correct, the Tudor time onward, ending with one of your son, Sir Homer.'

'Oh, you don't want to set any store by them. It was definitely Sir Randolph King who bought Wyley Manor. From some people me and Horace met when we were on honeymoon in Nice, as it happens. They sold it so that they could go and live in the South of France. Brash, y'know.'

'And before that?'

'I don't really recall the details, but I believe that their family bought the whole thing from an aristocrat who had gone to the dogs in the middle of the nineteenth century.'

'To the dogs, Lady Polly?'

'Lost everything. Every penny. Sold the whole thing – furniture, curtains, paintings – lock, stock and barrel. Had to.'

'And these furnishings were still there when Sir Randolph bought the Manor?'

'Lord, yes. Don't know who the portraits are of. The aristocrat's family maybe, or whoever owned the place before them. Needn't assume they're all related.'

There was a pause. Crispin Turner moved his gaze to the landscape outside the window.

'So, it would be true to say,' he dropped casually, 'that Sir Homer is a relative newcomer to the aristocracy? *In extremis*, it would be unlikely to rally round or suppress things for him?'

'Not them. They wouldn't rally,' said Lady Poll, not understanding.

'The folly is a curious construction,' said Crispin Turner, as if inspired by the view. 'Is it used for anything?'

'What?' Lady Polly was beginning to be irritated by the questions.

Crispin turned back to her.

'Perhaps another tot of vodka would hasten your recovery, Lady Polly?'

He poured some into her water glass.

'When it is finished I will rinse the glass out so that Cook doesn't have the opportunity to . . . interfere.'

'You are a good boy, Crispin.' Lady Polly was all smiles again.

'The folly, is it used for anything?'

Lady Polly shook her head. 'Not any more. Sir Homer used to play in it when he was a child. Don't know doing what.'

'Sometimes, in the morning, I find footprints in the dew, leading to and from the folly. The door is locked, so perhaps somebody has a key?'

Lady Polly shrugged. 'Sir Homer probably has one. The footprints, we must assume, belong to the mad people.'

The early service at St George's on Sunday mornings was attended only by the particularly devout, which made for a small congregation. The ten-thirty service was quite a different matter, for then Wyley turned out in force to kneel before God and contemplate the pleasures that breakfast had given and that lunch was still to bring.

John Feather's sermons were morally undemanding and usually avoided current affairs. If there had been a particularly appalling flood or earthquake in some distant corner of the globe, Wyley would sometimes be encouraged to feel sorry for its victims, as indeed it did, sorrow costing nothing, but generally speaking all that was asked was a sober consideration of how beastly human beings sometimes were and how nice they should be. As John Feather spoke, St George's parishioners would wish devoutly that these beastly people would mend their ways and start to be a bit less selfish, after the sermon they would pray for them to do so, and then they would return home to their roast pork and the radio news with the sense that they had contributed to making the world a better place.

John Feather was aware of this. He was aware, too, how little Wyley felt itself responsible for the world beyond its small confines. There was nothing to be done about it, however. Tell the upturned faces that famine and drought, unemployment and racial violence were not, perhaps, the unfortunate coincidence that they were fondly believed to be; suggest to Wyley that its pale hands were not quite as clean as was supposed and numbers would fall off. People would find a more understanding vicar in Rocester, one more attuned to the modern way of life, or they would cease to come at all. Any church-going, any nod in the direction of an ethical dimension, John reasoned, was better than nothing.

Today, he looked down from his pulpit, affectionately, upon the flock who, in the light of his gentleness with them, would be sure to accept today's loving rebuke.

In the second row, behind Homer King – Lady Poll was absent today – Marjorie Sand was sitting with a slight smile upon her face, the smile of one whose suspicions are confirmed, which she always sported during Sunday service. Next to her on the pew was her tight, liver-coloured plastic handbag. Seymour not being at home, she was tolerating the presence of Simon and Veronica Tarrant beside her, Veronica in a Laura Ashley frock and Simon in a blazer and cravat, both set to rush off and serve traditional pies as soon as the service ended. The Wise Lady Tea Rooms did not offer luncheons on Sundays, though it did a roaring trade in cream teas later in the day. Miss Sayle, in navy, swallowing constantly, was accompanied this Sunday by an anaemic niece who was going to spend the afternoon making scones for a pittance. Tom Callan, the butcher, was seated heavily beside Mrs Callan and their four children. At the end of the same pew Miss Evans from the post office was perched, inexplicably, dabbing at her white blouse with a handkerchief. Scattered throughout were the mothers; with them today their usually absent husbands, pallid from the commuter trains that ran daily from Rocester to London, from London to Rocester. Some had brought their blanched offspring, others had left them at home to help the Helgas and Gretchens lay the tables and pod the peas. In a pew, on her own, at the very back of the church, was Melanie.

As he considered these raised faces, John Feather felt overwhelmed by a vast, incomprehensible, pity.

'Hebrews, Chapter thirteen, Verse one.'

Marjorie Sand made a grab for the bible she always brought with her.

'"Be not forgetful to entertain strangers: for thereby some have entertained angels unawares."'

A barely audible sigh went round the church. The mothers looked ever so slightly less moribund, their children, not understanding, fidgeted, their husbands' backs stiffened. Tom Callan screwed his fist into a fleshy bundle. Simon Tarrant looked about him, surprised, as if to check it was not only he who had heard what the rector had said. His wife made an exasperated tutting sound.

'My dear people,' John Feather continued, feeling a not unpleasant rush of adrenalin, 'our small community is, at this moment, host to a group of individuals who have decided to pause here in their travels. Since their arrival I have been saddened and puzzled by the uncharitable reactions of a village that claims to be Christian, and which has even refused these travellers one of man's basic human needs.' He scanned his parishioners' expressions. Homer King's face had gone a deadly, furious grey. 'I have asked myself what strange and primitive fears can be preying on Wyley that, at the end of the twentieth century . . .'

John continued in a similar vein. It was the beastliness sermon really, though this time aimed at Wyley, and Wyley was angry. Though, more than this, Wyley was amazed. It was accustomed to thinking of itself as good, had, indeed, ample evidence for doing so: there was nothing it read in the newspapers – whichever paper it chose – nothing it saw on television to suggest that its views were different from the norm. Even the Labour party, when it entered Wyley's consciousness, rarely claimed that things diverged greatly from how they should be. Dissent was a distant rumour from a time mercifully long past.

A fidgeting erupted. Pews creaked. Watches were wound and shaken, handbags gone through, the hymnal read with interest. Everyone felt John Feather had gone too far. No one knew how to stop him.

Only Sir Homer King sat stock still. Singled out for particular and impertinent criticism, he should have been experiencing a focussed rage, aimed at a rector who, paperback books and prints notwithstanding, had greatly lost sight of his place in the scheme of things. The sensations running through him, however, were very much more alarming.

Flora, whom he had thought safely locked away for the time being, was responding to the tension of the scene and filling Sir Homer with tremendous excitement, a kind of spiritual vandalism that wanted to see what exactly happened when all control was withdrawn or lost. Would John Feather suddenly stand on his head, scatter flowers like Ophelia, swear and blaspheme? If one social convention fell, did all the others crash down with it?

Sir Homer experienced a sudden, mesmeric fascination with the stained-glass window, which had witnessed his own baptism and looked down upon the expensive coffins of his grandfather, Randolph King, and then his father, Horace. It seemed, though, that he was seeing it for the very first time. St George, those curling locks, the circle, glimpsed through flowers; the window was calling to Flora and she, the bright butterfly, was responding, was about to emerge from the pupa that was Homer King.

As John Feather's voice continued, Sir Homer's panic increased. His whole body became one giant heartbeat. Sweat ran down his back. His skin was too tight. It could not hold her in. At any moment he would do something strange and fanciful and absolutely beautiful. And then, thank God, something happened.

The Lord moved in mysterious ways, but not that mysterious. He set a series of riddles, which it was the job of the Christian to answer. Since her interview with John Feather the previous morning, Marjorie Sand had been busy deciphering. Now, with this, John Feather's manifestation of his hideous state of sin, if not actual possession, the last piece of the puzzle was given to her. It was clear that the words that God had put into her mouth, when she had warned him of a change of leadership, if he failed to guide his flock, were to be fulfilled. She, Marjorie Sand, was God's chosen one.

It was all so clear to her now. Had she not been one of the first to encounter the travellers, and had they not been asking for water, the symbol of baptism, which they, as the unelect, had correctly been denied by Sir Homer King? God had obviously sent Marjorie this as a sign of the imminent threat to His people. John Feather had been suspiciously hesitant in giving his blessing to the children of Wyley; that he had given it eventually was something of a stumbling block, but there were false prophets, after all, and it was probably to do with that. Besides, he had definitely forbidden – and, indeed seemed startled and horrified by – the image of Jesus upon His cross. He had blasphemed by suggesting, Marjorie shuddered, that Christ was a sort of hippy.

He had refused to exorcise – no question why that was – and he had denied access to the church hall: denied the Promised Land to God's people, because he could not go there himself; or rather he could but, for some reason, he didn't appear to want to.

After she had left the Rectory, Marjorie had spoken to Sergeant Tulliver, who had somehow recognised her as Christ's anointed, for he had agreed to put pressure on John to change his mind about the hall, though, unfortunately, he had not met with success. So this morning, still obviously under the auspices of the Holy Spirit, Marjorie had visited Simon and Veronica Tarrant, and they had given her a coffee and a very pleasant oatmeal biscuit, and agreed to have the public meeting in the room they used for wedding receptions. At no cost!

There was no question that Marjorie was heading in the right direction. Now the warm flow of Christ's love was filling her body, soaking it in heavenly outpouring.

Marjorie Sand rose to her feet and began to sing, with closed eyes and swaying slowly. Her arms were stretched out stiffly, her hands open, palms upwards. John Feather was completely upstaged.

> ' "City of God, how broad and far
> Outspread thy walls sublime!
> The true thy chartered freemen are
> Of every age and clime." '

Thin bubbles of spit rose, grew and popped at the side of her mouth. It was hymn number 375, the one the congregation were to sing next. In spite of her mystical state, Marjorie attempted to imbue the words with tacit reproach.

> ' "One holy Church, one army strong," '

she continued. She heard the rustle of the other members of the congregation reaching for their hymnals. Voice after voice fell in behind her own as more and more people stood up. They did not want to, and would not, listen to what the rector had to say.

'"How purely hath thy speech come down
From man's primaeval youth!
How grandly hath thine empire grown
Of freedom, love and truth!"'

By the time Marjorie had reached the third verse she knew that everyone was standing, everyone was singing along with her, for all the world as if the sermon had never happened.

At the end of the hymn she opened her eyes, gathered up her handbag and bible and began to walk slowly down the aisle, towards the door of the church. This was when another sign was sent to Marjorie, for Sir Homer King also left his pew and lurched out behind her, staggering under the mighty power of the Spirit, and after him came the rest of them: the accountants, stockbrokers, architects, civil servants, the wives and children, the tradesmen and shopkeepers; all of them following Marjorie Sand, all of them recognising her dominion, and God's.

Out in the daylight they continued walking. Not the usual Sunday gaggle outside the church and the slow progress to cars and Sunday lunch, or into the Rose and Crown, but a glazed march, with eyes straight ahead and a sense of purpose that rather dwindled as keys were removed from pockets. Except in the case of Marjorie Sand who, once through the door of Magpie Cottage, fell down upon her knees in prayer, asking God for advice as to how to proceed and thanking Him for the harshness of His judgement upon the unrighteous, His hatred of the stone circle.

God's reply was unequivocal, and considerate, for Seymour Sand's examinations would very shortly be over and it would be convenient for him to come down from Oxford. The need was for reinforcements, for the campaign must intensify. Marjorie was to summon Seymour by telephone and tell him to be in Wyley as soon as possible. She rose from her knees and dialled the number. As it rang she saw, in her mind's eye, the dreaming spires, the elegant buildings: the city of intellect harkening to her call.

When someone answered they checked Seymour's room and, finding he was out, asked if she could phone back later.

*   *   *

John Feather looked down from his pulpit at what remained of his congregation in the hollow, empty church, namely Sara and Melanie. Martha was working at the Rectory; Joyce Atter, the Rectory cleaner, who would probably have been loyal, went to the Methodists in Rocester.

He was suddenly struck by the ridiculousness of the complaints about 'dwindling congregations' that one read in the newspapers, when probably even the letter-writers would cease to go to church if the clergy told the simple truth. The points that John Feather had made, today, at Wyley, were only the foothills of the mountains of the unsaid.

John was shaken and ashamed.

What a fool he had been to think that he could venture, with impunity, where others, for various murky reasons, did not; to believe himself the High Priest of the stone circle.

In Wyley there was no real circle such as, he saw now, the stones were meant to signify. No enclosing arms, reaching hands, supporting and accepting links of love. Wyley's stone circle was British society in the middle of the nineteen-eighties. Self-centred; divisive; its foundations the police, the army, the uniquely cruel government it had voted for. All human structures were crumbling, except for these, the least desirable.

Broken, John's eyes met those of his wife. Sara's plain features smiled at him, and she nodded, silently asking her husband's forgiveness for having forgotten, for a day or two, what an admirable person he was and how lucky she was that he had chosen her. John was someone into whose care children should be given, whose ideas should be properly perpetuated. Sara decided, then and there, to do whatever might be necessary to procure him the baby that was rightfully his.

It was a long time since Melanie had been in St George's during a service. She'd come because Martha had been so full of John's wonderful sermon he was going to preach on Sunday, and how it would set everything right between the village and the travellers. Now she felt an idiot for having believed it could, for having thought that Miranda was just being paranoid when they talked among the herbs in the Rectory garden.

The transformation was complete, and this was the other

side of it; once you had seen, you could not go back to not seeing. Wyley and the travellers had been brought together in the cauldron of the circle. The travellers had made the landscape of Wyley colourful, exciting, beautiful, unfamiliar. They had also contorted the faces of Wyley's citizens, so that the awfulness of the characters that lay beneath the skin was totally visible.

Melanie had known many of these people all her life. She'd never liked them much but she'd never been afraid of them. Her stance had been scorn, amusement. Now, as they walked past her pew, out into the sunlight, each face that she saw was new and different. Lips pursed with prejudice, or pulled into the tight smiles of self-righteousness, teeth were exposed in the savage grimace of anger. The children mimicked their parents, not yet knowing the feeling that accompanied the expression, but learning, already, how to set the social muscles to convey those sentiments that they were imbibing slowly at their dining-room tables.

What was her own face doing? Melanie quickly explored its contours knowing, as she did so, that it bore traces of the jealousy she felt towards whatever relationship was forming between Martha and Josh. How easy it would be, in the light of this, to walk with Wyley, which was the bigger side, after all, the socially endorsed one, the one she was born into. No one would reproach or condemn her. No one would even know. If Josh had his eyes on Martha, Melanie Flowerdew owed him no allegiance. She even had an excuse at the ready, in that, when she had discussed things with Miranda, she had shown no inclination whatever to act to defend the camp.

Melanie looked up at the stained glass window, but did not see it. Instead, all the possible lives that might have been hers presented themselves to her, not vocalised or in the form of images, but as the sensation that her brain was full of ghosts. It was clear that you chose the person you wanted to be in life, and that this decision must be made with care and information.

Wyley had chosen its madness; it was not an unfortunate historical accident that everyone could be sorry about later. In its insanity it was dangerous and unpredictable. Whatever reaction she might provoke, it was Melanie's responsibility to warn the travellers about what was going on, as well as she could understand it herself. Whatever she might feel about Josh and Martha must be set aside for the time being.

11

Midnight

Remembering childhood from old-age must be like this, thought Flora: a bright, busy, self-contained place, familiar yet intangible. If she had stood at the door of her mother's closet and looked in through the key-hole, or been able to see the whiteness of the sheets, feel the sweat of the night clearly, even in the erasing powers of daylight. But sequins are made for chandeliers, not for the blandness of morning and afternoon; you cannot take a pebble out of water and expect it to shine.

From her position, hidden in darkness, the travellers came and went with the flames. Here or there would be a tattered sleeve, there a triangle of rug, the fur of a sleeping dog. They were rich, Renaissance colours when the fire lit them; almost perfect until the flute stopped playing and the voices started up.

It was a long, repetitive discussion that veered off into unexpected directions. Sometimes they lapsed into pidgin. Flora got to know the voices. There was the girl they called Karen, who had come to the Manor for water. The boy with the public school accent was Paul. Josh was a little apart from the others, the darkness treasured him, the firelight kept him for last. Only once did it present him for more than a brief moment, stretched out, his chest bare, the smooth circles of nipples that made one think of tenderness and bruises. The one who played the flute was Miranda; she came from somewhere foreign, or another part of England. Ralph, who didn't say much. An overgrown urchin, with bare feet, distorted by pregnancy, whose name was Emily. And Melanie Flowerdew, who had started the wretched discussion.

There was one word which kept recurring, until Flora, boredly, took to mouthing it with them: 'stones'. She imagined the word turning and turning in a cement-mixer until, all connotation battered away, it was nothing but a symbol anyone could put in their pocket.

'The stones fucking want us here,' said Karen. 'It's up to them what happens next. We followed the ley-line . . .'

'Not very easily,' said Paul. Flora wondered what a ley-line was, picturing a sort of intelligent rodent.

'We're here, aren't we?'

'Anyway, what I would say is that the stones are something of a tangent. I agree with Melanie. The public meeting gives us a perfect opportunity to explain our position and thereby deflect any possible hostility or violence that might be coming in our direction.'

'Sez you. What do you think, Ralph?'

There was a pause, then, 'I dunno, it's probably not relevant really. It's just I think about our caravan, I mean I can't feel it would have made any difference talking to the bloke, really.'

'Exactly.'

'I've already said, this is not our problem.' This was Miranda. She was tall and sturdy; Flora found her rather alarming. 'If Wyley is fucked up, why should we come here and have to deal with it?'

'But you're not dealing with Wyley, you're protecting your-selves.' Melanie Flowerdew. The firelight illuminated her face, an oval, faultless white. Two intense eyes. What, Flora asked herself, did girls like Miss Flowerdew do with their lives? Perhaps they became secretaries.

'You think it's any kind of protection having the best argu-ment?' The words came out of the darkness, a little way back from the others. It was the voice of Josh, clear but with a strain in it, as if he were finding it hard to sound normal. 'And where has reasonableness got us? Look what happened when we went to see that Homer King shit.' Homer Kingshit.

'Josh is correct. I don't concern myself with what they say at their public meetings, any more than I care what they write in their newspapers about us.'

'But Miranda,' Melanie Flowerdew, a note of despair in her voice, 'isn't that the whole point?'

'It's a political cause for you,' Josh in the darkness, 'but for us it's a way of life.'

The flames dyed Melanie's cheeks scarlet. 'I don't like to think of what they could do to you.' Her voice sounded shaky.

'We've had it before, luv. They trash your things but they usually stop short of grievous. Don't want to be bumped up, like Miranda here,' said Karen. Flora did not understand her.

'Be quiet, you lot, I'm trying to sleep.' A child, from inside one of the buses.

'And how do you think we can talk out here, with you making all that noise sleeping?'

'Oh, get stoned, Mum.'

'I am already stoned.'

'Then play something on the flute.' Yes. Yes.

'I will play something if you promise to stop that racket in there.'

'Leave off, Mum.'

Flora was glad they had stopped talking. Melanie Flowerdew tried to make them continue but fell silent. Maybe she realised, as Flora had come to, that the purpose of the conversation was to discuss, not to resolve. Now the soft, wistful sound of the flute, an instrument that always made Flora think of the woolly edges of old felt, curled through the woodland, its sound seeming to come from behind a thick, sealing door. Flora thought of the gravy advertisement on the television, where the smell was a little beckoning hand. She sought in her mind for the name of the tune, not knowing that it was a tune with no name, not knowing that Miranda was jamming, not knowing what jamming was.

Then Emily started to sing, jamming too, weaving her voice in and out of Miranda's flute, opposing, contradicting, agreeing, harmonising.

'That Homer King shit. That Homerking shit. Thathomer King-shit,' she sang, doing what Flora had done with the same words, that were strange in the woodland, until they, like the stones in the cement-mixer, were only sounds without connotation.

The scent of the music. Sweet, sweet, like the most floral of aftershaves, quite near to Flora. Behind a bush behind a bush behind her. And then, as well, muffled laughter from the same bush, muffled laughter through a hand. The stretching, leafy twigs stirred, though there was no wind. Flora froze. Was she being followed? Was somebody watching her watching? Or, like her, were they merely regarding the travellers? A bush to the side of the first one moved also. Were they creeping, or were there several, many? She thought of the munchkins in *The Wizard of Oz* that she had been taken to by Nanny, on the day Mother broke her ankle. When you entered a darkened room the whitest thing in it seemed to glow, then you saw the second whitest thing, the third, until the darkness was full of spots of light. At any moment she would pick out the person, object, thing, and find that it was only the representative of many others. It could be just Chummy, though.

Flora drew her foot backwards, barely breathing and slipped into the night. She would not return to the folly directly but go through the woodlands, skirting the edge of the circle. She paused. Something else paused, also. Whatever it was seemed to be intent on moving with her, but perhaps she could lose it. Was the scent really after-shave, or the sweetness of breath? Or was it just the combined perfumes of the gardens of Wyley, sending their pleas to distant nocturnal insects? It could be just Chummy, though.

Josh was wrong about that, they weren't a political cause for her.

Melanie was walking back alone, through Sir Homer's woodland. It was the long way round, but she felt like walking and it took her through the circle. It wasn't fully dark, the time of year when the sun never fucked off entirely. The trees were still charcoal silhouettes against a paler sky; she was walking through a black and white landscape.

It wasn't a political cause and Melanie wasn't a political person. Causes were whales and road-schemes, the toxic toad, not this complex muddle of ideas and opinions, at the centre of which was just a great, uneasy feeling that things – Christ, a billion things, were not as you reckoned they should be. Political causes were easily depicted on a t-shirt. What would Melanie write for this, if this was a cause? She remembered a bit of graffiti that shuddered on a grimy wall as the train from Wyley came into London, quite faded. God knew when it was written, looked like they'd built the wall around it: '90% is Shit'.

'The personal is political,' Martha always said. But she just trotted it out, like she did so many other things, so that it was easier to ignore it as a lump rather than madly sort through, the way Martha did her clothes when she was looking for clean knickers. Still, if that was true, if the way Melanie felt about the travellers was extendable beyond emotion, then she supposed you could say it was political. Though fat lot of good that was, anyway, since the travellers were set on passivity, since what she'd said had been chucked around and then ignored.

Melanie sighed and threw both arms up floppily in the dusk. At least she had warned them, and that was where she figured her responsibility came to a stop.

The sky was getting lower now, its whiteness slipping between the trees, signalling open fields. Melanie paused to wipe her brow. A moth's quivering wings brushed her face. She jerked her head away from it and, as she did so, saw, out of the corner of her eye, a standing form, parallel to her, but some distance away. By the time she was still again it had vanished.

Softly, Melanie took a step backwards, so that she was hidden by the thick trunk of an oak tree. There was no reason to assume that the person was malevolent, she told herself. She was just being careful. Her sharp eyes searched for the form, failed to locate it. The trees, leaves and bushes distorted under her gaze. Fallen branches became the arching bones of extinct creatures, silver birches were faced totems, the network of twigs was a fretted cuneiform. Probably, of course, they had done the same as her, the quickest, most effective way of disappearing in a woodland. There was no way they could have retreated that quickly. Melanie turned and looked at the darkness, behind where she had spotted the person. Something stirred in it. Something crouching. A bush moved by a breeze that was non-existent. An animal, perhaps. Or another person.

Maybe whoever was parallel with Melanie had not, in fact, seen her, was not hiding from her at all, was, instead, trying to avoid somebody who was following them.

Melanie wanted to sigh loudly, to be cross with her fear, with her pounding heart and rushing adrenalin. This was Wyley, after all, not some desperate other place, where people were pursued through woodlands, left to die in pretty streams that churned and leapt around their corpses. This was only Wyley.

The howl was deafening. It seemed to last minutes but could only have lasted for seconds. Raw and animal, it was the sound of agony, of stinking terror, the wide open mouth of grief, the sound of happiness lost or denied. It slashed a thin strip of horror from Melanie's mouth down to the pit of her stomach. As she took her first step forward she could not feel the foot she landed upon. She knew she was running, she knew her body was carrying her, because she could hear her shoes on the leaves and breaking twigs. She knew she was out of the woodland because she could hear the hollow sound of meadow grass.

The stones were looming markers. She hurtled between them and they closed behind her, made a thick wall between her and it. Up the slope of the field and then, somehow, clinging onto chinks between the bricks, or moss, or maybe only to panic, over the churchyard wall, falling onto the grass, lying there panting.

When she stood up and looked back at where she had come from, the stones seemed to have a studiously innocent, nonchalant air. 'We don't know where she is. What century are we talking about?' they would say to whoever paused, out of breath, to ask her whereabouts. The person would be convinced for, as soon as she was out of danger, they had lightly stepped back into their original positions and now there was only air between them.

12

Something Quite Horrible

Sergeant Tulliver was engaged in the task of sniffing his laundry when the phone rang in his office. It was Marjorie Sand.

'I am perhaps overstepping the mark here, Sergeant,' were her first words. 'This call must be strictly between ourselves. Sir Homer has made it expressly known that he does not want the police involved.'

'The mark, Mrs Sand?' queried the policeman, his mind still on his laundry.

'I mean that I know myself party to information that is not of this earth, and that gives me certain privileges,' said Marjorie Sand, clearly eager to elucidate.

'I take it there has been an incident, Mrs Sand?' asked the sergeant swiftly, guessing the supposed origin of these privileges, and reluctant to discuss the topic.

'Yes, there has. Something quite horrible has taken place in the Manor grounds, in the circle itself, to be precise. We must, you will say, assume a human hand has been at work. I, however, would urge you against being so hasty. Lady Polly has been most upset by it, most upset. Dr Oliver has been called and says he will look at her after morning surgery – unless she takes a sudden downturn, in which case it will be sooner . . .'

As he listened to her speaking, Sergeant Tulliver glanced out of the police station window. Either morning surgery was over or Lady Poll had taken the downturn, for Dr Oliver's car was purring along the road in the direction of the Manor, Dr Oliver looking businesslike inside. Then a face partly blocked it out and a hand rose in a wave and Martha, on her way to the camp to get information, smiled at him. He saw the pale shadow of her naked breasts under her white t-shirt. Why, he wondered, in a brief flash of self-doubt, was he allowing this to happen? In his ear Marjorie Sand continued, detailing the nature of the wounds, commenting upon the large amount of blood, her voice replete with a thrilled horror at what she described.

'Very well, Mrs Sand. Ta for keeping me informed. I will stroll over and have a word with Sir Homer.'

'Oh, he won't be there. Not until later this afternoon. He said he was going to the Rocester council offices to monitor progress on the travellers. He is very shaken, though he attempts to hide it. Were I not Lady Polly's closest friend I would not have guessed. The hand of The Lord is upon him, of course. You might want to speak to Melanie Flowerdew as well. She was the one who discovered the body.'

Marjorie Sand's status at the Manor may have allowed her particular insight into Sir Homer's feelings, but she was wrong in supposing herself unique. There was another who had made similar surmises, or appeared to have. He, too, was uppermost in Lady Polly's affections so perhaps gained his perspicacity similarly.

Crispin Turner's concerned expression. Sir Homer saw it repeatedly as his knuckles whitened on the steering wheel, as twig after twig swished against the side of the car, cottage after cottage leapt into vision and vanished. The lovely route to Rocester, the back road, for until two the council offices would be deserted, save for gossiping secretaries tearing bits off their sandwiches.

Sir Homer passed the solid and beautiful Tudor house, at the end of a drive and half-hidden by trees, which was the possession of his old acquaintances, Harald and Wanda Edelstein. Away from the house, and covered by all manner of creeping and climbing plants, was Wanda's studio. There she weaved 'rugs and garments inspired by her frequent trips to the Far

East and South America' as *Vogue* expressed it (there had been a photograph of her, surrounded by her yarns). Harald weaved too, metaphorically speaking, connecting by the supple thread of finance Swiss lenders, German entrepreneurs, Chilean businessmen, a tacit framework of understanding that emanated from his quiet office in the City and encircled the globe.

The thought was calming. Perhaps, Sir Homer considered, there were ways of saving the situation. Perhaps those Etonian resources, which he had hitherto viewed as providing 'gloss' or 'finish' to his character – if one could use such words without trivialising the end result – had something in them which was more . . . animal than he had realised; their major purpose being to give one a brute, unerring instinct when cornered.

'Animal'. 'Brute'. Sir Homer thought of all the blood. First those terrible sensations in the church and now this. He thought of Crispin Turner's quizzical face turned to his own, noting and then, discreetly, pretending not to note the look of horror.

Sir Homer drove past the house of a man who hosted a current affairs programme on BBC 2. How would a politician cope with the situation, he wondered? His grip on the steering wheel loosened slightly. Now he was being rational, thinking things through: here were ample useful examples of how to behave when in danger of being found out.

The first thing he must do, he decided, was to admit – to himself – that things were fast becoming out of control. It was hard, following this normal route, wearing his suit and in his expensive car, to bring himself even to think of Flora, but it must be done. He must take as his inspiration all those men he knew, or knew of, whose courage had allowed them to overcome financial or sexual scandals (or both), criminal accusations, etc. and to return, undiminished in anyone's eyes, to their rightful positions in society.

He had been wrong, he realised, in assuming that Wyley was the danger, any more than Britain was the danger to these men of stature. Wyley would not be a problem unless he himself made any errors. Essentially, Wyley would do what it was told. The public meeting could be used in order to consolidate his very special place at the pinnacle of Wyley society, to plant this idea ever more firmly in the public mind so that, if anything untoward happened, Wyley would be looking elsewhere. Here his friendship with Thomas Bright must be exploited.

At the thought of those two lovely words Sir Homer surprised himself with a sort of yelp that was somewhere between a sob, a hiccup, and an expression of rage. Flora was out of control, but was she really wreaking revenge for her long exclusion by acts of horrible violence? Must he believe that of her, when she was usually so gentle? In the past she had never minded, not really.

The Jacobean retreat of a retired opera-singer went past. Sir Homer pulled his expression into order. Almost nothing was different, this was what it was important to remember. The structure was substantially intact. It was just a matter of dealing with where things had gone awry. The world that Sir Homer would inhabit after the travellers had gone would be the same as he had inhabited before they came. It was they who had changed things and it was they who must be dealt with. The social mechanism ground exceeding small but, in this case, there had been too much delay. Pressure must be brought for it to get on with things. He must act logically, step by step, never succumbing to hysteria, never forgetting exactly who he was.

As the country turned to scrub, and the architecture plummeted to modern bungalows with caravans outside their garages, many-bathroomed new estates clustered around very attenuated greens with pretend wells, and then the grubbiness of 1930s station villas, it became easier and easier to remember.

The Rocester council offices were to be found at the end of a small, residential estate not far from the station. The location had previously been occupied by rows of nineteenth-century slum-dwellings, whose eradication had been a matter of considerable civic pride, and the visitor to the council offices, having managed to find the front entrance, was enjoined to contemplate this fact by a commemorative stone that had been unveiled by the Mayor of Rocester in 1972.

Sir Homer, however, had visited the council offices before. At the large reception desk, behind which three girls typed idly and answered the telephone, he firmly pronounced 'Sir Homer King to see the chief executive,' to the one who looked as if she might be in charge.

'You got an appointment?'

Homer King raised an eyebrow ever so slightly, his confidence growing, the familiar sense of his superiority reasserting itself in the kind of location where he was accustomed to using it.

'I'll go and see if he's around.'

'Around'. Sir Homer contemplated the preposition with satisfaction, reflecting how little the chief executive would like it. The chief executive, it implied, could simply be hanging about in the corridors doing nothing in particular.

The chief executive and Sir Homer had not taken to each other, especially when they had both been involved in a Rocester council committee for the prevention of crime. This was because the usually simple allocation of the position of superiority had not operated properly. That Sir Homer had status was unquestionable, but the chief executive, in his own eyes at least, had power, and he was not sufficiently conversant with the workings of the capital to realise that status and power were one and the same, that the first implied the second, and that therefore Sir Homer was quite simply above him in every possible way. This put an understandable strain on their relationship, to which Sir Homer responded with an air of *noblesse oblige* and Mr Taylor with a chill politeness. In the semi-social gatherings that they both attended, such as the annual dinner of the Rocester C.I.D. at the Station Hotel, Sir Homer's charm and its resultant popularity were such that Mr Taylor, foraging in his brain for consolation, discovered there, quite undisturbed, a bitter hatred of the British class system, at least in as much as it affected himself.

In the minutes that he spent waiting, Sir Homer had time to decide that the way of his natural inclination was undoubtedly the best way forward with Mr Taylor. Any attempt to placate, any show of unease or desperation would merely be fodder for Mr Taylor's sense of his own importance. If, however, he could make the chief executive feel lacking, inadequate, the chances of success would be that much greater.

The girl reappeared and Sir Homer was shown the way to the chief executive's office, along corridors whose flat, neutral carpets, had an inexplicable tendency to trip one up, perhaps because they created a mistaken expectation of texture, past numerous, gaping receptions labelled 'Reception A Housing'; 'Reception B Planning': a short, sad alphabet that ended in 'G'. At various points along the way people queued hopelessly, seated upon brick benches topped with tight plastic, reading shiny pamphlets entitled 'Rocester: The Way Forward' or 'Have You Got A Problem With Alcohol?' or just staring at posters of the Colorado beetle.

Mr Taylor's office, perhaps inspired by the example of the carpets, seemed to have been created with the intention of tricking the sensory perception of the visitor. He was a tiny little man, barely more than five feet in all, and he sat behind an enormous expanse of grey desk. The idea, Sir Homer assumed, was that one would think that Mr Taylor only appeared small because he was so far away. The illusion failed and, on other, less pressing, occasions, Sir Homer had idly wondered why and what would work, moving Mr Taylor in his mind backwards and forwards across the room, behind narrow low desks, wide low desks, high wide desks, until Mr Taylor seemed to him only a minor chess piece in the hand of a player. As indeed he was.

'Sir Homer. I'm afraid I wasn't expecting you so I can't talk long. To what do we owe the pleasure?'

Sir Homer noted the rebuke and did not ignore it or apologise.

'You were not expecting me because I did not make an appointment. I assumed that, in these difficult circumstances, your door must be open at all times to the people of Wyley.'

'Quite so,' said Mr Taylor, beaten, making a steeple of his two hands and implying, with a grave nod, that had Mr Mulch, say, or Miss Sayle of The Wise Lady Tea Rooms, suddenly, in their distress, decided to take their problems to the chief executive, he would have been as available to them as he was to Sir Homer.

'My reason for coming is that there is shortly to be a public meeting in Wyley, which I have been asked to address.' Sir Homer carefully avoided making his interest sound in any way personal. There was, after all, no need to explain to the chief executive why the choice of speaker had fallen upon him and not upon someone more intimately connected with the administration of the Rocester area.

'And?' Mr Taylor smiled a chilly smile, not appearing to understand being his main tactic in such situations, as if he gained a point for every excess word uttered by his opponent.

'I am simply seeking information. There is, as far as I can see, no sign of the byway camp being moved on, though the people are, to the best of my knowledge, illegally located there.' Sir Homer tapped a foot impatiently. Mr Taylor appeared disappointingly encouraged.

'The situation is complex,' he replied.

'I believe one of my education should be able to grasp the rudiments,' said Sir Homer, smiling. The chief executive was a grammar school boy.

Mr Taylor shifted, seeming to decide that the satisfaction to be gained from irritating Sir Homer was less than that to be gained from outlining to him the nature of his position.

'The police are unable to move the travellers on because there is nowhere for them to go.'

'Nowhere for them to go?' Sir Homer was incredulous. 'There's the whole of England.'

'According to part two of the 1968 Caravan Sites Act,' continued Mr Taylor, trying to suggest, by his tone, that Sir Homer's outburst had been unbecoming, 'the council is obliged to designate a local site for gipsies which, were they to be found illegally camped, they would be required to move to. It is not obliged to designate a site for New Age Travellers. They are therefore free to remain where they are.'

Sir Homer felt a chill fear run up his spine. He quickly endeavoured to hide it.

'I have been given to understand by the Wyley police station,' he said, remembering his reassuring conversations with Tulliver, 'that the Rocester police force is shortly to take action.'

Mr Taylor shrugged. 'You were misinformed.'

'Oh, this is preposterous.' Sir Homer steadied his voice hastily. Mr Taylor leant back in his chair in a pleased manner, even starting to swivel it a little. 'What does it matter what the damned people call themselves?'

'What indeed?' said Mr Taylor regretfully. 'But the police are refusing to act.'

'Could you not claim,' asked Sir Homer after a pause, 'that the general public call them gipsies even if they call themselves New Age Travellers?'

'Unfortunately not.' Mr Taylor produced, from his long drawer, Friday's copy of the *Rocester Gazette* and passed it to Sir Homer, who read it with distaste.

WYLEY SAYS 'NO' TO NEW AGE TRAVELLERS

Wyley village this morning was reeling under the shock of the arrival of a convoy of so-called New Age Travellers in its midst.

Police estimate that between 30 and 40 travellers have arrived in Wyley with the intention of celebrating the solstice there.

'It's an awful shock,' said local resident, Marjorie Sand, whose son, Seymour, is at Oxford. 'Wyley is a peaceful community and we intend to fight.' Mrs Sand has started a petition which she intends to present to Rocester M.P. Thomas Bright.

'It says "so-called",' suggested Sir Homer, handing back the newspaper and producing a handkerchief from his pocket, with which he proceeded to wipe his soiled hands.

'Not in the headline. And besides, they are similarly referred to in an article in today's *Guardian*.'

'There is an article about Wyley in the *Guardian*?'

'I believe so,' Mr Taylor replied. 'I have not read it myself. I suppose the *Guardian* must have a contact at *The Rocester Gazette*.'

This seemed unlikely.

'No,' said Sir Homer, after a pause. 'They will doubtless have picked it up from Sunday's *Times*. A journalist phoned me on Saturday. I put him on to Thomas Bright.'

'There is also,' said Mr Taylor, trying to look unimpressed, and opening another drawer, from which he produced a journal, which he held by one corner, as if fearing contamination, 'this.'

It was a copy of the *New Social Worker*. The chief executive drew Sir Homer's attention to page eight, where there was a long article on the topic of property in general and stone circles in particular, which purported to be a reply to his piece in *The*

Commentator – though why they bothered Sir Homer was at a loss to imagine: nobody in England would be likely to read both publications. Beneath it was an article, signed simply 'Josh', reprinted by kind permission of Kristof Smit, *Planetary Pathway*, which urged people to trespass on every stone circle they could find, Sir Homer's included. In the firelight. The tender nipples. Sir Homer cleared his throat sternly.

'You see,' said Mr Taylor, 'there is ample precedent.'

'They are cognisant of the situation?'

'Probably not, though they will have guessed that we are unable to proceed. At some stage they may seek legal advice. There are always solicitors . . .' Mr Taylor's voice trailed away on a note of regret.

'In that case,' said Sir Homer, thinking fast, 'the situation is quite straightforward. You must simply designate a site specifically for New Age Travellers.'

'Ah.' The chief executive shook his head as if he had suspected this moment would come, as indeed he had, with no little pleasure. 'That, I reiterate, is not our responsibility. We would be loath to take measures which we have, from past experience in the case of gipsies, usually found to make us unpopular.'

'But when this is known you will be unpopular in Wyley.'

'Damage limitation,' said Mr Taylor sorrowfully. 'Why extend it to elsewhere?'

'But once the travellers are gone you will be popular in Wyley again.'

'Residual resentment, however unreasonable,' said Mr Taylor, 'tends to dog the workings of government. Besides, this would amount to giving an open invitation to all New Age Travellers to come here. Rocester would become a hippy paradise.'

'Surely,' said Sir Homer, extremely irritated, 'even hippies prefer some places to others.'

Mr Taylor, stung at the thought of his neat maisonette not five minutes away, rose.

'Sir Homer, you must excuse me.' He put out a tiny hand. 'And please assure the people of Wyley that we wish their campaign the very best of luck.'

Sir Homer automatically shook hands, but left the room in

stiff silence. He got lost in the corridors and, when he eventually found his way out, had to walk round the building to get back to his car.

He was in a rage, a white, tearing fury; what Nanny would have called 'a tantrum'. Most of it was directed at Sergeant Tulliver, whose glib promises that all was proceeding as it should had taken him in, prevented him from acting, given things the time to get out of hand. He cursed the policeman and he cursed himself for believing him. Why had he put his trust in men of the lower middle-classes – Sergeant Tulliver and Mr Taylor were, after all, mere executors – when he could, all along, have been raising his eyes to the example which had, astoundingly, only occurred to him today, of men such as Thomas Bright?

Inside his head Homer King could hear Thomas's voice: 'The thing you must remember, Homer,' he was saying, 'is that the law is all very well for little things and little people, but when all's said and done, you don't spend your life playing in nobody's garden but your own, do you? That sort of thinking didn't build the empire, did it?'

Sir Homer started the engine and headed for home.

On entering the Manor, his mood was not improved by the information that Miss Trannock relayed to him. Dr Oliver had been and had confirmed that, though shocked, Lady Polly was in no danger – this was a disappointment and a nuisance: if she were still unwell on the day the Manor grounds were due to be opened to the public, should they proceed? If they did, would it be seen as brave or condemned as callous? Perhaps they could put out a message to the effect that Lady Poll's desire was that the fun should go on. If she were up to it, she could maybe wave from her bedroom window. At any rate, it was yet another thing to deal with. Miss Trannock also informed Sir Homer that the news was all over the village and many old folk tales about the circle had been remembered, or made up as a result. A local anthropologist had phoned; she had noted the number. Last of all, Sergeant Tulliver was waiting for him in the conservatory.

'Shall I bring you both coffee, Sir?' asked Miss Trannock.

'No,' said Sir Homer. 'Bring coffee for me.'

He found the policeman standing looking out at the orchard

where ripening plums and apricots hung from the branches of newish trees and, against warm bricks, espaliered peaches stretched their crucified arms. The conservatory itself was a riot of growth. Cactuses flowered there. Umbrella plants grew four feet high. Spider plants threw off child after child. A precious orchid produced one freckled, meaty bloom.

'Sit down, Tulliver,' said Sir Homer as he entered.

Sergeant Tulliver lowered himself into a chair whose straw back fanned out around him. It creaked, as if in discomfort.

'This stable, Sir?'

'What?' Then Sir Homer realised that Tulliver was referring to the chair. 'Of course it is.'

Miss Trannock entered with the coffee on a tray. She proceeded to place the coffee pot, jug of cream, sugar bowl, one cup and saucer and silver spoon upon the glass table. The men watched her in silence. The dark liquid was poured into its recipient.

'Could you bring a cup for the sergeant, Miss Trannock. If you would like coffee, Sergeant Tulliver?' asked Sir Homer.

For he had suddenly perceived in that silent moment, looking at the utensils, that the policeman was a tool, like any other, and this had been enough to dissipate his anger. You do not squander rage on tools. You just use them. Like Thomas. Like the prime-minister.

Here, he perceived, was a person who, by the very nature of his work, loved secrecy and would be able to be relied upon to carry what you told him to the grave; not because of an inherent sense of honour but because of the narcissistic pleasure he would derive from his little sack of knowledge. If, moreover, the violence had really been committed by Flora, who better than Sir Homer to throw the policeman off the track?

Sir Homer remembered now how they had taught him at school – tacitly – that, if you handled things correctly, there would never be any need for you to exert yourself visibly in order to achieve your ends: they could always be performed by proxy. Even governmental power was, in its way, quite brash: the principal boy singing a loud song in front of a crudely-painted backdrop while, behind him, other, quieter people changed the scenery. To be on a government committee, for example, you needed no other qualification than to have been chosen; and who would anyone choose but their friends? Even where you wished to participate openly you need only expend the minimum of effort. Someone else could sail your ship to the countries you discovered; you could man your polo team with highly-paid professional players; natives would, for virtually nothing, carry your bags up the mountain that you wished to conquer. It was called knowing how to delegate. It was called team spirit. Fate, you were told, had decreed you to be a leader.

Sir Homer started to be charming.

'Good of you to come, Sergeant. It's about this morning's discovery, I presume.'

Heartened, Sergeant Tulliver took his notebook out of his pocket and the stub of a pencil, which he licked excitedly.

'Just a few questions, Sir Homer. First of all, could you describe the exact nature of the injuries? Never know. Could come in handy. Especially if there's a repetition of the incident.'

Sir Homer shrugged. 'I didn't look closely. One doesn't want to dwell on these things.'

'Well in that case' – the policeman looked disappointed – 'perhaps you could allow me access to the body?'

'I'm terribly sorry, Sergeant.' Sir Homer shook his head firmly. 'The unfortunate creature will, by now, have been buried by Mr Mulch. In the circumstances we felt it best. My mother, you may have heard, was greatly distressed, to the point of illness, by the event.'

'We could exhume it,' said Tulliver, hopefully.

'I'm afraid that is out of the question. The body is now providing nourishment for onions and I feel it is best that things remain that way.'

There was a pause, during which the policeman wrote in his notebook.

'Do you think, Sir Homer,' he asked, looking up, 'that the wounds were inflicted by a human or an animal?'

Sir Homer appeared to reflect.

'The head wounds,' he replied eventually, 'were as if from heavy blows to the skull. This would suggest human origin, though maybe badgers or foxes do such things to their prey, I don't really know about these matters. The back, however, had been ripped at, as if something had perhaps tried to drag the animal away to its den, or possibly to eat it, though, for some reason, it did neither.'

'Bit off more than it could chew.'

'Precisely.'

Sergeant Tulliver leaned back in his chair, an ominous expression on his face. He was so out of place among the pale cane and the foliage that Sir Homer could imagine him part of some iconoclastic modernist collage. With an expression of fixed amiability upon his face he awaited the next question, though he had already guessed what it would be.

'Usually, Sir Homer,' said Tulliver at last, 'we find that the victim of a crime has a good idea who the perpetrator of said crime is, or might be. Of course this does not qualify as proof but it is, nevertheless, useful if suspicions are voiced, so that the force can have them at the back of its mind. A suspicion is, in a way, a proof without evidence. And where evidence is lacking, it can sometimes be supplied.'

'*Quod erat demonstrandum*,' said Sir Homer.

'Pardon?'

'You are telling me, Officer, that the police find themselves in the position of knowing what must have been the case while the law, unfortunately, requires them to demonstrate what might be, to all intents and purposes, undemonstrable. In short, you are petrified, like statues, between "must have been" and "was".'

The officer looked momentarily offended at the notion that the force could be petrified by anything, especially a pair of verbal constructions, but then, apparently intelligent enough to ignore what he had not understood and respond only to what he had, which anyway seemed to be supporting what he had just said, he replied, 'Exactly, Sir Homer.'

Sir Homer fixed his eyes upon the orchid, which hung from its stem by the thinnest of pink threads. He liked it in this room when it rained and the outside world became merely a green blur, the only clarity the slow plants and his own breathing. He could imagine himself in a bottle, bobbing upon sharp waves.

'I think, Sergeant Tulliver – or should I perhaps say I feel? – that the encampment is to blame. They, after all, have a dog, a mongrel I imagine, and we have no reason to suppose that it is kept under control. On the contrary. Apart from the farm dogs theirs would be the nearest to the Manor.'

'Did anyone report having witnessed any of the New Age Travellers or their dog within the vicinity of the event?' asked the policeman, his voice becoming squeaky with excitement, a cluster of beads of sweat erupting across his face.

A man full of resentment, observed Sir Homer. It was evident that Sergeant Tulliver was ready and willing to trample among the thickets of natural justice, on his own and Sir Homer's behalf. He was held back only by the need for permission. This permission had to come from somebody the policeman deemed superior, but it really didn't matter who.

'Oh no,' said Sir Homer. 'Nobody that I know of witnessed anything. But really, Sergeant, would you expect them to? I don't know, do thieves wait around to be discovered? And doesn't the deliberate absence of these people increase rather than diminish the evidence against them?'

'But where did the crime take place?' asked Sergeant Tulliver.

'Beneath the Wise Lady stone.'

'On private ground,' said the policeman, reluctantly.

Sir Homer raised his eyebrows. 'Are you suggesting, Sergeant Tulliver, that that would make any difference to them? They have already trespassed upon my land on at least one occasion that I know of.'

There was a pause, during which the officer wrote some more and thought a little.

'You know what, Sir Homer?' he said after a moment, shifting in his chair. 'I've got a feeling that these people have had it too soft in Wyley. I've got a feeling that there's a danger they'll get to like it so much that they'll stay for bloody ever – if you'll excuse my French.'

'Of course,' said Sir Homer. 'But what can be done?'

'Suppose,' the policeman squirmed some more, 'suppose I was to frighten them just a little? For one thing, it seems to me it's my job to protect the local girls, case they want to get their mits on them. Suppose I just stepped into the gap, as it were, and speeded things up a bit?'

'Why not? It would only be doing what was right, after all.

Wyley would thank you, Sergeant Tulliver. If they knew, which of course they would not.'

'Well, that's what I'll do, then.'

'The minimum, Sergeant – to start with.'

Miss Trannock entered with another cup.

When the policeman had gone, Sir Homer sat for a while, newly serene. What would Tulliver do? He vaguely wondered. How did you frighten people who needed to be frightened? He remembered, with revulsion, the filthy food at the C.I.D dinner: the watery, gritty prawn cocktail, made with tinned prawns and browning lettuce, the grey wad of steak with its accompanying tinned carrots, the unspeakable trifle. And then there had been the endless jokes – no ladies being present – about policewomen and police dogs, the housewife and the vacuum-cleaner salesman; jokes which, in the end, were really about themselves in a different gender.

'I thought it was a baby, put there by the mad people,' said Lady Polly.

'There was rather a lot of blood for that,' said Crispin Turner, watching a martin swoop past the bedroom window. 'Sir Homer seemed quite upset by it.'

'A new-born, I mean,' said Lady Poll, 'put there by the mad people.' Her tone threatened hysteria.

'No, no, Lady Poll,' said Crispin, turning into the room again and seeing nothing but the imprint of the light. 'It was only Chummy.'

Lady Polly rallied. 'Lot of blood, as you say, Crispin. Maybe it was a badger got him.'

Crispin smiled, sadly. 'I don't think so, Lady Polly. I'm afraid we must assume it was a person. The nature of the injuries.'

There was a silence.

'Plucky gal, to have brought him home,' said Lady Poll. 'Forgotten her name. Where does she live?'

'Her name is Melanie Flowerdew. She lives in a house by the village green,' replied Crispin, who knew where every-one lived.

'Plucky gal,' repeated Lady Poll. 'Her mother sells hats, I believe. Bit spattered herself. Did she take a taxi?'

'No,' said Crispin, 'I believe she walked. She left after you had fainted, Lady Polly, after Dr Oliver had been called.'

'It was the shock,' said Lady Polly stoutly.

'It was a shocking sight,' Crispin agreed.

'Thought it was a baby, but it was just the dog. It's got Homer in a real bate. Don't know why. He never liked the creature. Never liked anyone much.'

'Do you think, Lady Polly,' asked Crispin, 'that it might inspire him to contact his friend, Thomas Bright?'

'Possibly,' said Lady Polly. She fingered the lace along the edge of her lemon negligee then, to Crispin Turner's surprise, gave a sudden chortle of laughter. 'Funny things, men,' she said. 'Could you hand me my glass, Crispin? Not that one, the one by the po.'

Crispin reached under the bed.

'Funny?' he queried. 'You mean men in general, or Sir Homer, or someone else, Lady Polly?' He seemed to hold his breath.

'I saw them measuring their things,' said Lady Poll, all beaming smiles at the humorous memory.

'What "things", Lady Polly?'

'Their things,' replied Lady Poll, impatiently. 'Their tassels. The door to Tommy's room was open and they'd got their things held up against each other to see whose was longest.'

Crispin's eyes shone palely. 'When was this, Lady Polly?'

Lady Polly shrugged. 'Men!' There was another peal of laughter.

'How old was Sir Homer when this event took place?'

Lady Polly shrugged again. 'Not very old. Thirty-eight, forty.'

13

Martha

Downstairs the washing-machine was churning, though Melanie doubted it would get the blood out. Otherwise, the house was silent. Martha had gone out by the time Melanie got back, leaving a note to say that Hamish was with Camilla Pearson's Conchita; the other mothers sometimes, grudgingly, permitted Hamish to be looked after by their au pairs, but not often, and only when asked.

Melanie was wearing her nightshirt. A pillow lay across her stomach. She'd managed to get home before she threw up. Soon the story of what had happened would be all over the village. Marjorie Sand would be dispersing it. It wasn't hard to guess what she would be saying: evil spirits, flying over Wyley. Maybe even Satan himself, who Marjorie sometimes called 'the Beast' and to whom she seemed rather attracted.

Melanie sighed. God, wouldn't that be easy. Then everybody would know where they were. But this wasn't a spirit, this was a human being. Not even an evil one, perhaps. Not even an evil morning; a soft, misty one, with birds singing cordially. A cock crowing at some distant smallholding. The stones themselves were bland, as Melanie walked towards them through the dew. They could have been performing some function as prosaic and daily as the washing-machine in the kitchen.

At first there had seemed to be nothing out of joint. The

events of the night before might only have been a false alarm. Then, however, beneath the Wise Lady stone, Melanie noticed the crumpled form. Martha's child, she thought, ridiculously; the aborted foetus. But it had fur, a gaping, animal jaw. This was not birth; it was death. It was the dog that belonged to the Manor. She recognised it from when she was there asking about the flowers.

Dazed, Melanie picked the creature up and started walking. It was heavier than she had imagined and the Manor felt a long way away. She attempted to be discreet and entered through the hole in the hedge that the travellers had used, looking around for Mr Mulch. He was not to be seen, and then she noticed that Sir Homer, Lady Poll and Marjorie Sand were standing on the lawn staring at her, out there to admire the domain probably.

Amidst the hysterical commotion that followed, through which Melanie moved automatically, one stern thought supported her. It had joined her on the way, its solemn, stony face keeping her from crying or fainting or shouting, or doing any of the things that everyone else was doing – from any extreme reaction, in fact. The thought was this: it had not been enough to warn them.

Melanie returned to it now, in her bedroom, after having stripped and stuffed the clothes in the machine and sponged herself down. Her pale face made her lips very red, her slim hands rested on the pillow. If the body had not been a dog's but Hamish's. Such things happened; children were not immune. Or Josh's. Millions as young as him, or younger, had died in wars, or for other violent reasons. Suddenly it was not hard to see what people used to go on marches about.

Miranda's words in the Rectory garden came back to her: 'There'll be no one to stand up for us.' Melanie plumped the pillow savagely. But how did you stand up for them? She was fucked if she knew. And why the hell didn't they just stand up for themselves? For a moment Melanie felt angry. Here she was, lying on the bed, thinking and thinking about the travellers, worrying about them as if she were some kind of mother, while they were probably looking for magic mushrooms in the fields, mushing up chick-peas to make hummus, discussing something or nothing, fiddling with the buses, playing music. At the thought Melanie's anger deepened and changed. Her vocal chords tightened, so that when she said it out loud, her voice was a furious whisper: 'They have a right to do those things. It is Wyley's problem.' And, of course, she was Wyley, too. You got so used to listening to people you didn't agree with shooting their mouths off that it was easy to forget that.

How did you stand up for them? Who could tell her? Melanie considered the Feathers. John was the sort of person you could imagine addressing debating societies at whichever stupid university he went to – though his sermon had gone down like a ton of bricks and, besides, he was a clergyman. Sara was just Sara, a getting-on-with-it, muddling-through sort of person, not one who would be there manning the barricades. In the sixties, which Melanie supposed was the last time people had really believed in anything much, Sara and John wouldn't have been going on demonstrations or to rock festivals, though they might have written letters to the newspaper.

Melanie supposed she could have asked the travellers, but knew, as soon as she thought about it, that Miranda would refuse to answer, seeing her question as the beginning of some sort of Zen journey that she had to travel alone. Paul would give her a stack of books. Karen would advocate tapping into her anger. Emily and Ralph wouldn't have anything to say on the topic, which left only Josh, and she could not speak to him.

That press cutting in Martha's room, the woman with the long straight hair and the spiky eyelashes. She would know what to do. To her it would be second nature. She'd refer to 'demos', like Martha did, and have a head packed with memories of radical things she'd seen and heard. What were those things?

Melanie imagined Martha, her hair longer, sitting cross-legged, in jeans, smelling of patchouli, perhaps even rolling a joint. 'Yes,' she was saying to the blonde woman with the spiky eyelashes, 'I can make the posters. We'll meet at my place tomorrow, late.' Or something like that, though that didn't amount to much and, anyway, the room Melanie envisioned was full of intense, committed people. Looking like prats, but intense and committed.

'The thing people don't remember about the sixties,' said the old hippy on the documentary Melanie watched that time with

Martha, 'is that, as an era, it was intensely practical.' And Martha said, 'Oh yes. It was.' And Melanie said, 'So, how come you got yourself knocked up?' And that had been the end of the conversation.

She wished she hadn't said that now. She wished, instead, she'd asked how exactly it was 'practical', because the word must have shifted meaning. For Melanie it signified getting rid of things that you couldn't see as productive – and, of course, being able to feed yourself and earn a living. She should have asked Martha about it, because, if she had, she might have some idea as to what she could possibly do to protect the travellers.

Melanie let her breath out through her mouth with an exasperated sound. There really was nobody to ask except Martha, though it went against the grain. In her mind's eye she replayed the visit to the camp. Maybe Josh hadn't been admiring Martha, or, if he had, it had been in the way you admired a picture or a piece of scenery. Maybe desire had nothing to do with it.

Melanie threw the pillow on the floor and jumped off the bed. She got dressed and went to pick Hamish up from Conchita.

Martha didn't go straight to the camp, as she had planned to. Instead, after waving at Tully, she went to the church meadow and sat down under one of the stones. With her eyes shut and her head raised towards the sun, she felt like a kind of flower, absorbing light. There was so little time she spent alone. It was ages since she had simply sat like this. She rubbed her white hand along the bony spine of the stone and remembered when there had been hours in which to sit and think, or sketch.

Well, she shouldn't have got pregnant if she wanted time to herself – she could hear Melanie's sharp voice cutting through her reflections – if she wanted time at all, in fact, as it turned out. 1968: the summer when everything ended. At least for her. It seemed to go on for everyone else. When she had found a moment to look up, from three or four years spent drying rompers, dresses, socks, sweaters, on a clothes horse in front of a gas fire, the Vietnam war was all but over. Opinions had diverged. Martha could not follow the arguments, when she heard them. Mostly she could not understand what there was to argue about, or how the issues were relevant to what, in those days, they called 'an unmarried mother'.

She lifted her thin hand to her face and rubbed her forehead, because the stone had suddenly made her feel flimsy. Alone, the only thing to do was to rely on what felt good, or felt right, or, when winter seemed to go on forever and Melanie squalled in her carry-cot, what didn't feel too bad. Martha opened her eyes and gazed, starkly, straight ahead of her, as she had gazed at the dank future.

Men had been – and still were – the only fairground ride that was left. Now there was Tully, whose violent sexuality made her feel awake, who was secure and dependable, who, like her, had missed the past; more of it than Martha, in fact. She had had that summer, that short, beautiful relationship, that festival. How could she want to paint or draw again, after it was over?

She had never stopped caring, though, since it was all there was left to do. In the sunshine, beneath the stone, the thought gave her satisfaction. The causes were quieter, calmer, more rational, but they were better suited to a different time. The activities they asked of you could be performed between doing other things. She separated her rubbish into piles for recycling, drove to the bottle-bank, and stopped reading the newspapers.

Martha put her hand back on the stone and encountered a soft beard of moss. In a way she wished that the travellers had not come to Wyley, then she could have carried on forgetting. It was half her life away, after all, that secret time, before she had only herself to blame.

Her hand carried on downwards, over the ribs and undulations of rock. The smell of the travellers' woodsmoke had brought back the festival: a valley lit by fires; girls in big, floppy hats and ponchos padding by on bare feet, and she was one of them, thin and serious and self-contained. Melanie was conceived beneath bobbing stars, a hot network of muscles, a busy universe that was inside Martha's head as well as above it. When it ended, when they said, 'See you' and she walked off, in her long, patchwork, wrap-around skirt, and he stuck his thumb out by the motorway, Martha discovered that she had left most of herself behind there, among the falling marquees and the rubbish.

Martha stood up. What was her excuse? She had forgotten

what information she was supposed to be gathering. How long they were staying, that was it. Well it didn't matter whether she asked or not because she knew the answer: as long as they felt like. It was the old rule of thumb, the one everybody used to go by. You didn't let on if you felt differently. Almost automatically, Martha raised both her arms and placed them in the crevices of the stone. She leant her cheek against it; it was warm. She pretended to herself that she could hear a heart beating.

When she arrived at the camp, it was deserted, except for the boy they called Josh. He was lying on a rug with his eyes closed. Martha looked down at him, seeing again the resemblance that had fascinated her the other day. How many men had she slept with? Tens? Hundreds? It was hardly surprising that, sometimes, the pattern should be repeated.

Josh opened his eyes. 'Mum?' He squinted into the sunlight, looking surprised.

Martha shook her head. 'No, Martha. I came before, with my daughter and Sara Feather, the rector's wife. This time I've brought nothing but myself. Did I wake you?'

Josh sat up. 'I was only half-asleep. It's just I thought you were my mother for a moment. You look a bit like her.'

Yes, Martha supposed that was possible, he must be about the same age as Melanie. Something inside her recoiled, however: she felt too young to be mistaken for anybody's mother.

'You have a family? I mean, people wouldn't think you did.' Which was true. To Wyley, the travellers had materialised one day from nowhere.

'Just a mother.' Josh stretched his brown limbs. 'You probably wouldn't like her. She's pretty fucked up.'

'Oh,' said Martha, thinking of the tangled mess that was her own life, 'I think most people are, when you get down to it.'

'Do you?' Josh's beautiful eyes looked up at her. Martha had forgotten what it was like to be listened to with any attention; she had also forgotten how important such ideas were when you were eighteen. She sat down.

'I've always found it hard to understand autobiography. I

mean, being able survey your life as if it were a clear stretch of landscape,' she said.

'So you think being fucked up might not be a bad thing?' Josh asked, almost eagerly.

'Oh no,' Martha shook her head. 'I don't mean that. I just mean, for most people, it's kind of inevitable.'

There was a pause.

'Is there a village round here, with a name sort of like Wyley,' asked Josh, 'with a pub in it, by a cricket pitch?'

'I don't know,' said Martha. 'It depends on the distance you're talking about. In the county there could be hundreds.' Her voice trailed off at the end of the sentence. It was a desperate thought all of a sudden: hundreds of villages like Wyley. She glanced quickly at Josh. He was brushing some twigs off his back. 'Here,' she said. His skin was warm and flawless. Her fingers encountered the rise and fall of his breath. She could smell his perspiration. 'Come back to the cottage,' she said, 'I've got some ordnance survey maps of the area.'

'All right.' He leapt to his feet, nearly knocking her over.

As they walked, side by side, Martha tried to imagine a life without doors to be locked and keys to be mislaid. As they passed the police station she thought she saw, out of the corner of her eye, Tully watching. It didn't matter. She had an excuse: she was gathering information.

'It's pretty weird,' said Josh, once they were safe inside, 'being in a house again.'

'Yes,' said Martha, 'I suppose it must be. Up here.' He followed her up the staircase. She pushed the door open and smiled at him. 'The bedroom of a fucked up person.'

'I don't know, I think it's nice,' said Josh. His voice had gone cautious and awkward.

'So do I.'

The window was open and the scent of the honeysuckle and roses had blended with the pungent odour of an old bottle of patchouli. The clothes on the carpet were a tangle of colours and textures. Martha suddenly felt carefree and adolescent, inspired, in part, by Josh's discomfiture, as if it were somehow her raw material, to do as she liked with. A long part of her life ago, she remembered, boys had been nervous of her mere presence. It had been gorgeous to feel that trembling mix of fear and desire. You wondered if they would try to. They wondered if you would let them.

'You're a virgin,' she said, abruptly.

Josh blushed. 'In a way,' he said.

'Why?' she asked, wonderingly. 'When you're so beautiful.'

Josh's blush deepened.

Martha approached him and raised her hands to his naked shoulders. She had never been older than seventeen – not really, not with any conviction. As she closed her eyes and their lips touched and she smelled the patchouli, it could have been the past again, where someone was selling essential oils and secondhand tie-dyes. As they fell onto the unmade bed, it could have been the ground under her back. Not the ceiling – with the damp stains where rain had come in last winter – but the stars above her head. The boy who undressed her so frantically could have been Melanie's father. It could have been pieces of paper, not sheets, onto which he rolled, panting – pieces of paper covered with paintings and sketches, shiny photographs. It could still have been a clear future, when she turned over onto her stomach, gasping: a future in which she was painting, making a quiet, ringing sound as she shook her brush against the side of a jam jar of water, watching the colour swirl through it. A future in which Melanie and Hamish were not there at all. She could have been looking at the reflections of fires and tilley lamps on the dampish grass, and hearing the thump of music as her heartbeat got slower, instead of thinking that it was time to put the pillow-cases in the washing machine.

'I'll make some tea,' she said, and searched around the floor for her dressing-gown. 'Oh, the maps are somewhere in there.' She picked up the shoe-box and put it on the bed beside him.

And she went downstairs as if nothing had happened, as if the world before and the world after were not vitally different. She had seen him and wanted him and she had taken what she wanted. How he felt about it was up to him.

Was this the way it had been done once? Josh wondered if he had been conceived in a similar manner – two people, essentially minding their own business. 'You men,' said Miranda, 'you need to drive your fast cars and climb your high mountains. Women's lives already have enough danger.' On the floor, half-covered by a paperback, Josh noticed, for the first time, a packet of contraceptive pills, and felt relieved and guilty. Martha had made it not only possible but easy. She had been absent and urgent at the same time. It was just an act, like any other, no mighty significance attached to it.

Lying on the bed, hearing the quiet movements in the kitchen below, Josh perceived the vast gulf between sex and love, and realised how very easy it would be to muddle the two. He sat up and pulled the shoe-box towards him, though its interest had diminished in the light of this new experience. Looking for explanations for the past was just a wild goose chase; what could it matter to the warm, exciting present what had happened on a confusing day, long ago, in somewhere like Wyley? Why his mother had been crying, who the other woman was and why she was crying too. Fifteen or so years later it could scarcely be important.

In the box there were some photos, an old lady and a little kid. Maps. Josh got them out and laid them on the bed; they were mainly local. A scarf, an earring. He kept on digging, in case there were more maps at the bottom. Then suddenly. 'Shit!' He was holding in his hand a press cutting on which was a photograph of his mother.

For one crazy minute Josh stopped being in Wyley, in Martha's bedroom. The discovery was so surprising that it crashed him down in its own context. He was at home, in his mother's house. He was looking at a copy of the picture that she kept on the kitchen wall, the one that had bubbled and got stained; his mother, with long blonde hair and spiky eyelashes, ridiculously out of date.

'It's camomile,' said Martha, entering the room with two chipped mugs in her hand. 'Did you find anything useful?'

Josh raised his eyes from the picture. The present suddenly felt very uncomfortable. He had the sense of being where he was because of somebody else's volition.

'Why have you got this?'

He watched her face carefully. Did a look of alarm cross it? It was hard to say. She put the mugs down on the floor.

'Oh, that,' she said carelessly, sitting on the bed. 'I knew the photographer.'

Josh looked back at the picture.

'It isn't credited.'

'I mean I probably knew him. I recognised the style. It was someone I knew quite well.'

'How well?'

Without thinking, Josh reached out and grabbed Martha's arm. It felt bony under her dressing-gown. She looked at his hand, absently, as if it belonged to somebody else and then, quite unexpectedly, gave a little gasp. Her long fingers flew to her lips.

'How well?' Josh repeated urgently. 'I want to know. That picture's of my mother.'

There was a loud bang downstairs, the front door being slammed shut behind someone. There was the sound of a clear and animated voice speaking.

'It's Melanie,' said Martha. 'You'd better split. Now.'

The picture dropped from Josh's hand and fluttered onto the floor.

'What if she sees me?'

Martha stood up. 'It won't matter. You're not the first,' she added.

Melanie sat Hamish in his high-chair and lowered her lips onto his little forehead. His mouth widened into a grin and he made a small, pounding motion with each of his plump arms. Melanie laughed. She was optimistic now. On the way back with Hamish she had been thinking about women speaking to women down the generations. One imagined the particularly wise and mysterious – old hags and young mystics; one imagined the passing on of knowledge that was convoluted and secret. But perhaps it was, in fact, only something fairly ordinary and everyday, that had somehow not got written down, or had got written down in so many ways, in so many different places, that it was difficult to gather it all together, easier just to ask.

'Martha,' she began, in her head, in a voice newly sensible. 'I'm frightened for the travellers. I believe they're in real danger. For reasons of their own, that I only partly understand, they don't want to defend themselves at the public meeting, so I'm going to defend them. I feel as if . . .' What? As if there was a force, waiting to be unleashed, that the right words would bring crashing out to flood everywhere? Yes, but that could not be counted on to start working the day after tomorrow. It was rather an unformed sense that all this violence had somehow missed its destination and that people must, at a buried level, know that. In which case it could perhaps be deflected.

Anyway, Martha would understand what she was saying because she simply had to. Melanie had never asked Martha's advice before, which meant that she should have a good lot ready and waiting.

It was hot in the house. Melanie opened the back door and then went and pushed the front door wide, to get a cross draught blowing. As she turned, with her back towards the garden, a sound on the staircase made her look up.

It was Josh. He had paused, at the sight of her, on one of the middle steps. He was wearing only a pair of jeans. His cheeks were flushed and his hair ruffled. Light caught it from a window to the side of him, spilt gold across it; the current of air lifted it into fluttering wings. Their eyes met and she smiled instinctively. It did not seem strange to find him there; almost, in fact, as if she had expected it, as if he had been delivered to her.

'Josh?' she said.

At these words he regained motion. His eyes dropped and he hurried down the stairs, walked past her without speaking. Out in the street she heard him break into a run.

'Melanie,' said Martha, pausing on the same step, also flushed and tousled. 'Did you pick Hamish up from Conchita?'

Melanie breathed in quickly. She opened her mouth to speak but, at that moment, the house darkened. A form blocked out the light from the garden.

'Hallo, love,' said Tully. 'Just on my way over to the Manor. They've had a bit of trouble. Spotted that lad scuttling off. Here a while, wasn't he?'

'Was it a long time? I didn't notice,' said Martha, assuming nonchalance, her voice unsteady.

'No,' said Tully. There was a pause. 'Well, you've done your bit now, love,' he eventually continued, 'and I think, in future, that boy's worth avoiding.' There was another pause, a longer one. 'You will avoid him, won't you, Martha? And you, Melanie?'

'I think Tully's right, Melanie,' said Martha quickly.

'Melly! Melly!' Hamish's arms were bouncing again, but this time out of agitation. Melanie ran out of the kitchen, through the back garden, scrambled over the wall and hurtled across the village green. Two pale-haired au pairs, sitting on a bench, turned their heads at the sound of her sobs.

There was only once place to go: the stone circle.

14

A Midsummer Night's Dream

For the rest of the day Josh felt feverish. An overload of thoughts and emotions. When he got back to the camp he went and lay in the Pisces and watched the paper mobiles rotate, until he could imagine himself stuck inside one, each aspect of his existence balanced lightly and mysteriously upon the other. The trouble was that it was impossible to know what was supporting what, which was cause and which effect.

He had lost Melanie at the precise moment that it would have been possible for him to claim her. He could have given her love – physical, emotional: any fucking type she wanted, he could have given it. Now she probably saw him as just another of Martha's one-nighters. Except it hadn't been night, it had been afternoon; a glorious afternoon; sex, full and joyful and totally unexpected – like that other time, in the caravan. He would never stop being grateful for it. If it hadn't been for Martha's sudden gift he would have gone on not having anything to offer to Melanie.

But, of course, if it hadn't been for Martha's gift Melanie wouldn't hate him.

Josh spun the story round his head with the mobile until it got old. At sunset Miranda brought him a cup of herb tea and Paul read him some bits out of a newspaper.

He didn't think to ask what was in the tea and soon after Paul had gone out to the fire he fell into a strange sort of half-sleep.

His mind continued working, but now it fused past and present. Melanie became Martha, became his mother. He was among caravans, but it wasn't a fair, it was a festival. Then he was walking along Wyley High Street. In the church meadow the stones were large and benign. They told him to cross the road and look in the shop windows.

When he woke Josh realised, with a start, that it was dawn. He must have slept for about ten hours. On their mattress, Paul and Miranda were sleeping. Curdie was on his futon, flat out under his steam-engine duvet. Josh crept outside.

He had a pee in the woods then stirred up the fire, put the kettle on and waited for it to boil, watching the mist disappear from the woodland and thinking.

In the night his brain seemed to have done a kind of sorting and certain things had become clear.

'Split': that word again, which he'd scarcely noticed when Martha'd said it, because he was thinking of Melanie, had been tossed to the surface of his consciousness. No one could claim possession of a word, it was true, it was an old word, worn down by many tongues. But what a coincidence! It must surely be the case that his mother had had some kind of link with Martha. Either they knew each other, or they both knew the man who had taken the photograph he'd found in the shoe-box – the strange, disturbing photo that was old but depicted his mother's youth, related to past history but new in its significance. The second conjecture seemed more likely. It was what Martha had claimed, and it could explain, or go some way to explaining, the row in Wyley – if it was Wyley.

Josh poured the water into the teapot and tried to piece that day together in his mind. He rinsed off one of yesterday's dirty mugs and poured the tea.

Perhaps the trick was to see time, not as an intervention, but as a coincidence. Now, in 1985, he was young, but he could just as easily be old, or middle-aged. Even the stone circle had been new once. Even Martha and his mother had been seventeen once. Had they come into conjunction years ago, in Wyley, in the same sort of way as he and Martha and Melanie had come into conjunction the day before – or at least in a way that was kind of similar?

Maybe it was too big a jump to assume that the woman in the pub had been Martha. On the other hand, there was circumstantial evidence to suggest it. Maybe, of course, the man who went with them that day wasn't the photographer. But, in that case, why would Martha have been alarmed all of a sudden? Why had she become evasive?

Josh sipped his tea wondering how Melanie was feeling about him now. Could you stop loving a person quite suddenly, or was love something that stuck around pretty much indefinitely?

When he'd finished the cup he cut a hunk of bread and spread some peanut butter on it. He ate it standing up. Everything that was happening now was happening in Wyley. He wished that he could be sure that the past had happened here, too. The best way of doing that would be to go back to the Rose and Crown and check it out again but, of course, he'd be chucked out as soon as he crossed the threshold, and the local rozzer would have a perfect excuse to get him down the staion and give him a going over. Josh was not unfamiliar with police powers.

'You better, mate?' asked Karen, coming out of the Aquarius. 'You've boiled the kettle. Great.'

'Look, Josh. Look,' said Curdie. He was walking down the steps of the Pisces on his hands.

'Now our son can earn a living, we will never starve,' said Miranda, following him. 'Paul and I can carry the hat around.'

'If something told me to look in shop windows, what do you think I ought to do?' asked Josh, cutting more bread. He had suddenly remembered that bit of his dreaming.

'You should look in shop windows, of course,' said Curdie. 'Grown-ups are so fucking stupid.'

'Curdie,' said Miranda. 'You know I don't like it when you use that word.'

'But you are grown-ups,' said Curdie. 'At least, to me you are.'

At Oxford, Seymour Sand and his cohorts were accustomed to turning their thoughts and conversation to the less visible aspects of the spiritual domain. It was therefore a surprise to them, when the taxi drew up outside Magpie Cottage early that evening, to discover that Wyley's pagan invasion was manifest at every turn.

As the three men got out, and as Seymour handed the driver a minuscule tip, a small group of fairies passed them on the pavement, discussing finance in loud voices. Crossing the road, they perceived a man and a woman in priestly robes who, encountering the fairies, exchanged greetings and then accompanied them into the Rose and Crown. There was something in the air, too – something strange and subtle. It troubled Seymour and his two friends, all of them members of the Society Of St Jude, all of them devout to the very tips of their untouched bodies, and gave Seymour reason to be glad, as they worked out each one's share of the taxi-fare, that he had brought reinforcements.

How equipped the Society of St Jude might be to meet the challenge he did not consider, though he maybe should have done. The Society was of a cerebral nature, a group of young men (women were not permitted) who came together to listen to sermons given by guest speakers, after which they really did drink sherry, a glass or two leading them to become loquacious upon the topic of God's immanence. Christianity, but not in its most muscular form.

A man with an ass's head, finding himself unable to get it through the door of the Rose and Crown, removed it, revealing a normal, red, bulbous face: in a suit he'd be an accountant, perhaps, or an architect. The Dark One, it seemed, had indeed gained ground in the Home Counties in Seymour's absence.

'Mother, what enchantment is this?' he questioned sternly, as the door to Magpie Cottage opened and Marjorie Sand stood aside to let the men enter. As she closed it behind them the hooting laughter and braying voices of the possessed members of Wyley society grew silent – thanks to the hefty double-glazing – though two people, dressed as sprites or something, continued to speak together in a kind of dumb-show, just outside the window.

'This, Seymour? Oh, this is nothing,' said his mother, indicating that they should be seated at the table, where a ham salad had been laid and a tin of beetroot put out in a flowered bowl. 'Didn't you notice the posters in all the shop windows? It's a fancy-dress evening, organised by the Tarrants. Who are, incidentally, looked upon favourably by the Almighty. Aren't you going to introduce me to your friends?'

The two men, both in starched collars, raised their faces to Seymour expectantly.

'Cuthbert and Algernon,' said Seymour, nodding his large head at each in turn.

'I am Mrs Sand,' said Marjorie. 'You will have to be in with Seymour. I've put up two camp beds. I think you will find it snug but comfy.'

Cuthbert and Algernon assured her that they would be comfy indeed. Seymour sat and, in a lengthy grace, requested blessings upon their endeavour and other, rather technical things that Marjorie Sand gave a ready Amen to, though she had not understood a word, for it was spoken in Latin.

'"A sweet Athenian lady is in love with a disdainful youth,"' read Paul. '"Thou shalt know the man by the Athenian garments he hath on."'

'Do leave off, Paul,' said Josh, who'd had an afternoon of this. He was wearing a sheet, knotted on one shoulder and tacked, in purple thread, down the open side. Karen was painting his face.

'Josh is going to Babylon, to Babylon, to Babylon,' chanted Emily. She lay in the hammock, stroking her great mound of belly. Beyond her, the woods were filling up again with a greenish-grey light. The sun was flooding the low sky orange. Melanie had hated him for nearly two days and a night.

'I just don't think they painted their faces in Athens,' said Paul, irritatingly.

Karen lowered her stick of greasepaint. 'Well, we're painting his fucking face now, right? Else he might as well go as he is and get chucked out before he's over the door-step.'

'But what I can't understand is why you want to go,' said Paul.

'He wants to,' said Miranda, 'and that is his own business. But you'd better cover that tattoo, Josh, or they'll know who you are straight away.'

'C'n I come, Josh? C'n I come?' asked Curdie, who was darting around the fire.

'No, Curdie. They'd suss it immediately if there were two of us.'

'This should do. I mean, it's not very clean.' Ralph emerged from the bus, holding a large, red shawl. Under his arm was Carmine, completely naked and slightly smeared with diesel.

Karen took the shawl and draped it across the shoulder that had the tattoo.

'You'd better pin it,' said Miranda.

'A knot will do,' said Josh.

'On Solstice Eve,' said Karen, 'I'll paint everyone's faces. How's that?' She leant back and admired Josh's face.

'They'll notice the hair,' said Miranda.

Karen bent down, picked up a yellow and silver scarf, and tied it in the shape of a turban on Josh's head.

'Athenians didn't wear turbans,' said Paul.

'Athenians didn't go to some fucking Shakespeare do at the Rose and Crown either, did they?' said Karen.

'It's great, Karen,' said Josh. 'Thank you.'

'Remember your name's Demetrius,' said Paul.

'I'll remember,' said Josh. He walked slowly to the end of the byway and hid behind an oak tree until he was sure there were no cars coming.

When he got to the High Street the pub already looked busy; a row of shiny Range Rovers, Daimlers and Ferraris lined the pavement outside. Nevertheless, Josh decided to wander around a bit first. The more people there were the less chance there was of being spotted.

He went into the church meadow and, sitting under one of the stones, smoked a joint. The stone was still warm from the day's sunshine. Perhaps it was the grass or perhaps the fever had come back, but every one of his senses was particularly alert. His nose could differentiate the scents of the various flowers in the cottage gardens. Conversations in the street came to him loud and animated.

He must have been there for longer than he realised because, when he stood up, the stars had come out and an icy white moon was high in the darkening sky. He walked through the churchyard and read the names on the tombstones.

By the time he returned to the High Street it was even busier. Lights had come on in Wyley's cottages and houses. Josh walked past the Rectory and saw Sara Feather, standing at a downstairs window, watching the costumes going past. He crossed the road. In the sitting-room of a compact little cottage three pale men were spooning tinned peaches into their mouths. As Josh stood looking at them, one turned to the window, but stared completely through him.

There was a burst of applause as Josh walked through the door of the Rose and Crown. In a corner an effete young man was bowing, in his hand was a mandolin. People turned back to their drinks and, a moment later, Josh spotted the man fighting his way through the crowd.

'Dying for a slash, love. D'you know where they've hidden the kasi?' he said, as he passed by where Josh was standing. Then, running his eyes appreciatively down Josh's body: 'Catch my ad in the back of *The Stage* if you ever need a minstrel lay, dear.'

He disappeared.

'Where's Vero been hiding you, then?' The woman addressing him wore a green body-stocking draped with paper flowers. 'Fuck's biz?' She offered Josh a glass. He shook his head. 'Do you speak, or are you merely decorative?'

'I live in the woods,' said Josh, without thinking.

'Of course, how silly of me. Well, we all do, don't we?'

Josh pushed his way into the crowd until he found a position from which he could see almost everything. Unfortunately, it was near to the bar, where the landlord and landlady were holding court to three men dressed as fairies, a rounded man with a donkey's head on his lap and three women in the costume of country yokels.

'I suppose everyone's a bit like this down here,' one of the women was saying. 'Ooo ar and mugs of cider. Though they're not much in evidence tonight. Haven't scared them off, have we?'

'Sebastian's put the tit in Titania. Haw haw haw,' said the rounded man.

'Well, who put the cunt in Scunthorpe?' replied the oldest fairy.

'I don't know. Haw haw haw. But I do know who put the prick in Tarquinia. Soon be pudding time unless Marcus knows what's what.'

'Jolly, you're absolutely awful.' The landlady appeared to be slightly drunk.

Suddenly she looked straight in Josh's direction.

'He's rather scrummy. Who brought him?' she asked loudly.

'The babe in the wood?' said the woman in the body stocking, who joined them at that moment. 'I don't know, but he's got a lovely bum.'

'Had trouble with my toga. That's what took the time,' said the minstrel to the landlord. 'Shall I allow them to gossip, or pipe up a rousing ditty?'

'And of course shares rocketed,' said one of the fairies. 'He was making money hand over fist. A cool ten million in an afternoon. Now that's what I call making it work for you.'

'Vero's pissed,' said Jolly.

'No, I'm not. I'm just vivacious.'

'Nothing like a big word to cover a little embarrassment. What's lover-boy looking at? Never been in a pub before? Hey, Vero, better check he's eighteen. Could lose your licence.'

'No danger. We've tamed the local bobby.'

Their attention was making Josh uncomfortable but he thought it would probably attract even more if he made a sudden exit. So far nothing looked familiar.

'I say,' said the landlord suddenly. His wife's behaviour appeared to be making him tetchy. 'Don't I know you? You're not Nigel Rutger's boy who's just left Harrow, are you?'

Josh pretended not to have heard.

The minstrel struck a plaintive chord.

'"Alas my love, you do me wrong,"' he began in an uneasy countertenor.

'He lives in the woods,' said the woman in the body-stocking. 'I say,' she waved her drink in Josh's direction, 'Earth to young Athenian. We want to know who you are.'

'And whether you fuck,' said the landlady.

'Damn it, Veronica!' exclaimed the landlord.

'Oops,' said Jolly.

But Veronica had walked over to Josh and was running an exploring finger down his chest. Josh glanced about him desperately. He was going to have to get the hell out.

'I don't . . .' he started to say. The landlady undid his shawl and sent it fluttering to the ground. There was laughter. Now everyone was watching.

'Damn it, Veronica!' exclaimed the landlord again, giving Josh an indignant look. Then, spotting the tattoo, 'Good God, I do know who you are. You're one of the travellers.'

The way to the door he'd come in by was completely blocked by people. He'd just have to hope that there was a back exit, too. Josh made a dash for it. Veronica's hand, thrown backwards by his movement, hit a tray of glasses, sending them flying.

'Stop him,' shouted the landlord. 'He's jolly well breaking the law by being here.'

Numerous hands reached out and grabbed at Josh. His turban was pulled off.

'Bundle,' shouted Jolly, picking up a bottle of champagne, giving it a shake and spurting it in Josh's general direction. People in different parts of the bar, hearing the word, and not knowing that anything out of the ordinary had happened, took this as a sign that it was time to start trashing the place. In a mood of increasing hilarity, bowls of *amuse-gueules* were picked up and thrown in faces. Somebody grabbed the minstrel's mandolin and smashed it on a table. Jolly and two of the Titanias found the fire-extinguisher and let it off. A randomly-thrown martini bottle hit a mirror and sent it crashing to the ground. One of the barmaids got a black-eye from a stool hitting her head-on.

'Oh God. Oh God,' said Veronica.

'Sorry old sport,' said Jolly. 'Getting a bit out of hand.'

'Oh, it's not your fault, Jolly.' She looked down at her cut fingers. 'It was that fucking traveller.'

There was a back door. It led into a garden. Josh paused for a moment. He seemed to have been forgotten in the clamour. This was certainly his last chance for a look and he must take it.

Most of the tables were occupied, but the atmosphere out here was quieter. At one of them a couple, he in doublet and hose, she in a long dress and ruff, were doing a line of coke; by the wall of a separate, barn-like sort of building, another couple, both in tutus, were kissing passionately. The door of the building was open, revealing several, rather self-conscious serving-wenches, pushing their hair back from their foreheads and attempting to carve cuts from a whole pig, whose gilded body nestled behind a sign which said 'Dinner and glass of wine £20'. In front of him, on the other side of a low wall, partly illuminated by the houses surrounding it, was the cricket-pitch.

Josh blinked. His head had started spinning. It was the same pub. The place he remembered was Wyley. Tomorrow he would go and see Martha and, afterwards, he would know everything.

'He's still out there! Let's get him!'

'Do him over!'

'Punitive buggering.'

Josh ran, scattering chairs and tables, leapt over the low wall and lurched across the cricket-pitch. He fell, scrambled to his feet and looked over his shoulder. He was being pursued by a fairy, two large, male yokels and, further behind, Jolly, carrying his ass's head. The expressions on their faces, out in the open, away from the tempering influence of witnesses, were dangerous. This was the hunt, the thrill of the chase. They were out for blood. At best, they'd beat him up. At worst, they'd dump him down the cop-shop for the rozzer to do the same thing.

There was nowhere to escape to. Josh scanned his options desperately. He could't return to the street, there'd just be more of them. If he kept running, the chances were they would catch up with him – they were already gaining ground.

Fleetingly, Josh wished that the stones hadn't led him to the posters and to the idea of disguise, that they hadn't brought him to Wyley to decipher the past. Fleetingly, it struck him as buggersome. A favourite statement of Miranda's went through his mind: 'Magic is lateral.'

The only thing to do was to try and hide in one of the gardens that backed onto the pitch. Josh put on a spurt, darted into the shadow of a wall, and scrambled over it as quietly as possible. He landed on a rose bush, leapt forward and fell onto an uncut lawn, beside Melanie Flowerdew, who was sitting on a chair, in a white cotton nightgown, looking at the moon.

'Well, you certainly keep popping up all over the place.' Melanie surveyed him coolly. 'You'd better get into some shadow again or they'll spot you.'

There was a sound of voices. Josh rolled, noiselessly, behind a large bay tree.

'. . . got the little twerp and put his head down the bog. That's him.'

The two yokels and the fairy peered over the wall.

'No it isn't, it's a girl.'

'Oh, Lord. Not up to all this exercise.' They were joined by Jolly, panting. One of his ass's ears had fallen off.

The four of them stared at Melanie.

'I say,' said the fairy eventually, making to start climbing over the wall, 'there's been a spot of bother at the pub. Some local lads went loco and trashed the place. One of them ran in this direction. Not seen him by any chance? Thought we might check round the garden for you.' He paused. 'I say, you're awfully pretty. Might give him the wrong idea.'

'I say get the hell out,' said Melanie. 'This is private property.'

The fairy took a step backwards. All four men looked hurt and puzzled.

'It's only for your own good,' said one of the yokels.

'I'll look after my own good,' said Melanie. 'Now push off.'

There was a silent moment while the men appeared to be trying to think of a way not to lose face. Then, 'Frigid little bitch,' said the fairy. 'What she needs is her bottom smacking,' said Jolly. 'I think he might be over there,' said a yokel. They set off at a run.

'I'd give them a minute to make idiots of themselves. They'll soon get bored,' said Melanie, without turning. 'There, they're heading back to the pub.'

Josh rose to his feet and came out from behind the tree. In the moonlight she looked almost luminous.

'Melanie,' he began.

Still she did not move.

'Now you can go, too,' she said.

15

An Alibi

She would have liked to think he looked a prat, walking off in an old sheet, confused, perhaps hurt even (he and Melanie Flowerdew were friends, weren't they?). But he didn't. He looked gorgeous, could have fallen out of a legend. She wanted to run her fingers down his naked shoulder.

Well, she'd probably look gorgeous if she hadn't spent most of yesterday afternoon bawling her head off in the stone circle, and most of today in her bedroom, avoiding Martha and thinking till she had to take an aspirin.

For the first time ever, the stones had let her down, so there'd been no point in going back to the circle. She supposed that, when she took her broken heart there, she'd been expecting a sort of human comfort, guidance, maybe, about how to act and what to feel. When she got to the Wise Lady, however, she realised suddenly that she was running to a lump of rock. That was what you got for muddling stones up with people. Probably that story she'd been told when she was a tiny kid, about the woman, the bride, appearing in the middle of the circle, was another great big misunderstanding: a play of sunlight on mist, a trick of vision.

You wanted someone very wise to show up. You even had a feeling that heaps of wise people were out there somewhere and that they simply hadn't made their presence known. But, in the end, there was only Martha and, before her, Grandma, and, presumably, before Grandma, some other muddled woman, with her own ideas and desires, not much good at fitting the role allocated to them. You just had to make do – which, God knew, she'd had a lot of practice at.

Josh shooting over the wall confirmed what, in those tortured hours, Melanie had struggled to avoid admitting: that Martha was marginally better than a stone to talk to, still the only source of information she had on political activity, and, most of all, that her own involvement in whatever was going on between the travellers and Wyley could no longer be purely personal.

In the beginning she had thought it would be possible to salve her conscience with just a warning. Then she had heard that scream in the woodland and found the dog's mangled body. Afterwards she'd assumed that, once she had made the noble decision to ignore whatever was happening between Martha and Josh, everything would be easy – because the decision was noble. Now it was clear that Josh was in love with Martha it was difficult, to the extent of impossible, to go on wanting to defend the travellers.

There were so many points at which you could wash your hands of involvement. Maybe she would have done if she hadn't read the message in those men's ridiculous, menacing faces. They forced her to realise that the ethics of the situation would be the same even if nobody she cared about was under threat. Most people were somebody's child or lover. It looked like she got saddled with being, as Grandma would have said, her brother's keeper.

Miranda maintained that all that was going on wasn't about the travellers, it was about Wyley; but maybe, in the end, it was about something bigger, and the fuss about the solstice and the stones was only a small manifestation of it.

Melanie got off her chair and sat down on the grass. It was one of the hottest nights of the hottest summer ever. After a while she stretched out under the bay tree that Josh had hidden behind. She was not happy but at least there was something to be said for this kind of unhappiness. Her eyes closed and she fell asleep. Throughout the night she dreamed of the things that she'd seen and thought about while she was awake so that, when she actually woke up, drenched with dew, it seemed as if they could have just been part of her dream, too.

Martha was in the kitchen, mashing tofu for Hamish's breakfast. Her hair was wet and it dripped down her toxic toad t-shirt.

'Oh, Melanie,' she said, 'you're soaked.'

'Is there any water in the kettle?' Melanie asked. At the sight of Martha her courage almost failed her. She reached for her tobacco and papers on the kitchen table.

'I've made a pot of barleycup.'

Barleycup was gritty and tasted of hot water. Melanie got the coffee down from one of the shelves and put a tablespoon of it into a mug.

'Coffee can cause palpitations,' said Martha.

'Good,' said Melanie.

They sat at the table in silence, Melanie drinking her coffee black, so that it would have absolutely no nutritive value that Martha could be relieved about. She stuck her roll-up in the side of her mouth and lit it noisily.

'Look,' she said, 'you know that clapped-out pillock we saw on telly?'

'Which one?'

'Oh, Christ. Forget it.'

'No Melanie, I am interested. It's just there are so many.'

'The one who went on about the sixties being practical.'

'Yes,' said Martha. 'I remember him.'

'Well, what did he mean?' Melanie took a gulp of coffee, watching her mother over the rim of the mug.

Martha thought for a moment, absently spooning some tofu into Hamish's mouth, which he spat out.

'I suppose he meant it got things done.'

'What things?'

'Well, it ended the Vietnam War. Then there was civil rights. Feminism was later. But there was ecology. Vegetarianism.'

'Oh, hooray.'

There was a silence, then Melanie said everything in a rush, before she could think about Demeter and the toad t-shirt and Hamish's tofu.

'I want to know how they did it. I want to be able to

change things, too. I want to know how to fight for what I believe in and not have to watch people take shit from the bastards.'

Martha looked surprised and nervous.

'There's a recycling meeting in Rocester at the end of June,' she said, 'if you want to get involved.'

Melanie blew some smoke out from the corner of her mouth exasperatedly.

'Not like that, Martha. Properly. I want to make a big difference in Wyley straight away. Today. At the public meeting. Tell me how.'

'I wish you'd eat some more, Hamish,' said Martha. 'It's mainly down your bib.'

'Tell me how,' repeated Melanie impatiently, watching Martha mop up Hamish's fat little cheeks.

'That,' said Martha, steadily, 'I don't know.'

There was a silence. Melanie was horrified.

'You don't know? Stop it, Martha, he's clean now. Tell me how.'

Martha turned and looked at her.

'Honestly, Melanie, I really don't. There were things going on that I went to, but almost everyone did. Someone else organised them. And then, in '68 I got pregnant with you. There wasn't time to do much but that, and when there was time I was too tired. I'm not the person to ask. I doubt there's anyone to ask in Wyley.'

'The world, if all you fucking ex-flower-kids are right, was exploding around you, and you were too tired to be involved? You mean I've spent two days agonising over whether to ask you your stupid ideas and you can't tell me anything?'

At the sound of Melanie's raised voice Hamish's face screwed into a nervous grimace. He started to whimper. Martha stood up and lifted him out of his high-chair and onto her lap.

'Why should you have to agonise about talking to me?' she asked.

'Oh, for Christ's sake. "We're not like mother and daughter, we're more like friends."' Melanie put on a soppy accent. 'Not to mention Josh.'

There was a pause. A shadow crossed Martha's face.

'He was a virgin,' she said eventually. 'I've always liked virgins.'

Melanie blushed deeply. She looked out of the window. Her fucking eyes were filling up with water.

'Melanie,' said Martha, 'it never means anything when anybody has sex with me. Or, when it does, it only means children. People like travellers, they go away. They're not worth caring about. Really. They don't care about you. Believe me.'

The phone rang. Martha dumped Hamish back in his chair and went to answer it.

Melanie sniffed loudly and wiped her face with the back of her hand, but she felt better. Now she thought about it, none of the men could have cared much about Martha. She herself was born at the old Rocester General, with Grandma apparently fussing round the waiting-room. Hamish was born upstairs, with Dire Straits as the sole pain-killer and her in the kitchen waiting for it to be over. On neither occasion was any man involved in the matter.

She went over to the sink and splashed some cold water on her eyes and forehead. It was true that, from Martha's description of things, Josh's role didn't look that admirable. She didn't like to think of him as just another of a long line of males who worshipped at Martha's shrine and then buggered off somewhere. She thought of psychic Joodi, of the septic nose, who'd never figured out that men who ran around on their wives weren't awfully likely to be faithful to their mistresses.

It was tricky. Every inclination was in favour of forgiving Josh and trying to battle a way into his affections; all she needed was an adequate reason. Martha said that travellers, people like Josh, didn't care, went away, but was that always the case? How could that square with him being a virgin?

The beautiful are not only loved, they are also easily excused.

Melanie reached over and tickled Hamish under his chin. She felt that she had learnt a bit about sex, if not about politics. Playing things by ear was now the only option, in both cases.

She poured some milk into her coffee and gulped it down, then rinsed the mug.

'Who was that?' she asked when Martha came back into the room.

'Oh,' Martha said, looking sheepish, 'Tully. We were going to go to Tesco's together but he's going to be a bit late.'

Her tone made Melanie suspicious.

'Why?'

'There was some trouble at the Rose and Crown last night. They've got someone under arrest.'

'Someone?'

'Oh, all right, Melanie.' A haunted, nervous look came over Martha's face. 'It's one of the travellers, but I really don't think we should get involved. I'm sure Tully's only writing down the details.'

Melanie stood. 'What else might he be doing?'

'Nothing, nothing at all.'

'It's Josh, isn't it?' A sick, tingly feeling ran through Melanie's body.

Martha began to delve in a cupboard for her stacks of saved newspapers.

'I think so,' she said, her voice slightly muffled.

'Martha, you know what Tully's like. You've got to go to the police station and make sure nothing happens.'

Martha's head reappeared. She looked tired. 'Nothing will happen, Melanie. If you want to have a relationship with a policeman you can't be interested in what they do all the time. And I don't want you to do anything either. It's for the best. Honestly it is.'

Melanie dashed upstairs and pulled on her jeans and a t-shirt. She ran out of the house, slamming the door behind her.

When she got to the police station the desk was unmanned. The room smelled of pencils and was full of an uneasy silence. Then, from the back of the building, she heard a dull thump and Tully's voice, low and breaking, with what sounded like suppressed excitement. She had heard him speaking like that when he was in bed with Martha. For a moment Melanie wondered if he was having sex with someone.

'You go near her, right, you go near her again and it's over for you. You give me the littlest excuse. And don't think things like that don't happen. Because they do. You so much as think about Martha. You so much as set foot in the circle, that's it. Over.'

Melanie thought she heard Tully panting. There was another thump.

Melanie shinned over the counter, knocking some old biros onto the floor. The back room went silent again. She opened the door into the office. It stank of a deserted sandwich. She entered the house proper. She tried a door. It opened onto a spare bedroom with an unmade bed and bare white walls. Josh lay on the carpet in a foetal position. Tully, his sleeves rolled up, was bent over, sweating, in a corner. His arms were covered with bite marks.

Melanie smiled, carefully. 'Did he trip?' she asked, looking at Josh.

'What do you want, Melanie?' Tully wiped his forehead and straightened.

'Oh,' Melanie replied, 'Martha wanted me to give you a message.'

'Why didn't she phone?'

Josh struggled to his feet. Tully eyed him regretfully.

'She tried but there was no answer. I suppose you were busy. What's he done?'

'Who?'

'Him.' Josh looked as if he might throw up.

'Caused a disturbance in the Rose and Crown yesterday evening. Damage to property.'

Melanie assumed a puzzled expression. 'He can't have done. He was with me yesterday evening.' She stopped, then began slowly. 'I do remember, though, some people from the Rose and Crown asking me if I'd seen the local lads who'd caused the trouble. They were searching for them round the cricket pitch. Josh isn't local.'

Tully appeared dubious. 'He was with you in what capacity?' he asked.

'He's my boyfriend,' said Melanie.

'You could identify the people who said it was local lads caused the disturbance?'

Melanie thought of the fairy, the man with the donkey's head, the two yokels. 'Oh, yes,' she replied.

'You would be willing to swear to your version of events in a court of law?' Tully clearly didn't believe her but he also seemed to realise she knew that that wasn't what mattered.

Melanie nodded.

'The Tarrants,' said Tully, after a pause, 'recognised him by the tattoo.'

'Lots of people have tattoos,' said Melanie.

There was silence. Josh doubled, coughing. Tully looked him up and down, checking for visible damage. Melanie held her breath. Bruises too blatant, any blood and Tully's only option would be to proceed through the system. He knew now she'd make sure he couldn't make it stick – and she might just possibly be able to cause problems for him with Martha – but a lot of creative thinking could be done when somebody was locked up in a police cell. The drawback, from the policeman's point of view, would be that the charge would be specific to Josh and couldn't have anything to do with the stone circle or the other travellers. Josh was deathly pale, he was unable to speak, but there didn't appear to be any marks on his body. Tully could let him go and nobody need be any the wiser. Who would believe a traveller's word against a policeman? Melanie hadn't witnessed any actual violence. There was also a good chance, perhaps, that he'd frightened Josh enough to make the travellers decide to leave.

'Right, well listen to this.' Tully suddenly made a hideous attempt at a paternal tone. 'I don't want you having any more to do with the suspect, right?'

Melanie shrugged. She looked at Josh. 'It was only sexual,' she said.

'And you, I meant what I said about behaviour to local people and trespass. I'm going to keep you here and take your statement, then you can go. You can go now, Melanie. I'll take yours if I need it. What was your message from Martha?'

Melanie thought wildly. She could see the look of terror on Josh's face. With a shock she realised that he was frightened that Tully would kill him.

'That she'd walk down and meet you and wait around here,' she said. 'She should be here any minute.'

They crossed the road, separated, then met on the village

green. Josh was still pale, he looked horribly shaken. His eyes were massive.

'Thanks, Melanie,' he whispered.

Melanie said nothing because she was afraid of crying.

'Will you be all right?' she asked, eventually.

'Yeah.' He tried to put some energy into his voice. He started to head off in the direction of the camp.

'Josh,' she called after him. He turned. 'Did you bite Tully? There were bite marks on his arm. Did you bite him?'

Josh shook his head. 'Nelson did,' he said, slowly, bitterly. 'That's our dog. We found him dead this morning. The policeman killed him.'

Melanie broke out in a sweat.

'Why?' she asked.

'To frighten us. To make us go away.'

'Has it worked?' There was a sob in Melanie's voice that she couldn't suppress.

'I don't know,' Josh replied.

16

The Public Meeting

It had been a busy two days for Sara Feather. Ever since her resolve, in St George's church, to procure for John the child he deserved, she had been doing a lot of research. Twice she had visited Rocester Public Library and had read up, as much as she could, on child law and adoption. There were, it emerged, two major problems. One was that the sources were rather out of date. The other was that she did not seem to have anything concrete enough to take to a court of law. Emily, in spite of her way of life, looked healthy. The fact that she might not drink plenty of milk was clearly inadequate – though it might have done in the United States. The possibility of a life of persecution and hostility did not appear to be sufficiently unusual to merit the courts' intervention.

The only hope was that things might have come on a bit since these books were written. Sara made a list of phone numbers and decided to ring them after the public meeting. This, in itself, would possibly furnish evidence of the dangers Emily's baby could expect to confront from the very start of its existence – though, of course, she hoped that it wouldn't.

Another thing that had kept Sara occupied was John. She thought of him now, as she sat at his desk studying the phone numbers. Since the upset in the church he had rather collapsed. Oh, he functioned as usual, but he managed to look awfully hard done by. His face was strained and pale (which made it even more handsome); he shaved but you felt as if he hadn't. He spoke in a reproachful sort of tone. Sara cooked him poached eggs on toast and made sure he didn't have to answer the telephone.

In the garden Miranda was weeding. Sitting on the ground beside her was Melanie Flowerdew.

Sara shook herself out of her reverie. Staring at a phone number wasn't going to give her a baby and watching Miranda and Melanie wasn't very productive. She searched around for something useful to do. She thought she might get out a few books that John could look at when he'd finished his nap. He was threatening to dispense with the sermon this coming Sunday. A bit of reading might inspire him to do otherwise. After all, surely the whole point was that you were willing to suffer for your beliefs.

Sara chose a book about the early church fathers, the writings of two or three people who she was pretty sure had been burnt at the stake, and Cardinal Newman, because she dimly remembered he hadn't had a very nice time, either. Then something caught her eye: a book on mythology she couldn't remember having seen before. She took it down. The page fell open at the beginning of a chapter on Frija, the Teutonic goddess whom John had researched for *A Guide To Wyley*. What was it he had told Sara about her? Nothing much except that she was the wife of Odin. She might have been worshipped in the circle and was associated with midsummer's day. And that was really all there was to be said.

Sara started the first paragraph anyway. After a minute her cheeks became hot. She read on with growing interest and excitement, and a resentment that she was unable quite to explain or to suppress. What was John talking about?

It was true that there wasn't much information in the British tradition, but there was plenty elsewhere. Frija was important enough to have a day of the week named after her to start with: Friday. Her Roman counterpart was Venus (Vendredi), the goddess of love and procreation. Frija was not always faithful to Odin, but she still protected marriages and made them fertile. She was the mother of the gods; it could also be argued that she was Mother Earth. In this form she was worshipped under other names in a variety of places: Anatolia, Syria, Iran, Babylonia, Greece, Denmark, Germany, Cyprus and, of course, England. She was very much older than Christianity.

Hadn't John read this? Or had he just read it and not found it interesting? Sara felt disproportionately upset, but even more angry than upset. It seemed to her that John had – wittingly or unwittingly – made a definite attempt to exclude. In doing so he had deprived people of information that may have been useful. She snapped the book shut and decided to go for a walk to the church meadow.

'Melanie,' said Miranda, the two of them entering the study half an hour later, 'he is truly okay. Stop worrying.'

'I'm not worrying. I'm just concerned.'

'Concerned my arse. You are in love with him.' Miranda started dusting.

Melanie plonked down in a chair.

'How can I be in love with someone who's slept with my mother?'

Miranda looked at her, wide-eyed. 'Josh has had intercourse with your mother? But that's incredible.'

'Why? Because Martha's so old?'

'Martha is not old. No, because this is the first time he has ever had sex with a woman.'

'Right. So what? Martha said he was a virgin. She likes virgins.'

Miranda raised her eyebrows and gave a half-smile. 'You think he hasn't tried before?'

'You mean . . . ?'

Miranda nodded. There was a pause. Melanie looked confused.

'But why couldn't he?'

Miranda shrugged and went back to her dusting. 'Nothing biological. Only one, simple reason: he thought he couldn't. He tried with a littul girl, probably younger than you even. He knew nuthing about intercourse. Neither did she. There are things a littul girl cannot do that can be done by an older woman. How much do you know about intercourse, Melanie Flowerdew? Would you have been able to help poor Josh with his erection?'

Melanie was embarrassed.

'You mean you think he's cured?' she asked eventually.

'In as much as there was anything the matter with him. He did some wise choosing.'

'What do you think it meant to him?'

'How would I know? I don't live inside his serious head. Why don't you ask him?'

Melanie said nothing. Miranda finished the bookshelves and started on the desk.

'So are you going?' Melanie tried to sound casual.

'I don't know.' Miranda lifted the telephone and dusted underneath it. 'Stonehenge is not far away. Solstice eve is tomorrow. We are angry and depressed. Our harmless dog is dead, Josh is recovering in the hammock . . .'

'I thought you said he was all right.'

'He is all right, he is recovering. We are angry and depressed and anger and depression are not a good way of heralding in a new era. The Wise Lady wants us to be here but what use are we to the era if our bodies are walloped and our homes are smashed up? Your Wyley policeman is more dedicated than we realised.' She put down her duster and picked up a piece of paper by the telephone. 'And now there is this.'

'What is it?' Melanie got up and went over to have a look. It was a list of telephone numbers. 'Oh, that's nothing. That's what Sara does, fucks around helping people, whether they want it or not.'

'No, Melanie,' said Miranda, 'it's more than that. Look at the name at the top: Emily. Remember when you and your mother and Sara Feather came to the camp, how she wanted doctors for Emily who there's nothing wrong with?'

'It's not so fucking strange to have check-ups when you're pregnant. Even Martha did.'

'But look at all these numbers, Melanie. Look at the name. You know that Sara Feather believes she is infertile?'

Melanie was stunned. 'She told you that?'

Miranda shook her head. 'She didn't have to. I see it in the way she looks at children, the way she looked at Emily.'

They stood in silence, staring at Sara's notes. Melanie was

dubious. 'Sara Feather's a bit of an idiot, but she's all right really.'

'A lot of problems are caused by people who are "all right really". Something must be done.' Miranda carefully replaced the piece of paper.

Melanie returned to her chair. 'You could leave, I suppose,' she said. 'I mean, if that's what you think you'll do anyway.'

'No.' Miranda recommenced her dusting. 'Your busy British law would pursue us. This must be dealt with first of all. The only thing that will make Sara Feather forget Emily is if she has her own baby.'

'Well, you can't magic up one of those,' said Melanie.

'Can't I?' said Miranda.

By late afternoon the sky had thickened. It was terribly hot and threatened rain.

'Think it was the Day of Judgement, wouldn't you?' said Joyce Atter, meeting Melanie as she was leaving the Rectory. 'Who's to say it isn't?'

A sort of frenzied excitement engulfed the village. The door to the Rose and Crown was open and men in white overalls went in and out. Melanie heard Veronica Tarrant's voice from inside the building.

'Do you have to bang so bloody loudly? This must be finished within the next half hour. We've got a public meeting this evening and if we can't open I'll sue for loss of earnings. Marie, get some of the chairs from the garden and put them in the barn, there aren't enough.'

Seymour Sand and another couple of wankers passed Melanie on the pavement. Seymour didn't recognise her but one of his companions put a tentative hand to Melanie's bottom. She whacked it off. The three men turned and looked at her. 'Whatever was that about?' said Seymour. 'Search me,' said the young man.

When Melanie got home she brought the chair in from the garden. She felt stiff from having slept on the ground. Her head had started to ache again. She was nervous about the evening. She took a couple of aspirins and lay on her bed. After a while she heard Martha and Hamish come in.

'Melanie?' called Martha.

'What?'

'Oh, you're up there. Do you want some tea?'

'What sort?'

'I can do you a bag of the ordinary.'

'All right.'

Five minutes later Martha appeared with a mug. She put it on the floor and sat on Melanie's bed.

'You don't look well, Melanie. Are you sure you want to go to this meeting?'

'Of course I'm sure.' Melanie reached for the mug and took a sip of tea. 'Unless,' she said, 'you have a better idea?'

Martha raked her fingers through her hair.

'No, Melanie, I don't. I mean, I'd try to help, if I thought it was appropriate.'

'Why isn't it appropriate?'

Martha hesitated, then spoke quickly, 'Wyley isn't so bad really. I have to live here after the travellers are gone, and it's best they do go, for both of us, Melanie. You do have to continue after people go away.'

'I don't see why.'

'There was you and then Hamish,' said Martha quietly.

'I mean I don't see why they have to go away.'

There was silence.

'Anyway,' said Martha, 'there's nothing I can do.' She made for the door but turned when Melanie spoke.

'You know the kind of man Tully is. You know he beat up Josh, don't you?'

Martha's face snapped shut. 'You don't know that for a fact, Melanie,' she said, almost crossly. 'Maybe he was just frustrated. I mean, he seemed awfully confused about when we were going to Tesco's, but he was nice in the car. He bought a cornet for Hamish. I mean, he's never been anything but good to me. He lives inside the law. You don't want to get involved with people who live outside it.'

After Martha had gone back downstairs Melanie set her alarm for seven p.m. and went to sleep. It was raining when it woke her. She got dressed and made herself a sandwich in the kitchen.

'I don't know why you're bothering to come,' she said to Martha as they set out.

'Tully wanted me to,' she replied.

They dropped Hamish off with John Feather, who wasn't going to the meeting, and made their way to the Rose and Crown.

Everyone in the pub was talking about the wonderful job Simon and Veronica had done getting the place shipshape again so quickly. All trace of the builders had vanished. The packed bar glittered with copper horse-brasses. A new mirror reflected a hundred faces. Veronica Tarrant, in a cotton frock, well made-up, sat chatting and sipping a tomato juice and feeling pleased with herself.

For her and Simon the evening was already a triumph. Though staunch supporters of the prime-minister and vigorous opponents of any forces that might seek to undermine her, however vague, their decision to offer the room had not been entirely disinterested. Sir Homer was guest of honour. He had not yet availed himself of Veronica's mutton pasties and was perhaps unaware of the projected monthly dinners. He wrote a restaurant column in a national journal. It was Simon and Veronica's secret intention to invite him, and any other dignitaries who might be present, to share a bottle of Sussex wine with them after the meeting.

There was, moreover, the matter of the bar takings. The meeting was not scheduled until eight o'clock but since well before seven both bars had been full.

A little too full in fact. Marjorie Sand's curranty eyes, darting about the room, registering the arrival of Melanie and Martha, noted also that representatives of Wyley's vestigial working-class, especially its teenagers, along with some of their friends from the council estate in Rocester, had arrived in unlikely numbers – perhaps in the hope of a television news team – and were drinking rather heavily. Tom Callan, the butcher, out of his bloody overalls, at the end of one of the heavy, oak tables, was dominating quite a rowdy group, on the outskirts of which Miss Evans drooped over a port and lemon.

Marjorie Sand did not rejoice in numbers, was, indeed,

unaware of their potency. She would have been at a loss to say exactly what she desired of the meeting, but it was not this. In fact the idea that she was the inspiration for this drunken rabble rather sickened her. She had wanted a stern gathering of dignified minds: many Seymours, many Sir Homers, with just one or two family tradesmen to denote the support of the rest of their class (safely ensconced in front of its televisions). Nor had it occurred to Marjorie Sand, whose politics were confused and hysterical, that, without a discernible goal, the meeting would be inclined to create one. Used as she was to the milder pastime of religion, she had somehow thought that a gathering of Wyley's dignitaries might, in and of itself, achieve something.

In this frame of mind the familiar presence of Melanie and Martha was something of a comfort – though she liked neither of them. It was even a relief to note the arrival of Sara Feather, shameless though it was. And, of course, there was always Seymour, who was placidly sipping a soda water and commenting to his two friends on the novelty of being in a pub. Sir Homer was not to be hoped for until the last minute but there was Sergeant Tulliver, taking it all in, and Crispin Turner, drinking a bitter lemon. Mr Taylor, the chief executive, was a sudden, exciting surprise and, gradually, a procession of mothers and their husbands took their places in the bright bar, blinking, as if they spent most of their time underground.

By the time Dr Oliver was present Marjorie Sand felt more relaxed and was able to reflect that here was a superb illustration of democracy in action and that, for the crowd scene, you must, unfortunately, tolerate the crowd.

Sir Homer King arrived – sorry he was just a little late but his schedule had been thrown out by a rather lengthy interview he'd done with the *Guardian* earlier in the day. Veronica went up to shake hands, and Sir Homer shook hands with lots of people and nodded around the room, with an assumed diffidence that many found charming.

'Mr Taylor, how good of you to drag yourself away from Rocester. And on such a filthy night.' With these sentences Mr Taylor's gesture was reduced to the level of a dismal chore, executed out of obligation. 'Can we call on you at question time?'

'Actually,' said Mr Taylor, fingering a piece of paper in his pocket, 'I would be willing to make a speech.'

'We would not think of imposing on you,' said Sir Homer.

Martha bought herself a half of cider and a pint of lager for Melanie. Melanie gulped it down quickly and then felt sick.

Veronica Tarrant went through the crowd. 'We're ready to move into the barn. Could you leave your glasses in the bar, please?' Because their presence would make the meeting seem casual, and because Sir Homer was there. Many failed to comply. Many even went so far as to order another to take in with them.

There was a long table at the far end of the room with bottles of Evian and a subtle vase of flowers, behind which Sir Homer placed Mr Taylor. The speakers had come in, talking to one another, giving the customary impression of being unconscious of their position – some more successfully than others; Tully was positively quivering with self-importance.

Melanie, in her seat halfway down the room, looked around with growing horror. Too much excitement was in the air. So many people were drunk. Somebody tripped and sent a chair over on its side. Less than two fields away Karen would be swinging a crystal above Carmine's tiny nose. Paul would be reading, Miranda strumming her guitar or plaiting coloured thread into Curdie's hair. Josh would be stretched out, pale, on a mattress.

'We're ready to begin. We're ready to begin.' Marjorie Sand flapped her arms crossly. 'Oh, dear. Oh, dear. This really isn't very good.'

Sir Homer stood up. There was a volley of shushes. He knew the value of going last and had intended that he should. If, however, he could take control from the very first, then he would insert a few, solemn words at this stage, before sitting down to let the audience become bored with the mediocrities. After that would come the pithy moment when he would charm and amuse and show Wyley how lucky it was to have its very own Homer King.

He smiled cordially.

'Thank you, everyone, for coming out on this filthy night in order to discuss something that is of importance to us all – and, indeed, not just to Wyley.' There was a pregnant pause to allow the village to take in the fact that an interest in its concerns really did emanate from as far away as Westminster, and that Homer King was its medium.

'Since I am here merely in the capacity of a concerned citizen of Wyley, let me first of all give the floor to Sergeant Tulliver, who will be able to enlighten us on the legal position.'

Unfortunately, however, Sergeant Tulliver's English was designed not to give information but to elicit it. It took the crowd some time to understand exactly what he was telling them, and then they were incredulous: the police force did not intend to act!

Sensing an undercurrent of criticism, Tully reiterated the problem lengthily, attempting, once again, to illustrate that no one, especially the police, was to blame, and that included Rocester Council.

This was a wise move, since it shifted focus away from what Sir Homer, at last taking the opportunity to introduce Mr Taylor, elegantly termed 'the executive power' to Rocester Council, which he termed 'the legislative'. This, of course, was not true. Mr Taylor was every bit as executive as Sergeant Tulliver (though tended not to like to see himself in this way) and, just this once, in order to duck the glances of blame which seemed to be heading in his direction, he was quite inclined to leap to his little feet and say, 'If I may just intervene for a moment, Sir Homer . . .' when Sir Homer, sensitive to atmosphere, introduced the next speaker, namely Mrs Sand: very active in Wyley affairs and particularly assiduous in her attempts to keep Wyley free from street crime and 'on the straight and narrow'.

But Marjorie Sand did not budge.

'I would prefer to go last, Homer,' she said, in the voice of an almost-member-of-the-family, allowed to use his first name, a hard-earned recompense for sitting on Lady Poll's squashy sofa and smelling her farts while she admired the bird drawings in aged books that weighed half a stone.

'Marjorie, come now, I must insist,' said Sir Homer, without showing a shred of his irritation.

'No, no. I am determined to have the last word.'

So Sir Homer had to go next.

'I spoke, just before this meeting, to our M.P., Thomas Bright,' he began. A rustle went round the room. The mothers and their husbands sat up a little, as if they had caught a scent. People took cogitative gulps of their drinks, making a useless semblance of being unimpressed. 'He is indeed, as are others, extremely concerned at what he sees as an increasing problem in our society. I mean the fact that, while most of us go about our business, there are those who think they can just walk in and have the lot, that the law somehow doesn't apply to them, that in the name of a few watchwords – such as "freedom" and "equality" – they think they have the monopoly on understanding, they have the right to disrupt a law-abiding community with their filthy ways.'

Thomas Bright had not, in fact, said this, and Sir Homer would have been surprised if he had, convention demanding that one did not inflict one's fellows with the iteration of views that you could unerringly assume they shared. (Their conversation had actually been of a more intimate and frivolous nature.) Still, he might have done, and had he been sitting at the table, he would now be nodding in agreement with Sir Homer.

Melanie leapt to her feet. Standing, she was utterly alone, the centre of a large circle of expectant eyes. She swung her gaze quickly around the room. Only Martha had not raised her head. Melanie noticed how the light shone off her thin hair.

'Sir Homer, hasn't Sergeant Tulliver said that the police are unable to act because the travellers are protected by the law?' Her voice came out small and strained.

'Speak up,' shouted someone from the back of the room.

Sir Homer looked at Melanie with a mixture of amusement and distaste.

'There will be questions afterwards, Miss Flowerdew.'

'But I feel a point has been made that needs looking at more profoundly.'

'Profound we shall be, Miss Flowerdew, I assure you.' There was laughter. Melanie sat, trembling. Martha stretched out a thin hand and clasped Melanie's briefly.

'There are more seats at the front.' Marjorie Sand bobbed up and pointed a long finger, but people preferred to remain within easy access of the bar.

In the end Sir Homer King suggested nothing except the appropriateness of hatred and the wonderfulness of Sir Homer King. He swung Thomas Bright's name before the crowd until it lulled them into a passive sense that, somewhere in London, there was somebody who thought of Wyley and felt for its sorrows, and who knew of these sorrows only because of his contact with Wyley Manor.

Sir Homer, along with many of his class, felt a distaste for violence solely when it was perpetrated by or against himself – an exception being made for the very weak, such as slaves, servants and dogs (and history had disposed of two out of these three options). If, on the other hand, a group of drunken louts, inspired by moral, if not legal, justifications, decided that their evening would not be complete unless they kicked in the long-haired skull of a troublesome hippie, then Sir Homer need only shake his head sadly and challenge anyone to locate anything in his speech that could have encouraged them to do so. If, on that occasion, the police, otherwise occupied, arrived just a little too late and the ringleading louts were, in due course, imprisoned for involuntary manslaughter, say, then it would only give added credence – as if it were needed – to Sir Homer's articles in *The Commentator* on topics of the day such as the decline in moral values, the lack of respect for the law and the need for stiffer prison sentences.

He sat down to resounding applause and it was with a sense of anticlimax that the audience watched Marjorie Sand rise, unevenly, to her feet.

Surprisingly, however, she did not disappoint. Sir Homer had been more subtle about his feelings but Marjorie Sand felt no such compunction. In instinctive rhetoric she outlined shrill irritations, piercing their silvery points beneath the skin of Wyley normality. Where did the travellers go to the toilet? Wyley felt the vague, foreign threat of diseases they had thought were over forever. At the very least their children's shoes would be caked with human excrement. Wyley's local taxes would go sky high in the need to pay for extra policing. Could anyone leave their home without fear that it would be broken into? Locks would need to be more numerous and tighter, alarms more urgent. The young, enticed into the fascinating woodlands, would become a generation of lotus-eaters, drugged to the point of inability to do anything except get the bus to Rocester to sign on.

The mothers gasped at this imprecation of their children, whose blue-eyed, pyjamaed bodies lay beside rabbits and teddies, beneath twirling clowns, in rooms where friezes of sea-lions and monkeys danced. They gazed, with doleful ferocity, at their flaccid husbands and wished that napalm could fall from heaven upon the parents of Carmine and Curdie.

Marjorie had not finished, for she had saved the major culprit for the end of her speech.

'I would like to conclude by reading you this,' she said, picking up a pair of wiry glasses. ' "Are they astrological clocks? Great temples for the worship of forgotten gods? Places perhaps for ritual sacrifice?" These words were written by our own rector in *A Guide To Wyley*, as a description of the stone circle that we have so long had to tolerate.' She removed her glasses and waved them at the crowd. 'I do not know about you, but I do not want to live in a place where people feel that, because of the presence of some stones, they can come into a Christian community and worship whichever god, or gods, they feel like. Nor do I believe that, in this day and age, we should be looking approvingly upon the idea of ritual sacrifice and paganism. The stones, the stones are to blame.'

Marjorie had started to screech and nobody was thinking that she looked ridiculous.

'The stones approve. The stones are the cause. It's the fault of the stones. They approve of ritual sacrifice. They are the cause. They are the reason why our dogs will be savaged and our children will be drugged and our population will riot. It's the stones. They've done it.'

When she sat down there was not even applause, just a deathly silence, for her invocation of the circle as all that was Other had accurately defined what the villagers felt. The Wise Lady was a hideous manifestation of everything which was different from themselves and, from within the confines of an ever-more-strenuously bounded normality, differences must be viewed with increasing horror.

Should she defend her husband, wondered Sara Feather. Marjorie had misrepresented what he had written, claiming he had condoned when he had merely described – a common enough fallacy – but would it really have mattered if he had condoned?

The questions began.

A mother, who had read about such matters in the papers, asked whether there was a danger of the hippies flicking fleas onto her children. Sergeant Tulliver, scratching at the thought, said he believed there was every possibility and that children, in particular, should be kept away from the camp and from everyone in any way involved with it.

'How do you flick a flea, Tully?'

'You will be able to ask your question in a moment, Miss Flowerdew, there are other people before you,' said Sir Homer.

'It's Ms Flowerdew. I want Sergeant Tulliver to tell me how you flick a flea.'

As she spoke she was aware of Martha watching her.

The policeman smirked. 'I imagine, Mizz Flowerdew, that you pick it up and you throw it.'

'So you don't flick it?'

'Not strictly speaking, Mizz Flowerdew. But the action, I maintain, remains the same.'

'And how long does it take to catch a flea, Sergeant Tulliver?'

'I don't know, Mizz Flowerdew, having never had a flea.'

There was a burst of laughter. Sara rose quickly.

'If I may just make a comment. I have worked in London, in the Inner City, with the children of the very poor, and I think you will find that the article must have been a fabrication.' She sat down. There was a brief silence.

'I think, to summarise, we can say that, though the details of any given example might not be correct, the point remains that the travellers are a sanitary risk.'

Sir Homer's comment met with general approval. Mr Taylor was asked if the council would collect the travellers' rubbish and replied that the council would act under advisement.

After three more questions on similar subjects Sir Homer, reluctantly, recognised Melanie's hand.

'Why are none of the travellers here?'

'I imagine,' said Marjorie Sand, 'that they were frightened to come.'

Martha gave a start. She looked quickly across at Tully but he did not meet her eye.

'Were they invited?'

'Why, no, of course not,' replied Marjorie, in huffy tones, clearly feeling that the discussion was straying into irrelevancies.

'Do you think England's a democracy?'

'Of course it is.'

Melanie was flushed and her forehead damp with perspiration.

'Then should people who are directly involved in this situation either not come to this meeting because they don't know about it, or because they are too frightened to?'

'Too bloody right.' From the back of the room.

'Ms Flowerdew,' Sir Homer, suave and polite. 'This is not a political meeting.'

'She consorts with them,' yelled Marjorie Sand suddenly, pointing a quivering hand at Melanie.

Melanie's nerve was failing her and tears were pumping into her eyes.

'In a democracy should they be frightened?' she screamed at the shaking Marjorie Sand. 'Well should they? Fucking should they?'

'Ms Flowerdew, the chair cannot recognise questions voiced in an uncivil manner,' said Sir Homer, coldly. Melanie went unanswered.

She sat down, trembling, the room seething around her and very hot.

In the slight abeyance which followed Crispin Turner rose to his feet.

'Is it not true, Sir Homer,' he asked, 'that your intimacy with the Right Honourable Thomas Bright dates from when you were at school together?'

'Yes, it is,' said Sir Homer, puzzled.

'Thank you.' Crispin Turner took his seat again.

There was a buzz of conversation. The crowd sensed anticlimax. Soon the meeting would be winding up and everyone must disperse back to their dull houses, with nothing to do but lay up the morning's breakfast and consider that nothing had changed. It was intolerable. Marjorie Sand's words, worming through their brains, seemed to have promised an answer to the unbroken tedium of tomorrow – the daily-shouldered cross of the commuter train, dank with bodies and boredom; the foreignness of the Paulettes and Gretas; their obtrusive homesickness; tourists who blocked one's path with handbags so that you nearly tripped with tea-trays; tourists who asked for stamps to difficult countries; the permeating smell of boiling mutton and the tedium of sex; ignorant inquiries about wine. All those millstones around the collective neck, all those milestones of calendars and birthdays, undesired invitations, had become suddenly interesting at the thought that they needed to be defended.

Then Tom Callan, whose bloody face was feeling the dead chill of a dozen frozen carcasses, shouted across a concluding Sir Homer, 'Let's pull them down.' People leapt to their feet. Everyone realised the rightness of it.

Except Sir Homer who, though torn, could not permit frenzied incursions across his land to create gaping holes and massive boulders to be disposed of and, at the back of his mind, open the possibility that such incursions might happen again.

'The stones are private property,' he asserted quickly.

Sergeant Tulliver, too, stood up, uncertain as to whom he was supposed to be defending from whom, but knowing that it would involve reinforcements and a humiliating borrowing of the Tarrants' telephone (how much better if it could have been foreseen. Then the crowd would have flowed out into the street only to find turning blue lights and the sound of the disembodied deities that talk down police radios).

'The stones are protected by law, which means that anyone attempting to interfere with them, in any way whatsoever, will be liable to arrest by Her Majesty's Police Force.'

'As an ancient monument,' said Mr Taylor, uncertain of his correctness, but feeling that the council, too, must stake its claim, 'the stones fall under the auspices of Rocester Council.'

'Well, they're falling under our auspices tonight,' shouted Tom Callan, all bravado until he could be sure of followers.

There was a scream, tearing the vocal chords, eradicating the youth of the face, creating the lines that would one day make this young girl an old lady – a wise old lady. A scream that made a large silence.

'They're nobody's stones. They don't belong to any of you.'

Then, 'Onward Christian soldiers! Yes yes yes,' screeched Marjorie Sand, breaking the spell and everyone made for outside where the rain was falling. A woman got trampled. Somebody fell and bloodied their head. In the stampede Melanie was separated from Martha. She was carried through the doorway by the surge of the crowd and deposited in the street.

Tom Callan, the first out, had found a rope from somewhere. Seymour Sand and his two sidekicks were continuing the hymn, rather ponderously, as if to make it clear that their support would be moral as opposed to physical. Lashing rain sizzled on people's sweaty faces. Fathers were removing jackets and handing them to mothers.

'This way! This way!' Marjorie shrieked, waving the point of an umbrella.

'You're all insane!' shouted Melanie. Nobody seemed worried. In her mind's eye she saw The Wise Lady, fallen on her side, a rapacious crowd, buoyed with its success, looking around for other victims, seeing the small light of a tilley lamp across the fields, arriving at the camp . . .

'Press!' she yelled. 'Press! You're being photographed. That bloke over there,' she pointed into the darkness, 'he's got a camera.'

'Be courageous against the pagan idol,' retorted Marjorie Sand. ' "There is nothing covered that shall not be revealed." '

A nervous silence fell, broken only by the singing of Seymour and his companions. It was an own goal. People strained their eyes in the direction that Melanie had indicated. They would rather that covered things should remain unrevealed. It was one thing to be courageous under cover of darkness, quite another to see yourself, engaged in an act of dubious legality plastered across the front of the *Guardian* or, worse still, the *Telegraph*. If the press was there, might there not also be hidden television cameras? The fathers retrieved their jackets and put them on over their sopping shirts. People began sloping off into the darkness.

From inside the Rose and Crown one of the bar-staff called time. Sir Homer and Mr Taylor shook hands distantly, and then with Sergeant Tulliver, who first wiped his palm down his trouser leg. They congratulated each other on having managed to contain a difficult situation. Veronica Tarrant, having checked that the bar was clearing, came over and invited Sir Homer and Mr Taylor to taste the planned bottle of wine, cold-shouldering, none-too-subtly, Tully, who was only a policeman. Sir Homer looked at his expensive watch and regretted that he would have to leave, owing to the poor health of his mother, which everyone understood and sent good wishes about. Mr Taylor, however, had just enough time and the irritated Veronica, who had witnessed the salmon swimming out of her net, led him off to the now empty bar, where Simon was, optimistically, putting out some olives.

Seymour, Cuthbert and Algernon stopped singing, the two guests glancing awkwardly in Mrs Sand's direction and wishing they had remained in Oxford. But Marjorie was not downhearted.

'The Lord has sent us His message,' she pronounced. 'We shall return to Magpie Cottage and make a cup of tea. We have a busy night ahead of us. Cuthbert, Algernon, I hope you have brought wellingtons?'

17

Frija

'Thank God for the media.'

Throughout the village there was the sound of front doors being shut and bolted. Marjorie Sand and her entourage disappeared into Magpie Cottage. Sir Homer's car purred away, spitting thin droplets of water from its wheels. Tully, after scanning the street for Martha and seeing only Melanie, trudged off in the direction of the police station.

Melanie looked around for Martha, too, and thought she spotted her going into the church meadow. Anyway, Martha had said she'd pick up Hamish so all Melanie had to do was go home.

It stopped raining quite suddenly. Melanie started to walk. She was utterly exhausted. Still, she'd achieved her goal. The camp was safe for the night. Wyley seemed to be exhausted, too. Lights went out in bedroom windows. Tomorrow was another working day. Nobody had the energy to maintain their hatred now. That wouldn't rekindle until morning and then the things that they had considered doing in darkness would appear ill-judged and strange.

Melanie sighed. How fucking typical to be more frightened of a camera than of hostility and prejudice. The idea of shouting 'press' had come to her spontaneously. She had been able to control Wyley because she knew Wyley. The travellers wouldn't have had a hope in hell.

*   *   *

John Feather was reading a book when the door opened. Sara closed it behind her softly and entered the sitting-room.

'How's Hamish?' she asked.

'Asleep.' John pointed to the pillow where Hamish lay covered by a blanket.

'I'm surprised Martha isn't here yet. Do you mind waiting up for her?'

John shook his head. 'How was the meeting?'

'Oh,' Sara ran her hand across her forehead, 'bad. I mean, I think it's fair enough to put yourself at risk, if that's the way you want to live, but one thinks of the children. Even if they're not actively discriminated against, people believe they've got fleas and lice and whatever.'

'Well, that's just stupidity. There was an outbreak of lice last year at Wyley Primary.'

'I know. I suppose they reckon that travellers' children get a different sort of lice from their own children. Anyway, I'm concerned. I think there's an argument for intervention.'

But John's eyes were straying back to his book.

'I'll pop up,' said Sara.

'Good night,' said John.

When she had gone, though, he stopped reading. He heard her footsteps on the stairs with a kind of dismay. A tap was turned on in the bathroom. Soon Sara would button up her cotton nightgown and fall into a sleep that was perhaps sorrowful but essentially tranquil. Gosh, how wonderful to be as simple as Sara Feather.

It had begun to occur to John that religion, as a means to an end, was not an awfully effective one. Until last Sunday the boundaries within which he worked hadn't greatly bothered him, but then he had never attempted to cross them before. Now he was a king fallen from power, with nothing to console him: an adequate little marriage; a pleasant, though barren, wife; a minor domain, in which his word went unheard. He supposed he would continue to be rector in Wyley, or somewhere similar, and get used to it again. He just wished he could accept, as calmly as Sara, that nothing interesting or exciting was ever likely to happen.

The phone rang. John made to get up but Sara answered it in the bedroom.

The front door opened and closed. There was a tap on the sitting-room door. Martha entered.

John rose to his feet.

'Good heavens! Martha, whatever's the matter?'

'I've been to the stones,' said Martha. She sank onto the carpet in a bedraggled mass. Damp scarves, soaked t-shirt, dripping hair.

'I thought it had stopped raining.'

'Not long ago.' She started to cry.

'Whatever's the matter?' John repeated. He, too, sat on the carpet, something he had not done in many years.

'Oh, I don't know, John.' Martha produced a lace handkerchief from a pocket and wiped her eyes. John Feather watched her. 'I keep thinking of the past, and how much happier I was then.' She buried her face in her hands. 'You might not believe it now, but I've known people like travellers. I understand them. I know that they've probably got it right and we've probably got it wrong.' She gave a large sob. 'I know Melanie hates me for not standing up for them, but it truly is hard to remember and, anyway, they've got to go. It's important that they do. For Melanie in particular. I'm trying to protect her.'

John reached out and pulled Martha into his arms. He had the warm sense that this was the kind of thing a rector should be doing, listening to the troubles that really emanated from people's hearts.

'Go on,' he said steadily.

'Tully's not perfect.' Martha gave a hiccup. 'Nobody's perfect. I think I really do love him, though. He'd have radioed if everybody hadn't gone home. It was right not to do it straight away, a local policeman has to turn a sort of blind eye sometimes, to take things into his own hands. But then I went to the church meadow and . . .' She subsided into sobs again. John ran his fingers up and down her arm. 'I went to the church meadow, because I felt so upset, and I remembered . . . There are better lovers than Tully, I mean gentler ones. But in the end you have to choose something strong and constant, even if it isn't what you really want.'

'Better lovers?' asked John after a short silence. He looked down at Martha's body. Her drenched t-shirt clung to her. He could see the perfect outline of one of her nipples. 'That is to say, gentleness is important to you in a lover and Sergeant Tulliver is not providing it?'

Martha raised her head and looked into his face. Some new awareness had suddenly caught her attention. She appeared to forget about Tully, quite spontaneously, in the interest of it.

'Oh, yes,' she said, 'though excitement's important, too.'

John Feather went from zero to ninety in the space of a second. This was not the gradual stirring of interest he was accustomed to. His hand had left Martha's arm and was toying with the nipple. His crotch was aching.

'And what is exciting?' he asked.

Martha, consoled, smiled a wide, dazzling smile, glittering with tears. She raised her lips to his ear and told him. Most of what she said was new information.

'Cooee. Cooee. Is anybody at home?'

'Holy shit!' John leapt to his feet. Martha tumbled onto her side. The door flew open and he was facing the quizzical gaze of Marjorie Sand, very aware that his jeans did not do much to hide a bulging erection. He lay a hand casually across his genitals. Marjorie's eyes followed it.

'Good evening, Marjorie,' he said, waving the hand in the air. Marjorie's eyes remained on his crotch.

'I had come, John,' she said, 'to give you the chance to join in a blessed task. What is Martha Blandish doing on the floor?'

'Yoga,' said Martha. She stood and picked up Hamish. He did not stir. 'I was telling John about some positions.' She gave John another dazzling smile. He wondered if his zip was going to burst. 'But I'd better get back now or Hamish will wake up. Good night.'

'Good night, Martha,' said John. He and Marjorie stood in silence until they heard the door close. Then, 'She was in need of moral guidance,' John said valiantly.

Marjorie let a full minute pass before she uttered.

'I came to Dennis Sand a virgin,' she said. John's erection abruptly subsided. 'Not once, in all our years of marriage, did I waver from my marital vow.'

John nodded. 'I can believe that Marjorie,' he said nervously, wishing she would keep her voice down. But worse was to come. Her pitch rose.

'First paganism and now adultery.'

'Marjorie, could I please request that you lower your voice? Sara is trying to sleep.'

'It's partially Sara's fault, of course. I acknowledge that,' said Marjorie, ignoring him. 'Delaying having a child may be fashionable but it is hardly the prerogative of a rector's wife. It is the kind of behaviour that encourages a man to wander.'

'I don't really feel, Marjorie, that this is any of your business.'

'Oh, but it is, John. It is. The rector's situation affects us all. There is no doubt in my mind that you chose Sara specifically because you believed she would be a good wife – and mother.'

John became angry. 'I reiterate, Marjorie, that this is none of your business,' he said, aware that a little self-righteousness might also serve to obfuscate. 'For your information, however, and for that of any of my flock who care to gossip about it, it is an unfortunate and disappointing truth that Sara is unable to have children. Happily, however, her ability to have children was not why I chose to marry her. I chose Sara because of the qualities in her that I felt would make a good rector's wife.'

The front door slammed. They both jumped.

Outside, a warm wind that had blown up was swirling the trees. An intense moon disappeared behind clouds, then reappeared and flooded the landscape with blue and silver. The ground was dry again. Sara's hot cheeks cooled. It was so different that she could believe that John and Marjorie and their damaging conversation were not minutes and feet away but in another dimension altogether, a dimension in which links could be made, events could have consequences. Out here, where there was only the wind and the moon and the ancient stones, nothing mattered. There was just a vast, beautiful indifference. Maybe this was what she had loved about the stones all along: their lack of requirements.

Sara tried, and almost managed, to join in the indifference. Perhaps it was the words that failed her. Just as she thought she was slipping away, everything came back from that other world. Indifference didn't seem to be something you could join in with. Nor did anything else, come to that. She had thought she was wife, if not mother, and all she had been was a kind of glorified caretaker.

The chill way that John, in his calm, intellectual voice had said those words. And to Marjorie Sand, of all people. 'Poor Sara. Of course she's besotted with him. (Well, who wouldn't be? And with her looks she probably couldn't believe her luck.) He chose her for professional reasons, you know, though it must still be a disappointment that she can't have children.'

She had almost forgotten about the phone call but still her feet brought her automatically to St George's. She passed through the lych gate and into the graveyard.

The trouble was, she realised, that those schoolish virtues you had been assured would hold you in good stead for the duration were absolutely no use in the adult world. Being a good sport; not making a fuss; smiling through: pretence, lies.

She was not smiling now. The gravestones swam and distorted. She fingered the large, rusty key that she had taken from her handbag and placed in her pocket. It was to a side-door. Something was happening in the church, they had said, though it all seemed quiet enough. Perhaps it was a practical joke.

The graves around her were white in the moonlight; their proclamations struck her as bleak and stoic – not making a fuss. 'Gone to meet his Redeemer': 'Well, I'll be off then. No no, it's fine, don't worry about it. Only hurts a very little. I don't mind, really, knowing that I'll never see a log fire again or hear the dawn chorus.' It was horribly unkind, and Christianity, at that instant, seemed unkind, too. A religion with a perfect, oh so unattainable, family at its centre, to remind everybody of how much they had failed. A religion in which even a virgin had a baby. There was so much more comfort in a faith whose only creed was the abacus of the seasons, which celebrated not that which suffered but that which endured. If your poor body could not stand more than seventy years' assault there was something which could.

Sara wondered whether to go back with the just-wanting-a-breath-of-air excuse. John, relieved, would assume that she had not heard – or allow himself to assume. Marjorie would

have gone on her self-righteous way, gloating over her nugget
of gossip. Things would return to normal. Except that normal
didn't seem very normal any more. Normal seemed ugly and
bizarre. Normal, when you got down to it, wasn't normal.

She decided she had better go to the church and then make
up her mind. It would be terrible if anything happened to the
stained glass window.

The door was unevenly dampened by the rain, all the thick
slices of wood different shades of grey in the moonlight. Sara
put the key in the lock and was about to turn it when, to her
surprise, it swung open. She stepped down into the church
feeling, through her shoes, the irregularity of the flagstones.

'Good heavens!'

The figure on the altar turned and looked along the aisle to
where Sara was standing. With the moon behind it, it was only a
dark silhouette, just catching an edge of light where the bulbous
stomach bulged outwards.

'Hallo.'

'What on earth are you doing?'

'Looking at the Lady. The moon's shining through her. It's
pretty.'

Sara was irritated. 'I told you last time: It's not a lady, it's a
man.' Then it occurred to her how ridiculous the conversation
was and how irrelevant. This girl had broken into the church
and was standing on the altar, which must be blasphemous.
Sara should be telling her off or calling the police. She hurried
up the aisle. By the time she reached the front pew Emily had
turned back to the window and was, again, watching the slowly
travelling moon.

'You're so lucky,' she said.

Sara stopped short. 'Lucky? Me? Why?'

'The Lady lives here with you.'

'Oh.' Sara felt absurdly disappointed and illogically angry. She
had wanted good news and all she had been given was what she
had already.

'And you've got a nice husband. I've seen him. He smiles a
lot and always looks worried.'

John to perfection. Sara sat down on the pew and started to
cry.

Emily lowered herself into a sitting position, paused to rest for a moment, then slipped off the altar and walked over to Sara. She surveyed her curiously.

'Why are you crying?'

Sara did not reply to the question. 'Who is the father of your baby?' she blurted out instead, looking at Emily fiercely.

'I don't know. Could be lots of people.'

Sara nodded, bitterly, taking a grim satisfaction in the utter injustice of it all. 'What I can't understand,' she said, 'is why it had to be you and not me.' She produced an embroidered handkerchief from her pocket and started dabbing ineffectually at her eyes and nose. 'I deserved it. I worked to deserve it. And I'm not lucky. My husband doesn't love me.'

Emily looked surprised. 'Does he say so?'

'No, of course he doesn't.' Sara's voice was muffled by the handkerchief.

'Then he probably does.'

'He doesn't say that either.'

Emily shrugged. 'What's to say?' She perched on the altar rail. 'Whose fault is it?'

'Whose fault is what? Shouldn't you be lying down or something?'

Emily shook her head. 'That you can't have a baby.'

'Nobody's fault. At least that's what the doctors said.'

'Why do you blame yourself then?'

Sara looked up. Above the altar the moon was leaving them. Soon they would be plunged into darkness. Yes, it was true, she did blame herself. It was hard, almost impossible, to imagine a defect in John. To think that way would be bordering on insult, so she insulted herself instead.

'My husband thinks it's my fault,' she said.

'Rectors and doctors,' said Emily. 'Who can believe them? You're too nice. You try too hard.'

'I wouldn't have thought it was possible to be too nice,' said Sara, gruffly. She was thinking of the randomness of those microscopic sperm you saw on television documentaries, swimming towards happiness or sorrow, riches or poverty; all of them swimming towards death.

'The trouble with Wyley,' she said suddenly, 'is that they don't know where responsibility begins and ends.' She gave a funny little shriek of laughter, putting her face down into her wet hands and talking through her fingers. 'And neither do I. I put it in all the wrong places, I suppose.'

'Probably,' said Emily.

'Do you know,' said Sara, 'I'm sick of jumble sales, and Bring and Buy, and I would like to lie in late on a Sunday morning, and eat toast and Marmite in bed, and read the *Observer*.' She felt rather reckless.

Emily did not reply. 'Why did you do that to the door?' she asked instead.

'Do what to the door?'

'Try to open it with a key?'

'I thought it was closed.'

'It wasn't, it was open.'

'I didn't know that.'

Emily took Sara's hand and uncurled the damp fingers. She placed a tiny piece of paper upon it. On the paper was a circle. Inside the circle was a black area, shaped like a tadpole or a comma, with a white dot in it, and a white area, similarly shaped, with a black dot in it.

'This is a present,' she said.

'What do I do with it?' Sara asked.

'You eat it,' said Emily.

Sara did not watch her go. When she turned her head to the back of the church Emily had vanished. The wooden door was open. The wind had completely died down. She looked back at the piece of paper. It was a drug, of course. She could give it to Sergeant Tulliver and Emily would be arrested. Perhaps her baby would be put up for adoption. The answer to her problems had, literally, fallen into her hands. So why did she feel nothing?

Sara stared and stared at the pattern. She realised that she recognised it from somewhere. The yin and the yang. The feminine and the masculine. The coming together of opposites to make a complete whole. In the still church she smiled to herself, bitterly. What could be more opposite to her, to Wyley, than Emily and the other travellers? Could anyone possibly imagine a situation in which they would, together, create a unity? Never in a million years.

Except . . . Emily had trusted her. She had put hand in hand and completed the first curve of the circle. She was possibly too stupid to do anything else but, anyway, wouldn't it be churlish to take her present and use it against her?

The next moment, however, this struck Sara as silly. After all, she was planning on using the authorities to take away Emily's baby, wasn't she? What was the difference?

She raised her eyes to the window. The moon lingered still, longer than she had expected. She wanted the baby, she wanted its happiness. She was secure in her list of telephone numbers on the desk in the study. Let them do the business.

Time passed. At one point Sara thought she heard footsteps in the churchyard, but that was perhaps her imagination.

How quickly things could crumble, how noiselessly. She had no Christian faith left to speak of – that slipped away without her knowing that it had until this evening. The same with her marriage. Outside – who could say? – perhaps Wyley itself lay in ruins. No farms or cottages, no Wyley Manor, no Rose and Crown. Only the stones. Only the manifestation of a belief in process for its own, beautiful, hopeless sake.

Almost without thinking Sara placed the piece of paper on her fingertip and put the finger in her mouth. What did it matter anyway? It tasted of nothing.

She waited. Still the moon waited with her. No changes took place for a long time.

Then a tingling began, the same sort of tingling she had felt that day in London and on the night the travellers arrived, except now it was only in the tips of her toes and fingers. She became suddenly fidgety and preternaturally alert. She stood up and walked backwards and forwards in front of the altar. The moon really, really should have gone by now, rather than doing what it did, which was to shine brighter and brighter: the entire church was lit, as if with spotlights.

Sara raised her eyes to the window. St George glowed. The flowers of his robe were jewelled colours. She paused. Wait a minute. The flowers weren't part of his robe at all. His robe was a misty white and the flowers were outside. They were in the meadow surrounding the stone circle. And, what was more, St George wasn't a window. He had stepped down, smiling joyfully, knocking the roses off the little sill, and was hovering above the altar. He had a secret.

Sara tried and tried to work out what it was, but her eyes kept straying to the sill and she kept thinking, again and again, that it really wasn't a very good sill and that to persevere with it had been lunacy all along, especially if St George was prone to wandering around his church and knocking the vases off. There wasn't more gravity in Wyley than other places at all. There was exactly the same as everywhere else in England. It was just that, in most churches, their saints stayed put. In which case the sill should have been made bearing that in mind.

Her eyes met St George's. He shook his head, managing to convey somehow that it was a very good sill *if you used it for its purpose*. Which was not to put flowers on.

'Oh, God! Oh, God!' It was a very good sill for bread. St George nodded. And the odd vegetable, he added, as long as you chose solid, sturdy sorts of ones. A very good sill for offerings. Which meant, of course, that this was not St George at all. That was the secret. The curling locks. The long robe. Not a saint, not a god: a goddess. Frija.

'I'm sorry,' said Sara. 'This is most embarrassing. I'm awfully sorry.'

But Frija only smiled, goddesses being used to people muddling their names up. We make our own angels, she added.

And Wyley had indeed vanished. When Sara reached the church door there was no graveyard, only grasses. When she turned to wave good-bye to Frija, there was no church either. Instead there was a massive stone. Sara glanced across the valley; grey-blue in the moonlight, The Wise Lady stared back at her companion stone, which was not going to survive. Even as Sara's eyes returned to it, its flanks became ribbed; it was a pillar. It fell on its side and became small boulders, these became a wall, which became the wall of St George's in the middle of its graveyard.

Of course we make our own angels, thought Sara. No point in sitting about waiting for them. She jumped out of the churchyard and fell into the field. She could smell the scent of wild herbs and meadow flowers. The air was full of moths. She knew she was being followed but it didn't matter. Up in the sky there were a trillion crystal stars.

'I know you're there,' she called, without looking backwards. 'And I know you're a man because I can hear the weight of your footstep. You can walk with me, if you want to.'

'I will, thank you,' the man replied. She paused to let him join her. 'Do you remember me?' he asked.

'No,' said Sara, for his face was only a composite of shifting features.

'I'm Paul. Miranda is my lady. She's been working for you.'

'Look,' said Sara. They had stopped beneath The Wise Lady. 'They're having a firework display tonight.' The shooting stars left rocket trails.

'They do that every night, up there. It's just we don't always get to see it.'

They sat on the grass and a while passed. Eventually there didn't seem to be any point in having any clothes on.

'Wow! Oh, wow!' said Paul. 'All that hair. It's crazy. It's terrific. I've never seen so much of it.'

'It seems rather animal,' said Sara.

'Yes. Exactly. Terrific.'

'John's never done that to me,' Sara said after a moment.

'If you were my lady I'd never do anything else.'

'He's a rector,' said Sara, then she was silent. She slid along smooth lines of feeling; surging, subsiding, surging, subsiding, surging, surging, surging.

'Wait just a second,' said Paul. 'Yes, that's it. Oh, Christ. Oh, fantastic.'

Sara screamed. Never before. Her first ever orgasm. An almighty one. Each cell in her body was dancing. Paul gave a final, massive thrust. Sara felt billions of vibrant points of life rushing inside her. Across the valley she heard the clock of St George's begin to chime. She was lying on Paul's chest.

'Are you all right? Everything will be normal again tomorrow, you know. I'll stay with you till then.'

'Nothing will be normal ever again,' replied Sara.

Tomorrow least of all. When the stars had faded and the dawn had come, she would make her choices. Their lack of children was not her fault. It was neither of their faults, but especially not hers. She knew that beyond any doubt because, for five minutes now, she had been pregnant.

18

The Folly

'Dig, dig, dig!' cried Marjorie Sand.

It was dawn. Except for her and the three men the circle was empty. A pale lemon light coloured the eastern horizon. The stones were great charcoal masses of darkness surrounded by a woolly mist. Cuthbert and Algernon, who had done little digging in their lives heretofore, thought, ever-more-wistfully, of the elegant city they had hurried away from. Dennis Sand, the lucky recipient of Marjorie's maidenhead, had had, it turned out, what Mrs Sand termed 'awkward' feet. His wellingtons – finally and unfortunately located in Magpie Cottage's attic – rubbed their heels and blistered their toes. Their hands were becoming calloused. And still the stone did not budge.

Even Seymour's ardour seemed to have flagged.

'Are you sure, Mother,' he questioned, 'that the Lord really does want us to fell this boulder?'

'Oh yes, Seymour,' said Marjorie. 'I am merely his vessel. It is His will we perform.'

And Marjorie, if anyone, was in a position to know. She had hatched the idea, inspired, in part, by Tom Callan, but actually led by God. After her indignant return from the Rectory, while the men – flesh weak but spirit polite – dozed among the china, Marjorie Sand leafed through her Bible for justifications, precedents and handy hints. There was Babel, of course, and

Samson in the temple, but there were also heaps of others. By the time Marjorie had finished, the Bible read like a demolition manual. She stirred the men at first light, opening the door of Magpie Cottage onto a dewy, vacant world. They would destroy one of the pagan idols, or at least topple it over, Seymour would say a purifying prayer and then they would have breakfast.

Later, Marjorie would deal with John Feather's appalling rudeness to her after Sara's disappearance. Goodness knows, she had ammunition enough.

Unfortunately, however, the stone was proving more recalcitrant than Marjorie had envisaged. They had chosen one of the smaller ones, thinner than the rest, with a slightly pointed top but, even so, its root went down deeper than they had thought. It had never occurred to any of them, least of all Marjorie, how deeply lodged the stone circle might be in Wyley's earth.

Amidst the lemon a pale streak of tangerine now appeared. A cuckoo called. There was a sense of awakening that only served to intensify the men's tiredness. The spades slowed. Backs were rubbed.

'I think, Mother,' said Seymour, 'that we should probably cease before somebody sees us.'

'No, no, no,' cried Marjorie.

'There's someone over there,' said Cuthbert.

They looked across the fields in the direction he had indicated. In the distance, almost entirely obscured by the mist, there could have been a figure walking in the direction of Wyley Manor.

'Well, we'll start again tonight,' said Marjorie, shooting a cross little glance in Cuthbert's direction. 'Pack the earth back loosely so our work isn't spotted.'

'This afternoon,' said Algernon, 'me and Cuthbert are expected back at Oxford.' Marjorie's eyes bored into him. 'We've had a lovely time,' he added, nervously.

The sound of the birds woke Sir Homer.

He had never greatly cared for the dawn chorus. Whatever birds did in summer – laid eggs, or made nests or something or other – he saw no reason to wake people by singing about it. Especially since the first thought that came into his head was an irritating one, irritating enough to ensure that he would not be able to get back to sleep again: the stupid ineffectuality of the policeman. One would have thought that it was little enough to ask that Sergeant Tulliver should be able to frighten people effectively. It couldn't be that difficult, even if you had to do it with discretion.

Sir Homer pulled himself into a sitting position. Light came in through a chink in the heavy velvet curtains. Killing the dog had not only been unoriginal but in the worst possible taste. It had also suggested links with the Manor, should people choose to make them. Tulliver had, mercifully, neglected to mention it when he had phoned the previous afternoon, in his excitement about having arrested one of the travellers and 'done him over', whatever that meant. At that moment, it had seemed to Sir Homer that some progress was finally being made, but then the policeman had admitted that he had let the traveller go again. What on earth was the point of that? If you were going to arrest people you must detain them.

To the best of Sir Homer's knowledge the travellers were still happily ensconced in the byway, indulging in the hedonistic revels they were doubtless prone to indulging in, and with no intention of budging. And, all the time they were there, the danger that Flora might be discovered remained.

Thank God for Thomas Bright, that silver smokescreen. Thank God for the public meeting, for the interview with the *Guardian*! It was the way of all great men, and, of course, the prime-minister, to angle things in such a way that they chose the focus of people's attention. How fortunate Crispin Turner's question had been. Though he had found it curious at the time, Sir Homer now realised that it was merely a courtesy between servant and master, designed to underline, lest there be any doubt, the profundity of Wyley Manor's association with Thomas and, by implication, with the workings of government. It could not have been better timed.

Sir Homer was invaded with a warm glow of satisfaction. He would just have to start again with Tulliver, making his instructions precise, placing no trust in the policeman's imagination. Until then the situation was stable. The warm glow continued. Stable enough, in fact, to allow for slight indulgences.

Half an hour later he was standing in the folly, in his pink slip with matching panties and brassiere, deciding what to put on. The curtain was undrawn and sunlight streamed through the window. Flora loved the sunlight and it was too early to fear prying eyes. So intent was he on his task that he did not hear the footsteps approaching the folly.

Tomorrow he would go and see Martha and, afterwards, he would know everything: that was what he'd said to himself the day before yesterday. By now he'd expected to know all about what had happened that time in Wyley: if it had been Martha; what she and his mother had been crying about; how the photographer, if it was the photographer, fitted into the whole thing. The nearer he'd got to the answers, the more important they had become. Then the policeman had beat him up and he'd been too sick and frightened to go back to Martha's house. Now he wasn't sick any more, just stiff and there were bruises all over his stomach, but he was still frightened.

A large part of him wanted to get the hell out. If it wasn't for Melanie Flowerdew, he'd have backed up the inclinations of Paul and Ralph and Miranda and they might even have hit the road already. It was solstice eve. By midnight they had to be in a stone circle. They were all pissed off with Wyley. There was no hope they'd be allowed to get on with their rituals quietly, and there were too few of them for the rozzers to leave off because they were outnumbered. All common sense said to head in the direction of Stonehenge – whatever The Wise Lady desired of them, they weren't in a position to give it. There they'd meet up with lots of other convoys; some of them were bound to get through. It was just, he couldn't bear to leave her.

Josh had been knocked around enough to know that he was not immortal. He had learned how uncertainly life squatted the human body, always ready to fuck off to some other dimension. He knew how easy it was to get killed by mistake. He wasn't convinced that Sergeant Tulliver would go the whole hog and do him in, but he was sure that he would get close enough that it might happen accidentally.

Not to hear the birds singing in the woods on mornings like this, the patter of the rain falling on the ground, bashing on the bus roof, then stopping. And, later, Miranda, Paul and Emily's voices, as they got the fire going again.

What had they been up to? No point in asking. Miranda would just have told him to mind his own business.

'Are you sure this is going to work?' Paul asked. 'If it does it's one of the scientific break-throughs of the twentieth century.'

'The twentieth century? The twentieth?'

'You know what I mean, though. You could give it to the poor and sell it to the rich. Use the money for setting up communities – growing vegetables, making pots and jewellery, proper education.'

'You can't sell magic,' said Miranda. 'And it's only for occasional use.'

'Are you sure it will work?'

'Well, if it bloody doesn't you can fall back on your own devices, like you did with me.'

'A boy or a girl?' asked Emily. 'You hold a crystal over your stomach and watch the way it turns.'

Through the thin scarf that covered the bus window, Josh had been able to see the light from the fire. For a second it seemed to him that it changed colour, the vivid green of a Roman candle. A sweet, poignant scent filled the air. Herbs. Meadow grass. Hay. Sweat. Blood. Pollen.

'There. It's ready. Drink it.'

'What about those spiky things floating in it? Do I have to swallow them?'

'Yes,' said Miranda.

And then their voices were gone and it was just getting light and the birds were singing. And now he was walking through the woods and thinking how, whatever Karen had to say about any other dimension, however blissful they were there, however stuffed full of nirvana, it would take a lot to beat a summer's morning, even if you were shit-scared and fed up with mysteries. This was the right place for love. He couldn't imagine it being better anywhere else.

Love clung to the earth and refused to be celestial.

Love unlocked memories. Josh discovered that there had been times when he had been happy and simply not known it. In fact, he had thought himself unhappy. Those nights when he had lain in anonymous arms, had sex with faces he could not remember. The lighting of the gas with a box of matches carefully put in place for the purpose, the half bottle of cheap wine with the cork pushed back in it in the fridge, the setting of an alarm clock: all these things seemed pervaded with decency, himself a privileged witness to have been allowed to see the simple, intimate details of the lives of strangers. If it wasn't permanent, if it wasn't love, if it wasn't what he had ultimately wanted, well it had never pretended to be.

Josh emerged at the edge of the woodland, crawled under the brambley hedge and into the misty field, where the low sun was just beginning to turn the water drops pale blue. He made for the footpath – though the quicker way back to the camp would have been along the edge of the field – beckoned by his compulsion to tread paths that had already been asserted, however faintly.

When he reached the path, however, he paused just parallel to the folly. It would never have crossed his mind to walk up to it and look inside were it not for the fact that somebody's passageway across the wet field from the Manor garden was clearly marked by the deeper green of the pressed grass. He walked forward, his boots creaking moistly.

It hadn't been comfortable sleeping on the ground. They had woken, shivering, well before the sun. They'd walked up to the Rocester road and stuck their thumbs out when a lorry went past, still with its lights on. It stopped. The driver was taking a lorry drivers' shortcut. He was heading North, to Glasgow. He and Paul chatted. Sara thought of how exciting North sounded, dark and earnest, while South was a riot of colour and light. West was plains and East was spices.

The lorry driver dropped them off at a transport caff outside Rocester. They had large mugs of tea and bacon sandwiches. They talked for a long time about a variety of things. Paul told her why he thought drugs should be legal and what he saw as the role of mythology in modern society. Sara told Paul about her unsatisfactory wedding night in Cornwall and her sense of inferiority to her intellectual husband.

'Women often feel inferior,' said Paul. 'They're taught to. Don't buy into it.'

Don't buy into it. Sara felt ridiculously happy. Yes, it really was that simple: 'Not today, thank you.' She told Paul about Frija.

They got a bus back to Wyley. It was full of head-scarved cleaners from the Rocester council estate. When they alighted in the high street St George's was striking seven.

'Good-bye,' said Paul. 'It's been fun.'

'Yes,' said Sara, 'it has. Be careful. Or rather . . .' She looked at her watch. June 20th, 1985: Solstice eve, according to Miranda. 'Happy solstice for tomorrow, wherever you are for it.'

John hadn't locked the front door of the Rectory, presumably in case she'd gone without her key. Sara went softly up the stairs and put her nightgown on in the bathroom. She slipped into the bedroom. John was lying on his back, naked, under only a sheet. She studied him as he slept, seeing his character laid out, disordered, across his face – vulnerability, arrogance, compassion, eagerness, frustration, pride. As soon as she woke him, all those attributes would arrange themselves into the face he met the world with. Sara was moved. She wanted to touch him. But, before getting into bed, she went and stood at the open window. The heat was returning. She smelled the scents that the earth gave off as it heated: the rich, fruit-cake aroma of apple orchards; roses; deeper still, a fleshy smell that was perhaps only her own body, or last year's rotting petals. You could see the stone circle from up here. The stones floated in mist, mountain tops above cloud, islands in a white sea; a cidery sunshine dyed them amber.

'Sara?'

She turned. John was sitting up in bed, still half-asleep.

'What's going on?' he asked, rubbing his eyes. 'What's happening to us? To me? To Wyley? You'll never guess what happened after you left.'

Sara shook her head. She sank into the rocking-chair by the window, her hands crossed over her stomach.

'I went for Marjorie. Oh God, you should have seen me.'

'You mean you hit her?'

'No, at least, not literally. I came back at her with the Bible. I'd just had enough of her quoting it at me, as if it belonged to her, so I quoted back. She screamed judgement and wrath. I countered with mercy and forgiveness. It was the Old Testament versus the New, I suppose.'

Sara laughed. 'Which won?'

'God knows. She went off in high dudgeon, issuing all kinds of threats. I couldn't believe I'd done it. Do you think the stones really are making us all a bit crazy?'

Sara began to rock, slowly. 'No, we're making ourselves crazy.'

There was a silence, then John spoke, nervously.

'I don't know how much you heard last night Sara. I think you maybe only heard the last thing I said, which you must have known I didn't mean.' He glanced at her quickly, trying to read her expression, hoping, it appeared, that she would just let it go and they would be able to forget about it, or at least tuck it back in its neat container.

'But you did mean it, John.' Sara smiled, rather sadly. 'You chose me for my serviceable merits.' She shrugged. 'Rich men marry young women for their beauty; it's virtually the same thing. Most of us probably want to be chosen for "ourselves", whatever that might be. I don't know how many of us are.' She continued rocking, watching him steadily. He was stumbling.

'There's something else,' he said. 'You might as well know, and then you can decide whether or not you want to stay with me.' And he told her about Martha.

Sara listened with surprise, and a carefully concealed amusement. She had taken LSD, seen visions, made love with a stranger in the stone circle, conceived a child, hitch-hiked to Rocester. John had had a fumble with Martha Blandish on the sitting-room floor.

For the first time in her life, Sara felt very powerful.

'Well, John,' she said, when he had finished. 'I am not going to leave you. I am merely going to make an effort to love you less. And you must make an effort to love me more – and better.' She walked across the room and pulled her nightgown over her head and dropped it on the carpet. 'You must be frustrated,' she said.

'I didn't know it could be like that,' said John half an hour later. 'I mean, when Martha . . .' He stopped himself. 'I mean, I didn't think, for us . . .'

'You know,' said Sara, before they fell asleep, 'I've just had an idea. A surprise. A wonderful surprise for the opening of the Manor grounds.'

St George's struck eight, nine, ten, eleven. Sara opened her eyes to the sound of Melanie Flowerdew yelling up the stairs.

'Are you ever getting up or am I going to have to keep on answering the phone to your poxy parishioners? Martha's gone to the doctor's with Hamish for his check-up and there's already been six calls. They're all het up about St George's.'

'What about St George's?' Sara came downstairs in her dressing-gown. She tried not to blush when she saw that Melanie was eyeing her curiously. 'I'll make some tea. Do you want some, Melanie?'

'Long as it isn't herbal.' Melanie followed her into the kitchen.

'So, what's happened at St George's?' For a crazy minute Sara wondered if the whole of Wyley had spontaneously realised the truth about Frija: that, in nine hundred years or so of devotion, they had actually been worshipping a pagan goddess.

'The clock's started working.'

'Oh. Yes, I suppose it has. How funny.' But it didn't seem strange at all really. 'So, what are they asking?'

Melanie's green eyes stared at her impatiently. 'Why it's cranked up now, when that pillock from *Country Manner* couldn't get a squeak out of it. Oh, and Marjorie Sandbox has phoned to say that it's a sign of God's anger.'

Sara got the mugs down and poured a cup of tea for her and Melanie, and one to take up for John.

'What an odd way to show one's anger,' she said. 'Marjorie's God certainly does move in mysterious ways. If you don't mind dealing with things for about another twenty minutes, Melanie, I'll have a quick bath and get dressed.'

'Oh, all right.' Melanie took the mug Sara handed her. 'But what shall I tell them?'

'Tell them the clock-mender said the repairs might take a while to work.'

'Do you think they'll buy it?'

'It's more likely than it being the wrath of God. What Wyley believes doesn't usually have a lot to do with truth or logic.' Sara glanced at the newspaper on the kitchen table, turning it over to read the headlines.

'That's something else they're hot under the collar about,' said Melanie. 'Sir Fat-arse is going to be shitting himself.'

'"Crack-down on Unions"?' asked Sara, startled.

'No, it's a few pages in. There's this interview with Sir Fat-arse himself, wanking off over what pals he is with our stupid M.P., and going on and on about his land and his sodding stone circle. But they've got another piece with it. It's called "In the Footsteps of the Past" and it's by a professor from some university or other. Here.' Melanie found the page. She and Sara bent over it.

Above the first article was a picture of Sir Homer, looking at once pleased and portentous, as if he had just issued some particularly clever warning. Above the second was a picture of a fat, vigorous woman, in a rain-hat and wellingtons, holding a trowel, captioned 'Professor Morrow, on a dig in Northumbria'.

Sara skimmed the article. Professor Morrow, it emerged, was convinced that the byway outside Wyley, where the travellers were now camped, was the remains of an ancient road that had once crossed what was now Sir Homer's land, travelling through the stone circle itself. She had come to this conclusion firstly through study of the literature on the distribution of artefacts in the Wyley area and, latterly, from her own observation of the patterns of the landscape, made during a Sunday she had spent in Wyley two years earlier. At the end of the article she made a spirited argument for reinstating the ancient thoroughfare and thereby granting public access to the The Wise Lady, concluding:

'Before land enclosure, before barbed wire, before the "No Trespassing" signs of the present century, men and women had the right to wander where they pleased, without let or hindrance. Now even our public highways are liable to sudden closure at the whim of the authorities. Pathways, however, were meant to be walked upon and the road to be an open one.'

'Gosh,' said Sara. 'No wonder they're upset.'

'Yeah,' said Melanie. 'Mrs Blade went on like Sir Homer's land was her own back garden.'

'The thin end of the wedge, I suppose,' said Sara. 'Sir Homer is going to be very upset about it.' She closed the newspaper and picked up John's mug of tea. 'Literally, Melanie, twenty minutes.'

'Okay,' said Melanie. She went back to the study. Sara started the bath running and put John's tea on the bedside table. He was still asleep.

The phone rang. It was picked up, then she heard Melanie calling again. She went to the top of the stairs.

'What is it?'

'I think you'd better get John to take this one. It's some pissed off old geezer. He says he's the bishop.'

19 ∫

Clarification

Josh had stared at Homer King, in a pink petticoat and with drooping rubber breasts, and in his imagination there had blossomed a massive sunflower, at the centre of which was the stone circle. Each stone was a seed. There was a fair. Men and children rode on roundabouts. Josh danced with Melanie and Martha. Sergeant Tulliver danced with Nelson. Paul and Miranda danced with the rector and the rector's wife and Emily and Emily's unborn baby. Karen and Ralph formed a small ring with Carmine, bouncing in their arms, and Curdie, his feet off the ground. All the people from the Rose and Crown did a hokey-cokey in a long train, whose window-frames were arms, in and out of the stones. The two nutty women at the Manor and the pale men and women and children, who you saw in Wyley High Street, joined hands in an enormous chain.

Sir Homer King presided, on the arm of a kind gentleman, to make sure he didn't trip up and that his stilettoes didn't sink too deeply into the grass.

The Wise Lady Free Festival. Every Solstice. The Pathway To The Millennium. Everyone Welcome, Including Dogs And Other Animals.

Josh kicked one of the tyres of the Aquarius.

'Whoa there. Hang on. What's happening?'

Ralph's oily face appeared.

'Sorry, Ralph. Didn't think you were under there. Pissed off.'

247 •

'Kick that generator then, mate. See if you can get any life into it.' Ralph pointed a black finger in the direction of a heap of old rust.

But Josh didn't feel like kicking anything else – except himself. And, even so, he knew he'd done the right thing.

It was just that it had all been so fucking possible. The Lord of the Manor himself, done up in his transvestite gear, mouthing 'What do you want?' in a voice tight with shock and fear. 'Get on with it. What do you want? Money? Housing? Access to the stones?'

Look like he wouldn't keep the secret without being bribed and the danger of the policeman would disappear. They could celebrate the solstice in the circle in perfect peace. There would be no need for fear, no need to leave Melanie. Shit, they could even insist on a fucking festival. It was at that moment he'd seen the giant sunflower and all that Wyley could have been if it had just let itself. For one split second, like sodding Moses, he'd glimpsed the promised land and then . . .

Then he'd seen the inside of a caravan. A paraffin lamp. The lighting of a small stove. He'd smelled candy-floss and frying onions, heard the distant music of the fairground. He'd remembered various squats round Brighton. Joss-sticks burning. Thrashing shadows in the light from half-broken gas-fires. He simply couldn't do it. He couldn't threaten someone because of their sexuality. Not even for Melanie. Not even for the solstice. That was something he was just not capable of.

Which didn't mean he didn't wish he was.

'Nothing,' he'd mouthed back. 'I don't want anything.'

Miranda and Curdie appeared, walking through the woodland with a large basket of mushrooms. Carmine was on Miranda's back in a papoose. Karen must've gone off somewhere.

'Found any magic ones?' Josh asked, as she deposited the basket on the ground.

'No,' said Miranda. 'But we have got ceps for our solstice dinner.'

'We're going to celebrate the life of Nelson,' said Curdie. 'Look at this one, Josh. It's a whopper. We're going to send his dog spirit on the way with a blow-out. Karen thought of it.'

'Where is she?'

'Gone for a walk,' said Miranda. 'She is angry with us for thinking of leaving Wyley. She trusts in her ley-line. Get a cloth, Curdie, and we'll wipe them clean.'

'Where's Paul? He wasn't here when I got up.'

'No,' said Miranda. There was an expression on her face that told Josh to back off. 'You had departed by the time he came home. Now he's gone up to the Manor.'

'What for?'

'To see that man, Homer King. He's going to ask him, for the last time, if we can use the stone circle tonight. If he says no, we had probably best not stay in Wyley. The policeman they have here is a dangerous spirit.'

Josh thought of leaving Melanie. 'He's not a spirit. He's just a complete bastard. Policemen don't have spirits.'

'Maybe, Josh, evil spirits have policemen. Anyway, the result is the same. Wyley will not give us a successful solstice.'

Curdie came out of the bus with a cloth. He and Miranda started to wipe the mushrooms.

'Paul hasn't got a hope,' said Josh.

'He must try anyway.' There was a pause. Nobody spoke. Miranda wiped the mushrooms swiftly. She seemed to be thinking deeply about something. After a moment she appeared to come to a decision. 'Josh,' she said, 'I do not interest myself in your sexual business. However, there is danger near to us and so there is something I must say to you. Martha Blandish: she cannot be trusted. She is not a bad woman, I think, but she is a young soul. Young souls can easily work mischief.'

Josh shrugged, awkwardly. Sensing that he was dubious, Miranda stopped what she was doing and looked straight at him, until he felt forced to look back at her.

'I do not joke. When I was working at the Rectory I heard this Martha speaking with the policeman and the rector – who is a young soul, also. She told them she would come to see us, on Monday morning, to find out information. She promised she would not tell us of any legal rights that belong to us.'

A nasty feeling rose in Josh's stomach.

'What legal rights was she talking about? Why didn't you mention them before?'

Miranda returned to the mushrooms. 'We know what we are

not permitted to do,' she said. 'We know that, what we are doing, we are only doing because they have found no way of not permitting us. That is what your English legal rights amount to. You were the only one at the camp on Monday morning, Josh. Perhaps Martha Blandish did not visit us?' She stopped and looked at him again. Josh said nothing, but felt his face grow hot. Miranda resumed her work. 'I only repeat my warning. Do not trust a young soul. It is undecided and plays games which are very perilous.'

There was a dull thud as the generator fell on its side. A couple of the parts dislodged and rolled along the grass. Josh set out at a run along the byway, towards Wyley. Martha Blandish owed him some answers, and fuck the policeman.

After he had finished speaking to the bishop, Sir Homer King made his way to the drawing-room for morning coffee. It was important to behave as usual. The exertion of his influence in one quarter must remind him of his similar influence in others, and how desirable a thing such influence was. As he passed the Manor's gracious staircase, those ancestors, that might have been his, looked out upon him encouragingly, as ruff dwindled into cravat and on into tie.

How ironic that, when the thing he most feared had happened, Sir Homer's first emotion had been relief. No need now to be anything but Flora. He would keep Wyley Manor, allow nobody inside his stone circle; the travellers, or anyone else who wished to, could destroy his reputation. The old hag upstairs might go or stay, as she pleased. If she took it into her head to change her will, then all that would have to be done was to get her certified as senile, or mad as a hatter, or whatever the law required. Dr Oliver would comply. How foolishly strenuous Sir Homer's recent efforts had seemed to him in the beautiful sunshine: dogs and policemen, secret pathways under hedges, public meetings and interviews with the newspapers. Relief, nothing but relief, now that it was all over.

But then his mind spontaneously changed direction. Public meetings. Interviews with the newspapers. Thomas Bright. Thomas Bright everywhere. His name constantly upon Sir Homer's lips. 'I spoke, just before this meeting, to our M.P.,

Thomas Bright.' The new-bug journalist from Eton: 'Talked to Tommy Bright the other day. You two are still in touch, I daresay, how could you not be?' How could you not be? Old gossip that he had thought forgotten and that he himself had been vehemently confirming and renewing. Foolish, foolish, foolish. He had sought to protect Flora by evoking the name of Thomas Bright. And now, as a result of his stupidity and selfishness, if Flora, Sir Homer King, was publicly disgraced, Thomas Bright, M.P. for Rocester, was bound to fall with him.

Any sacrifice must be made to prevent it.

'What do you want?' he asked. Josh did not reply. 'What do you want? Money? Housing? Access to the stones?'

An expression came onto Josh's face that it was impossible for Sir Homer to read. It was gone by the time he spoke. Nothing. He wanted nothing. And, with that, he simply walked away, leaving Sir Homer with no choice but to believe him.

Air wafted into the drawing-room from the open French window. In a vase on the walnut table a group of casually arranged roses opened slowly. Cook entered with the coffee. For the first time, Sir Homer examined her face for the possibility of incipient treachery, wondering, as he did so, if there were ever a revolution in England of the muddled and bloody kind that happened in more distant places, to what extent Cook's loyalty would remain intact. To betray a Homer King or a Thomas Bright, for example: was this an idea that Cook would have scorned? Mulch? Miss Trannock? Those quiet facilitators of Sir Homer's existence abruptly took on personality, had feelings, ideas, noticed things, exercised judgement. He decided to give them all a small rise in salary.

'I'll bring the biscuits, Sir.'

'Don't worry with biscuits today, Cook.'

'Very well, Sir.'

She exited silently and Sir Homer bent forward to pour himself a coffee, wondering about Josh's possible motivations. Were some people quite simply good? This seemed preposterously unlikely. As he leant back in his armchair his attention was drawn to a copy of the *Guardian*, casually placed on the sofa. This was not a newspaper that usually found its way to Wyley

Manor. One of the staff must have purchased it, knowing about Sir Homer's interview. Crispin Turner most likely.

Sir Homer picked up the paper and found the page. The style of the article was mildly facetious, Thomas Bright's name a terrible, recurring chorus. His eye was drawn to the piece below and the photograph of the hefty archaeologist. Chagrin turned to rage, which turned to horror – a horror that was further exacerbated by the sight of two sandaled feet on the carpet by the French window and the knowledge that, after all, Josh had been lying.

The wonder was that Sir Homer had believed that Josh would keep his secret, a boy who came from a world where promises and lies were easy, uncircumscribed by any danger of calumny or disgrace. He had related the story to his companions and they had been struck, like Sir Homer himself, by the ridiculousness of not driving a bargain. They had egged him on to go back to Sir Homer with their conditions, but he didn't have the courage to, so this one had come instead. Now Sir Homer would be forced to give the travellers everything they wanted, to permit the hideous incursion the wretched archaeologist recommended in her article. No breath of scandal must be allowed to damage Thomas Bright.

'I came in the back,' said Paul. 'I didn't want to disturb anyone.'

'That was absolutely correct. Sit down.'

Paul hesitated. 'Are you sure? I'm a bit grubby.'

'That doesn't matter.' But it did. Dried mud fell off the trousers and settled on the armchair. Sir Homer reflected that, odious though Chummy had been, he had not been dirty.

'Coffee and biscuits?'

'That's awfully nice of you.'

Sir Homer rose and summoned Cook, who returned with another cup and saucer and a plate of biscuits. When she had gone, Sir Homer poured Paul's coffee. He expected him to fall on the food, to wolf it down, scattering yellow crumbs out of the sides of his mouth, the way that suddenly-fed beggars did in Sunday afternoon dramatisations of Dickens. He was surprised when, instead, Paul accepted the cup and saucer as if he had used such implements before, and placed only one biscuit on his plate.

'My name's Paul.'

'Homer.' Sir Homer swallowed and thought of those white sheets of long ago.

'I won't eat much because we're celebrating the death of our dog tonight. Or rather the murder.'

'You celebrate murders?' asked Sir Homer, drily, unsurprised.

'You mean like on Poppy Day? No, we're celebrating Nelson's life, I suppose I should say. We're sending his spirit on its journey joyfully.'

A horrible pang ran up Sir Homer's chest.

'Do you have any idea who killed him?'

Paul nodded. 'The policeman.'

'Oh.' Sir Homer's mind went back to his interview with Tulliver in the conservatory, among the plants. He despised the policeman for having got caught. 'Do you believe all that?' he asked, changing tack.

'All what?'

'Spirits on journeys, that sort of thing.' Sir Homer waved a hand slightly, in order to indicate other spiritual matters.

'Some of us believe it more than others. My approach is largely metaphorical. I suppose I believe in it as much as I imagine you believe in the Church of England. Perhaps I had better explain in more detail and then we can go onto the reason why I've come.'

'I know why you have come,' said Sir Homer quickly. Paul looked surprised. 'And there is no need for you to explain your motivations. I would probably not understand them.' He remembered how at school they had been told that, in the Middle Ages, people believed that the earth was flat, and that, if you went beyond the known world, and reached the edge, you would fall off into nothingness. The idea had caused a lively interest and a great deal of discussion. Sir Homer had liked to envisage these foolish people, in flimsy canoes, paddling purposefully towards the ultimate waterfall. Except, of course, that the world was not flat. It only seemed to be.

'But I'd like to explain, if I may,' said Paul. 'With all due respect, I don't think you are aware of what you possess.'

Sir Homer glanced around the clear room and out to the garden. 'I think I am aware of what I possess,' he said, thinking of other things, too – the London flat with its thick, olive-green silk curtains; his rarely-occupied but hallowed desk in the *Commentator* offices (most *Commentator* articles were written from rural or foreign retreats); his charm; his reputation. Thomas's reputation.

'If, however,' he added, squeezing every last drop of the satirical from his tone, 'you would like to inform me, then I am at leisure to listen.'

'To us . . .' Paul began.

'Us?'

'People like me.'

He made an expansive gesture and Sir Homer imagined them, row upon row of hippies, a faulty thread in the fabric of society. It was a bit like it would have been to realise that he had head lice.

Sir Homer nodded for Paul to continue.

'To people like me, stone circles are holy places. We bring to them, as I said, a variety of ideas and hopes, like anyone brings to any religious centre.'

'My stone circle, then, is deemed similar in that respect to Rome, Jerusalem and Mecca, for example,' said Sir Homer, unable to keep himself from adding, 'and suppose the centre of my worship was in the middle of one of your vehicles and I insisted on occupying it once a year, regardless of your wishes.'

'Then I hope we could talk about it and work things out so you could do what you wanted,' said Paul.

'Should you ever possess any kind of property,' said Sir Homer, 'you will find that you will be less inclined to generosity. It is easy to make magnanimous gestures in the abstract.'

'That's unfalsifiable,' said Paul, 'though you may be right. Anyway, what I mean is, we use this focal point as a celebration and consolidation of all that we would like to achieve.'

'You must forgive me for finding this rather ineffectual,' said Sir Homer through tightened lips.

'Oh, I do. For instance, I have never been able to understand what people hope to achieve by going to church. Though I suppose a church is a good sort of example in that one doesn't consider it private property and, in theory at least, anyone can go there at any time.'

'They are locked against thieves,' said Sir Homer swiftly.

'Supposing,' said Paul, smiling, 'we promise not to steal any of the stones?'

Sir Homer King studied the young man's face. What a waste. In other circumstances such an individual, obviously intelligent, might have been someone that Sir Homer could have wanted to know. 'You are squandering your talents,' he remarked.

'That's what my father says.'

There was a silence. Sir Homer determined upon bringing matters to a conclusion.

'You wish to celebrate the solstice in my stone circle,' he said, 'and you do not believe that I am in a position to refuse your request.'

'In the light of what I have said, no. We'd go there late tonight and be around to see the dawn.'

This struck Sir Homer as sly. No open threat of exposure, not even an implication. Had the conversation been recorded there was nothing upon which to build an accusation.

'And what will you do if I do not comply?'

Paul shrugged. 'I don't know,' he said, chillingly and, again, slyly.

Sir Homer stood up and walked over to the French windows. He stared at the gentle woods that cushioned his gaze from the stones, those compulsive antennae that sent out a signal at a pitch too high or too low for him to hear. Might one presume that the tourists, regularly disengorged throughout the summer to look at the church's two stones and, if it was open, to wander, dully, around the church, pushing thin pennies through the slot of its collecting box for lepers, had also heard the signal? Or were they, as seemed more likely, only ticking off another item in their pursuit of the antique?

'And next year?' he asked bitterly, turning to look at Paul. 'And the year after that? Am I to expect your regular return, my own particular migratory parasite?'

'I can't say about that. We'll celebrate the solstice, of course, but how and where I don't know.'

'If you are to celebrate anything in my circle I will need your assurance that you will not return next year. Can you give me that?' Sir Homer's voice quavered. He became aware that he was trembling.

'I don't like making decisions on behalf of the others.' Paul looked uncertain.

'I need to know now or no agreement will be undertaken.'

Paul thought a moment. 'All right. I can square it with them.'

Sir Homer turned back to the window.

'I'd better go, I suppose. I want you to know, though, how much I appreciate this.'

Sir Homer glanced round sharply, an exclamation on his lips. He stifled it and Paul said nothing more. He left, as he had arrived, through the French windows, down the lawn, and under the hedge.

Josh arrived at Martha's house, kicked open the front door and made his way to the kitchen. He stood, panting, by the kitchen table, where Martha was unloading groceries from recycled plastic bags. He picked up a carton of free-range eggs and slammed it onto the floor. It cracked open. Yolk and white trickled out.

'You'd better get out of here, Josh,' said Martha. 'I don't want you to visit again.'

'What're you going to do, call the police?'

Martha continued to unload her groceries. 'I will if I have to. Really, believe me, I'm not lying, it's better if you go now. For me. For you. For Melanie.'

'You fucking betrayed us. You knew we had some kind of right to be in the byway. You came to the camp and acted all friendly, you fucking seduced me and all the time you were on their side.'

Martha ran some water onto a cloth and picked up the dripping egg-box.

'It isn't a question of sides, Josh,' she said. Her calmness enraged him.

'Of course it's a question of sides. That's what it's all about. Sides are the fucking issue.' Without thinking, he raised a fist and smashed it into the kitchen door. The wood shattered. It was agonising but it made him feel better. He collapsed into a chair. 'I just want to know the truth,' he said, 'and then I'll get out of here.'

There was a long, long silence. Martha dropped the carton into a pedalbin and squatted and wiped up the mess. He watched her.

'What truth are we talking about?' Martha asked. She rinsed the cloth and replaced it on the tap. She put away the last groceries, folded the bags and put them in a drawer. She sat down at the table.

'Do you want some ice on that?'

Josh glanced at her, resentfully. She looked more like a mother than a lover, much older than he remembered.

She sighed. 'I didn't tell you about any legal rights because I forgot about them. There wasn't anything to say anyway, it was terribly vague.'

'We need to know everything.' He spoke through clenched teeth. 'You came to get information.'

Martha smiled faintly. 'I didn't ask any important questions, did I? I even had to remind myself what I was supposed to be doing at the camp – it wasn't why I went there. You see, there was no question I could have asked that I didn't already know the answer to.'

'Yeah, you know all the fucking answers.' Josh's fist was throbbing like shit. 'I'm not going until you tell me.'

Martha leant forward and tried to look into his downturned face. 'Will you go if I tell you that it's better you don't know about me and your father and mother, and that it's vital that you don't go near Melanie?' Josh raised his head. Martha nodded. 'Yes, it was us that day in Wyley. Now go, please go, celebrate your solstice, get out of Wyley.'

Her face was pale and frightened. 'No,' said Josh, 'I'm not moving. Unless you call your policeman and get him to beat me up again.'

There was a pause.

'I want to know the truth,' Josh repeated. 'Let me know that and then I can make a decision about what's best for everyone.'

Martha buried her head in her hands and rubbed her face violently.

'There's no choice but that,' said Josh.

There was another silence. He could hear the sound of distant children's voices on the village green. Martha cupped her hands under her chin and looked at him. 'All right,' she said, hopelessly. 'Make your decision. Listen.'

A peace descended upon the room. Josh breathed loudly, his mouth slightly open.

'In 1968,' said Martha, 'I was seventeen.' She paused a moment at the memory. 'Most people were then, or not much older. I mean, they seemed to be. I was going to go to art college. I drew all the time, and I painted. In 1967 I even sold a picture. It was a charcoal of The Wise Lady. Anyway, it was probably because we both liked art that made me fall in love at that rock festival, that summer in 1968. We wore long skirts then. I had a patchwork one. And bare feet. We really did put flowers in our hair, but mine's thin, so they fell out a lot.

'He was an artist, too, and a photographer. He liked photography especially. I remember he took a picture of me wearing one of those big floppy hats we all wore, and a poncho. We didn't know I was pregnant when he took it. He was the only man who was anything more to me than marking time, though I suppose I've felt affection since, love I suppose you could call it. He knew about all sorts of things, but it was more the way he could pull them together to make new senses. After he was gone the world got muddled and I didn't have the heart to make any more pictures. In fact, I hated them. His name was Jacob Flowerdew.'

Josh let his breath out slowly. 'That's my name, Jacob.'

'Yes,' said Martha.

'Does Melanie know?' Josh asked.

'She knows she was conceived at a rock festival with a stranger. She doesn't know why her surname is Flowerdew.'

'Why not?'

Martha thought a moment. 'Conceiving a baby,' she said, 'is only to do with two people, whatever anyone believes later. As soon as Melanie knew she'd got a different name from mine she just thought it was silly.'

'So where does my mother come into all this?'

'Jacob and me went different ways after the festival. That was the way it was done then, or we thought it was. I never knew much about him, really, though I had his baby. I suppose he'd met her a year or so before he met me. I suppose she'd got pregnant too and had his baby.'

'Me,' said Josh, though it felt like a different person and sounded like somebody else's story. It was old and he was young.

'And Wyley?'

'That was later. '71, '72 perhaps. He'd come to see the stones I expect. Perhaps he even remembered my sketches of them. Though he was surprised to see me. Well, you didn't expect people to stay long in the place they'd started.'

'You fought with my mother about him?'

Martha nodded. 'Wasn't it hopeless and silly? But I was still young, even then, and worn out. Melanie was a terrible baby. Your mother was young, too. We were both in love with him.'

'He sounds like a shit.'

'No,' said Martha slowly. 'Though there wasn't any point in fighting over him. I thought he was hers. She thought he was mine. The truth was he was nobody's. He didn't belong to anyone. That was what we both realised suddenly. I can't remember who started crying first. We were in the same boat, you see, so there was nothing to argue about. He wasn't a shit, he was a free spirit. Free spirits always have an edge to them.'

'And the picture?'

'I cut it out of an old newspaper that I found lying about a few months later. I liked your mother, Josh. I felt for her. Over the years I kept it because I thought that probably she was making a better job of things than I was. I liked to think of her, sort of unchanged and young and untroubled, while I worried and got older.'

'It didn't work out like that.'

'I know.' Martha glanced at the clock. 'I've got to go in a minute. Melanie's covering for me at the Rectory. But now you can see, Josh,' her voice became pleading, 'now you can see what I'm talking about when I say you've got to leave Wyley as soon as possible. It's all been so difficult. I couldn't help Melanie at the public meeting when she went there to defend you, or rather, I maybe could have a bit. I could have perhaps remembered something, or maybe I couldn't, I don't know, it was all so long ago . . .'

'She went to defend us?'

'Oh, Josh,' Martha wailed, 'she's in love with you. Which is why you're going to have to leave here. I hoped you would leave because of the meeting. I didn't know Melanie would be so forceful and the whole thing would be such a shambles. And Tully. Well, Tully's just rather careless. He wouldn't hurt you properly. Not properly. I couldn't get involved because that would involve Melanie. Though that didn't work, either. She rushed down to the station as soon as she knew you were there. Nothing's worked to get rid of you. Telling you the truth has been my last resort.'

Josh was confused. 'Why does this mean we've got to go?'

But Martha had stood up. 'Think about it,' she said. 'Just think about it. And then please please please, get out of Wyley.'

He heard her go upstairs and then her footsteps in the room above. He heard her come downstairs again.

'Martha,' he called, but the front door slammed shut behind her.

So that was the past. Josh continued to sit at the kitchen table. He thought of his mother and her absurd self-extinction, Martha and her discarded art. He thought of his father, the free spirit, and he realised why his mother had tried to stop him from going to the fair every year. It would have been the fair that his father left with, or something like it. But the fair had taken Josh anyway. After that night with the man in the caravan he hadn't wanted to go home again, back to the place where nothing happened.

Josh wished he could take that little chunk of time and give it a shake, and tell it not to be static. He hoped his father was still wandering somewhere, even if he sometimes hurt people. He was sure, beyond any doubt, that he had been taking them to see the stones on the day they met Martha. And it was the stones that had brought Josh here too, thirteen or so years later. Because of them he had met Melanie Flowerdew.

Realisation dawned. That was what Martha was getting worked up about. That was why she wanted to get rid of him. Melanie Flowerdew was his half-sister.

Josh smiled to himself. Stupid. Old. Other people's problems.

How could it make any difference to them? How could it do anything but bring them closer to each other? It would only be easier to be lovers when you knew, already, that you were brother and sister. Yin and yang. Feminine and masculine. The muddled past dealt with and discarded.

Leave Melanie Flowerdew? Whatever was Martha talking about? Melanie had always been there for him. She'd hidden him after the Midsummer Night's Dream thing at the Rose and Crown, even though she was suffering because he'd slept with Martha. She'd come to the police station as soon as she found out he was in there. No question. Before that, she'd tried to get them to defend themselves at the public meeting. When they refused she'd gone and done it herself. Successfully, from what Martha said. Josh choked. He wiped his arm across his eyes swiftly.

The front door opened and closed. Melanie Flowerdew walked into the kitchen, saw him, and her face lit up. She was beautiful. Josh knew, in that minute, he had been forgiven.

'Oh, you're here. That's what Martha's so het up about. I passed her in the High Street but she didn't want to talk to me.' She noticed the splintered panel that Josh had put his fist through. 'Did you do that?' Josh nodded. 'Wow.' She looked impressed. 'That's what Martha does to you.'

Josh stood up. He pushed his hair back from his forehead. Melanie stopped smiling and her face took on a serious expression. She blushed. Josh looked into her eyes. They were green. His were hazel.

'I've got something to tell you,' he said. 'Actually, lots of things, but one in particular.'

He wanted to say how wonderful he thought she was, how wise and lovely. He wanted to say how much he liked her changing expressions and the sound of her bolshie voice and her courage. In the end, though, he just told her that he loved her.

For a moment she said nothing and he thought she might still be angry, and then she started crying.

He held her in his arms and kissed her black hair. He boiled a kettle and made them both a cup of coffee. They sat together holding hands and he told her about his mother and Martha and Jacob Flowerdew. He told her about the man in the caravan and the other, similar encounters with gentle strangers. He told her about the girl in the phone box, and about him and Martha. It was like recounting stories that they had each already heard and each forgotten.

After a while they went upstairs and undressed and got into bed together.

As he took Melanie Flowerdew's virginity, as he felt the stickiness of her blood on his body, Josh imagined that they were not in her bedroom, but in the stone circle. Night or day, dawn or twilight, there they were, among the grasses, escaped from time because time was too immense to matter, no death or regret there, no past to clear up after. If anything pleased The Wise Lady, it was surely this, to see them together.

They fell asleep and woke when they heard Martha's voice calling up the stairs. Josh tried to avoid seeing her stricken expression as he walked past her.

20

A Ride

St George's clock struck six. Early evening drinks at the Edelsteins', with its usual mix of the semi-famous and semi-talented, and Sir Homer would much rather not have gone. Everything, however, must continue as normal and this was as good a place as any to begin to account for the travellers being permitted to celebrate the solstice in his circle.

Sir Homer was well aware that his gesture would demand explanation, not to mention justification. Should he try to pass it off as a bit of self-indulgent whimsy on his part? Something that he fancied might be amusing? The thought of Wanda Edelstein's large, mittel-European face flanked by two heavy, lantern-like earrings, bought for a song in some distant market, staring incredulously down its aquiline nose at him made this option unappealing. On the other hand, to claim an iota of allegiance with the forces of disorder, a modicum of comprehension concerning the travellers' motives, would be no better. Could he, he wondered, hint that matters were beyond his control; introduce, perhaps, the idea of some hitherto undisclosed archaic law, tiresome but unrepealed, allowing right of fallow, or whatever? This struck him as a rather good plan since it would mean that he would be pitied and sympathised with.

'Oh, poor Homer.' He imagined Wanda's hand, loaded down with Indian silver, patting his maternally. 'You shall come and dine with us at Rules and tell us all about it. We will pay, won't we, Harald?' Turning to her husband as if he were floating a few inches above her, then lowering her head, seemingly disorientated to find him standing on the carpet, raising to his lips a blini anointed with smoked salmon and sour cream. 'We will pay. Yes we will. We insist.'

Sir Homer's black Jaguar glided towards the fork in the road by the war memorial. Could he coerce his friends' credence in an ancient law's tenacity, he wondered? Another, more possible, scenario presented itself.

'But, my dear Homer, what are they thinking of at Dudley & Brownsmith? Harald will get you an appointment with Cuthbertson, Little & Thyssen.'

Was there, Sir Homer wondered, a sort of non-statute, unwritten law, binding but inretrievable that even Franz Thyssen would be unable to search out and eradicate? Maybe. Maybe not. All in all everything was hideous. Insupportable. Totally and utterly unjust. Were it not for Thomas . . .

It was indiscreet but when, suddenly, a tall form, emerging from the front garden of one of the cottages, caught the corner of Sir Homer's eye, he pulled to the side of the road, lowering his shoe so heavily onto the brake that the car came to an abrupt halt, just outside the village school.

Once a year Sir Homer King went there to give out prizes on speech day, a dull duty that he had been constrained to take on the year after Lady Polly had a fall in the playground. He would have been instantly recognised if there had been anyone there to see him but, thankfully, even the most enthusiastic teachers had now gone home and the mongoloid adolescent who did the sweeping had likewise returned to wherever he emanated from. The only people visible were Sir Homer King and Josh, who had come to a standstill, surprised at the sight of a Jaguar stopping beside him.

Sir Homer leaned over and spoke through the open window.

'Get in. I want to talk to you.'

Even as he said it he realised there was no point in expecting a response but, to his surprise, Josh opened the door and lowered himself quickly onto the black leather upholstery, fastened a gleaming seatbelt and, as the car pulled off, ran a roughened hand over the mahogany dashboard. Sir Homer pressed a button and the sun-roof closed. Josh watched it. He pushed another button and the windows sealed shut. Josh watched this as well, with such evident fascination that Sir Homer wondered if he were perhaps under the influence of some drug that imbued the commonplace with particular and silly significance. He glanced quickly at Josh's face, and then away again. He had rarely been in the presence of happiness and found it disconcerting.

They drove for a couple of miles, neither of them speaking. Then, 'I never thought I'd get to go in one of these,' said Josh and Sir Homer King – realising that here lay the key to his compliance and that he was, to all intents and purposes, giving a hippy the ride of his dreams through a gorgeous summer evening in one of the most select slices of countryside in England, perhaps in the world – burst out in a torrent of muffled rage.

'Do you think that I am doing this for your amusement, or for mine?'

'I don't know why you're doing it,' said Josh mildly. 'I'm just enjoying the experience, that's all.'

Sir Homer was struck at that moment by two sensations. One, incredulity that anyone could 'just enjoy' experiences without wondering what was the catch, the other a hunger to touch the happy beauty of Josh's young face. He swallowed them both.

'I cannot, of course, expect you to understand concepts that to me are second nature,' he said, as calmly as possible. 'And now you have the option of ruining a reputation that it has taken me many years to build and foster you will doubtless be tempted to if I am anything less than courteous. I must, however, speak and you must hear what I have to say.'

'Okay.' Josh yawned and stretched his long, bare arms.

'If you wish to celebrate whatever pagan nonsense you adhere to in my circle this evening, I obviously have no choice now but to agree, but let me say that I allowed myself to think that maybe some vestigial traces of a Christian education might lurk in the otherwise ethically bereft confines of your personality.'

Josh took a large breath. His face broke into a massive grin. 'I didn't expect this,' he said. 'It's great. Everyone'll really appreciate it.'

There was a silence. They drove past a tumbledown barn

among whose rotting hay a black and white cat slept in the sunshine. Sir Homer hardly dared to believe what he might be hearing.

'They don't know already?' he asked softly.

Josh thought. 'I suppose they might, if you mentioned it to Paul. I don't know.'

'You yourself, however, have not spoken to your colleague?'

'Colleague?'

'Paul,' said Sir Homer, trying to avoid sounding either eager or impatient.

'Nah, I haven't seen him at all today. Miranda told me he was coming to see you.'

There was a silence. Sir Homer's mind worked quickly. It was evident that Josh had not yet betrayed him; it also looked as if he truly did not intend to. 'Can you,' he asked, 'reiterate to me the promise you implied this morning?'

'About what?'

Sir Homer said nothing.

Josh looked momentarily irritated. 'I won't let on about you being a transvestite, if that's what you mean.' Sir Homer winced. 'I can't prove that or anything. But I won't. I never would. You just don't if people don't want you to, though it's not something to get hung up about, anyway.'

Sir Homer stopped the car. They were still not far from Wyley now because he had been circling the village, no great distance from the topic of their conversation: the only thing that they would ever have to talk about, the only place where their interests could possibly overlap. It occurred to Sir Homer that there must be as many as ten or fifteen other stone circles in the United Kingdom and that it was only random, unhappy chance that had brought this boy and his companions to The Wise Lady. A different decision and their paths would never have crossed. This thought engendered a fresh rush of resentment. He forgot that they had singled out, not Sir Homer King, for their special attention, but his stone circle. He forgot as well that, scattered across the land, there were many other Homer Kings (some of whom he knew) who also possessed things that other people might feel they had a right to and who were equally deserving of being spared the horrible incursions that are always possible, though mercifully unlikely.

It could be that the travellers did not make decisions, though, that this reckless devotion to 'experience' for its own sake led them to wander, errantly, until some drooping contour scooped them up and trawled them in. A wobbling universe that could only be made sense of by attaching all kinds of significance to objects and events – stone circles, solstices, etc. – as people had done in primitive times. Was Josh, even now, constructing a view of his day in which some kindly god or spirit, or churning karma, decreed that today he would get to ride in a car that he had never thought he would ride in? The idea was distasteful, not least because Sir Homer King was not accustomed to viewing himself as the tool of other, greater powers.

How could one believe that, not three miles from here, Wanda Edelstein was raising her heavy hands to light beeswax candles, carefully placed in the bronze candlesticks that she herself had designed and had made up by a craftsman in Stavanger? Could one imagine even a world that could accommodate this silent youth and Harald Edelstein, turning his Cartier watch to his jowly face and saying, 'Homer is late.' Quite quite impossible.

And yet Homer King now believed that Josh was telling the truth and had not betrayed him and, moreover, never would, in any circumstances, for reasons that he perceived were as binding upon his . . . conscience, one must call it, for want of a better word, as other ideas might be upon Sir Homer's. This much he perceived, but no more. What those reasons were he could not begin to imagine.

'Tell me one thing,' said Sir Homer, his hands resting on the steering wheel, looking at Josh, whose lips were full and whose cheeks were flushed and beautiful. 'If I hadn't given you permission to enter my stone circle tonight, would you have done so anyway?'

Almost he hoped that Josh would say no, but Josh nodded. 'Yeah. The stones want us.'

Sir Homer's lips tightened into a grim expression. 'You may enter my property at eleven o'clock precisely. I'll drive you back to the village.'

*   *   *

'So you see,' Paul concluded as Josh walked up, 'it proves my point. It's just a question of asking people to listen to you and then explaining things to them. He was quite reasonable, and now we get to celebrate the solstice in the stone circle.'

'My baby is going to be a solstice baby,' said Emily, swinging in the hammock.

'We can drive the buses in about an hour before midnight. We can light fires and watch for the sunrise.' Paul was grinning all over his face.

'What's he gone and changed his mind all of a sudden for?' asked Karen. She was working on a garland of dried flowers. Josh sat down beside her and lifted the tea-pot to see if it had any tea in it. It didn't.

'My magic tongue,' said Paul brightly.

'The kettle's going to boil soon,' said Miranda.

'S'pose people do change, sort of,' said Ralph, sucking on his roll-up, which had gone out. He plucked it from his mouth and picked a hanging bit of tobacco out of its dampened end then hunted through his pockets for his matches. 'I mean, when you think of what you were like when you were a kid, you know I was sort of really, really interested in insects, but then my Dad got this old motorbike and I got interested in that, and it kind of went on from there. I don't think about insects much now.'

'Exactly what I mean,' said Paul. 'Sometimes you've just got to accept that good things do happen.'

'You think we should believe that, just because you get it into your head to go and talk to Sir Codfish, he suddenly turns into a fucking socialist?' said Karen.

'Stranger things have happened.'

'Not much.'

Paul watched her fingers working on the garland. 'Why can't you just feel good about this?'

'What's to feel good about? Why should we make a big deal about being given our basic rights?' asked Karen. 'And why should we have been all set to run away if we didn't get them?'

'Jeee-zus. They aren't basic rights to him. To him we have no rights at all. It's as if he's giving us an enormous present.'

'Presumably he feels the same way when he pays his paltry taxes.'

'Presumably he does. But what does it matter? The way forward is going to involve understanding people like Homer King.'

'What is there to understand? Greed, egotism and selfishness. Did I leave anything out?'

'You left out humanity,' said Paul primly.

'Oh, Christ.'

Josh reached for the Rizlas and started to roll a joint. He didn't want to hear Karen's voice. Now he had Melanie he was vulnerable. He couldn't even risk thinking of Homer King not being legit. He remembered the session in the police station: the pain, those punches in the stomach so he couldn't breathe or speak, the humiliation.

It was puzzling, why Homer King had changed his mind. Josh's heart began to hammer. He lit up and took a deep drag, held it in as long as possible and let it out, coughing.

'Where have you been, Josh?' asked Miranda.

'About,' said Josh, not wanting to give details.

'You got out of a black car at the end of the byway.'

'Yes,' said Josh. 'It was Homer King's. He drove me round a bit.'

The others stared at him, incredulous.

'Brill!' said Curdie.

'So what did he say?' asked Paul.

Josh shrugged. 'Said we could go into the circle at eleven.'

'There.' Paul was triumphant. 'Confirmation.'

Josh felt better. Maybe Homer King had simply been grateful for his attitude and wanted to return kindness for kindness. Maybe Paul, similarly educated, had been able to talk to Sir Homer in a way that they both understood but that Josh would never have arrived at, however long he'd tried. Was there, he wondered, not just an accent but a whole language that he hadn't ever heard? Would changing things be simple if you could manage to tap into that language?

It occurred to him that there was no way in which he understood Homer King. He didn't even know where to begin considering him, so there wasn't any point in trying to figure why he did what he did. He was only a shadow, defined by what he possessed. You could guess where he'd gone to school and university, you knew he had power (though that power was, itself, hazy; he wasn't a judge or a politician, for instance). But what did he do? What experiences had shaped his personality? What did he eat, and when, and, when he did eat, what did he call the meals?

When you got down to it, Josh knew as little about Homer King's life as he did about the lives of nomads or aborigines or people in the South American Rainforest or on the edges of the Nile. Less, in fact, because, with them, there were quite a few points of contact and, anyway, you could always read about them in books. But there were no books about Homer King. Of course, there was a whole load of stuff about stately homes and acts of parliament, but if you went to a library and said, 'I want a book on this species', they wouldn't know where to start looking. Nobody wrote about it because it was just too normal.

Now a definite crime was about to be committed. Sir Homer knew the exact form it would take and the exact hour at which it would be enacted. He was completely in control of things. This was not vague, unprosecuteable trespass. It was planned and premeditated. What it lacked in threat could be provided by a more-than-willing police force, which would arrive precisely on time, with all the legal equipment it needed in order to do exactly as was wished of it.

The entire situation would be cleared up quickly. Thomas Bright would be safe forever. Sir Homer could say this without any doubt because he had realised suddenly that, when the travellers left, Flora would go with them. She had seen too much of the kind of world she would like to inhabit to be able to stay in Wyley. And, as an added protection, Sir Homer would give Thomas up. From now on, they would only meet at official functions.

He stopped the car outside Wyley police station and, before getting out, dialled the Edelsteins' number on his car-phone.

The maid answered.

'Edelstein residen'.'

'Homer King here.'
'I call Mizeez Edelstein.'
'There's no need.'

But the receiver had been placed on the exquisitely simple Shaker table that Harald had had imported from Pennsylvania for Wanda's fortieth birthday. Sir Homer heard Wanda's voice in the background. 'How often must I reiterate it? You must take messages. It's not hard. I myself am a foreigner. You have been here six months now.' Then, the tone taking an elastic leap, 'Homer. You are not disappointing us I hope?'

'Not at all. I am, however, going to be a little late. Twenty minutes, perhaps slightly longer. Will you accept my apology?'

Wanda Edelstein would.

Sergeant Tulliver liked animals. He wasn't potty about them, like Martha was, but he'd always had it in mind to get himself a dog. So it had pained him more than a little to get rid of the mongrel that hung around with the travellers. It had made him feel a bit sick, even. But there was no denying that the dog bit him, and dogs that went round biting people were dangerous to the community, and it was the duty of the police force to deal with that kind of problem. Not to mention, thinking of eyes, the eye for an eye thing, that had always struck him as more sensible than what you had at the moment. If the travellers wanted it that way, they could have it that way. They killed Lady Poll's dog, Sergeant Tulliver killed theirs. There was no way you could argue with the logic of that, no matter how many degrees you'd got.

On the other hand, it must be admitted, some people didn't frighten easily. Living in the country must be making him soft. He'd forgotten how hard it was to cause an effect on that sector of society. Dog dead. No hysteria. No tears. Least of bleeding all, no fucking off. Tully imagined what Martha would do in similar circumstances. It'd send her round the twist, quite literally. They might have to put her away for a while in The Queen Elizabeth in Rocester – no, hang on a sec, that was closed down now, well somewhere like it, and give her electric shocks so that the part of her brain that thought about dogs died on her and she felt better again. The policeman wondered if the bit that thought about dogs was the same bit as thought about rabbits and guinea-pigs and cats that they put shampoo in the eyes of and monkeys they gave cancer. If it was, good riddance, Martha'd be better off without it and he wouldn't have to look at her tits always plastered with something covered in blood or caught in a trap.

No, one must be honest, it plain hadn't worked. Wasted effort. Still, there was no need to let on to Sir Homer King, who was striding into the police station, looking very pleased with himself thank-you very much, and who would probably be thrilled to bits. Tully wouldn't be able to say they'd gone, since they hadn't, but he could drop a mighty hint that they were dead rattled.

'Evening, Sir Homer. To what do we owe the pleasure?'

Sir Homer wasn't as cordial as he had been the other day. They were like that, that kind of people.

'Good evening, Tulliver. I need to speak to you, as briefly as possible, I haven't a lot of time. Can we go somewhere where we won't be interrupted?'

'Policemen are always being interrupted, Sir Homer. It's the nature of the job.'

'Somewhere where we are less likely to be, then.' With strained patience.

The sergeant opened the counter and led Sir Homer into his office. He pulled up a chair for him, brushed some crumbs off the desk, put the plate with the old sandwich on the floor and seated himself in his customary chair. In this position he felt in charge.

'S'pose you've heard about the dog,' he said triumphantly, lolling backwards. 'Forgot to mention it on the phone. I was the one that did it. Given them a nasty scare that has.'

'Yes,' said Sir Homer, dryly. 'I know you did. And so, incidentally, do they.'

The policeman was startled.

'Come again?'

'They know you did it. Due, I presume, to the bite marks on your arms.'

Tully stared at his arms as if the marks had suddenly appeared. 'Anything could have done that,' he said, defensively.

'Yes, indeed. I imagine you are frequently bitten, by all manner of things: cats, rabbits, hamsters, people.'

'It happens,' said the policeman sulkily.

'Anyway, the miserable failure of that ploy of yours – not very original, was it? – is not what I have come here to discuss.'

'I represent all of the people,' said Sergeant Tulliver, feeling that this point was somehow relevant.

'Indeed you do. And it is on behalf of all of the people that I am here. I have some information pertaining to the travellers' projected activities that I feel might be useful to you.'

'Not planning on picking flowers again, are they?' said Tully rudely.

If Homer King noticed the insult it did not register on his face.

'I have information – that I know to be accurate – that the travellers are planning a mass invasion, a mass trespass, onto my land, most specifically the stone circle, at eleven o'clock tonight.'

Sergeant Tulliver's ears pricked up. 'Am I not right in recollecting that trespass has already happened previously?' he asked cautiously, trying not to show his excitement.

'Indeed it has, Sergeant.'

'And you instigated no procedure against it?'

'What was the point? You yourself informed me it would serve no purpose.'

'And in what ways is this occasion different, Sir Homer?' queried the policeman, experiencing a queasy renaissance of respect.

'Well firstly, Sergeant, it is to be a mass invasion. I could well experience concern for the safety of myself and my property, a fear that violence would be the result of a gathering such as this. We do not, after all, have any idea as to the number of people that can be expected; we may suspect that all manner of crimes are intended to be committed.'

'Disorder,' yelped Tully, his forehead breaking out in a sweat. He reached for his telephone. 'We can get a warrant on these grounds, Sir Homer, we really can. It'll allow us to search the bastards' property soon as they set foot on your land.'

'Oh yes,' said Sir Homer. 'It is of the essence that it be quick and immediate.'

'Christ knows what we'll find,' continued the policeman.

'Enough to get them put away, no doubt about it. We've got them by the balls, if you'll pardon my French.' He hesitated a moment, holding the receiver in his hand. 'Just one thing, though, Sir Homer. How do you know this is going to happen? I might have to convince my superiors. The courts, you know, they can get fussy about these things. Course, there's a lot we can do without a warrant, but there's more we can do with one. It's a sort of a safeguard for all concerned. You are sure, aren't you?' he finished nervously.

'Oh yes,' Sir Homer replied. 'Quite sure. You see, they are coming onto my land because I, in effect, invited them. That should set your mind at rest, Sergeant Tulliver.'

'You invited them?' The policeman's mouth dropped open.

'It was time that matters were brought to a head.'

'I can't tell my superiors that.'

'No, indeed you can't. And, if you do, I shall strenuously deny it. But surely, Sergeant,' the tone became ironic but Tully, dazed, did not notice, 'you can find some plausible explanation as to how this information came into your hands? Anonymous notes from several different sources perhaps? Maybe you've been spying on them – that should help towards a promotion. Anyway, I have no doubt you will think of something.' Sir Homer produced, from his waistcoat pocket, a silver fob watch. 'And I am very late for a drinks party.'

Sergeant Tulliver barely registered his departure. A hot glow of pride that had begun at the ends of his boots was welling up his body and settling inside his thumping heart. Proud, yes, he was proud: proud to know someone like Sir Homer King who was, after all, fit to be a leader of men; proud that he had been singled out for his confidence.

The limp telephone receiver stiffened to attention. He'd had an idea already. Martha had been to the camp and overheard about the invasion and the projected criminal activity and she'd told him. If you wanted proof she'd been there, you could ask the rector's wife, or the rector. It was the God's honest truth and who better to give it you?

Melanie heard the gate click open and heavy footsteps walking up the path. She heard a hammering on the front door and

Martha answering it, the muffled droning of a dead musician coming out of the sitting-room and then abruptly ceasing.

She would not go downstairs now, definitely. Perhaps she wouldn't go downstairs at all this evening, just lie in her room, that was still full of Josh's presence, and listen to St George's mark the hours.

In the end it had been easy to forgive him. She had done it without realising. Miranda's information about his sexual past and the sight of him, beaten up by Tully, had made it happen. What Martha had said about herself had played its part too; she was right, she was impermanent, only a temporary pleasure. And that too couldn't last much longer. Martha was getting older. One day no one would want to have sex with her.

Melanie rolled on her back and stretched luxuriantly. Her legs felt weak, as if she had been swimming. Her body smelled of perspiration. She'd go and have a bath later but, for the moment, she wanted to revel in all that was animal. In this mood, she could even find it in herself to forgive Martha.

Who was drunk in the sitting-room with Tully.

Hamish had been crotchety but had eventually dropped off, his tired, grumpy wails leaving Martha with the sensation that all her energy had drained away. She should carry him upstairs to his cot but she couldn't be bothered, so he slept hunched in an armchair.

She'd even taken some of Melanie's tobacco and made herself a roll-up, which she held between the ends of two of her fingers and puffed on lightly. She'd fished an old litre bottle of wine out of the back of one of the cupboards.

She felt used up. Unable to protect Melanie from the repercussions of her own, disastrous existence; accused by Josh, harangued by Josh and then let down by him. When you were over thirty you didn't even bother with big words like 'betrayal'.

How long were they staying? It was a simple question. Anyone could have asked it. Just like any one of the travellers could have asked . . . who? Well, someone . . . what exactly their legal rights were. And, as she had said to Josh, she wasn't there for all that, anyway. It was beside the point as far as she was concerned. She'd just wanted to smell wood-smoke again and to see lots of Indian things that sparkled.

Josh assumed that she must want to be on their side, but Martha couldn't be sure. It wasn't that easy to decide between a past that had deserted her and a present and future that would at least be adequate and stick around. The indecision about that was what had made her willing to attempt to seduce John Feather; it stopped her having to think about it.

By the time Tully arrived, she had drunk nearly a quarter of the bottle. Once they were seated on the sitting-room sofa she threw herself into his arms and started to cry.

'There, there, love. What's this about?'

It was then that Martha saw, in her mind's eye, Josh walking down the stairs, past her and away, leaving behind things that couldn't be got rid of, like his father before him.

'One of the travellers came here and upset me,' she said.

Tully's body stiffened. Martha realised she had made a mistake and hoped he wasn't going to be angry with her. She suddenly felt a bit dizzy.

'Which traveller was that, love?' Tully's voice sounded in the distance. Martha didn't speak. She hoped that, if she was silent, it would somehow change the situation. 'Was it that young one who was here the other day?' Still she said nothing. 'Was it?'

Martha nodded.

The record came to an end but the arm of the record-player remained on it. Its slow, regular heartbeat accentuated the silence. Eventually, Tully began again, very softly. She had to strain to hear him.

'Those travellers, you know, I've been given anonymous information that they're planning on invading Sir Homer King's land tonight.'

'To celebrate inside the stone circle?' Martha spoke into his chest, cautiously.

'Ostensibly,' said Tully. 'Ostensibly, yes. But this information that has come into my possession suggests that their intention is rather more than that. I've been told we can expect violence – and other sorts of trouble.'

'Oh,' said Martha. She didn't want to talk about the travellers or the solstice or the circle. What she wanted was to be held in Tully's arms, to feel his fingers sealed together around her. She was relieved he wasn't angry.

'And this is where you come in, love,' he continued quietly. 'I'm going to try and get a warrant to search the buses, if they come onto Sir Homer's land. Now I might need a bit of back-up on this, but that shouldn't be any problem, since you'll want to nail them as much as I do, since they've been round upsetting you.' He stroked the back of her neck and she felt cared about and protected. 'That won't happen again, I promise.'

'Will they go away?' asked Martha. 'Will they leave me alone – and Melanie?'

'If we can clear up a couple of little details, yes they will. Never asked you about what you found out at the camp, the day you went there, have I? Quite frankly, love, I reckoned you were going for your own reasons, something you wanted to get out of your system, so I didn't bother to.'

'Oh, Tully,' Martha blew her nose on a piece of recycled kitchen-roll, 'that's how it was.'

'They're clever, those people. Didn't find anything out, did you?'

Martha shook her head. 'Nothing. But really, like you said, it wasn't what I went there for.'

There was a pause. The needle bounced.

'Went with the rector's wife as well, didn't you?' said Tully. 'Thing is, we've got a problem. The information I've got at present is anonymous, and that makes it not very useful. What I need is a real person, as it were, to verify it – probably wouldn't be called on, of course. Bit of trespass doesn't matter, it's this danger of violence I'm worried about. As things stand, without verification I can't protect Wyley.'

Martha listened to the throbbing beat and tried to sort things out in her mind.

'I don't think the travellers would be violent,' she said, and felt the pressure of Tully's arm on her back increase, almost imperceptibly.

'No, no, neither do I,' he said after a pause. 'But things start out innocent and then other people move in, and it all turns nasty. Best for the travellers, too, our travellers, as it were, if they got out before there are difficulties.'

'Who are these other people?' Martha asked, uncertainly. She had thought that they were the only people.

'Ones you don't want to know about,' said Tully. She imagined them: large, shady, faceless individuals, a threat to Wyley. She thought of Josh gone and Melanie getting over it, the travellers dealt with, out of the way, before these anonymous people could take over. 'Thing is, I might need you to say that you've heard the travellers planning the invasion, when you were down there with the rector's wife,' said Tully. 'You and I know you didn't, but someone did. And that's what counts. Legally speaking.'

He reached out a boot and kicked the record player. It subsided with a yelp. A large silence filled the room.

If there was a threat of violence and Tully could do something to help stop it . . . ?

'I don't want anyone to get hurt because of me,' said Martha. 'You didn't do anything to Josh inside the police station, did you, Tully? Melanie thought you did, and he seemed to think so too, but I thought it was probably a misunderstanding.'

'Hurt? Martha, love, this is Wyley, not Outer-Whatsit.' Tully patted her protectively. 'Listen, Martha, this mightn't result in a promotion or anything, but it could mean that, when something comes up, I'm singled out for special consideration. And that could affect you as well. I'm an ordinary sort of a bloke, and I know you've got a lot of ideas that strike me as pretty fancy. But that's all right. We make the wheels turn and you, well, you do other things. I know it hasn't been very long but I think we've both reckoned that we might think of tying the knot at some stage. You've got two kids, and that's the kind of bind that doesn't appeal to everyone. But it doesn't worry me. I could give Melanie a firm hand and Hamish won't ever need to know that someone else was his father. So how about it?'

Martha raised her eyes upwards to look at him. Unbidden, a memory dropped into her mind. She was very young. It was summer. She was laughing into a camera. The shutter clicked. The camera was lowered. A pair of green eyes laughed back at her. Black hair. Green eyes. They laughed across the years. They did not grow old, as she, who was left, grew old.

Hamish stirred and rolled over.

'Smelly Tully,' he said. 'Smelly, smelly, Tully.'

Tully gave him a look.

'So, how about it?' he repeated.

21

Another Proposal

Lady Polly was feeling much better. She had got up today and made a circuit of the garden with Mulch, giving him instructions as to how she wanted the grounds to look by the time they were opened to the public. She had received a brief telephone call from the rector's wife, that she had not quite understood, but the import of which appeared to be that Mrs Feather wanted to choose different flowers from the ones that Melanie Flowerdew had chosen for her to decorate St George's.

'Melanie Flowerdew got the ambulance when I fell off the rostrum. Plucky gal, Melanie Flowerdew,' remarked Lady Poll, before replacing the receiver, and Mrs Feather, rather startled, agreed with her. To Miss Trannock she said, 'Tell Mulch to expect a visit from a lady about the flowers for the opening,' and then forgot the whole conversation.

For lunch, which she took in her room, she had a pink meringue and a dry martini with a skewered olive, which Crispin made for her.

'I should like a pug, in a pleasant shade, Crispin,' she remarked as he placed the glass on the embroidered tray cover.

'Then please allow me, dear Lady Polly,' said Crispin, 'in due course to present you with one.'

She sat in the garden during most of the afternoon, except for a brief foray to the edge of the ornamental borders to stop

Mulch doing something he shouldn't. While she was having tea and watching a rather confusing quiz show on the television she heard Crispin's Land-Rover drive off and wondered whether he had gone to get the pug. Not long afterwards she heard Homer leave also. She poured some brandy into the top of her silver hip-flask and tried to answer the questions.

At eight-thirty Lady Polly retired to her room, where she put on her nightgown and peacock bed-jacket and installed herself by the open window with her gin and binoculars. The evening was hot and full of jungle noises. It reminded her of her visit to India with Horace, before independence. She raised the binoculars to her eyes and scanned the vista for mad people, taking a while to steady the image.

Beneath The Wise Lady the sunlight had dyed the grass scarlet. For a terrible moment Lady Polly thought it was blood. The stones were marked with triangles and rectangles of blue shadow, here and there a streak of lemon light.

And then she saw them: dark forms, perhaps a dozen. Mad people.

Homer was not at home. Lady Polly felt a sickening fear fill her body, and a ginny queasiness. Crispin had gone out in the Land-Rover.

'Mulch?' she called, uncertainly. But Mulch would be in his potting-shed or busy with the compost.

'Cook? Miss Trannock?' But they had doubtless retired to the outer reaches of the kitchen.

'Crispin! Crispin! Crispin!' Lady Polly's voice came out as a despairing wail.

The bedroom door opened softly.

'Yes, Lady Polly?'

She toddled over to him on her still-beautiful legs, weeping.

'Mad people. Mad people. Dozens of 'em.'

'Calm yourself, Lady Polly.' He took her hand and led her back to the chair by the window. 'Those are not mad people, they are the police. They are there to protect us, should anything happen.'

'Police?' asked Lady Polly, uncertainly.

'Yes.' Crispin Turner knelt at her feet, stroking her hand.

'Have you brought the pug?'

'The pug, Lady Polly? Oh, no, but I have ordered it. They are much in demand.'

'I think,' said Lady Poll, 'I need something to steady my nerves. You are sure it is just the police, Crispin?'

'Just the police, Lady Polly.'

Crispin bent and poured some gin into the empty glass on the carpet. He handed it to her.

'Chin,' said Lady Poll loudly, and took a large gulp.

'And now, Lady Polly, that you are feeling calmer,' said Crispin, 'I have a question that I wish to put to you. You will observe that I am kneeling.'

'Get the chair from the bathroom,' said Lady Poll.

'No, no, Lady Polly,' smiled Crispin Turner, 'it is not because of that, it is because I wish to ask of you the greatest favour that can be bestowed upon man by woman.'

Lady Poll looked down at Crispin's smooth features.

'I will not become your mistress,' she said haughtily.

'No, Lady Polly, of course not, and I would never desire it,' said Crispin. 'I am asking you to become my wife.' From a secret pocket he produced a small velvet box, which he opened.

'Goodness,' said Lady Poll, 'that looks like that ring of mine that went missing.'

'An exact replica,' said Crispin. 'But say that you will wear it and be my bride, Lady Polly. I can protect you from the mad people and ensure that nobody hides your sherry.'

Not long after nine, Sir Homer returned from the Edelsteins', not very pleased with the way in which the situation was developing.

He had imagined that for perhaps half a dozen travellers, half a dozen police would suffice, in fact be ample. He had thought it would be a quiet affair. Barely through the gate into Sir Homer's field, under cover of darkness, they would be silently arrested and gone by morning. Instead, still two hours before the invasion, he had spotted eight policemen between the village school and the war memorial and had been informed, when he pulled up to speak to the officers who were constructing a road-block at the fork of the Rocester road and the high street, that there were already another twelve patrolling the circle.

'I was under the impression that this was to be a discreet operation,' he said crossly.

'It is,' said one of the officers. 'Sir Homer King, isn't it? We met at the Rocester C.I.D. evening. Don't worry, Sir Homer, we are limiting police activity to the stones and the village centre. Don't want the travellers to get wind of us.'

'And the road-block?'

'Oh, you can pass through it, Sir Homer. It's to avoid, as much as possible, any contact between the village and the camp. We've got Wyley sealed off until 0200 hours. There's another at the other end of the village.'

Sir Homer stopped the car in front of the Manor wondering, irritably, why the police could never do anything without making a performance of it. What he needed now was a glass of claret. He was less than delighted to discover Crispin Turner waiting for him in the hall.

'Can't it wait until morning, Turner?'

'I don't think so, Sir Homer.'

'Oh, very well then.'

Sir Homer led the way into the sitting-room and poured himself some wine without offering anything to Turner.

'Sit down,' he said curtly. 'What is it?'

He lowered himself into an armchair and looked at the man expectantly. But Crispin Turner did not sit.

'I have some news, Sir Homer,' said Crispin, 'which I hope you will be pleased with.'

'Get on with it,' said Sir Homer, imagining something to do with vegetables.

'Your mother, Lady Polly King, has tonight done me the honour of consenting to be my wife.'

'What!' Sir Homer leapt to his feet, slopping wine on the armchair and the carpet. 'This is a preposterous, not to mention macabre notion. Have you taken leave of your senses?'

Crispin Turner in possession of the entirety of Sir Homer's rightful acres. The Manor his. The grounds. The garden. Every antique ornament, every stick of furniture. The Manor Farm completely organic. Sir Homer left with merely his flat in London. Taken away by one from his own section of society. Sir Homer was almost floored by the hideousness of the betrayal.

'My mother is mad,' he said sternly. 'Attempt to marry her and I shall have her certified insane and incapable of making decisions.'

There was a silence. Crispin Turner smiled lightly.

'Wyley appears, at present, to be much in the thoughts of the nation,' he said. 'Our member of parliament, Thomas Bright, has a high profile in the newspapers. I remember, Sir Homer, at the public meeting, how impressed Wyley was to hear of the closeness of your association with the good gentleman and the longevity of your intimacy. I think your mother's mind is as sound as anyone else's.'

Sir Homer went pale. 'You have no proof of anything,' he said swiftly.

'That,' said Crispin Turner, 'is a thesis that I would be very wary of putting to the test, Sir Homer. And now, let me bid you good night, with the assurance that I wish that all may continue cordial between us. After all, I shall be your stepfather.'

When the door had closed behind him Sir Homer collapsed into his armchair and wept silently, his shoulders heaving. His own class. His own fellow Tory. And if only, if only it could have been about Flora. Then he would have sent Crispin Turner packing and dealt with the public disgrace in the solitude of the Manor. No, it had to be Thomas that Turner found out about. Sir Homer had lost his home. He had lost the one person that he had ever loved. He had lost Flora – she was leaving with the travellers.

Sir Homer got out a silk handkerchief and wiped his eyes. His mind replayed the events of the day: Josh watching him in the folly, Paul's visit, the conversation with Josh in the Jaguar. Josh had not lied, and Paul had not attempted to blackmail him. It was all Crispin Turner's now, lock, stock and barrel; there was no reason whatever that they should not use the circle. And perhaps, if they stayed a little bit longer, he would find out a way to keep Flora.

Sir Homer hurtled into his study, sat down at the desk and quickly looked up the number of Wyley police station. The phone rang and rang. He glanced at the clock. Just coming up to ten. Through the window the sky was pale gold and the trees and bushes charcoal. Eventually, Sergeant Tulliver answered.

'Ah, Tulliver.' He attempted to imbue his voice with authority, but somehow it wouldn't come. It sounded thin and ineffectual. 'Rather unfortunate but, for various private reasons that I won't trouble you with, I am going to have to withdraw my information of earlier this evening. I'm afraid there will be nothing you can do to prevent the celebration.'

On the other end there was silence. Sir Homer felt uneasy. Sergeant Tulliver spoke.

'If I recall, Sir Homer,' he said, with a nasty edge to his tone, 'we never had any conversation, not this evening, and there was nothing that you told me. It's quite another witness upon whom we are basing our police operation.'

There was a light tap on the bedroom door. Melanie yelled for Martha to come in.

'Yeah?' Melanie was lying on the bed, wearing a night-shirt. Her hair was slightly damp. She glanced in Martha's direction, ready for an argument, but her eyes were transfixed by what she saw: Martha had got old.

A sexless, powerless Martha: Melanie hadn't expected it to happen so quickly. But here she was, pale, her eyes rimmed with red, the odd wrinkle. Had this been coming on for ages without Melanie noticing it?

'Melanie,' said Martha, 'I think I've done something awful.' She sat down on the bed. She was trembling.

'What?' asked Melanie nervously. 'Is it to do with Tully?'

Martha nodded. She sniffed. 'I think it was because I got confused when he asked me to marry him . . .'

'Tully asked you to marry him?' Melanie thumped her head against the pillow. In the events of recent days she had almost forgotten that this was on the cards. 'What did you say?'

'I said I needed time. My head started aching. It's still aching. He wants an answer tomorrow.'

'And what will you say then?'

'Yes, probably.'

'But Martha, why? What's wrong with your life the way it is?'

Martha looked at her with an expression that was at once bitter and nearly amused.

'I'm lonely,' she said. The words fell in the room with quiet finality.

'Lonely? But the house is full of me and Hamish.' Melanie stopped. And there was Joodi. There were the ecology meetings in Rocester, but nobody ever came back to Martha's house. Martha sometimes dropped Hamish off with one of the mothers' au pairs, but didn't get asked in. Apart from Tully there probably was no one really concerned about Martha, not since Grandma died.

The constant male desertions began to assume a different light. Miranda's words came back to her: 'Your mother's very young. She must have been about your age when she had you.' Melanie didn't like to think about their significance.

'And I'm tired,' said Martha. 'The washing-machine started to make a clanking sound the other day and I don't know what I'm going to use to pay for having it fixed. Tully's got a steady salary.'

'So have you,' said Melanie. But hadn't Miranda mentioned something about this as well?

Martha looked at her again. 'How much do you think it pays, Melanie? And it relies on the Feathers being there. I don't think it's very likely any other sort of rector would want me.'

'Oh, shit.' Melanie looked out of the window. A large white moon was rising over Wyley. St George's struck eleven. She'd never really, in her heart of hearts, believed that life actually was hard for Martha, though she'd indicated it often enough. Melanie hadn't been listening. Too busy scoffing and criticising, a voice whispered in her ear, and thereby pushing Martha – and Hamish – into the arms of Tully.

'What about your art?' she asked, without thinking.

Martha looked startled, then she sighed.

'So Josh told you everything.'

'About Jacob Flowerdew, my wandering father, and all the rest, yes. I suppose Josh and me are what you always call "the children of the sixties".'

'No.' Martha shook her head slowly. 'Jacob and Josh's mother and me are the children of the sixties. You are our children.'

Melanie thought a moment. 'You were in love with him, weren't you?' she blurted.

'Yes,' said Martha.

'And that's why I was named after him?'

Martha nodded.

'So it wasn't anything to do with not wanting to feel responsible for me?'

Martha made a limp gesture with her thin hands. 'Melanie, did I ever act like I didn't feel responsible?'

There was a pause.

'But isn't proper love worth having?' Melanie asked. 'And not settling for less?'

'I don't know,' said Martha. '"Proper love" hasn't been much good in my existence. I haven't seen Jacob Flowerdew since you were a toddler.'

'Well, then,' Melanie felt her old impatience rising, 'maybe men aren't the answer. What about your art?'

Martha shrugged. 'What about supporting you and Hamish?'

There was a silence. 'Martha,' said Melanie uncertainly, 'did you ever think of having an abortion?'

'No,' said Martha. 'With you I couldn't. And with Hamish, once I'd had one baby it was impossible to consider an abortion.'

'Before that, though? Before it was legal?' She watched Martha's face carefully. 'In the stone circle.'

'Oh, Melanie, you're not talking about that old story? That was around even when I was young. It's just an old wives' tale.'

Melanie bit her lip. The idea that Martha could have done such a thing had always seemed too horrifying to contemplate. Now, for the first time, she wondered what kind of desperation would drive a woman to self-abort in the snow. And she wondered also why she hadn't asked about it sooner. Perhaps so that she could go on blaming Martha for not giving her a father, for forcing her to be independent early on?

Though neither of these seemed so bad, now that she thought about them calmly. And anyway, the one who had suffered most was Martha. 'Your mother's very young. She must have been about your age when she had you.' No lolling around or dreaming. No painting or drawing or wandering through the fields or staying in bed as long as she felt like.

'Why couldn't you have had me aborted?' she asked. 'Wouldn't it have been better?'

'Maybe,' said Martha evasively. 'But something happened, and after that I knew you were meant to be here.'

'What happened?'

'Oh, you don't want to know, Melanie.'

'If I don't want to know that, what the fuck do I want to know?'

Martha took a deep breath. 'A few weeks after I got pregnant I saw the Goddess.'

'You what?'

'I saw the Goddess. I was gathering mushrooms.'

'Her robe was made of mist, the sun was shining on her and she was smiling,' said Melanie.

Martha nodded. 'After that I knew that you had to be born.'

'What sort of mushrooms were you gathering?' asked Melanie.

'I can't remember.' Martha smiled. 'It was a long time ago.'

There was a silence that lasted perhaps five minutes, during which Melanie thought about her mother. Now she had seen Martha as a victim of time and circumstance, it was easy to feel that this knowledge alone could make her stop being one. But of course it didn't work like that. You wanted some kind of soaring image of freedom but the bloody truth was that freedom was financial. Without enough cash, no magical transformations and no real choices. It was time to set Martha free.

'Melanie, I've got to tell you about the awful thing I've done,' said Martha. She started crying. Melanie was startled. She'd thought the awful thing was thinking about marrying Tully. 'I wanted to protect you from Josh,' Martha sobbed.

'Protect me? Why, for God's sake?'

'Melanie, he's your brother.'

'Half-brother, and what the fuck does it matter? Is the world so chock-full of love that we can make a fuss about where it sodding comes from?'

'Oh, I don't know, Melanie. I suppose not. I mean, it's too late anyway, and I didn't think about that. I was so confused by Tully, and I'd drunk some wine. And then I was frightened about the other people.'

'What other people?'

'Well, I don't think there were any, actually. Tully must just have imagined them. The only people are you and me and the travellers and the police and Wyley.'

'The police?'

'Oh, and I didn't notice the time. It's probably too late to stop it anyway.'

'To stop what? Martha, tell me what happened between you and Tully.'

Martha told her.

Melanie jumped off the bed and scrambled into her jeans and t-shirt. Abruptly she bent and kissed Martha. She ran down the stairs, almost falling, and out of the house, in the direction of the war memorial. There she came to a standstill. At the fork of the Rocester road and the High Street was a road-block. Four policemen stood sentry and two others, on motorbikes, spoke into walkie-talkies. There were three police cars and a police van in the High Street. In the distance she could hear the sound of an ambulance.

'Sorry, miss, you can't go down there. Access is restricted to the police and the emergency services.'

It was too late. It was too late to save them.

Melanie belted past policemen and policewomen, vehicles and onlookers and into the churchyard. A massive noise was coming towards Wyley from the Rocester direction.

It was too late. It was too late to save them. Back on the road she heard an enormous sort of crashing sound.

Her footsteps clanged on the pathway between the grave-stones. She hit the wall at full pelt, out of breath, her mouth full of liquid.

Oh, Christ. Oh, Christ. She couldn't believe what she was seeing.

22

The Stone Circle

At ten o'clock Sara Feather looked out of the window at Wyley High Street. Everyone was out on the pavement. The blue lights of a line of police cars twirled silently, streaking veins of colour across the white faces of the Wyley mothers who talked in clusters. From time to time one of them would leave their group and go and speak with a policeman or policewoman. Then the policewomen would assume pally expressions and the policemen preoccupied ones. The mother returned to her companions with her information, or lack of it.

Miss Sayle from the tea-rooms exchanged comments with Tom Callan and Miss Evans from the post office. The Tarrants, Simon and Veronica, strolled up to Sergeant Tulliver, Veronica in Liberty print and thin cardigan, held round her shoulders by a pearl button, Simon in khaki Bermudas. But Sergeant Tulliver was busy and only gave curt answers to their inquiries.

The door to Magpie Cottage opened and Marjorie Sand appeared. Sara saw the blue light bounce off Marjorie's ornamental plates as she and Seymour cautiously made their way into the front garden, Seymour inexplicably carrying a spade. They looked up and down the High Street, had a hurried consultation, and went back in again.

A police van arrived. The police remained inside it. Sara couldn't see them very well but they appeared to be wearing riot gear. A couple of motorbikes weaved their way through the people trailing static.

Sara dropped the curtain and turned away with a sigh. How silly. How very, very, silly. She went back into the study to put the lights out. She could have gone and remonstrated with the police, she supposed, or John could have done, but it wouldn't make any difference, and anyway it was unlikely that anything would happen.

Her conscience gave a little twinge. Would she feel differently if she weren't pregnant? Wouldn't she be worrying frantically about Emily's baby? Oh yes, probably, she thought, but other people's problems – including their babies – were not her concern any more. Her eye caught a piece of paper with a list of telephone numbers on it. She tore it up and threw it in the bin, put the light out and went upstairs.

'What's going on in the High Street?' asked John as she entered the bedroom.

Sara started to undress. 'Oh, a terrible fuss with lots of police cars and whatnot,' she replied. 'But I expect it will all amount to nothing. Though I do hope they get to celebrate their solstice.' Images of things she had seen in the inner city entered her mind; she pushed them out of it. Sara wanted to leave the travellers. They did not feel very real to her any more, even Paul and Emily. It was the nature of travellers to be like this, she reflected: curious for a while and then forgotten. They did not have the solidity of surroundings and therefore could not be classified in your consciousness. Here today and gone tomorrow. It was probably this that irritated Wyley most of all.

John Feather watched his wife undressing. She seemed to have got much prettier all of a sudden. She slipped her nightgown over her naked body and came to lie beside him. He put the light out.

'Well, Marjorie Sand has done her worst,' he said into the darkness.

'Or Sergeant Tulliver,' said Sara.

'Or Sergeant Tulliver,' John agreed, remembering the veiled threats when he refused the church hall for the public meeting. 'Anyway, whoever it was used Homer King as their agent. The bishop made no bones about it. He and Sir Homer were at school together: that was what seemed to be uppermost. It was clear that whatever took place between me and my parishioners was only a secondary consideration. "The Manor might expect to rely on the support of the Church in times of difficulty. This support has not been forthcoming." We're out. They've got what they wanted.'

There was a pause.

'Have they? Do you really think so?' said Sara. 'I prefer to believe that we've got what we came for and that something's telling us that it's time to move on.'

John smiled. 'And that Something's medium is the bishop?'

'Yes,' said Sara. 'Well, at least we've got a month or so for packing,' she added. 'Do you remember how we always used to say the old trunk was the kind that missionaries took to Africa and that, if we ever became missionaries, we had the trunk for it already?'

'Did we ever want to be missionaries? I'd forgotten.'

'Oh, I don't know if we really did, not exactly. I certainly wouldn't want to now.'

'No,' said John, 'neither would I.' He yawned. 'Well, I won't miss Marjorie Sand. Though she's lost a lot of her sting now that we've seen the worst that she can do to us. I honestly can't think why I got so upset by her. Heaven knows, her type springs up everywhere; they kill off their husbands, castrate their sons and then concentrate on disseminating venom in the name of God. Cathedral cities are crawling with them.'

'You make her sound like some kind of horrible insect.'

'Yes, I suppose I do. But she's not that. She's something worse altogether. What is she?' John considered for a moment, then it came to him. 'She's the spirit of misdirection. She gives the illusion of knowing where she's going, but really it's all a gigantic, confused mess.'

'At least it's not your responsibility,' said Sara. 'The clearing up, I mean.'

'Not after this particular version. But there's always a Marjorie Sand, just like there's always a Homer King. You meet them again and again.'

'In that case,' said Sara, 'the important thing is not to let them get too strong a hold.'

'I know. It's just so hard to identify, to know which of the dozens of things they're doing are going to have repercussions. There must be a place for them doing something. For example, I don't know, would it really matter that much if Marjorie were allowed to parade around with her crucifix at the do in the Manor grounds? It's not as if anybody believes in it or anything.'

There was a silence as they both took in what he had said. John Feather thought about the kind of God he hankered after, the 'God of concrete, God of steel,' that the hideous hymn valiantly and hopelessly asserted. It was all very well to harp on about gardens but the modern world needed a practical God who was familiar with the workings of the London Underground and the pavements of Brixton, a God of dole offices, God of streets. The problem was that God did not want to, perhaps could not, leave his garden, was, in the end, as all gods are, an agrarian god. As Greek as ever he, she, probably they, wished only to frolic, heartlessly, through the seasons, refused to forge the world into a better approximation of how one might wish it to be because it was, quite simply, not their job.

'I wish,' he said, 'that I could believe like them.'

'Like who?'

'Like the travellers. I envy their certainty that they know something that it's worth committing their lives to. Laid out bare it probably isn't much, but it seems to me now as if I would have liked something I could fervently believe in; something that wasn't woolly and undemanding.'

'Well then,' said Sara, 'I think it's time for a change of direction.'

'Yes,' said John, 'it probably is.' Would the future be messy, he wondered, or could they slip out of their present lives, unscathed, with only their needs, their belongings and the burdensome desire to be useful to hold them back or to push them forward?

John and Sara Feather fell asleep. St George's struck eleven. Then 'God Almighty, whatever's going on?' John yelled. 'That noise. What on earth is it?'

At a quarter to eleven Sergeant Tulliver took up position on the edge of the circle, beneath the first stone they'd come to once they'd opened Sir Homer's gate and driven across his field. Let them come in a bit of a distance and the lads could get them completely surrounded. No retreating and pretending it had never happened.

The policeman glanced behind him at his back-up. Well, not his back-up, actually, because he wasn't in charge, strictly speaking, but reinforcements from Rocester, like there were in Wyley High Street, keeping everyone out. Only the understanding eyes of other coppers to see whatever happened.

He was going to get that boy for going back to Martha's. This time there'd be no Melanie Flowerdew to show up and make like she'd stir things for him if he didn't let the boy go. This time there'd be no getting off scot free. Tully saw Josh in his mind's eye. His beauty felt like a personal affront. With a mashed in nose and a limp, or perhaps in a wheelchair, he wouldn't look so beautiful any more, and maybe other people would think twice before they thought they could drive round English roads in beat-up buses.

Sergeant Tulliver looked up at the thin form of the stone he was standing under, past its slightly pointed top to the big shiny moon with its white circle of light, outside of which you could see a million stars. Or a billion, probably. Or a trillion. Or a trillion trillion. Or a squillion. His radio receiver gave a sudden burp and a voice said, 'They're coming.' But he didn't need it to know they were on their way because he could see them in the moonlight. He hid behind the stone and peeked out at them. St George's was striking eleven.

One of the girls opened the gate at the end of the byway. She wore a long skirt and had bare feet. Her face was painted with little flowers and her hair was a mess of beads and plaits. Tied to her back in a bundle of fabric was a baby.

She got back in the bus and, after a pause, it proceeded in a straight line towards the stones, followed by the other one, bobbing over tussocks, their lights illuminating the grass. If you made it illegal to have paintings plastered across your vehicles, thought Sergeant Tulliver, none of this would happen.

Nearer they came, until he could see their faces. Earrings, nose rings, stars, moons, necklaces, patterns. Tulliver felt his mates' excitement.

They were twenty feet away from him now. The byway gate opened again and five coppers entered the field. They closed the gate behind them and two of them leant up against it.

Sergeant Tulliver stepped out from behind his stone knowing, without turning round, that another dozen or so policemen were doing the same thing. He registered the expressions of alarm with a burst of almost sexual pleasure. The buses came to an abrupt standstill. The travellers remained inside. From what he could make out they appeared to be talking.

After a minute one of the men made his way down the steps and stood in front of his vehicle. In that sort of light, with his large nose, he looked a bit like a Red Indian.

'Look,' he shouted, 'we've been given permission to celebrate the solstice here.' Sergeant Tulliver smiled to himself, thinking of Sir Homer. The man continued. 'We don't want any trouble. We only . . .'

He stopped. There was the sound of windows smashing. A filthy creature in a boiler-suit from out of the second bus came running in Tully's direction. His cheek was bleeding.

'Stop them. There's more behind us. Stop them. They're breaking the windows. The glass is falling on Emily.'

'Right, boys. Get them.' But already the ones with Tulliver were dashing at the buses with their truncheons and the other travellers were hurtling out of them. The girl with the baby was running towards the centre of the circle but a policeman had got her by the arm and was about to fell her. A pregnant one tumbled onto the ground and a big blonde made to wipe the blood off her forehead as two of the lads tried to drag her away. A kid was crying. Someone kneed the poncey one in the groin. The beautiful boy was standing, frozen, staring at all the blocked exits.

Tulliver experienced a rush of self-righteous pleasure. Resisting arrest. Resisting arrest. That was what you called it. This one was his. In his mind's eye he saw the boy's pretty face scarred and spoiled. He'd walk funny, if he walked at all. Martha wouldn't even drop a penny in his hat.

Tully caught the boy's eye. The boy stared back at him like he knew it was inevitable. No need even to rush about it. Savour the moment. The crystal tinkling of the breaking windows was music. Coppers were everywhere. Tully began to move slowly in Josh's direction. This one was his to do what he liked with.

There was a rumbling sound. Startled, the policeman looked up. The sky did a sudden sort of darkening. The earth tipped over sideways. He heard someone yelling, 'Jesus H. Christ!' Another shouting, 'It's coming down. Get back for Christ's sake.' Tully saw the point of the stone, silver in the moonlight, falling towards him. He plunged forwards, waiting for it to split his back in two, felt his foot twist strangely and the impossibility of further movement.

In the seconds before he lost consciousness he was also aware of a massive noise moving in the direction of the stone circle.

'What the fuck is that?'

It was Paul, who'd got his breath back and managed to struggle over to where Josh was standing. The policemen's interest in the travellers had momentarily abated at the sight of Tulliver trapped under a fallen stone. A cluster of them was attempting to free him. It was only a question of picking them off now, anyway. They were completely surrounded. The policemen who were holding them loosened their grip on Miranda and Karen. Miranda wrenched her arm away and helped Emily to a sitting position.

'Dunno. Police van, probably. They'll separate us. Should've thought of a meeting place.' Josh felt like he could kill someone. God knew what would happen to Emily and to Carmine and Curdie. They'd be lucky to see them ever again. Almost every window on the Pisces and Aquarius was destroyed. How much dole would it take to get those fixed? But then the buses would probably be confiscated. It was a shitty world. Okay, the stone had saved him, but it might as well not have bothered.

'No,' said Paul. 'That's not a police van. It's something much bigger. Massive, in fact. It's a fucking great noise. If you ask me it sounds like about a thousand . . .'

There was a cracking sound, a large amount of wood splintering. The policemen looked up in alarm. Things crashed onto tarmac. Four or five police sirens started up near the war memorial. There were masses of lights. Single ones. Continuing along the road. Turning into the byway. The yells of policemen leaping out of the way as the gate was smashed through and the lights came towards the circle, illuminating it like a stadium, row upon row upon row of them.

'A thousand motorbikes.' Dazed, Josh finished Paul's sentence. Unbelieving, he watched as the policemen managed to get Sergeant Tulliver out from under the stone and set off at a run across the field, dragging him behind them, casting nervous glances back at the circle.

A massive Harley stopped next to Josh.

'Hey, man,' said a guy with a bulging stomach and a beard and fringed jacket with 'Eat Shit' written on it. 'We're here for The Wise Lady Free Festival. Read about Wyley in all the papers. Mind where we camp?'

'Anywhere,' Josh managed to say. 'Anywhere.'

'Jesus,' yelled Paul. 'Jesus. Will you look at that? The police have buggered off. They're totally outnumbered.'

Josh turned in the direction of the byway and wondered if he was dreaming. Behind the bikers was a seemingly endless trail of cars and buses which just kept on coming.

He looked back at the circle. One of the buses had stopped there. A road crew was getting out of it, unloading large pieces of wood and scaffolding to make a stage. Tents were being got out of the boots of clapped out vehicles, along with cooking equipment and firewood.

A flare went up and dyed the sky above Wyley scarlet.

'One. One. One, two,' said a sound-man into a microphone. A Rasta picked up an electric guitar and played a screaming chord on it.

'Hot knives. Hot knives,' yelled another Rasta, unloading his wares from an ancient beach-buggy without a licence plate.

'White Lady,' called somebody. 'White Lady.'

'Look.' Paul pointed. 'Now they're coming from both directions.'

Josh looked across the fields. Paul was right. The whole landscape was seething with people. At one edge of the circle a small village of teepees was being laid out on the ground, ready to be erected, and a street of stalls was going up: 'Sorrel's Psychedelic Kaftans' were scattered across the grass, Greenpeace were unloading piles of Toxic Toad t-shirts from a van with a picture of *The Rainbow Warrior* on it; 'The Cosmic Cobbler' unfolded her trestle tables talking to people from the Anti-Nazi League and Rock Against Racism. Somebody doing tattoos was writing a sign on a piece of cardboard. Gay Vegans From Sheffield had lit a gas-burner and were starting to cook lentil-burgers.

A band began a loud reggae number that vibrated off the stones and bounced off the stars and shook the walls of Wyley to their foundations.

'Acid. Hot knives. White Lady.'

'Get your Festival Eye here.'

'Kill The Rich. Kill The Rich.'

A painted caravan, pulled by a dapple-grey horse, came to a halt beside Josh and Kristof Smit got down from it with a bundle of copies of *Planetary Pathway* under his arm. His beard was longer than ever. He was accompanied by a large, jolly lady who carried a trowel and a bucket.

'Josh. Josh. Thank-you so much for your article,' he shouted above the music. 'I was given it by Becki of Legalise Marijuana. Not at the Spring Tree festival, as it happened, but during a week's retreat at a Buddhist monastery in Wales – she's somewhere about, deciding where to put her stall, by the way. I'd like to think it was the article's publication in *Planetary Pathway* that made all this happen, but I'm afraid it's probably more due to its appearance in *The New Social Worker*, along with its companion piece, of course, and to the splendid article in the *Guardian* by my friend here, Professor Morrow. Never underestimate the power of the media.'

'This is wonderful. Wonderful!' yelled Professor Morrow, grabbing Josh's hand and beaming around her. 'Pathways have a way of reasserting themselves, you know. How I envy the archaeologists who dig here a thousand years from now. Think of the artefacts.'

'Josh! Josh!' cried Curdie, bounding over. 'There's a bloke over there who does fire-eating and he's going to show me how to do it. Come and see him. They're planning a sort of circus tent over where the Anti-Apartheid and Amnesty people are. Oh, and the other Convoy's arriving and they're going to set up an acoustic stage and there's some radical cabaret people here, too.'

'Emily's gone into labour,' shouted Miranda, coming up behind him.

'Is everything okay?' asked Josh. He felt like crying.

'Fine. She's being looked after by one of the radical midwives who came down with the Brighton Feminists. Karen, Ralph and Carmine are being checked over by a doctor from Medical CND. Karen's arm is bruised but the doctor thinks there are no other problems. And also I met a member of "The Bus Crazy Barratt Family". They came back from Afghanistan early. They reckon they have got nearly enough glass to repair our windows, and they have got some hardboard for the others.'

The number came to an end. There was riotous applause and whistling. Josh looked around him. In all directions there were lights, activity, colours, people laughing, shouting, doing crazy things, and still more and more people were arriving.

'Thanks. Thanks,' said the Rasta musician. 'One, two. One, two. Hi, everybody. Welcome. One, one. One, two. Welcome to The Wise Lady Free Festival. Pathway to the millennium. Everyone welcome, including dogs and other animals.'

Oh, Christ. Oh, Christ. Melanie Flowerdew leant against the churchyard wall and looked out over the valley. The scent of woodsmoke was beginning to fill the air. The light of the flames of the newly-lit fires reflected off the stones, so that the stones seemed to be dancing.

Perhaps they were. And perhaps there really was a doorway to somewhere else, just across the fields.

She climbed over the wall and into the festival.

23

The Solstice

The sun had not yet risen. The sky was pale blue, the damp fields full of mist. Melanie walked through the churchyard with its slanting stones, past the cold, grey form of St George's, and emerged in the sleeping High Street. Over the other side of the road the window of Callan's Butcher was a rectangle of buff material, with two empty milk bottles on the doorstep. The 'Closed' sign in the Wise Lady Tea Rooms looked strangely redundant in the absence of anybody wanting its coffee and homemade biscuits. The pale pink tablecloths were bare of cutlery. On the white windowsill a fly buzzed among the dried flowers and the corn-dollies, which were for sale. In two parked police cars a couple of policemen were sleeping. Another went past quietly on a heavy motorbike. He looked at Melanie but didn't stop.

She crossed the road and took the path between the Rose and Crown and the post office. An overflow was running onto it from a pipe in the pub wall. She headed across the dewy village green. No one was around. All she saw was a solitary cat, stalking delicately over the grass. The village pond was a reflection of the sky. In Martha's front garden there was a calm scent of roses.

Melanie entered by the front door, which had been left unlocked, and made her way upstairs, treading carefully on the one that creaked. In her bedroom she got a small bag out of the wardrobe and bundled into it a couple of pairs of jeans, some t-shirts, a cardigan and a book. Then she went to Hamish's room, opening the wooden door cautiously, so that it wouldn't make any noise. She grabbed a few of his clothes from the floor and put them in the bag with her own. She bent over his cot. He was in the very depths of sleep, his small, new lips parted, his little body curled in upon itself. She reached out a hand and stroked a plump cheek. 'Hame. Wake up, Hame.' He threw a short arm upwards. 'Hame. Wake up.' He rubbed his face with his fist. She smiled. 'Wake up, lazy bones.' Hamish's eyes opened. He smiled up at her and brought his two hands together in a clapping motion.

'Come on, there isn't much time.' She lifted his heavy body out of the cot and got him dressed, then she hoisted him onto her hip. In the kitchen she had a drink of water and gave Hamish his orange juice. There was an open magazine on the kitchen table, and a mug with some cold coffee in. She washed it up and wiped some crumbs from the sideboard.

She looked around her. This kitchen was almost Grandma's final resting place, and Grandma wasn't so bad really. She gave a quick sniff. Mind you, it was a pretty hopeless kitchen, full of nooks and crannies and unnecessary difficult-to-get-at places. Then there was the Aga. Old-fashioned and ponderous, redolent – according to Martha – of a whole pile of boring virtues that had probably never even really existed. She gave it a peremptory kick.

'Okay, Hame, it's time to be moving. Want a piggy-back?'
Hamish clambered up.

Outside it was still hazy but shoots of light were emanating from the horizon. The first bees had started a muted buzzing among the lavender.

Melanie retraced her steps. She reached the churchyard wall again.

'Hold on tight now, Hame, very tight. It'll be like flying.'
They hit the grass with a bump.
'You all right? Good.'
She made her way slowly across the meadow, which was dense with tents and benders, the ground criss-crossed with guy-ropes. Once or twice she had to retrace her steps. She had

to be careful to avoid tripping over people who were sleeping in the open, on layers of bin-bags, covered with blankets, beside the smouldering embers of last night's fires.

They passed a stall where a yawning punk with a green mohican was selling black coffee. Someone was playing acid rock, very softly. A woman, wearing only a pair of cut-offs was dancing, her hair tousled, her body boyish and dirty.

Along the horizon there was a saffron radiance. With Hamish on her back Melanie entered the circle. In the growing light the stones were white with cold, seaweedy shadows.

In jeans and leathers, in army surplus, Indian cottons, t-shirts, sandals, barefoot; hair matted, oiled, orange, red, streaked pink, stuck in long points, shaven, Rasta tufts; with tattoos, nose-rings, ankle-bracelets, necklaces, earrings; with young children in long, sagging sweaters matted with seeds and grasses, babies in bright colours; with boyfriends, girlfriends, mates, sisters, homosexual, lesbian, bi-sexual, heterosexual lovers, people emerged from their blankets or their shelters as the sky turned the colour of baked terracotta.

Melanie lowered Hamish from her back, picked him up in her arms and carried him into the very centre of the inner ring where she stood, motionless.

'Look, Hame. The sun's going to rise any second now. It's Midsummer Day.'

As she looked down at his face it took on an orange glow. In his two, liquid eyes, two suns raised their russet curves over the edge of the earth. She turned back to the horizon.

Now that it had appeared, the sun was changing very quickly. Already it had metamorphosed into a strong, bronze disc: old, well-used, a circular saw dividing light from darkness, slicing the year into its component parts. Perhaps this was what whoever erected the stones had been celebrating: the modest practicality of its workmanship with their own.

Up it went, sturdily, heavily climbing the sky, lighting the upturned faces of the New Age people, until it seemed to pause, just for a moment, on the curved back of The Wise Lady, wrinkling her with its illumination, making her old. The burden of light. The burden of time. Maybe once a year those ancient people had felt that, for a few seconds, they should share it.

When Melanie and Hamish reached the byway the birds had started singing in the woodlands and it was already beginning to be warm. The windows of the Aquarius and Pisces were in place. Their engines were running.

'Did you see it?' asked Josh as they clambered into the Pisces.

Melanie nodded.

'Ready to roll?' yelled Karen from the Aquarius.

'Ready,' shouted Paul. He switched on the Bob Marley. 'Right. We're out of here.'

The buses pulled away.

Martha woke with a start and heard the thumping of the music. She smelled the smell of woodsmoke and knew what must have happened. For a moment she felt a burst of old joy, then she sensed the emptiness of the house. She leapt out of bed and flung open the door to Melanie's room. Empty. She ran to Hamish's room. Empty as well. She grabbed discarded clothes from her floor, almost panting, ran down the stairs and out of the house, without closing the door behind her. St George's clock was striking eight.

She hurried across the village green, pounding on Melanie's footprints. Emerged in the High Street. She dodged round the back of a row of police cars and reached the other side of the road, paused for a moment, looking up at the sky, at the sound of a police helicopter. Then she ran through the churchyard, winding through the pale gravestones, along the thin walkways until she got to the wall, which she hurtled over, grazing her hands. She strained her eyes across the field, searching among the cars and tents and motorbikes, the buses, the teepees, the stalls, the stages, the dancers for a sight of them.

As she looked, however, something strange happened: her desperation vanished and Melanie and Hamish slipped, quite quietly, out of her mind. She became entranced by the patterns and colours, the austerity of the stones, cool in the sunlight, among the riotous activity around them. Her eyes were trans-fixed by a piece of blue shade, beneath the table of a boy selling organic ice-cream, and she started to move, in a trance, through the milling crowds of people – jumping, bouncing, throwing

their locks out into black aureoles against the powder-blue sky
– past the triangular teepees, through the perfumes – patchouli,
marijuana, frying onions, woodsmoke.

She reached an area of stalls, gazed at the jewelled colours of
the shoes of 'The Cosmic Cobbler', the livid sweets of a couple
of sweet-sellers. Somebody was shucking oysters. She stared at
their pearly interiors. A young boy was having his hair shaved
in a wavy pattern. A woman with candy-floss hair was plaiting
beads into the hennaed curls of another. Martha got a whiff of
Indian fabric and turned to see a row of paisley patterned dresses.
She found some money in her pocket and bought a hummus roll,
made with stone-ground flour. She took a bite into it.

It was then that she saw him, or thought she saw him. A
brief glimpse of green eyes, dark hair to his shoulders, and he
had vanished into the crowd. She thought of following him, did
almost, but realised suddenly that it couldn't have been him after
all, because the hair had had streaks of grey in it.

She walked on, towards the byway, fell over a guy-rope and
was helped to her feet by a biker with a skeleton tattoo. Further
on she felt a crunching under her feet. Looking down she saw
that the ground was covered in crystals of broken glass, almost
blindingly brilliant in the fierce sunlight.

The byway was empty, which was what she had expected.

Epilogue $\int$

Though she was not there to see it, Melanie Flowerdew's wish came true: Lady Poll did do something exciting at the opening to the Manor grounds. Or rather, Sir Homer did, on her behalf.

The opening was rather an attenuated affair that year, including only the Manor gardens, for the festival, which lasted about a fortnight and, at its height, numbered a hundred thousand people (the police estimate was fifty), was still in full swing. To a backdrop of wild dancing, nudity and rock music, the citizens of Wyley assembled upon the Manor lawn, full of Dunkirk spirit and dignity under duress, to hear, with astonishment, Sir Homer King's announcement that his mother – emphatically seated, and forced to remain so by a guard of Cook and Miss Trannock – was, to his extreme joy, shortly to be married to Crispin Turner. The quizzical applause which followed, and a rather half-hearted rendition of 'For She's a Jolly Good Fellow' were merely further indications – if such were needed – that though others might not know how to behave, Wyley did.

It was just a shame that certain people had to go and spoil things.

The first of these was Marjorie Sand who, as soon as Sir Homer had left this pleasant topic and gone onto more general subjects, such as the particular excellence of this year's roses, made a sudden dash onto the rostrum with a crucifix attached to a broom handle. What this was designed to achieve was never made clear because, barely had she reached the centre of the stage before she collapsed, foaming at the mouth, and had to be taken to Rocester by ambulance. People said it was stress and blamed the festival, but it put something of a damper on the proceedings.

Which was not relieved by the extraordinary behaviour of Sara Feather.

At three o'clock, the time at which Sir Homer's speech was due to finish, the doors of St George's were flung open. An hour or so later, having witnessed Marjorie Sand's departure and verified the claims for the roses, the people of Wyley drifted back to the village, where the Rose and Crown was selling strawberry teas, to the rage of Miss Sayle from the tea rooms. Before eating, however, most Wyley-dwellers, as custom demanded, went into St George's to see what display the church had put on to complement the Manor.

New horrors awaited.

Upon the altar was a foreign and somehow pagan blend of freckled orchids and giant sunflowers from Mr Mulch's special patch, the existence of which was unknown to Lady Polly. No floral screen hid the stained-glass window's portrayal of the stone circle. Upon the stone shelf beneath it were what looked like offerings: bread, fruit, vegetables. At either end of the shelf were two holders filled with burning joss-sticks. A Hari Krishna, in saffron robes, wandered in from the festival, went round offering people coconut-ice and trying to engage them in conversation.

All in all the festival and the travellers had a lot to answer for. Not just the aberrant behaviour of two of Wyley's more prominent citizens, but also, it was assumed, the vandalism that had caused one of the stones to topple; in spite of their manifest love of rectitude, this was a notion of which Marjorie and Seymour Sand never saw fit to disabuse anybody.

Sergeant Tulliver, the unfortunate victim of the vandalism, was given a desk job in Rocester and a special commendation for having had a stone fall on his foot. At the end of November, three months after Lady Polly King and Crispin Turner had been married by the new rector – Homer King giving the bride away and a completely recovered Marjorie Sand acting as matron-of-honour – Sergeant Tulliver was himself married, in Rocester Registry Office, to a divorced woman with two young children. By that time Crispin Turner had applied for, and received, a special restoration grant from English Heritage to return the fallen stone to its rightful position, along with a hint that, should he ever think of The Wise Lady in commercial terms, more cash might be forthcoming.

Sir Homer King was now rarely seen in Wyley. After his mother and her new husband had departed for their honeymoon in the Canaries, he had his possessions moved from the Manor to the rather more cramped quarters of his London flat, comforting himself with the knowledge that he had given all to save Thomas.

This comfort proved short-lived. In the middle of October Thomas Bright hit the headlines over an alleged misunderstanding between himself and a prostitute. When considered in court the incident, of course, came to nothing, but the glittering future that could otherwise have been expected was ruined. He was unlikely ever to progress beyond the back benches.

Also in the middle of October, Martha Blandish's house sold, at the top of the market. Martha invested most of the money and used the rest to help pay for her time at art school, not in London, but in Glasgow. The Independent Financial Advisor, who bought the place, tore out the original mullioned windows, installed double-glazing throughout, and had another bathroom put in. His wife, a woman of vast imagination, became fast friends with Veronica Tarrant. At Christmas she helped Veronica organise 'An Olde Englande Evenynge' with mulled wine and carols. Tickets only.

Possession is generally supposed to be nine-tenths of the law. But what is the other tenth?

When, at the beginning of a crisp new century, Randolph King bought Wyley Manor and its grounds, which included the Manor Farm, he was presented with the deeds at his solicitors' chambers in London, as well as a detailed plan of the limits of his ownership (though Randolph King was rather more interested in what was to be found inside that line than what was to be found outside). There was no question. No ambiguity. With the exception of the unfortunate footpath which, eighty-three years later was to cause such problems for his grandson, Homer King, everything belonged to Randolph.

Or at least nine-tenths of it. And in that outer, straggling, uncooperative tenth lies the difficulty. Tell a Masai that they have crossed the border between Kenya and Uganda and you have told them nothing. Tell any tribal people that their holy places are part of South Dakota or Central Australia or have been brought by a lumber company and you have told them nothing. Tell history that it must cease to have a magnetic pull upon the present and you might as well not have bothered to speak. Their ears are dust who dropped cooking implements and arrow-heads along the, now invisible, track that did indeed continue from where Rocester County Council deemed the byway to end. It cut through the woods that were a forest then, emerging in a clearing on the very edge of the stone circle, the forest pressing in upon it so that it must have been constant work to keep it back. At that time it was harder to rid places of what one considered undesirable – though, of course, the forest would not have been considered undesirable beyond the clearing. These people must have lived with the tension. Perhaps they even incorporated it into their way of looking at things.

At a certain point, therefore, what Randolph King might have thought or not thought about his ownership of the circle was irrelevant. The travellers were using a path that was older than, and exterior to, his dominion. A path that went back before England was England; before the existence of law, before anyone started putting bricks together to create what would become the village of Wyley; before Christianity had even been thought of. But that was not older than human voices. Not older than things dropped out of bags or pockets. Not older than memory, of a kind. Randolph King and his descendants could make things easier or more difficult for them. He could not stop them.

To stake a claim on perpetuity indicates greater optimism than wisdom.

One snowy day, just before Christmas, when Crispin was in London, discussing supplying organic vegetables to Selfridges, and picking up the pug, Lady Polly's solicitor, Mr Callow, arrived at Wyley Manor. He had been summoned there by Lady Polly without her husband's knowledge.

She received him in the sitting-room, where a wood fire was burning. They were brought a jug of egg-nog by Cook. Mr Callow admired the large Christmas tree.

'The presents under it,' said Lady Polly, 'are useful things for the servants.'

'Wise,' said Mr Callow. He sipped his egg-nog in silence.

'I have asked you to come here,' said Lady Polly eventually, 'because I wish to make a new will.'

'Wise,' said Mr Callow again. 'Upon your marriage, Lady Polly, any previous will became invalid. Presumably you wish to spare Mr Turner unnecessary suffering upon your decease.'

'Why?' asked Lady Polly crossly, topping her glass up.

Mr Callow looked confused. 'I was assuming, Lady Polly, that you wished to leave your estate to your husband.'

'Crispin,' said Lady Polly, 'is a neophyte.'

Mr Callow nodded gravely. 'Then it is to Sir Homer that you wish to leave it?'

'No,' said Lady Polly. 'Don't like him.'

'To who then?' asked Mr Callow, astonished.

Lady Polly did not reply immediately. Instead she looked out of the French windows at the snowy garden, which was already disappearing into a blue darkness, remembering.

Horace had been six months in India, doing something concerning the Empire, when Lady Polly made that freezing journey up north for Christmas, back to everything she had promised to forget; back to everything that she remembered each day of her life, ever more clearly; back to her first and only lovers.

She was a young bride then. She was bored and lonely. Of course she would derive comfort from reviving her moribund passions in the arms of the madmen who had initially 'satisfied her curiosity', as she had expressed it to Crispin Turner in June, when they were walking in the garden.

It was a cruel winter. The snow had been on the ground for six weeks when Polly King realised that she was pregnant.

Was it superstition that led her to The Wise Lady in search of help that bitter day? Or was it purely the kind of desperation that needs movement? Did she really do something to herself that made it happen, or was it only the terrible cold. Anyway, that was the end of the baby.

But not of the nightmare, the sense that she had betrayed the mad people and that they must somehow know and would one day return for vengeance, the constant awareness of how easy it would have been to fall from grace, to become an unfortunate family incident, to have to work in a hat shop, alone with a child. Like Melanie Flowerdew's mother.

'To Melanie Flowerdew,' said Lady Polly.

Mr Callow started. 'I beg your pardon, Lady Polly?'

'To Melanie Flowerdew,' Lady Polly repeated. 'Got the ambulance when I fell off the rostrum. Brought Chummy home. Had a deprived upbringing. Her mother has a house by the village green.'

'What specifically, Lady Polly?'

Lady Polly turned to face him.

'Everything. The Manor, the grounds, the farm, the stone circle, the pictures, the money, the furniture.'

Mr Callow cleared his throat. 'Traditionally, Lady Polly, property is passed down through families via the male line.'

'Tradition,' said Lady Polly, 'is something we make up as we go along. Draw up the papers. Let Melanie Flowerdew have a shot at it.'